Asda Tickled Pink

45p from the sale of this book will be donated to Tickled Pink.

Asda Tickled Pink wants to ensure all breast cancer is diagnosed early and help improve people's many different experiences of the disease. Working with our charity partners, Breast Cancer Now and CoppaFeel!, we're on a mission to make checking your boobs, pecs and chests, whoever you are, as normal as your Asda shop. And with your help, we're raising funds for new treatments, vital education and life-changing support, for anyone who needs it. Together, we're putting breast cancer awareness on everyone's list.

Since the partnership began in 1996, Asda Tickled Pink has raised over £82 million for its charity partners. Through the campaign, Asda has been committed to raising funds and breast-check awareness via in-store fundraising, disruptive awareness campaigns, and products turning pink to support the campaign. The funds have been vital for Breast Cancer Now's world-class research and life-changing support services, such as their Helpline, there for anyone affected by breast cancer to cope with the emotional impact of the disease. Asda Tickled Pink's educational and outreach work with CoppaFeel! aims to empower 1 million 18 - 24 year olds to adopt a regular boob-checking behaviour by 2025. Together we will continue to make a tangible difference to breast cancer in the UK.

Asda Tickled Pink and the Penguin Random House have teamed up to bring you Tickled Pink Books. By buying this book and supporting the partnership, you ensure that 45p goes directly to the Breast Cancer Now and CoppaFeel!.

Breast Cancer is the most common cancer in women in the UK, with one in seven women facing it in their lifetime.

Around 55,000 women and 370 men are diagnosed with breast cancer every year in the UK and nearly 1,000 people still lose their life to the disease each month. This is one person every 45 minutes and this is why your support and the support from Asda Tickled Pink is so important.

A new Tickled Pink Book will go on sale in Asda stores every two weeks – we aim to bring you the best stories of friendship, love, heartbreak and laughter.

To find out more about the Tickled Pink partnership
visit www.asda.com/tickled-pink

Penguin
Random House
UK

STAY BREAST AWARE AND CHECK YOURSELF REGULARLY

One in seven women in the UK will be diagnosed with breast cancer in their lifetime

'TOUCH, LOOK, KNOW YOUR NORMAL, REPEAT REGULARLY'

Make sure you stay breast aware
- Get to know what's normal for you
- Look and feel to notice any unusual changes early
- The earlier breast cancer is diagnosed, the better the chance of successful treatment
- Check your boobs regularly and see a GP if you notice a change

A FOUNDLING AT THE WARTIME BOOKSHOP

Lesley Eames

PENGUIN BOOKS

TRANSWORLD PUBLISHERS
Penguin Random House, One Embassy Gardens,
8 Viaduct Gardens, London SW11 7BW
www.penguin.co.uk

Transworld is part of the Penguin Random House group of companies
whose addresses can be found at global.penguinrandomhouse.com

First published in Great Britain in 2025 by Bantam
an imprint of Transworld Publishers
Penguin paperback edition published 2025

Song lyrics on page 99 from 'Wish Me Good Luck as You Wave Me Goodbye' written by
Phil Park and Harry Parr-Davies.

A CIP catalogue record for this book
is available from the British Library.

ISBN
9781804993712

Typeset in Baskerville by Falcon Oast Graphic Art Ltd.
Printed and bound in Great Britain by Clays Ltd, Elcograf S.p.A.

The authorized representative in the EEA is Penguin Random House Ireland,
Morrison Chambers, 32 Nassau Street, Dublin D02 YH68.

To the four shining stars who shoot sparkles of joy and delight across my sky: my beloved daughters, Olivia and Isobel, and my precious granddaughters, Charlotte and Anastasia. Thank you for all the love and laughter.

Prologue

April 1942

It was the dead of night and sleep had smoothed its velvet hands across the heads of most young women in southern England, easing them gently into the sort of slumber that would leave them clear-eyed and refreshed come morning.

But in the county of Hertfordshire, one young woman hadn't slept at all. Exhausted, shaken and ill, only her desperation drove her onwards. One part of the night's work was done and, so far, no one knew of it. The other part remained to be accomplished and no one could know of that either. With the clock ticking the available time away, she needed to act quickly but stealthily.

She'd planned for this moment. Normally, she shared a bedroom, but, knowing she'd need privacy, she'd prepared the small room that opened off the kitchen. It was little more than a flimsy lean-to – chilly and damp and used for storing tools, boots, a washing basket and the like. Over the past weeks she'd tidied it to create space for lying down if necessary and hidden old newspapers, rags, sheets and a cardboard box in there. Tonight, she'd added a pail of water, some clean clothing and a couple of small blankets which she'd cut from a larger blanket that was worn into holes.

Cupping the water in her hands now, she washed her face and used wet rags to wash the rest of her, shuddering because the water was cold, but that couldn't be helped. She used more rags to dry and protect herself from further staining, then pulled on underwear, a long white nightdress and her pale mackintosh.

She'd covered the floor in old newspapers which she bundled up and stuffed into a corner together with the sheets, which she hadn't managed to keep clean despite her best efforts.

The box sat on the floor still and she paused to consider its contents. But time was a luxury she couldn't afford. She needed to return from the second part of her night's work before dawn streaked pale fingers across the sky and stirred sleeping people into life.

She eased open the door and listened, but all was quiet in the rest of the tumbledown house. Picking up the box, she crept into the kitchen, where she pushed her feet into her shoes and let herself out into the darkness.

Only occasionally did moonlight gleam between clouds. This reduced the chances of her being seen but meant she needed to choose her steps carefully if she wasn't to stumble. The soreness didn't help, but she pressed on with as much speed as she could manage. It was a walk she'd made many times before but never in these circumstances, and she fretted at the thought of how long it was taking. For the most part she walked past fields and woods, seeing nothing more than a slinking fox and a swooping white barn owl.

But she tensed as she entered the outskirts of a village, her head moving from side to side to alert her to signs of people being up and about in the houses and cottages. A cat startled her when it jumped from a wall and she clutched the box close, fearful of dropping it and harming the precious contents. 'No time,' she muttered, as the cat miaowed for attention.

She reached the far side of the village at last and passed between tall gateposts. But here she hesitated. The drive was made from pale gravel that would crunch underfoot. She moved on to the lawn instead, though it was impossible to avoid the gravel for the final few yards. Tiptoeing over it, she finally arrived at the house and took the single step that led into a porch. It was a large, square porch with a sloping ceiling that rose to a central point. Enclosing it around the sides and most of the front was a low brick wall topped by fancy wooden railings.

She looked into the box again and felt her heart swell fit to burst.

Was she doing the right thing? The answer came back at her: she hadn't a choice. Lowering her face into the box, she kissed the contents, murmured, 'Sorry,' and put it down behind the wall where it wouldn't be seen from the road. She had a note in her pocket, written with her left hand to disguise her usual handwriting. She arranged it in the box so it wouldn't be blown away – and then stepped back.

Tears streamed down her face as she walked away. In her haste and distress, her foot sent gravel rattling across the drive. Glancing back, she saw no sign that anyone had heard but she quickened her pace anyway and ran sobbing through the night.

CHAPTER ONE

Victoria

Churchwood, Hertfordshire, England

Letting herself out through the kitchen door at the back of the house, Victoria stepped into the chill of early morning. Far from being unpleasant, it was the sort of chill that promised sunshine and freshness. Spring was spreading goodwill across the earth, turning overnight dew to sparkling diamonds, beckoning forth soft, pliant buds on bushes and trees, and encouraging birds to sing joyously of a winter survived and a busy season of nest-building to come.

When Victoria tallied up the good and bad aspects of the decisions she'd made, living here sat comfortably on the good side. It wasn't just the village of Churchwood that she liked but also this house that she was privileged to call home. For the moment, anyway. Foxfield was the largest and loveliest property in the village, a rambling Victorian confection with extensive lawns and majestic trees. Walking around the side of the building, she passed pale primroses sheltering under hedges like shy young girls longing for dance partners at a ball. There were blue forget-me-nots and colourful wallflowers, too, bolder than the primroses and swaying gracefully in the breeze.

She reached the tall gateposts that opened on to Churchwood Way. This was the village's main thoroughfare. In one direction it led to the triangular-shaped green, the church, the school and the shops. In the other direction it led to Bert Makepiece's market garden and then open countryside.

There were more flowers in the hedgerow opposite, which marked the boundary of a farm that belonged to Alec Mead. He was a grumpy man in his forties, but it was as a result of his badly behaved dog tipping Victoria off her bicycle and into a ditch that she'd met Naomi Harrington, the middle-aged owner of Foxfield. Naomi had given her a job as live-in cook-housekeeper, despite Victoria being only twenty-two.

As a child it had never crossed Victoria's mind that she might one day work in such a position. Her parents had shown every sign of having wealth. Their home had resembled Foxfield in size and graciousness. They'd had servants and given their only child a private education. But they'd been hopeless money managers and their wealth had been frittered away to nothing. Victoria had been taken out of school due to non-payment of fees, the servants had left due to non-payment of wages and the house had been taken away by the bank. Determined not to be beaten down, Victoria had made the best of the situation, looking after her parents in a much more modest home and working in a shop to bring in some much-needed income. After their deaths she'd worked as housekeeper to an elderly lady and then signed on for war work in a wireless factory in London.

A change of circumstances had moved her on from the factory but she'd had the good fortune to cross paths with kind Mrs Harrington. Victoria's position here wasn't a forever job – Naomi had been clear about that, since her own circumstances were uncertain – but with luck it would occupy Victoria for several years.

6

Victoria felt fondness and admiration for Naomi. Sympathy, too, for Naomi had her problems, not least her stockbroker husband, Alexander, who'd betrayed her in the most hurtful way imaginable. Victoria had met the man briefly and, despite his icy good looks and crisp way of dressing, she'd despised him on sight.

Fortunately, happiness beckoned for Naomi in the form of a second marriage to market gardener Bert Makepiece, but before then she had to navigate a divorce from Alexander, including the return of some of the money he'd fleeced from her. He wasn't making it easy. In the meantime, Victoria was sure Naomi was feeling the pinch financially, which made it all the more admirable that she was kindness itself to Victoria and the other waifs and strays who'd crossed her path. There were numerous waifs and strays at Foxfield just now.

Naomi wasn't the only person to sit on the good side of Victoria's tally of her life. She'd made other new friends in Churchwood. Among them were Bert Makepiece, Alice Irvine, Kate Fletcher, May Janicki, Janet Collins and vicar Adam Potts, who were the organizers of the Churchwood bookshop. This was the beating heart of the village, the place people headed not only for books, newspapers and magazines but also for story readings, talks, clubs and social events.

Ruby and Pearl, land girls who lived at Kate's nearby farm, had also become friends.

All in all, Victoria had much to be thankful for, and it was important to remember that when thoughts of a different sort of life crept unbidden into her mind. No one could have everything they wanted, and—

Her ears picked up the distant sound of a motor. Not Bert Makepiece's ancient truck, nor the grocer's sedate van. This vehicle was approaching at speed. Seconds later, it rounded a curve in the road and came to a sudden halt beside her. It appeared to be a military vehicle – open-topped and painted green – and there were two men inside. They wore the khaki uniforms of army personnel but there was something different about them . . . Victoria realized what it was as soon as one of them spoke. They weren't British. They were American.

'Well, ma'am. Aren't you a sight for sore eyes so early in the morning.'

The speaker was the passenger. He'd been holding a map but it fell into his lap as he looked her over appreciatively. It wasn't an offensive ogling – Victoria had been ogled offensively before so knew the difference – but a simple expression of liking what he saw. Even so, the driver shook his head and offered Victoria an apologetic smile. 'You'll forgive my friend his lack of . . . subtlety, ma'am?'

'I'll forgive him, seeing as America has joined the war on the side of Britain and her allies.'

'We sure are hoping to make a difference,' the driver said.

'That's right,' the passenger agreed. 'By kicking Adolf Hitler and his cronies all the way back to Germany and arresting him.' This man was the more flamboyant of the two with lively blue eyes, an easy smile and an air of finding the fun in life.

Yet Victoria found herself warming to the driver. He wasn't quite as handsome. Not quite as lively. But she liked the depth and thoughtfulness she read in his brown eyes and his steadier manner.

The passenger drew her attention back. 'Corporal Ralph Brady at your service, ma'am,' he said, introducing himself.

'Are you at my service?' Victoria asked. 'That's lucky. Because I can find plenty of jobs for you. Chopping wood, filling the coal scuttles . . .'

She'd taken him by surprise but the gleam in the driver's dark eyes showed he realized she'd been joking. 'She's teasing you,' he told his companion, sharing a look of understanding with Victoria, who smiled back at him.

'Figure of speech, ma'am,' Ralph Brady explained, a little chastened but still game for flirting.

'She knows that,' the driver told him. Then he addressed Victoria. 'I'm Paul Scarletti. Sergeant. I regret that I'm not at *your* service but I hope you may do a service for *us*, Miss . . .?'

Victoria declined to give her name, drawing another amused gleam from the driver. 'What service would that be?' she asked.

He reached for the map. 'Pointing us in the direction of a place called Barton. We took a false turn a few miles back and found ourselves in a narrow, winding lane with hedges on both sides and no room to turn. Quaint, but we're used to more open spaces back home.'

'We'd have had to back up all the way to Kentucky if we'd met a vehicle coming towards us,' Ralph said.

'I think you have a tendency towards exaggeration,' Victoria told him, smiling to take the sting out of it.

Paul grinned. 'She's got your measure all right,' he told Ralph. He turned to Victoria again. 'We kept going but Ralph couldn't get a fix on our new direction. Let's hope he turns out to be a better soldier than map reader.'

'You're mean,' Ralph protested. 'As for you, miss, I never expected an English girl to be so smart with her tongue. I expected more . . .'

'Reserve?' Victoria suggested. 'Coyness? Perhaps you formed an impression of English girls from a book you read? A book written in an earlier century?'

'I'm not a great reader, ma'am,' Ralph said. 'But if you're an example, English girls sure are pretty.'

Victoria rolled her eyes.

'Ralph here seems determined to set back Anglo–American relations,' Paul said.

'I paid her a compliment!' Ralph protested.

'There's a difference between complimenting someone and patronizing them,' Paul said. 'Isn't that right, Miss . . .?'

Again, Victoria refused to take the bait. 'If I may summarize the situation, I think the gist of what you're saying is that you're lost.'

'I wouldn't call us lost, exactly,' the passenger objected.

'What would you call it?' Victoria asked.

He floundered before saying, 'We're just temporarily uncertain of our position.'

'Which means you're lost but have too much male pride to admit it,' Victoria concluded. 'But you're in luck. This village is called Churchwood. Drive straight through until you come to a fork in the road. Take the left-hand road and you'll be heading towards Barton. Now, if you'll excuse me, I need to get on with my day.' She gestured back through the Foxfield gateposts.

'That's your house?' Ralph asked. 'It sure is beautiful. And that one' – he pointed towards The Linnets, where Alice Irvine lived with her retired doctor father – 'sure is cute.' Standing on its own with a profusion of spring flowers in the small front garden, it was a picturesque cottage with an old oak door and windows criss-crossed in lead.

'I only work here,' Victoria corrected. 'And, as I said, I need to get on. Welcome to England, gentlemen. Now I must bid you good day.'

'Good day to you, too,' Ralph said. 'And thanks. Our luck was in, finding you out here like a princess of the dawn.'

Victoria rolled her eyes again.

'I've no taste for flowery talk,' Paul said. 'But I'm glad I met you.'

Something in his steady gaze made Victoria feel self-conscious suddenly. Not liking to appear flustered, she nodded and turned away to walk in the direction of Foxfield. Behind her the vehicle roared off. Judging the moment when she'd be safe to look back, she turned again and watched a small cloud of dust rise up as the vehicle moved into the distance and out of sight.

The encounter had entertained her. Invigorated her, momentarily. But now a sense of anti-climax was descending and reminding her of the other side of her tally – the choices that would never be hers given that she'd taken on other responsibilities. Choices like romance, marriage, children of her own . . .

She'd taken on those other responsibilities willingly, fully aware of the sacrifices she'd have to make but feeling only mild regret. After all, she'd reached the age of twenty-two without ever feeling particularly attracted to any man. Which made it odd that a chance encounter with a stranger should make those sacrifices seem sharper just now.

She'd liked him, that was why. There'd been something deeply appealing in those warm brown eyes. But there was nothing to be gained by dwelling on it.

She was heading back around the side of the house when she heard something rather like the mew of a kitten. She paused, looking around the garden and listening in case the sound were to be repeated, but she saw and heard nothing except for the birds going energetically about their business. Assuming she'd misheard one of their calls, Victoria continued to the back of the house and entered via the kitchen door.

CHAPTER TWO

Beth

The train was busy considering the earliness of the hour, but Beth had been at the station long before it was due to leave and, being the first passenger to enter the compartment, had secured a seat by the window. More people entered – a soldier who was probably home on leave, a businessman, an elderly vicar and a woman she took to be his wife . . . Beth managed to return polite nods and smiles but was relieved to be able to turn away and stare outside as the train shuffled through the outskirts of London and into the countryside.

Not that she registered much of what she saw. Her eyes felt fiery from lack of rest since, with so much turmoil inside her, she'd slept little last night, tiredness doing no more than drag her into occasional troubled dozes from which she jerked back to consciousness with a racing heart and the sick feeling of remembering what had happened all over again.

Rising before dawn, she'd decided to waste no more time before leaving her nurses' home, her hospital and, best of all – or was it worst of all? – golden-haired, blue-eyed Dr Oliver Charles Lytton. What a fool she'd been to fall for him. Starry-eyed and hopeful, she'd even used up precious money and clothing coupons in buying a blue satin dress for what turned out to be their last evening together. It was the first glamorous dress she'd ever owned but it had felt entirely appropriate when she'd expected so much to come of a joyful night of dining and dancing.

Far from being the best night of her life, it had turned into the worst. Recalling it now, tears flooded her eyes but she blinked them away. Having cried so much already, she had no wish to squander more tears on the man who'd not only broken her heart but behaved as though it hadn't even occurred to him that he'd be hurting her.

All through that last evening she'd waited for him to say the words she longed to hear. She'd smiled and danced and, sparkling with happiness and anticipation, told him what a lovely time she was having. And when he'd walked her back to the nurses' home and turned her to face him, her breath had caught in her throat at the softness in his blue eyes as he gazed down at her. This was it, she'd thought: the moment he'd declare his love for her.

'We've had fun, haven't we?' he'd said, and she'd nodded, swallowing to keep her giddy expectations under control.

'But it would be a mistake to let ourselves become serious,' he'd finished.

The words had fallen on her like icy water and she'd gaped at him in bewilderment. 'You don't want to see me any more?'

'We shouldn't be tying ourselves down. We're young. We have careers. You're a great girl, though, Beth.' Bending, he'd kissed her cheek, and then, job done, he'd sauntered away, his carefree steps suggesting he'd ceased to think of her already.

The following weeks had been fraught with misery. As ever, though, concern for her patients had made her set about her duties conscientiously, suffering in silence as she watched Oliver move on to pastures new.

Oh, she knew now that he was a shallow sort of man who was careless of other people's feelings, but she loved him even despite it. And she couldn't hold off bitterness when she asked herself how she – a girl of average height and build with unremarkable brown hair and eyes, and nothing special in her features – could ever have competed with Nurse Cassandra Carlisle, who was a golden-haired, blue-eyed princess to Oliver's Prince Charming.

Needing to escape the torture of seeing him almost daily, she'd requested a transfer to a different hospital, only to feel surprised and rather conflicted when the request was granted.

'I'm moving to Stratton House,' she'd told Oliver, hoping hungrily for a sign that he'd miss her.

But he'd only smiled and declared, 'A new adventure! I'm sure it'll be wonderful.' Once again, he'd strolled away as though he hadn't a care in the world. Which perhaps he hadn't.

But enough brooding. She wasn't expecting the move to bring adventure, but at least it would put distance between her and Oliver and give her the chance to start the healing process that his constant presence denied her. It would bring a change of scene and pace, too, since she was leaving the bustle of city life behind her. The new hospital was in the countryside, not far from a village called Churchwood. She'd never heard of it before, but it sounded just the sort of small, sleepy place where nothing much happened and she could grieve for her lost hopes without disturbance.

The train reached St Albans. Beth stood, thanked the soldier who lifted her case from the overhead luggage rack for her and headed through the corridor on to the platform. Now to catch the bus to Churchwood.

CHAPTER THREE

Ruby

Sitting on the side of the bed, Ruby stroked the sleeping boy's hair back from his face – an urchin-like but much-loved face. 'Time to get up, sleepy-head,' she said gently.

Timmy stirred, opened his eyes and gave her a grin that tugged on her heart. She'd given up a lot for this boy, and every day since his birth she'd worried that their secret might emerge, but he was worth all that and more.

'I brought water up for your wash,' she told him.

'Thanks, Ruby.'

There was no bathroom at Brimbles Farm. It was a ramshackle place with a surly, scowling skinflint of an owner who had little sympathy for young boys who might eat him out of house and home and prove a distraction to work. But to Ruby and Timmy it had become a sanctuary.

A few years ago she could never have imagined herself living and working on a farm as a land girl. Brought up near the docks in London's East End, Ruby's notion of a lovely day out had once been to take the bus to the West End to look in Selfridges and the shop windows of Bond Street at gorgeous outfits she could never afford but liked to fantasize might one day be hers. Had anyone suggested that she might come to volunteer for digging in filthy earth or – worse still – shovelling compost, she'd have laughed at the absurdity of it.

Ruby was a city girl at heart and knew she looked like a city girl, too. Short and curvy, she dyed her hair film-star blonde, wore cosmetics, including vivid red lipstick, and varnished her nails to match.

But love and war were great incentives for change. Back in the autumn of 1939 Timmy had been evacuated to a farm in the Bedfordshire countryside, but he'd been treated unkindly and made miserable. In an agony of worry over him, Ruby had spent months fretting before she'd fixed on a plan for improving his situation.

It hadn't been the most foolproof plan. Looking back, the chances of making a safe and happy home for him on another farm by becoming a land girl must have been small indeed, since they depended on the goodwill of the owner or tenant farmer to whom she was allocated. After all, it wasn't usual for land girls to be accompanied by their little brothers.

Yet against the odds the plan had succeeded and almost a year ago Timmy had come to live with her. In part, this was due to the kindness of the farmer's feisty daughter, Kate, and fellow land girl Pearl, who'd made Timmy feel welcome. But mostly it was down to the farmer's eldest son, Kenny, whose morose personality hadn't blinded him to the attractions of Ruby's shapely figure and no-nonsense way of speaking. Kenny wasn't half as morose these days and affection had grown into love on both sides, so much so that a couple of months ago they'd become engaged to be married.

Walking downstairs now, the thought made her reach up to the ring she wore on a chain around her neck, fol-lowing the example of Kate, who'd once lost her ring in Five Acre Field. Kate's ring was a dazzling emerald

16

surrounded by diamonds. Ruby's ring was much more modest but she was delighted to have it.

Kenny was a marvel at farming, but social graces and conventions largely passed him by and it hadn't appeared to cross his mind that a ring was customary until Kate had pointed it out. Ruby had been upstairs when she'd heard them talking in the kitchen.

'You need to buy Ruby a ring,' Kate had said.

'Eh?'

'An engagement ring.'

'I don't have money for fancy jewellery! I'm not rich like your Leo.' Kate was married to a flight lieutenant in the RAF, though she was still living on the farm because her labour was sorely needed.

'It needn't be fancy,' Kate reasoned. 'Just pretty. Ask Ernie for money if you haven't got enough.'

Ernie was Kenny and Kate's father. All the Fletcher offspring called him by his first name, probably because *Dad* would have felt inappropriate for such a joyless man.

'You want me to ask Ernie for money for a ring?' Kenny scoffed.

'Insist on it,' Kate instructed. 'Oh, and maybe you should talk to Ruby about the sort of stone she'd like. Don't make assumptions because of her name.'

'Eh?' Kenny said again.

'She may be called Ruby, but it doesn't follow that she'd like a ruby ring. She might prefer a sapphire or something else.'

Doubtless creases formed in Kenny's forehead, signalling to the world that he was out of his depth with precious stones.

Ruby had taken pity on him after that, and suggested they visit a jeweller's together.

Ernie hadn't been pleased, of course. 'First you want

my money for useless fripperies and now you want to skive off work,' he'd protested.

But as was happening more and more at Brimbles Farm, they'd ignored him and taken the bus to St Albans. Kenny was a tall, strapping man but his head shrank into his shoulders when they entered the unfamiliar territory of a jeweller's shop. Ruby sensed he was terrified of making a fool of himself as well as afraid she'd ask for something grand.

A male assistant approached them. 'Good morning, sir. Madam. May I be of assistance?'

Kenny ran a finger around his collar as though it were strangling him. 'We're – um – here for a ring.'

'An engagement ring?'

'Um . . . Yes.'

'Congratulations. Have you a particular stone or design in mind? A diamond solitaire? A cluster of jewels?'

Sweat broke out on Kenny's forehead at the mention of diamonds.

'My name is Ruby,' she told the assistant. 'I'd like a ring that matches it.'

'A ruby ring. Of course.'

'I'm a land girl doing my bit for the war,' Ruby said. 'I'd prefer something small that won't get in the way of my work.'

'Of course.'

Kenny blew out air and she sensed his relief. But it didn't last long. The assistant gestured for them to approach a counter, slipped silkily behind it and brought out a tray of rings – all of which sparkled with diamonds as well as rubies.

She tried on several but was sure they must all be expensive. Kenny's sickly pallor suggested he thought so, too.

18

'Do you mind if I look around?' she asked. 'Walking helps me to make my mind up.'

'Certainly, madam.'

She crossed to another counter and looked down through the glass surface to the jewellery displayed below. 'Those are dress rings,' the assistant pointed out. Presumably, he meant that they weren't traditional engagement rings.

'That one is nice.' Ruby pointed to a simple gold band which had a small red stone attached. There were no diamonds or other embellishments in sight. 'May I try it on?'

'The stone isn't a ruby,' the assistant cautioned. 'It's a garnet, which is only a semi-precious stone.' In other words, far too cheap and humble for an engagement ring.

Ruby gave him a determined smile. 'Even so . . .'

He brought the ring from under the counter and passed it over. Ruby slid it on to her finger. 'What do you think, Kenny?'

He shrugged but Ruby saw hopefulness in his expression, too, since a stone that was only semi-precious might mean this visit wouldn't be financially ruinous, after all.

'We can adjust the size,' the assistant told her, but there would be no need for that.

'It fits perfectly,' she said. 'This is the ring I'd like.'

The assistant gestured Kenny to a corner. Ruby supposed he thought it would be vulgar to state the price in front of the bride-to-be. Ruby saw Kenny's relief deepen further when he heard the figure that was whispered. 'I'll keep the ring on, if that's all right?' Ruby called.

'Certainly, madam.'

Leaving the men to sort out the payment, she walked around the shop admiring glorious, glittering displays but feeling content with the gentle gleam of her little garnet. She might only be twenty-four but her experiences over the past years had taught her to value what was important: love and security.

'Ready to go?' Kenny asked, and she nodded.

Outside, he blinked in the daylight and breathed in deeply, putting her in mind of a prisoner released from a long period of incarceration. 'Let's go home,' he said, for work awaited him on the farm.

But he made no objection when she said, 'I'd like to buy something for Timmy first.'

Sweets rarely made it to Churchwood these days but she managed to buy two ounces of barley sugars. 'I'll pay,' Kenny said. 'Seeing as it's my day for spending.'

Aside from the occasional pint of beer down at the Wheatsheaf, he rarely spent any money. Not that he had much to spend, since Ernie allowed his sons only nominal wages and ploughed the rest of the farm's earnings straight back into it. Given that those sons were set to inherit the farm one day, Kenny had told her that he didn't consider he was being cheated of a fair recompense for his labour. It was just that his reward was being postponed.

They boarded the bus and Kenny almost threw himself into the first seat they reached but then, as though remembering his manners, stood back and said, 'After you.' He'd been a young child when his mother died and, having been brought up by the graceless Ernie, he had almost no finesse. But he was learning.

Ruby felt pleased with her lot as the bus pulled out of the station but Kenny began to fidget beside her. 'What's wrong?' she asked.

'That ring,' he said. 'Are you sure it's . . . Are you sure it's *enough*?' Was he thinking of his sister's magnificent ring?

'Quite sure, thank you.' Ruby was glad to see relief washing over him again.

She burrowed her head into his powerful shoulder and he put his arm around her to draw her close. He'd never be a romantic, sentimental sort of man but he loved her, of that Ruby was sure. It made her feel protected. Safe. And Ruby hadn't felt either of those things in years. Perhaps ever.

A month had passed since then and she was still satisfied with her little garnet and still satisfied with her life. Apart from the secret, of course, but, as the old saying went, what couldn't be cured had to be endured.

'Don't drop back to sleep,' she told Timmy now, 'and don't forget that ears need washing as well as faces.'

Timmy gave her another grin and she got up from his bed to go down the bare wooden stairs to the kitchen. It was the largest room in the house, the only other downstairs room being used as a bedroom now. There was nothing impressive about it, though. The kitchen cupboards had been painted a swamp-like green many years ago and the paint was chipped and scuffed. The stove was ancient. So, too, was the furniture – a shabby dresser and an equally shabby table. Ten chairs were arranged around the table but not a single one matched with another. There were shelves on the dresser top and in the alcoves beside the fireplace, but these were mere dumping grounds for tools, machine parts, tins of oil, rags, string and tattered catalogues of farming supplies.

Ruby and Kate had hopes of getting to work with fresh paint and beeswax one day when time and money permitted, but for the moment had to settle for tidying the mess and bringing in flowers and greenery to brighten up the dingy space.

Everyone had gathered for breakfast: Ruby's fellow

land girl, Pearl; surly old Ernie; Kate; Kenny; the next brother in line, Vinnie; and Fred who, along with his twin, Frank, was the youngest of the Fletcher boys. Expecting larks and adventures, both Fred and Frank had gone off to fight in the war despite being exempt as farmworkers. Frank was serving still but instead of larks and adventures Fred had lost his legs, an experience that had turned him into a bitter man.

Luckily, Pearl had performed wonders in lifting him out of his depression and getting him working on wood-carvings, which were beginning to sell and give him a small income. Not that Fred was a barrel of laughs even now, and not that Pearl was anyone's idea of a soothing nurse. On the contrary, she was tall, wiry and clumsy, with plain features and enormous hands and feet. But somehow her taunts and criticisms had worked better on Fred than any amount of sympathy, and it seemed to give him pleasure to taunt and criticize her in return. They bickered constantly.

Even so, Ruby and Kate had long suspected that Pearl and Fred had romantic feelings for each other. That they were in love, in fact. But, between their insecurities and awkwardness, neither seemed able to admit it and the romance never made any headway.

Kate carried the teapot to the table. 'Shall I fetch the milk?' Pearl asked.

'I'll manage,' Ruby told her, not wanting to risk Pearl dropping it. 'You sit down.'

Ruby placed a jug of milk on the table and Kate began to pour the tea while Ruby fetched the big bowl of por-ridge she'd left to keep warm in the oven. She carried it to the table, knowing that every last drop would be eaten. Mornings on the farm started early and they'd all been working for a couple of hours already.

'Save some for me!' Timmy cried, rushing downstairs and into his chair.

'I miss the days when we had as much bacon as we liked for breakfast,' Vinnie lamented. He was the Fletcher who most closely resembled Ernie, being small with ferret-like features and sparse, gingery hair. He could be miserable, too, though his mean streak had fallen by the wayside thanks to Kate, Pearl and Ruby stamping down hard on it.

'There's no point in complaining about rationing and shortages,' Kate said. 'We can only make the best of things and hope the war ends soon.'

'I like Ruby's porridge, anyway,' Timmy said, sending her a smile.

'So do I,' Kenny said, showing his loyalty, too. He spooned some of the porridge into a bowl and passed it to Timmy. 'Tuck in.'

'Thanks, Kenny,' Timmy said.

It warmed Ruby to see the growing affection between them. She'd made the right decision in agreeing to marry Kenny, though the wedding was bringing its own set of problems. Not the least of them was the tricky issue of whether to allow the past to come forward into the present when doing so might suck some of the joy out of the occasion and – worse – risk letting her secret escape.

Only a few people in Churchwood were party to that secret. Kate had guessed it. So had Kate's friend Alice Irvine, and Alice's retired doctor father, who treated people in the village for free when they were unwell. Kenny had been next to share the secret, since Ruby was going to marry him and it wouldn't have felt right to keep him in the dark. Fortunately, it hadn't changed anything between them. Ruby had also told Pearl, Vinnie and Fred. Pearl was a loyal friend and it had seemed

23

better to swear Kenny's brothers to silence rather than risk them picking up – and perhaps spreading – any suspicions that might emerge one day. Finally, knowing she could trust them implicitly, Ruby had confided in Naomi and given permission for Bert to be included in the secret, too. But that was all.

To Churchwood at large, Timmy was Ruby's brother. In reality, he was her son, born out of wedlock when she was just sixteen. The thought of the name-calling and disgust that would result if this fact became known haunted Ruby daily. It wasn't for herself that she was concerned. Ruby would simply lift her chin and stare boldly at anyone who insulted her. But Timmy deserved better.

It grieved her that he couldn't be like other children in calling her Mum openly. But at least Ruby could shower him with a mother's love even if she had to pretend to be his sister. It was a pity he had no one to call Dad, either, since he'd never even met the man who'd fathered him. But in Kenny he had a friend who seemed genuinely fond of the boy.

It wasn't a perfect situation but it had to be enough. Secrecy was everything.

CHAPTER FOUR

Victoria

Victoria hadn't been out for long but the kitchen was already astir when she went back inside after her early walk. Suki, Mrs Harrington's pleasant little maid, was there; and so was Victoria's friend Mags, a spirited red-haired cockney with Irish origins, who'd worked alongside Victoria at the wireless factory. Along with four other women, they'd shared a damp and shabby little house near the London docks until it had been condemned due to bomb damage.

Victoria had evacuated to Churchwood and, due to a misunderstanding, Mags and the other women had come too, bringing their children with them. In an extraordinary act of generosity, Naomi had invited them all to stay. The women worked in aircraft construction in Hatfield now, except for Ivy – a grandmother – who looked after the children.

These old friends also sat on the good side of Victoria's tally of her life.

'I'll go and check on my two then I'll be down to make the breakfast,' Victoria said.

Climbing the stairs, she entered the bedroom where 'her two' slept, though both were awake. If Victoria needed a reminder that she'd made the right decisions in her life, she had it now, because four-year-old Jenny jumped up to wrap her slender arms around Victoria's middle while eight-year-old Arthur grinned at her as he tugged on a sock, saying, 'I had the strangest dream last night. I dreamed a dragon was chasing me but you came and threw a bucket of water into its mouth to put out its fire and it slunk away again.'

'I'm glad to have been of use in Dreamland,' Victoria told him, smiling and feeling love for both children, though they weren't hers by birth.

Victoria had never met their father, who'd died before the war, but their mother, Joan, another cockney who worked at the wireless factory, had become a friend. Joan's sudden death from heart disease had left the children with no family at all and, knowing what it was to be alone in the world, Victoria had promised to take over their care. Arthur's start in Churchwood had been rocky but now both children were happily settled, and that was surely more than sufficient reward for sacrificing her freedom to choose a different sort of life.

She helped Jenny into her pinafore and cardigan, and then brushed her hair before tying it back with a ribbon. Both children were brown-haired and blue-eyed, unlike Victoria who had honey-coloured hair and green eyes, but no one had ever questioned whether they were hers. Why would they, when the death and destruction of wartime had turned many a family upside down? Not that Victoria pretended to be their mother. She'd never try to take Joan's place in their hearts. She was happy to have her own place as their friend and protector.

'Breakfast soon,' she said, and went downstairs to make it.

Mealtimes were always lively affairs with so many people in the house, but everyone was fed and watered, and made ready for the day ahead.

The London women were the first to leave: Mags, Jessie, Pat and Sheila. They packed their lunches into their bags, kissed their children goodbye and headed for the kitchen door via the scullery, where shoes and coats were kept. From there, they'd walk into the village to catch the bus to Hatfield and their jobs.

Before long, it was the turn of the older children to leave for school. There was a flurry of activity as they, too, put on shoes and coats.

Victoria walked them out of the kitchen door and around to the front of the house, standing at the gateposts to wave them off as they headed along Churchwood Way to the village school. She caught sight of Ivy and Flower coming in the opposite direction. Ivy was Flower's grand-mother and the only one of the London women to board out, an arrangement which gave her a little peace and quiet and allowed those left behind more space to spread out.

A childhood of poor nutrition had bowed Ivy's legs with rickets and made walking difficult. Not wanting the older woman to feel obliged to quicken her pace, Victoria decided not to wait for her and turned back towards the house.

That was when she heard it again. The faint mewing sound. Glancing around, she still saw nothing, but the sound continued. Getting a fix on its direction, Victoria moved towards the wooden porch that was built around the front door. Tucked into a corner stood a box. And inside the box was . . .

Oh, heavens!

CHAPTER FIVE

Beth

'Churchwood!' the bus conductor called.

Beth rose to her feet, gripped her handbag and suit-case, and made her way along the aisle to step off the bus and look around.

She guessed she'd been dropped in the centre of the village because opposite her was a sizeable green. Shaped like a triangle, its middle was occupied by a war memorial, benches and tubs of flowers. Behind it stood a pretty church together with a house she assumed was the vicarage and another building that looked like a school. There was a space between the vicarage and the school where the ground looked uneven, as though a building had once stood there. Perhaps it had been demolished for some reason – or destroyed by a bomb. Beth had seen many a bombsite, living in London. It seemed unlikely that this gentle village would be a prime target for enemy aircraft but, whether by accident or design, bombs were dropped in odd places now and then.

The other sides of the green – including the one where Beth stood – were home to cottages and shops. As far as she could see they included a grocer's, a baker's, a green-grocer's, a post office, a cobbler's . . . Adequate, if unexciting.

Two women stood chatting outside one of the shops. What were they discussing? The challenges of rationing?

The best way of starching their husbands' collars? Something along those lines, anyway, for Churchwood looked to be just the sort of sleepy place she'd imagined. Or so Beth thought until a shriek suddenly assaulted her ears and a woman ran past shouting, 'I've seen a ghost!'

Good grief!

The woman was tall and thin, her shoulders rounded and her hat and coat drooping with age. Surprisingly, the other women showed no alarm at her approach. 'What is it this time, Marjorie?' the one in a blue hat asked.

'A ghost, I tell you!'

Mrs Blue Hat exchanged glances with her friend. Disbelieving glances, it seemed to Beth.

'It's true!' the woman called Marjorie insisted.

'Where did you see this ghost?' Mrs Blue Hat enquired.

'Walking along this very road. Terrified me, it did.'

'What time was this?'

'I don't know, exactly. I'd got up in the dark to . . . to . . .' Marjorie's words trailed off as though embarrassment had overtaken her.

'Weak bladder,' Mrs Blue Hat suggested to her friend.

'Anyway,' Marjorie continued, blushing, 'I happened to look out of the window and there it was. The ghost!'

'What did it do?'

'I didn't stop to watch. I jumped back into bed and pulled the covers over my head. Not that I could get to sleep again. Not for hours. I was afraid it might come into my house. Into my bedroom.'

'How would it manage that?'

'Ghosts can walk through walls!'

The other women exchanged more cynical looks. 'I'm sure you *thought* you saw a ghost, Marjorie,' Mrs Blue Hat conceded.

'I did!'

'Either way, it did you no harm so it's best forgotten.'

'I can't forget a ghost!'

'Try,' Mrs Blue Hat advised. 'You don't want to be stirring up trouble, do you? Not again?'

This caused Marjorie to hesitate but she came back fighting. 'I know what I saw!'

'Excuse me, but do you need some help?' The voice came from Beth's other side, rousing her.

Turning, she saw a young woman who appeared to be in her early twenties, as was Beth. She was a fair-haired, slightly built girl, but she'd never stay unnoticed for long. Her blue eyes were too clever. Too shrewd. And despite the kindness of her smile, they were also too discerning to someone who was trying to keep her bruised emotions to herself.

Beth liked to consider herself a polite and helpful person but she was also deeply private and hadn't the knack of being open with her thoughts and feelings. She'd never been anyone's enemy but neither had she ever been anyone's closest friend. Her instinct was to retreat now with a courteous but firm 'No, thank you' since she was feeling so raw but, frustratingly, she did need help with directions. 'I'm looking for a place called Stratton House. It's—'

'A military hospital. I volunteer there.'

The girl made it sound as though that common ground would soon make them friends, but Beth wasn't ready for anything like that yet. She needed time to heal first. She especially wasn't looking for a friendship with someone who wore a sparkling engagement ring and gold wedding band. Another girl's happy marriage would only rub salt into the wound of Beth's rejection.

'Not that I'm a nurse,' the girl continued, 'though I suspect you may be one.'

Beth couldn't deny it without being rude. 'Yes,' she confirmed. 'If you could just point me in the right direction . . .'

'I can do better than that. I can walk with you for part of the way.'

'There's no need to put yourself out.'

'It's no trouble. I live in that direction.'

More rotten luck. Seeing no escape, Beth fell into step beside her. 'You mustn't mind Marjorie Plym,' the girl said, once they'd passed the tall woman. 'She's what you might call a character.'

A character? Beth would have described her as unhinged.

'I'm Alice Irvine, by the way,' the girl added. 'I'm from London originally but I've lived in Churchwood for more than two years. I love it here.'

Good manners required Beth to introduce herself in return but her reluctance must have been apparent because, after the shortest moment, Alice picked up the conversation again, giving no sign of resenting what must have looked like a snub.

'You'll find some wonderful people working at Stratton House,' she said. 'Matron is strict but kind, and I have two particular friends among the nurses – Babs Carter and Pauline Evans. I'm sure they'll be glad to help you find your feet.'

Doubtless Babs and Pauline were nice, but Beth craved solitude more than company.

'They'll be able to tell you all about our bookshop, too,' Alice added.

A bookshop *did* sound interesting. Beth loved reading, and one of the reasons her suitcase was heavy was because she'd brought four books along.

'It's actually rather more than a bookshop,' Alice

continued. 'We sell books and lend them out, too, but we also have talks, clubs and social get-togethers.'

A pity. Beth had warmed to the idea of there being a supply of books nearby but if she were to be expected to throw herself straight into attending social get-togethers, it would be too high a price to pay. She'd have to travel further afield to find a bookshop or library.

'This is where I live,' Alice said as they reached a pretty cottage.

A small sign by the porch announced its name as The Linnets. It was separated from a much grander house – Foxfield, according to the nameplate attached to one of its tall gateposts – by a rough sort of road.

'This is Brimbles Lane,' Alice explained. 'It'll take you all the way to Stratton House. It's quite a distance so if you'd like a cup of tea first, you're more than welcome to—'

'I'm expected at the hospital,' Beth said hastily, though she had plenty of time to spare. 'But thank you for the offer and thank you for the directions.'

She realized Alice's attention had been caught by someone or something else. Turning, Beth saw a short, middle-aged woman hastening over from the grander house.

'Is everything all right, Naomi?' Alice asked. The woman looked flustered and out of breath.

'Would you mind coming over to Foxfield, Alice? Your father, too?' she asked.

'My father?' This seemed to alarm Alice for some reason but she snapped herself to attention. 'We'll come straight away.' She turned back to Beth. 'I'm sorry to rush off, but I'm needed elsewhere. Good luck at Stratton House. I hope to see you again soon.'

Beth merely nodded and stepped away but the woman,

32

Naomi, called after her. 'Forgive me for interrupting your conversation so rudely! It's just that there's an emergency.'

Beth lifted a hand in acknowledgement but kept walking, turning up Brimbles Lane as directed.

So much for Churchwood being a sleepy sort of place. But hopefully, Stratton House would offer the calm sanctuary Beth craved.

She'd been walking for several minutes when she heard laughter up ahead. Rounding a curve in the lane she saw two young women in ancient breeches and shirts attempting to share a single bicycle. 'This is madness!' the one on the back was saying.

'I can do it,' insisted the other.

But she couldn't. The bicycle wobbled precariously before overbalancing and tipping the women on to the ground. Ouch!

Beth hastened forward. She was a nurse, after all, and these women must be hurt. She could see blood on the hand of one of them and both were rolling from side to side as though to ride out pain. She could see that one was shaking, too.

Gradually, it dawned on Beth that they were laughing. She stopped in her tracks as they sat up and then got to their feet.

'Oh, hello,' one said, obviously noticing Beth.

This was the taller one, the one who'd been at the front of the bicycle. Her build was wiry while her hands and feet were huge. She was plain-featured, too, with ruddy cheeks and thin brown hair. Yet, despite her bloodied fingers, she was smiling as though she hadn't a care in the world.

'You've hurt your hand,' Beth pointed out, amazed that the girl showed no sign of having noticed.

'This?' She gave the injury a cursory glance then

shrugged broad shoulders. 'I've had worse and I'll have worse again. It's only to be expected when you work on a farm.'

But the injury hadn't been sustained through farm work. It was the result of larking around on a bicycle.

The other girl stepped into Beth's line of sight. Beth had already formed an impression of a tall, slender figure but only now did she notice how beautiful the girl was, despite the fact that both she and her friend could have passed as scarecrows in their patched, shabby clothes. This girl's hair was a gorgeous shade of chestnut. Long and abundant, it was arranged in a loose braid down her back but tendrils had escaped to frame her lovely face. Beth had never seen such clear, fresh skin before. As well, the girl had expressive dark eyes, and her cheeks and lips curved smoothly.

'I'm Kate Fletcher,' she said.

'No, you're not,' her friend told her.

'That's right, I'm not.'

What? This girl might be beautiful, but was she also simple-minded? How odd this village was!

'I'm Kate Kinsella now,' the girl explained. 'I'm newly married.'

Ah. She wore no rings on her filthy hands but Beth could see there was an emerald ring and a gold wedding band on a chain around her neck. No, not one chain. Three. More oddness.

Beth didn't begrudge others their happiness but the last thing she needed was a series of blissfully happy brides parading in front of her.

'I'm Pearl,' the other one said. 'Actually, my real name is Gertie Grimes but people call me Pearl.'

Beth couldn't see why. Anyone less suited to the name Pearl was hard to imagine, but perhaps nothing was straightforward in Churchwood. 'Neither of you are seriously hurt?' she asked, keen to be on her way.

'No, but thanks for asking,' Kate said. 'Are you heading to Stratton House?'

'I'm told it's at the end of this lane.'

'It is. You're joining the nursing staff?'

Did no one mind their own business here?

'My brother Fred is a Stratton House patient,' Kate continued. 'He's been discharged home but still goes back for therapy. You may see him there.'

Ah. Beth felt a tug of sympathy for both Fred and his family.

'Don't stand for any nonsense from him,' the taller girl advised. 'Fred likes to whine but the best way to deal with him is to push his wheelchair into a cupboard or steal his food.'

Good grief.

'Thanks for the advice,' Beth said.

Nodding goodbye, she walked on. She was here to serve her patients to the best of her ability while also giving herself space in which to mend her damaged heart. She decided that second goal was more likely to be achieved if she visited Churchwood as little as possible.

CHAPTER SIX

Victoria

'Hmm,' Dr Lovell said. They were in the small, private sitting room of Naomi's house. 'I'd guess this baby is no more than a few hours old. A little premature and rather small but doing well. She's alert and moving, and her colour is good. You found her in that box?'

'It was in the porch,' Victoria confirmed. The box had once contained tins of corned beef but had been kitted out with a folded towel as a mattress and blankets, also folded to create layers of warmth. Both were faded and thin with use but spotlessly clean. 'This is the note that was left.'

She held it out since Dr Lovell was still cradling the baby, though the words had scorched themselves into her brain.

Dear Miss Page,
*   Please look after the baby as I'm unable to do so just now.*
Please, please don't let her be taken away. Her name is Rose.
Thank you for being kind.

'I'd say the writer tried to disguise their handwriting, wouldn't you?' Dr Lovell said.

'I think so,' Victoria agreed.

'I imagine the mother is a young girl who found herself

caught out by an unplanned pregnancy. Or a woman at the end of her tether, perhaps because she already has more children than she can manage.' He looked at his daughter. 'You haven't been aware of any pregnancies in the village?'

'None that would fit with the birth of this little mite,' Alice told him. 'It's interesting that the mother says she can't look after the baby *just now* and begs for her not to be taken away. It suggests she intends to come back and reclaim her when she's in better circumstances.'

'It's a pity she gives no indication of when that might be,' Naomi said. 'But I think we can assume she's a local girl or woman, since she knows that Victoria is a kind and safe pair of hands for the child in the meantime.'

Victoria acknowledged the praise with a smile.

'Whoever she is, I'm worried about her,' Dr Lovell said. 'Especially if she's a young girl who hasn't given birth before and knows little of the dangers of infection and bleeding, not to mention a placenta that may not have fully come away. She may need medical attention.'

'Do you think we should ask around the village for information or even tell the police?' Naomi asked. 'I know the mother may come back of her own free will, but if she's in need of medical care . . .?'

'She may come back soon if she only left her baby here in the panic of the moment,' Alice pointed out.

'And if we announce the baby's appearance to all the village we might frighten her mother even more and drive her even deeper into secrecy,' Victoria said. 'In fact, she may never admit the child is hers and that could be a tragedy for her *and* the baby.'

'It's tricky,' Dr Lovell admitted. 'We can't keep the child hidden indefinitely – the birth needs to be registered with the authorities, for one thing – but perhaps we could keep quiet about her for a little while and give the mother a chance to reconsider what she's done. What do you think, Victoria? You're the one who's been asked to look after the child.'

Yes, but she lived in Naomi's house and her working time belonged to Naomi, too. Besides, there was another problem. 'There are already a lot of people living in this house at present,' Victoria said. And Naomi couldn't be expected to take in another waif and stray.

'We could take the baby to The Linnets,' Alice offered, 'though it would mean going against the mother's wishes.'

'I'll be happy to keep the baby here for the time being,' Naomi said, 'if Victoria is willing to look after her? With my help, of course.'

How kind she was! Victoria nodded agreement.

'But the other people who live here will need to be in on the secret, too, since babies make their presence known by crying,' Naomi continued. 'That means children as well as adults. We can impress upon them the importance of saying nothing about the baby outside the house but can't guarantee that no one – the younger children especially – will blurt something out. But perhaps that's a risk that needs to be taken to give the mother a chance to reunite with her baby.'

'This whole situation is fraught with risks,' Dr Lovell said, 'not least to the mother, since she may be unwell. I don't feel it would be right just to wait for her to appear. Might efforts be made to seek her out? Discreetly, of course.'

'I suggest we keep our ears and eyes open and ask a few others to do the same,' Naomi said.

Alice nodded. 'I'll ask Kate. She's rather cut off from things at Brimbles Farm but might still see or hear something useful.'

'I'll speak to Bert, Adam, May and Janet,' Naomi offered. They were all members of the bookshop organizing team and used to working together in sensitive circumstances.

'I don't suppose there's anything I can do personally,' Dr Lovell said. Now he was retired he spent most of his time at home indulging a long-held interest in the study of ancient civilizations. 'But you know where to find me if I can help.'

Little Rose had begun to mew. 'I suspect she's hungry,' Dr Lovell ventured.

Which brought them to another problem. What to feed her.

'She needs her mother's milk or milk from a wet nurse,' Dr Lovell continued, 'but we'll have to make do without either. Is there a tin of condensed milk in the house?'

'Yes,' Victoria told him.

'Mix it with some hot water and a little sugar. You'll need a feeding bottle, though. One that's spotlessly clean. When I was starting out in medicine, around half of babies who didn't have access to mother's milk died, and poor hygiene in bottle-feeding was one of the reasons. We want to give this little lady the best possible start.'

'I could buy a feeding bottle in the village,' Victoria said, 'but it'll rouse curiosity as people are bound to wonder why.'

'I have a solution to that problem,' Alice said. 'Mrs Baxter twisted her ankle yesterday so I said I'd do her shopping for her. She's weaning her latest baby but he still has bottle feeds sometimes, so if I buy the bottle, people will assume I'm buying it for him.'

'Don't forget teats,' her father advised.

Alice left and Dr Lovell offered the baby to Victoria. 'Would you like to take her?'

He spoke gently and Victoria wondered if he'd seen something in her expression. A certain yearning for a child of her own, perhaps? The thought made her pull herself together. She'd made her choices and had no desire to appear weak and regretful to anyone else, not even a man as nice as Dr Lovell.

Dismissing her own feelings, she took baby Rose into her arms and rocked her into quietness. How exquisite the child was with her delicate eyebrows, soft eyelashes, tiny nose and rosebud mouth. Rosebud . . . Rose . . . 'I wonder if there's any significance in her name?' Victoria said.

Naomi looked struck by the idea, too. 'Do you mean Rose could be a family name?'

'Something like that.'

'It's possible.' Naomi seemed thoughtful for a moment before adding, 'I can't think of anyone in Churchwood who's called Rose, but the name could go back a generation or two. It's worth considering, anyway. I can't make a connection, but someone else might.'

Rose stirred again and Victoria bent to kiss her downy head, revelling in the smell of her and in the softness of her hands, which bore tiny fingernails as fragile as pale-pink seashells. But she was swift to control the yearning that came over her. She couldn't help her feelings, but she could help how she managed them. Her priority had to be to let Arthur and Jenny grow up in blissful ignorance of all she'd given up for them.

Alice returned and took a bottle and teats from her shopping basket. 'I came straight back to leave these, though I'll have to take Mrs Baxter's shopping to her soon.'

'They need to be sterilized before use,' Dr Lovell said.

'I'll see to it.' Victoria handed the baby to Alice, who stroked the little one's cheek only to stiffen suddenly.

'Oh!' she said. 'I've just remembered something.'

CHAPTER SEVEN

Naomi

'What do you think?' Alice asked, after she'd finished explaining what she'd remembered.

'I think it's possible,' Naomi said.

She waited only long enough to be sure that baby Rose was feeding well – a relief to them all – before hastening into the village on a mission that would require her to keep all her wits about her if she was to draw out information without giving any away in return.

She nodded to the people she passed and called out occasional greetings but didn't pause to chat. Instead, she headed for a drab little terraced house and knocked on the door.

It was opened by Marjorie, who looked as though she couldn't decide whether to be pleased or full of apprehension when she saw who was standing on her doorstep. The puce flush in her plain face spoke of conflicting emotions within.

'Naomi,' she finally said. 'It's lovely to see you, but I suspect you've heard about me seeing a ghost and I hope you aren't here to tell me I must have imagined it. I know what I saw.'

'May I come inside?' Naomi asked.

'Oh! Certainly. Forgive my poor manners, only I've had an upsetting experience.'

'Why don't you put the kettle on for tea and then we can sit down and talk about it?'

'I'll be glad to do exactly that, only I hope you won't take the side of the unkinder people in Churchwood.'

'Kettle, Marjorie.'

Naomi stepped into the tiny hall and hung her coat over the newel post of the staircase that led to the two bedrooms upstairs. Another step took her into the sitting room, where she waited as Marjorie busied herself in the kitchen. 'I've no biscuits, I'm afraid,' Marjorie called. 'No cake, either.'

'A cup of tea is all I need,' Naomi called back.

She looked around the little room with its faded carpets and curtains, and the sagging sofa that ate a person up when they sat on it. On every surface there were ornamental china nick-nacks, many of which Naomi had given as gifts, not because she liked them but because she knew they gave Marjorie pleasure.

Naomi always felt a mix of emotions in this house. The first of them was pity. Like Victoria, Marjorie hadn't been born to poverty. Her family had once been wealthy but their fortune had dwindled away long ago and, as a middle-aged spinster, Marjorie's financial position was modest indeed. The second emotion was guilt, because Marjorie had been a loyal friend for many years and, while Naomi did her best to keep up the friendship, she suspected that Marjorie still felt left behind in her affections now newer friends like Alice, Kate and even Victoria had come along. Finally, there was also exasperation, because Marjorie's love of gossip coupled with her desperate need for attention made her the most tiresome woman in Churchwood.

Naomi perched on the edge of the sofa and sent up a smile as Marjorie entered with the tea tray. 'Lovely!'

'I expect Ada Hayes and Phyllis Hutchings have been gossiping about me,' Marjorie said defensively as she poured the tea. Doubtless, it would be weak tea and not just because of rationing. Marjorie's tight budget meant even food and drink needed careful management. 'I love Churchwood, but I wish the people here didn't gossip so much,' continued the village's biggest gossip.

Naomi was used to Marjorie's lack of self-awareness, though, and was only stunned for a moment. 'No one has said anything unkind about you, Marjorie. But I heard something about a ghost . . .?'

'I *did* see a ghost, Naomi! I swear I did. People around here think I imagine things but they're wrong. They said I imagined seeing poor John Gregson when he was camping out in the woods and visiting his wife in secret, but time proved I was telling the truth.'

John Gregson had been a soldier who'd deserted following a breakdown due to the cruelty and bullying he'd suffered at the hands of both his comrades and his officers. Sadly, he'd been killed when a German plane had hit the Sunday School Hall but, after being shunned by much of the village, his wife and two young sons had come to be accepted thanks to the intervention of Alice and her father. Now Evelyn Gregson had become a teacher at the village school and the family was very much liked.

'Tell me exactly what you saw,' Naomi invited now.

'You *do* believe I saw a ghost? Some people say I couldn't have seen it because there are no such things as ghosts but—'

'I keep an open mind about such matters,' Naomi assured her. 'So . . .?'

'I saw it when I got up in the night to . . . When I got up in the night and glanced out of my bedroom window. The ghost was floating along Churchwood Way.'

'Floating? Not walking? I imagine that, if there are such things as ghosts, they can do both.'

'Floating . . . Walking . . . I was too shocked to pay attention to its feet.'

'What was it wearing?'

'Some sort of shroud.'

'Long and white?'

'Yes. Long and pale, anyway.'

'Was the ghost male or female?'

'Female.' Marjorie was more confident about that. 'Slightly built with long hair.'

'I don't suppose you noticed the colour of the hair?'

'Heavens, Naomi, you ask some difficult questions! I only saw the ghost for a moment when the moon came out. I suppose it . . . *gleamed* on the hair, so it was probably fair or light brown. Why? Have other people seen ghosts with different hair colours?'

'Not as far as I know. I'm just trying to get a complete picture.' Now for another question. An important one. 'In which direction was it travelling?'

Marjorie looked nonplussed.

'Looking towards Churchwood Way, did it move from your left to your right or the other way round?'

Marjorie held up her arms, her eyes closed like a medium invoking the spirits of the dead. 'That way,' she finally said, waving an arm from her right side to her left side.

That meant the so-called ghost had headed towards the far side of the village from Foxfield. There were several streets of cottages over there, and more cottages straggling along the road to Barton.

'It wasn't carrying anything?'

'Such as?'

'Anything. I'm just trying to visualize what you saw.'

'I don't think it was carrying anything,' Marjorie said. She paused before adding, 'I'm just glad it didn't see me. Imagine if it had turned to look at me. Its eyes might have glowed red like the devil's. It might even have floated towards me to do me harm. I'd have fainted on the spot. I might even have died from the shock.'

'It didn't see you, so you've nothing to worry about,' Naomi pointed out.

'It didn't see me last night, but what if it comes back?'

'I suggest you avoid looking out of your window, Marjorie. That way, you can stay safely tucked up in bed like the rest of us.'

'But I need to get up sometimes.'

'Then go about your business but get straight back into bed,' Naomi advised. Having got as much information out of Marjorie as she was likely to get, she turned the conversation to the more down-to-earth subject of rationing but didn't stay much longer.

Outside again, she looked towards Churchwood Way. Marjorie's house was a few yards down a side street. It faced the houses opposite, but Marjorie would still have had a view of someone passing along Churchwood Way if she'd looked towards it sideways.

Naomi didn't believe in the ghost story for a single second. But she did wonder if the so-called ghost might have been baby Rose's mother, fleeing after leaving her child at Foxfield. Marjorie had described her as slight with light-coloured hair, but Naomi decided to treat that description with scepticism. For one thing, the night had been mostly dark, especially given the blackout. For another, the long hair might have been a shawl thrown over the head as camouflage. And for a third thing, Marjorie's tales were never reliable. It was true that she'd seen poor John Gregson when he was hiding from the village, but she'd described him as a giant of a man when in reality he was a little below average in both height and build.

Naomi headed for the vicarage but Adam the vicar was out visiting parishioners. 'Will you ask him to call at Foxfield as soon as it's convenient?' she asked his housekeeper.

'I'll be sure to,' Mrs Harris told her.

Naomi went next to May Janicki's house and was relieved to find her at home. May looked serious as she heard the story of baby Rose and Naomi guessed that her thoughts and feelings were complicated.

Tall, stylish May had come to Churchwood from London a couple of years earlier. Brought up in an orphanage, she'd overcome her troubled start in life to marry a man she loved. Not wanting children, she'd also embarked on a successful career as a designer and manufacturer of fashionable women's clothes. But then her Polish husband, Marek, had taken in the three refugee children of his sister after they'd been smuggled out of Poland when life for Jewish people had become difficult there. He'd then gone off to fight in the war so the care of them had fallen to May. Forced into abandoning her career and moving to Churchwood to create a safe home for them, May had struggled at first but had become a wonderful aunt to Rosa, Samuel and Zofia. Even so, Naomi knew May still carried shame over the anger and resentment she'd felt in the early days.

Naomi guessed that May's struggles would make her sympathetic to Rose's mother and she was right. 'I know what it's like to flounder when children are forced on a person by nature or circumstance,' May said. 'I completely understand if this baby's mother is overwhelmed and frightened, especially if she's young with no husband in sight.'

'We want to help her but we can't do that unless we find her,' Naomi said, 'preferably before the baby's existence is revealed and a scandal erupts.'

'I've no idea who she might be, but I'll keep my eyes and ears open,' May promised. 'I'll be discreet about it, too.'

'That's exactly what I hoped to hear,' Naomi said. 'You meet other families at the school, which the rest of us don't, so it'll be particularly helpful if you could watch and listen out when you're taking or collecting Rosa, Samuel and Zofia.'

'Understood,' May said.

From May's house Naomi went to see Janet Collins, a woman she'd known for many years though it was only recently that they'd become friends after joining forces on the bookshop organizing team. When Naomi looked back on the way she'd treated Janet and many other people in the village until just a couple of years ago, she felt ashamed.

Naomi's mother had died when her daughter was small and, though her father had loved her, he'd been what many people called a 'common little man' who made a modest fortune supplying quack tonics to gullible patients. Naomi had loved him in return but been mortified by the sneers that came his way. In time he'd sold his business and tried to launch his daughter and himself into high society. How embarrassing that had been! Always awkward and plain, Naomi had been all too aware that she was of interest to no one, but her father had been blissfully unaware of the disgust he engendered.

Alexander's unexpected attention had come as a relief as well as a surprise. After all, he was debonair and good-looking and very much a part of the society that scorned Cedric and Naomi Tuggs. Foolishly, she'd allowed him to persuade her that he truly cared for her and, after her father died unexpectedly, she'd been glad to marry him, only to come to the gradual realization that he was a cold man whose only interest was the money she'd inherited.

Twenty-five years had followed and, with her confidence at rock bottom, Naomi had tried to compensate for her desperate insecurity by using her wealth and position as the richest woman in Churchwood to set herself up as the social leader of the village, lording it over pretty well everyone.

She was past that period of her life now, thank goodness. The change had begun with Alice Irvine's arrival in Churchwood. It was Alice who'd conceived the idea of the bookshop, but in her sweet yet determined way she'd refused to let Naomi take it over. Affronted and hurt, Naomi had declined to be involved – until Bert Makepiece challenged her to give Alice and her fellow organizer, Kate, a chance. In giving them that chance, Naomi had discovered that there was joy to be had in working with people as equals instead of mere followers. Best of all, she'd found friends who valued her as a person. Fortunately, neither Janet nor anyone else held a grudge over Naomi's former pompousness.

A mother, grandmother and deeply caring person, Janet was concerned for both baby Rose and the girl or woman who'd given birth to her, though she, too, had no inkling about who that might be. 'I'll be on the watch for clues, though,' she said. 'You can count on me to help to look after the little scrap if you need me, too.'

Naomi pressed Janet's hand in gratitude and then left to visit Bert Makepiece at his market garden.

He was a big bear of a man who dressed in ancient clothes when working and wasn't much smarter when he wasn't. 'Hmm,' he said, leaning on his spade and watching her pick her way around his growing beds. 'I'm no doctor, but I diagnose trouble.'

'Would you expect life to run smoothly in Churchwood?' she asked.

'I would not. First things first, though.'

He wanted a kiss. Bert always wanted a kiss when they met or parted and often in between times, too. Why not? She was going to marry him as soon as she was free from her first marriage.

Who'd have thought it? Certainly not Naomi after all the heartache she'd endured with Alexander. Being married for her money hadn't even been the worst of it. He'd caused her worse grief by depriving her of children. Finally, she'd been devastated to learn that, despite being married to Naomi, he'd entered into a bigamous marriage with a much prettier woman, Amelia Ashmore, and had two children with her.

Fighting back at last, Naomi had threatened to expose his bigamy if he didn't agree to a divorce and financial settlement. A fair settlement, that was. More than fair, since it consisted only of Foxfield and enough money to restore her trust fund to less than half its original value, Alexander having fleeced her of most of it.

It left Alexander with the London flat and all of his pension and investments, most of which he'd probably hidden away, but he'd still been furious at being caught out and resented allowing her any money at all. Unfortunately, the divorce and settlement were taking months to go through and Naomi feared he might still try to wriggle out of the agreed terms somehow.

It was frustrating, waiting to see what happened, especially as she was running short of money. But it helped to know that happiness awaited her eventually in the form of Bert – Alexander's opposite in almost every way. Bert's kisses not only excited Naomi in a way that Alexander's chilliness had never done, but his down-to-earth good sense and kindness made her believe that there was no situation they couldn't make at least a little bit better between them.

He kissed her lips and then murmured in her ear, 'I'd draw you close for a hug but I'm covered in soil.' He was in his usual garb of ancient shirt, patched trousers, limp sweater with holes in the elbows, and boots that were held together by tape. Naomi didn't care a jot about his lack of smartness. Alexander had dressed immaculately but had been a horrible person. Scarecrow Bert was worth a hundred of him.

'So,' he said, easing back. 'What's the trouble this time?'

'A baby.'

'Someone's having one who maybe shouldn't?'

'Someone's already had one. Victoria found her in a box in the porch this morning.'

'Goodness. A little girl, you say? I hope she's all right?'

'She's tiny but Archibald Lovell has seen her and believes she's thriving.'

'That's good to hear. I suppose you want me to help to find her mother?' Bert guessed. He was never slow on the uptake. 'Discreetly, too, I imagine?'

Naomi told him about the note that had been left. 'We want to give the mother a chance to reclaim her child without the sort of fuss that means no one will ever forget she abandoned her daughter, if only in a moment of panic.'

'I won't go barging in with questions, but I'll keep my eyes peeled and my ears to the ground. Cup of tea?' he offered.

'Lovely idea, but I'd better get home.'

Bert nodded. 'Maybe I'll call round later and see how things are going.'

'I'd like that.'

She reached up to kiss him again and then went on her way.

She was almost home when she saw the vicar approaching. 'Adam!'

He was a slightly built young man with a mass of untidy brown hair. He wasn't dressed much smarter than Bert, but his heart was pure compassion and sweetness. 'Mrs Harris told me you wanted a word,' he said.

'I do, but let's wait until we're inside before I explain.' She glanced over her shoulder as though someone might be listening even now.

'Intriguing,' Adam said.

'That's one way of putting it.' Naomi let them into the house and led the way into the drawing room, where adults and children alike were gathered around looking down into a box.

'Has the grocer had some sweets in the shop?' Adam asked.

'The box contains sweetness but not of the confectionery sort,' Naomi told him.

He stepped forward and the little crowd parted to give him access. 'A baby!' he said. 'Whose is it?'

'Good question. She was left in the porch.'

Adam looked incredulous. 'She's a foundling?'

'So it seems. Now we've found her, we also need to find her mother.'

She left him lifting baby Rose from her box and went into the hall to hang her coat in the cupboard. Turning away, she noticed an envelope on the hall table. The postman must have delivered it while she was out.

Picking it up, she recognized the scrawled handwriting of William Harrington, Alexander's seventeen-year-old son by Amelia Ashmore.

Naomi had met him only recently. Believing that she was fleecing his father instead of it being the other way round, he'd run away from school and come to confront her, only to lose his nerve and spend a week living rough in the woods behind Foxfield until Naomi had found him, pitied him, and taken him into the house to be fed and bathed.

She'd assumed Alexander's family must be blissfully happy, but through William she'd learned that this wasn't the case. Alexander was as domineering with his family as he was with Naomi, and William was thoroughly miserable. His father's temper scared him. He hated his boarding school and he was struggling under his father's expectation that he should set his sights on a glittering career – stockbroking like Alexander himself, or something like accountancy or law, none of which appealed to the boy.

Gradually, William had realized that Naomi wasn't the money-grabbing harridan his father had portrayed and became her friend, much to Alexander's fury. He'd also become Bert's friend and, after helping in Bert's market garden, had decided that he, too, wished to work in horticulture one day – again, much to his father's fury. It was thanks to Naomi's intervention that William had changed to a school that allowed him to leave at weekends, and now he divided his free time between home and Foxfield.

It was a strange and unexpected situation. William resembled his father in being tall, thin and blue-eyed, but he was nothing like him in personality. He was modest instead of arrogant, kind instead of cold, and good-humoured instead of critical. Naomi liked him very much.

What his mother and sister thought of the situation Naomi couldn't know, since she'd seen them only once across the restaurant at Marcroft's Hotel the day she'd discovered Alexander's secret family existed. She'd never spoken to them or exchanged letters. But her impression was that Amelia Ashmore was both beautiful and weak and her daughter resembled her.

William had written to Naomi only a couple of days previously and it was unusual for him to be writing again so soon. Had something bad happened at school? Or had his father upset him somehow?

She tore open the envelope and drew out a note. It was short but still hit her in her stomach like a fist.

Dear Naomi,
   I didn't tell him, I swear. Whatever he says, it wasn't me.
Love from William x

Him had to be Alexander. Oh, heavens.
What now?

CHAPTER EIGHT

Ruby

Ruby stirred the pan of stew she'd made for lunch. As a land girl she wasn't supposed to carry out domestic tasks, but since she much preferred them to filthy farm labouring, Kate had agreed that Ruby could swap some of her outdoor duties for some of Kate's indoor work.

Kate was good like that, valuing happiness above rules, and insisting that she had no objection at all to taking on more of the actual farming since she'd been doing it all her life. She was a good person all round, which was remarkable considering she'd been dragged up by awful Ernie. Dismissing school as a waste of her time, he'd treated her as a domestic skivvy and farm labourer from her early childhood, paying her not a penny until recent years and allowing her only the cast-off boots and clothes of her four older brothers.

For most of her life the village had shunned her, since the Fletchers had a reputation for being rough and rude, but Kate had gradually fought back. She'd made friends with Alice Irvine, who'd drawn her into helping to organize the village bookshop. More friendships had followed and just weeks ago Kate had married Leo, a dashing flight lieutenant in the RAF.

Leo was a man of means so Kate could have left Brimbles Farm that very day, but after a short honeymoon she'd returned to work since she knew the rest of them would struggle without her.

The thought of weddings prompted Ruby to take a scrap of paper from her apron pocket. On it she was drawing up a list of possible guests. Naturally, darling Timmy was the first on the list. Then came Kate and the rest of Kenny's family, even cantankerous Ernie who'd consider a wedding to be a waste of valuable working time. Fellow land girl Pearl came next. Ruby had met her during their six weeks of land girl training. To an outsider their friendship had probably seemed unlikely, Ruby being a poor East Londoner and Pearl's family being far more well-to-do. But it had soon become apparent that Pearl's size, clumsiness and preference for shabby breeches and fresh air over dresses and cocktail parties made her an irritation to her parents. Her daintier sister, a lover of fashion and gracious living, was their preferred daughter. With her confidence destroyed by constant criticism, Pearl had been chuffed to bits to make a friend in Ruby.

The list continued with Alice Irvine and her retired doctor father. Then Naomi and Bert and young vicar Adam Potts, who Ruby hoped would conduct the service despite neither she nor Kenny doing much churchgoing. There were other people in the village whom she'd like to invite – May Janicki and Janet Collins from the bookshop organizing team for two. Then there was Naomi's housekeeper, Victoria, and little maid, Suki. Ruby had also befriended the evacuee women who lived at Foxfield and were fellow Londoners, while Timmy had befriended the children, particularly Victoria's boy, Arthur. But extending the list to include all those people might make the wedding unmanageable, so Ruby had added question marks beside their names.

There were two more possible guests whose names weren't on the list yet. Ruby's parents. She hadn't seen them since leaving London to become a land girl and was in no rush to see them now, especially considering she wasn't sure she could trust them not to let something slip about her secret.

'Planning the wedding?' Kate asked, stepping into the kitchen from outside and walking to the sink to wash her hands.

'There isn't much to plan since it's going to be small.'

'My wedding was going to be small but look what happened there.' Kate's wedding had been taken over as a bookshop event and almost the entire village had come along to celebrate.

'You've lived in Churchwood all your life and you have friends here,' Ruby pointed out.

'I've only had friends for the last couple of years,' Kate countered. 'Anyway, you have friends here too now. Is that your guest list?'

Ruby passed it over, knowing that clever Kate wouldn't miss the omission of Mr and Mrs Turner's names.

Sure enough, Kate looked up questioningly.

'I haven't made my mind up yet,' Ruby said.

Kate nodded and Ruby appreciated her understanding.

'Have you thought any more about where to hold the reception?' Kate asked instead.

'I'm still thinking of here in the barn.' It was no thing of beauty, but Ruby couldn't see a way to hold the reception elsewhere. Not with so little money in the budget.

'I'm sure Naomi will gladly offer Foxfield,' Kate said, not for the first time.

'She has her hands full with the London families and will have her own wedding to host once her divorce comes through,' Ruby replied, also not for the first time.

'There's always the bookshop,' Kate said. 'We can always explain to people in advance that it's a private party,' she added. 'I'm sure people will—'

Kate's words were cut off as Fred flung open the kitchen door and propelled himself inside in his wheelchair.

He took one look at them studying Ruby's list and said, 'Are you talking about weddings? Please don't while I'm here. It's the dullest subject on earth.'

Pearl had entered behind him and must have caught every word. For a moment she didn't move but then she clomped towards the sink to wash her hands. 'Is lunch ready?' she asked. 'I'm starving.'

It wasn't unusual for Pearl to announce that she was hungry. But it *was* unusual for her to let Fred get away with being a misery. Had she taken his words personally – as meaning he had no interest in her romantically – and been hurt by them?

Pearl's confidence had come on in leaps and bounds since arriving at Brimbles Farm. She knew she was appreciated as a strong and willing worker and liked as a person, too. But as a woman . . .? Ruby suspected Pearl still had no confidence at all.

She was the first to joke about how her hands were as big as shovels and her feet as big as a man's. About how plain she was with her large nose, ruddy complexion and limp brown hair which she wore cut short. And if Ruby were to ask whether Pearl ever saw herself as a bride, it wasn't hard to predict what she'd say. 'Me? A bride? Can you imagine me stomping down the aisle on my big feet? Everyone would laugh because I'd look ridiculous. Me? A bride? As if!'

Yet Ruby was sure she'd seen hurt on Pearl's face before she'd hidden it behind a mask of unconcern, because there was a world of difference between the feelings Pearl allowed people to see and the feelings she kept hidden, even from herself.

As for Fred, Ruby was equally sure that he'd only pretended to scorn weddings because he couldn't imagine that Pearl or anyone else would wish to marry him now he was no longer the tall, strapping man of old. He was less obviously bitter these days but his confidence remained fragile, too.

Oh dear. With so many barriers between them, it was hard to imagine how Pearl and Fred could ever move forward into an openly romantic relationship. The look on Kate's face suggested she was just as exasperated with them as Ruby.

Ernie walked in with Kate's middle brother, Vinnie. 'Why are you all wasting time standing idle?' Ernie demanded.

Ruby stuffed the list back into her apron pocket and returned to the stove to fetch the stew. Kate brought bowls and a plate of bread to the table while Pearl brought spoons. She couldn't do much harm to spoons.

The moment the meal was over, Ernie barked, 'Back to work.'

But just then there was a knock on the kitchen door. Ernie growled when Alice Irvine stepped inside. 'You again.'

'Yes, me.' Alice smiled sweetly despite his boorish behaviour.

She was small and slight but her courage more than made up for her size. Ruby understood that Alice had been going into battle with Ernie for two years now, and always emerged the victor. 'Don't let me keep *you* from your work,' she added.

Ernie muttered something – probably a curse – and left the kitchen, pausing at the door to snarl, 'Don't stand there gawping, the rest of you! Get back to work.' He glowered at Alice but the hostility troubled her not a bit.

'Everything all right?' Kate asked, when only she, Alice and Ruby remained in the kitchen.

'I'm fine,' Alice said.

She was pregnant again after a miscarriage last year which had upset her terribly, but Ruby suspected she wasn't here to talk about herself. 'I'll check on the washing,' Ruby said, to leave the friends alone to talk in confidence.

She went out to the washing lines that were strung between the outhouses, but the washing wasn't yet dry enough for ironing. She lingered for a few minutes but other jobs awaited her indoors, so she headed back towards the farmhouse. Nearing the kitchen window, she paused to catch the tone of the conversation going on inside, hoping it would have moved on to commonplaces so she could enter without awkwardness. 'Apparently, Marjorie thought she saw a ghost walking along Churchwood Way,' Alice was saying.

Marjorie Plym's hysterics were nothing new. Ruby had just decided to continue to the door when Alice added, 'We're wondering if it might have been the baby's mother.'

Baby? Ruby thought. *What baby?*

'Poor little thing,' Kate said. 'What will happen to her?'

'We want to give Rose's mother a chance to step forward before we involve anyone else,' Alice explained. 'That's why we're only telling a few people about Rose at present.'

'She's in good hands with Victoria and Naomi,' Kate said. 'And Foxfield is private enough.'

'My father is worried about the mother's health, of course. We'll all be relieved when we know she's well.'

'I'll keep the secret in the meantime,' Kate promised. 'And I'll let you know if I have any ideas about who the mother might be.'

Alice changed the subject then. 'There's a new nurse at the hospital.'

'I've met her,' Kate said, 'though I don't think Pearl and I made a good impression . . .'

It was probably safe to enter now but instead Ruby walked back to the outhouses, her heart pounding and her head reeling.

A little baby called Rose had been abandoned at Foxfield and the mother was missing.

It was possible that the mother was a married woman who was panicking momentarily because she wasn't coping well with her family while her husband was away serving in the war. If that were the case, she might soon be helped to cope better and all would be well.

But what if her circumstances were different and she was unmarried? Ruby remembered all too well that giving birth to a child outside of marriage had been lonely and frightening. She was full of sympathy at the thought of what this mother might endure.

But she was also desperately worried for herself and, even more, for Timmy. If word got out about this secret baby, the gossip would be brutal. It might cause people to turn their eyes towards Ruby and her so-called brother and question their relationship. If suspicions and con-demnations reached Timmy's ears, he might fire up and blurt out the truth, thinking he was defending his own mother but opening himself to disgust, since nasty comments and contemptuous looks weren't reserved for mothers. On the contrary, they could be directed at the children who were born out of wedlock, though those children had had no say in the circumstances of their births. If they were directed at darling Timmy, a small boy who was innocent of any wrongdoing . . .

The thought lacerated Ruby's heart.

Should she talk to him, perhaps? Explain that, whatever happened, he shouldn't retaliate but simply continue to keep their secret?

But Timmy was so happy now and it would be tragic to cast a shadow over that happiness by burdening him with what might prove to be unnecessary anxiety. Ruby decided she wouldn't speak to him yet. Instead, she'd keep an eye on the situation and be ready to act quickly if it changed. Of course, there was a chance that she might not be able to act quickly enough, but Ruby could only hope fervently that that wouldn't be the case.

What a worry!

CHAPTER NINE

Beth

Dear Mum and Dad, Beth wrote.

Then she sat back in her chair with a sigh, trying to sift through her mind for nuggets of information that would interest them while being comfortable for her to share. The easiest and most important thing to mention was that she'd arrived at Stratton House safely.

Just a quick line to let you know that I've arrived at the hospital and all is well, she added. All wasn't well but Beth's parents knew nothing of Oliver Lytton and the way he'd disappointed their daughter. It wasn't her intention ever to cause them pain by telling them.

The nearest village is called Churchwood. I haven't explored it properly yet, but when I got off the bus I saw that it had several shops as well as a church and what looked like a school. The scenery is pretty here and, while the hospital is some distance from the village, the walk is pleasant.

The hospital itself is rather magnificent, being in what was once a stately mansion. I believe the style is called Palladian. The main doors are set in the middle on a wide stone terrace that can be reached by steps on either side. They're very tall doors with a balcony above which is held up by a number of pillars.

The main wards are on the ground floor in what used to be splendid reception rooms – a drawing room, a dining room and a library, among others. It's startling to walk in and see plain metal beds in rooms with chandeliers, wood panelling and floor-to-ceiling windows that open into the gardens. Naturally, the nurses' quarters are tucked into the attics. My room is small but I have it to myself, which is nice.

I mentioned the gardens. They're lovely – lawns and woods, mostly.

So far, so bland. What next?

I had an interview with the matron, who appears to be a very efficient sort of woman.

That much was true, but the interview had been awkward for Beth since Matron had probed into her transfer from London. 'You requested a change, I believe?'

'Yes. Having worked on a surgical ward I thought it would develop my professional skills to work with patients who are at the next stage in their treatment – adjusting to their injuries and trying to build strength and mobility.'

'I see,' Matron said. But she subjected Beth to a long and thoughtful stare and it was difficult not to squirm.

For a moment Beth thought Matron might ask for the real story. It was a relief when she didn't.

'Welcome to Stratton House,' Matron said. 'You're not on duty until tomorrow, so I suggest you use today to settle in and get to know how we work. I'll ask another nurse to show you around and answer any questions you may have. Be warned, Nurse Ellis. I run a tight ship here. But work hard and you'll find me a fair taskmaster.'

It was hardly a gushing welcome but preferable to being required to talk about her private life.

A knock sounded on Matron's door. 'Come in,' Matron called.

A nurse entered. She was the sort of person who brought energy into a room, her figure curvy without being excessively so, her dark eyes full of sparkle and her smile wide. 'Reporting as requested,' she told Matron.

'Thank you, Nurse Carter. This is Nurse Ellis, a new member of our staff. I'd like you to show her to her room so she can leave her things there and then take her on a tour of the hospital.'

'Of course, Matron. Would you like to come with me, Nurse Ellis?'

Beth followed Nurse Carter outside. 'I'm Barbara,' she was told. 'Babs to my friends.'

'I'm Beth.'

'Pleased to meet you, Beth Ellis. I hope we'll become friends.'

This must be one of the nurses Alice Irvine had mentioned. She seemed nice, a jolly, fun-loving sort of girl – Beth's opposite in many ways.

All her life Beth had tried to be approachable and helpful, but she'd never been able to throw herself into life with carefree abandon. She didn't know how. She supposed most people would describe her as reserved. Even a little dull.

'We're mostly a friendly set of people here,' Babs said. 'My closest friend among the nurses is Pauline Evans. I'll introduce you to her soon. We've made friends in the village, too, particularly with Alice Irvine, who comes here as a volunteer to run a library that's related to the bookshop in the village. She writes letters for the patients, too, and reads stories to them.'

'I met her,' Beth admitted, adding when Babs's eyes lit up, 'but only briefly.'

'We love the bookshop,' Babs continued. 'We go there for talks, clubs and social events. Pauline and I are going along tonight. One of the organizers, May Janicki, is giving a talk on fashion in wartime. She used to design clothes before the war. Make them in her factory, too. Now she looks after three refugee children who are the nieces and nephew of her husband but she still dresses as though she's going to be featured in *Vogue*. It's hard to dress nicely with clothes being rationed, but May gives us all tips and encourages us to swap clothes or cut them up for making into new things. You could come with us since you're not on duty,' Babs said.

'Thank you, but I need to write a letter.'

'Another time, then.'

Beth gave a non-committal nod and decided the best way to head off questions about herself was to ask questions about the hospital. She began with, 'How many patients do you have here?' and kept up the enquiries until the tour was over and a cup of tea had been drunk.

'If you'll excuse me?' Beth had said then. 'I need to unpack. But thank you for showing me around.'

I'm impressed with what I've seen so far of the staff and the facilities.

Beth broke off as someone knocked on her door.

'Only me,' Babs Carter said when Beth opened it. 'This is Pauline, the nurse I told you about.'

Pauline – a slender, fair-haired girl – waved and said, 'Welcome to Stratton House.'

Beth forced a smile. 'Thanks.'

'I just thought I'd knock in case you've changed your mind about coming to the bookshop?' Babs said.

'It really is fun,' Pauline added.

'Thank you, but I need an early night,' Beth told them. 'I'm on duty in the morning.'

How stiff and prissy she must sound.

But Pauline was sympathetic. 'It's tiring settling into a new place. And it's quite a trek to the bookshop and back.'

'Worth it, though,' Babs said. 'Not to worry. You'll have plenty of other chances to come along.'

'I hope you enjoy the evening,' Beth said.

The visitors left and Beth returned to her letter, only to sink down on to the bed instead.

She reached for the photograph of her parents that stood on the window ledge. It showed Edwin Ellis with his beloved pipe in his mouth and an arm around his wife. Beth had taken the photo on the old Kodak Brownie last year. 'Smile!' she'd commanded, and her mother had given a self-conscious laugh, whipping off her apron and patting her hair.

Beth's father was a postman back in Norwich, while her mother kept house and looked after her own mother, who'd lived with them since becoming a widow. Everything about the household was modest because money was tight. Not that any of them complained, because they expected no more and were content with their lot.

They were good, loving people. But Beth had never felt that they understood their only child. She'd mastered reading early and loved books and learning ever since, but her parents had considered it strange that she hadn't preferred to dress her dolls or play at house. They'd expected her to leave school at fourteen, as did the children of everyone they knew, to mark time in a modest little job – in a shop, perhaps – until a pleasant young man came along to marry her.

When she'd won a place at grammar school, she'd heard them talking about how lessons in preserving fruit and darning socks would serve her better than Latin and complicated mathematics. But they'd agreed that she could attend the school if that was what she really wanted, and they'd paid for her uniform without complaint, even though it meant tightening their already snug belts. They'd also let her stay on until she was sixteen so she could take her School Certificate. By then, Beth had set her heart on nursing.

'It means I'll be able to help people,' she'd pointed out to her parents. 'That's a good thing, isn't it?'

'Oh, certainly,' her mother had said, but she'd exchanged looks with her husband and it hadn't been hard to interpret what those looks meant.

Nursing was a noble profession but it wasn't for people like the Ellises, whose place in the world was small, humble and domestic. Though they'd never insisted that she live their sort of life, she knew her choices grieved them. Beth remembered them sighing wistfully whenever news came of the engagement or marriage of one of her contemporaries. There'd been equally wistful comments about local houses becoming available for rent.

Beth had never been opposed to marriage and motherhood. She'd even hoped to achieve them one day. But she'd wanted to tread her own path through a career in nursing first.

That was one of the reasons Oliver had seemed ideal to her. She'd envisaged them working side by side in the hospital, each admiring the other's skills and professionalism.

Remembering her starry-eyed optimism, misery dragged on Beth's spirits. And to think she'd wasted money and coupons on that blue dress. She rarely spent much on herself, preferring to help her parents and grandmother by sending her spare cash home since she knew how much it was appreciated. She'd brought the dress to Stratton House, but, doubting she'd ever wear it again, had left it folded into her suitcase where it wouldn't taunt her with reminders of what she'd lost.

She sighed. Misery was lonely, but Beth knew no other way of dealing with it except by herself. Oliver Lytton might have taken her out of herself for a while, but look what had happened there.

It was a pity she'd lacked the money for a holiday before coming to Stratton House. Breathing in sea air while taking bracing walks along the coast might have helped her to get over Oliver sooner, but changing hospitals had been the best she could do to give herself a change of scene and, hopefully, space in which to recover. It remained to be seen whether Stratton House and Churchwood allowed it.

Would Oliver be taking Cassandra Carlisle out tonight? A painful hollow opened up inside Beth and it was a struggle to hold back tears. But she got up to continue with her letter.

There's a carpet of bluebells in the woods here. I'm looking forward to walking among them . . .

CHAPTER TEN

Hannah

Waking with a start, Hannah lifted her head from the kitchen table and looked around her, slumping in relief when she saw that Simon and Susie were still safely playing together. She rubbed her tired face with her hands. Tired? She was exhausted. Sore, too. And sick at heart at the thought of what she'd done, not only during the night but also just then, when she'd fallen asleep while she was supposed to be caring for two small children.

She'd sat down after she'd found herself trembling uncontrollably, intending only to rest for a while. The trembling had begun hours ago but gradually grown worse. Fortunately, her father hadn't noticed when she'd served breakfast. He'd merely grunted as he'd left for work instead of bawling something like, 'Don't you go fancying yourself ill so you can take to your bed all day. I've got a job to do at Edmundson's and you've got a job to do here.'

His job was delivering meat for the wholesale butcher in Barton. Hers was looking after everyone here in the cottage they called home. It was a cottage in the middle of nowhere along the road that connected their nearest village, Barton, to Churchwood. Old and shabby on the outside, it was cramped and crowded on the inside, since it was much too small to house a family with six children in comfort. There were three bedrooms upstairs and two rooms downstairs in addition to the lean-to, but none of the rooms were large. The furniture was old and random, probably picked up cheaply years ago, but, although Ma had kept the place clean and Hannah followed her example, there was clutter everywhere – pots and pans that wouldn't fit in the cupboard, racks of clothes and nappies, Pa's toolbox, the sewing box, a few toys . . .

After her father had driven off in Edmundson's van she'd seen Michael, Milly and Johnnie, the elder three of her five young brothers and sisters, off to school and begun to clear up the breakfast things, but the trembling had grown so bad that she'd feared her legs might give way. At least the doze had steadied her a little.

Her thoughts flew to Churchwood. The box she'd left at Foxfield must have been discovered long ago. If only Hannah could know what was happening there.

Wincing, she got to her feet and crossed to the kitchen sink to drink cold water and try to revive her energy so she could serve Ma and the younger children lunch. They must be hungry.

Afterwards, she washed up the lunch dishes, rinsing them carefully the way Ma had taught her. Thoughts of Ma had emotion rippling through her. Kind and loving, Ma had done her best to make a happy home despite being married to a surly bully. She'd never been strong, though, and her first four children had put such a strain on her slender body that from an early age Hannah had needed to rush home from school to help out. 'Enough!' the doctor had ordered after Johnnie's birth. 'No more children!'

But Hannah's mother had fallen pregnant again and been sick from the start. The law said Hannah had to stay at school until she reached fourteen but, with her mother needing help at home, the law had to take second place to harsh reality. Hannah's education had been abandoned in practice, even if she'd remained on the school roll, but after she'd turned fourteen Ma had insisted that she should have a few hours out of the house each week to work in the Barton bakery.

'You shouldn't be stuck at home all day,' Ma had said. 'You need to get away sometimes and if you're earning even a few shillings you can save for your future.'

Hannah had been glad to work, though her few shillings had mostly gone to supplement the meagre housekeeping money her father handed over.

After Susie's birth, Hannah had heard the doctor having stern words with her father. 'I'm warning you, Jed Powell. Another pregnancy could kill your poor wife.'

But Simon had appeared not long afterwards and Ma's health had collapsed completely. Her weak heart had been put through more strain than it could bear. 'If she dies, it'll be on your head, Jed Powell,' the doctor had said. 'You'll be as much to blame as if you'd stabbed her with a knife.'

'It isn't for you to tell me how to live,' Hannah's father had argued.

'You need telling because you're a fool, Jed. Think, man, think. How will you cope with all these children and no family to help out?'

Ma had lived, thank goodness. But since she spent most days resting in bed, Hannah's little job had fallen by the wayside.

It was at the bakery that she'd first met Mattie Hamilton. He lived in Churchwood rather than Barton but had called in for a bun one day when passing. He'd called in for a bun several times after that, asking her questions about the best ones to buy. 'Which bun would you choose?' he asked one day, and when Hannah told him, he bought it for her.

'I can't accept it,' she told him.

'Why not? It's bought and paid for. Wrap it in a bag and slip it in your pocket for later.'

Hannah hesitated for a moment longer then did as he suggested. It would be nice to have a treat to eat. It was also nice to see the way Mattie's brown eyes grew warm with satisfaction. He had the kindest, loveliest eyes. The kindest, loveliest smile, too.

When she left the bakery that evening she found him waiting for her at the end of the road. 'I hope you don't mind, but I thought we might enjoy talking about more than the merits of this bun or that bun,' he said.

'I don't mind, but . . .' She glanced around to be sure no one was about to see them.

'You have strict parents who wouldn't like to see you with a boy?' he guessed.

'It's my father,' Hannah admitted. 'He . . .'

'Isn't a pleasant man?'

'I suppose it's wrong of me to say it but no, he isn't.'

'Don't worry. My mother isn't exactly Mrs Wonderful, either, so we're even.'

They set off walking. Mattie was much taller than her, since she was what Ma had always called a 'dainty little thing', but he matched his strides to her shorter steps so there was no awkwardness about it. He didn't touch her but simply walked at her side. Hannah was relieved. Not counting her brothers, she'd never walked beside a boy before. She wasn't sure what to expect but she wouldn't have been ready for anything more than this easy companionship.

On that first walk home – punctuated by a dive into some bushes when a vehicle approached, though it proved to be an unknown car rather than Edmundson's van – Hannah learned that Mattie was a carpenter who loved working with wood. That he had an older sister – long married – who'd left home years ago. 'Probably to escape my mother,' Mattie said. 'They don't get along, but then few people get along with her.'

'Does that include you?'

'She smothers me with love but that doesn't mean I'm blind to her faults.'

He was respectful when they drew near to Hannah's cottage. There was no clumsy attempt at a kiss that would have frightened her off. Instead, he smiled and said, 'I'd like to see you again. If you'd like to see me?'

'I would but—'

'We can be discreet,' he promised.

Mattie kept to his promise. He didn't touch her on their second walk, either, but as they set out to walk for a third time he offered his hand and said, 'Shall we?' and they walked along with her fingers clasped tenderly in his.

'I hope my hand doesn't feel rough to you?' he said. 'Working with wood toughens them up.'

'I like it.' There was something comforting and re-assuring about the feel of Mattie's fingers around hers. He was capable of strength yet with her he was gentle.

At the end of that walk he said, 'May I?' and kissed her cheek.

It wasn't until their fifth walk that he kissed her lips. It was a slow and hesitant kiss. But lovely.

Yet uncertainty must have crossed her face afterwards because he frowned and asked, 'What is it, Hannah? Am I going too fast for you?'

'No, it's . . . Are you sure I'm enough for you?'

'You're the person I want,' he insisted.

'But all the secrecy . . . All the time I need to spend looking after my family . . .'

'I'd like us to spend more time together. Of course I would. I'd like us to be open about seeing each other, too. But I understand things are difficult for you with your mother being sick and your father being . . . who he is. I hope our circumstances will change for the better one day, but until then . . . I think I'm falling in love with you, Hannah. All the time we're apart I look forward to being with you again. Feeling your tiny hand in mine, seeing your beautiful face . . .'

'I'm hardly beautiful, Mattie.' There was nothing striking about Hannah's appearance. She was small with no figure to speak of and nothing in her face to catch the attention.

'You're beautiful to me,' he insisted. 'Your hair—'

'Is dull brown.'

'It's a soft brown that reminds me of the woods and nature. Everything about you is soft and fresh, Hannah. Your lovely blue eyes, your cheeks, your mouth . . .'

'I'm not sure about all that,' she said, laughing with embarrassment.

'*I'm* sure.'

He certainly looked sincere and perhaps he was right in believing that it was the inside of a person that made their outside so appealing. It was the same for her. Mattie didn't have the clean-cut handsomeness of some men she'd seen – Alice Irvine's husband being one of them. Neither was he dashing like the pilot Kate Kinsella was courting. But Mattie was beautiful to Hannah.

'I think I might be falling in love with you, too,' she told him, and he grinned.

'That's all right, then.'

Soon, though, Hannah's circumstances changed for

the worse with Ma's health collapsing after Simon's birth. Giving up her job at the bakery meant there'd be no more walks home with Mattie.

'I'm the eldest child and the little ones are my responsibility,' she'd explained.

'I understand, but I hope it doesn't mean we have to stop seeing each other. I love you so much.'

They were both sure of their love by then.

'I still like to think we have a future together,' he continued. 'I know it's going to be difficult to meet but we'll find a way.'

They had found a way, sometimes meeting early in the mornings and sometimes late at night. But then Mattie had been called up to the army.

'Don't worry, darling,' he'd said, drawing her into his arms. 'Everything feels thrown into chaos just now. But it'll be all right in the end. We're young. We've got years ahead of us.'

The night before Mattie left, Hannah had waited for the sound of her father's snores and then crept downstairs, letting herself out into the night and running into Mattie's arms in the wood behind the cottage.

It had been a heart-wrenching meeting, for who knew how much time would pass before he was allowed home on leave? Months, certainly. Maybe even years. And forever if he were to fall in the fighting.

'Stay safe,' she'd urged him. 'Promise me you'll stay safe.'

'I'll do my best. All I want is a wonderful future with you, Hannah.' She'd sobbed and he'd held her close and kissed her.

And somehow the desperation of the moment had swept them further than it should have done.

'I'm sorry,' he'd said afterwards. 'I should never have—'

'I'm as much to blame as you,' she'd told him, but Mattie had shaken his head.

'I'm two years older. I'm supposed to be two years wiser. Besides, a man should look after the girl he loves. He shouldn't . . . shouldn't have . . .'

'Hush, Mattie. Don't spoil our last few minutes together with regret.'

'But—'

'I love you, and I believe you love me.'

'More than anything or anyone.'

'Then let's hold each other tight and cherish our last moments.'

They'd done just that but in time they'd needed to part. 'Here,' he'd said, pressing four half-crowns into her hand. 'Buy paper and envelopes so you can write to me. Shall I write to you?'

Hannah had wanted to say that of course he should write to her, but they both knew that if Jed Powell discovered his daughter was corresponding with a man, his fury would make life miserable for her and the whole family. He was usually at work when the post came – not that the family received letters often – but she'd still be taking a terrible risk if she encouraged Mattie to write.

'It's a pity I can't write to you at my mother's address,' Mattie had added, 'but you know what she's like.'

Hannah no longer had any friends to take in post for her since she'd missed so much school. She'd considered asking the baker if her letters might be sent there – he'd always appeared to value her hard-working attitude and cheerful way with customers – but feared he might object to doing anything underhand. In any case, she couldn't be sure that he'd keep the arrangement confidential. Hannah couldn't even be certain that one of her brothers and sisters wouldn't accidentally let slip that she'd received a letter.

'Write if there's an emergency,' she'd told Mattie.

'But not otherwise,' he'd agreed, and they'd shared forlorn looks. 'Please don't let it stop you from writing to me,' he'd said. 'I want to hear from you as often as possible.'

'I'll write,' Hannah had promised. 'I'll also shop in Churchwood sometimes in the hope of picking up news of you there.'

With a final hug they'd parted and Hannah had crept back into the cottage to curl up on her bed and weep in silence, because she shared the little bedroom with her sisters and didn't wish to wake them.

When she started feeling more tired than usual, she'd put it down to low spirits due to missing Mattie. Gradually, it had dawned on her that there was more to it than that, and panic had set in. Should she write to Mattie to tell him what had happened? Hannah had decided against it, scared that worrying over it might distract him and make him vulnerable to an enemy bullet or shell. Instead, she'd spent months hoping he'd be granted leave soon anyway so they could manage the situation together, starting with a wedding because surely her father would give his consent in the circumstances, even if he was furious about it.

After that . . . Hannah hadn't been clear on what would happen then. She still had little knowledge of how soldiers' wives were supported financially when their husbands were serving but assumed there must be some sort of provision which might give her options over where she lived.

If there were only herself and the baby to consider, she imagined she could take a lodging somewhere, supplementing her army allowance by cleaning or doing any other job that was possible with a baby. But she couldn't abandon Ma and the children. It wasn't only during the daytime that they needed her. It was also during the night, because she couldn't trust her father to help Ma or soothe a sick or troubled child. It wasn't in his nature and, besides, he often drank too much at the Wheatsheaf and fell asleep in his armchair afterwards while smoking. Once, he'd dropped a cigarette on to a tea towel, and if Hannah hadn't been there to throw water over the flames, the house might have gone up in smoke and taken the Powell family with it. When Mattie was home they might be able to work out a solution. But Mattie wasn't home.

The Powell family's ration books were registered in Barton so Hannah had only been able to use the Churchwood shops for unrationed food. She'd still visited as often as possible in the hope of hearing news of Mattie. On one occasion she'd even followed Aggie Hamilton along the street, listening as she talked to another woman but learning only that Mattie was a good boy who wrote often, though the censors made sure he gave away little about his duties.

Another time she'd followed Aggie into a shop but once again heard about Mattie in only the vaguest terms. And yet another time, feeling desperate, she'd walked past Mattie's house and seen his mother cleaning her windows. She hadn't been smiling but neither had she looked upset. Hannah had taken from that only that Mattie was still safe. It had been something – a huge relief, in fact – but oh, how she'd ached for his return.

Waiting and waiting, Hannah had done her best to hide her curving body even from her mother, who already had enough problems without Hannah adding to them. 'What are you doing?' her sister Milly had asked once, catching Hannah letting out one of her few dresses.

'Some of the stitching was unravelling,' Hannah had

fibbed. 'I'm going over it to stop it from bursting right open.'

With her looser clothes and a cardigan on top, Hannah had hoped it would take an eagle eye to discern her changing shape. Not that it was changing dramatically. Hannah had known enough to be sure she was smaller than most women at this stage and that had been a relief, until it occurred to her that the baby might not be thriving despite the gentle flutterings Hannah could feel. She had neither the money nor the courage to consult a doctor alone. Instead, she'd clung to the hope that Mattie would be home soon.

When he'd been absent for more than seven months and she was beside herself with worry, Hannah had finally written to tell him about the baby.

Darling Mattie,

I'm so sorry to give you worrying news but I'm expecting our baby in about two months' time and I really need your help. I wanted to tell you face to face when you came home on leave but that hasn't happened and time is running out. Might you ask for the sort of special leave people can get when there's trouble at home? Compassionate leave, I think they call it. Please try, Mattie. I'm not sure how much longer I can keep hiding what's happening from my father and everyone else.

Sorry, again, for worrying you.

With all my love,

Hannah x

She'd posted the letter the next morning. She'd had no idea how long it would take to reach him nor how long his reply would take to reach her, but she'd heard nothing. And then last night the baby had arrived.

Now she sat down to write another letter.

Darling Mattie,

Our baby came early. She's a little girl and I've named her Rose as it's a pretty name for a pretty baby and also my mother's middle name. I've left Rose in the care of that nice woman in Churchwood who took in those two children from London: Victoria Page. She's always had a smile for me if I've passed her in the street and a smile for Susie and Simon too. I know she lives in someone else's house but Mrs Harrington seems nice as well. After all, she took in several families from London, including I don't know how many children. I hope they'll keep Rose with them until you can return home and we can work out what's best to be done. Have you asked for that special leave I mentioned? Please hurry home, Mattie. I need you and so does Rose. You'll adore our daughter. I know you will.

With all my love,

Hannah x

PS I know I told you not to write except in an emergency but this is *an emergency. If you can't come straight home, please write to let me know what you think I should do.*

Wanting to post it immediately, she pushed herself to her feet only to clutch the table as she swayed with sudden weakness. How tired she was! How shaky, too. She took some deep breaths, knowing she had to steady herself somehow.

Posting her letter was only one reason for returning to Churchwood. Hannah also wanted to hear if word had got out about baby Rose. The more she thought about it, the more she worried that it had been foolish to think a baby could be kept secret in a house like Foxfield, which had so many people living there. And Miss Page might have been given no choice about handing the baby to the authorities – whoever they might be.

Hannah imagined the authorities as stiff, unyielding people who'd have scant sympathy for a penniless young mother who'd given birth out of wedlock and had nothing to offer her child except love. Probably, they'd place Rose in an orphanage or with a married couple who had no children of their own and wanted to adopt someone else's. Without Mattie by her side the situation made Hannah feel like a wilting plant, but she had to cling to the hope that Miss Page would keep Rose for at least a little while. If only Hannah didn't feel so sore and fragile!

'Come on,' she said to Susie and Simon. 'We're going out.'

CHAPTER ELEVEN

Hannah

It was hard work wheeling Simon to Churchwood in the ancient perambulator, especially since one of the wheels didn't turn properly. It became even harder work when Susie complained of aching legs and wanted to ride in the pram as well. But at least the handle was something for Hannah to lean on as she trudged along the Barton Road.

Reaching the turning to Sycamore Street, where Mattie lived, she looked along it at the rows of neat cottages. A woman was out sweeping her front path but she wasn't Aggie Hamilton. Hannah continued onwards to the Churchwood bakery. 'You stay with Simon,' she told Susie. 'I'll watch you through the window.'

The thought of lifting the little ones out of the pram and then back into it was daunting, given how weak Hannah felt. Besides, if she heard that she'd been seen last night or that Rose had been placed with the authorities already, she'd need a moment to get her emotions under some sort of control and could do that better alone.

But Susie began to whine. 'Want to come! Want to come!' she cried, holding her arms out imploringly.

Hannah sighed and lifted her down from the pram before taking Simon into her arms. Bracing herself, she entered the shop. No one shouted that here was the girl who'd abandoned her baby. In fact, no one gave Hannah more than a fleeting glance, and the conversation between the two women in the queue was about Farmer Mead's dog. Apparently, it had got free from the farm again and snapped at the postman.

The door opened behind Hannah and the tall, lanky woman who never stopped gossiping walked in. Marjorie Plym. 'Have you heard?' she asked the others excitedly.

Heard what? Hannah's heartbeat quickened.

'Alec Mead's dog got free and snapped at poor Mr Baldry,' Miss Plym announced.

'We already know,' she was told, and she slumped in obvious disappointment.

'Any more news to impart?' one of the other women asked, nudging her friend knowingly.

'You make me sound like a gossip and nothing could be further from the truth,' Miss Plym complained.

The others exchanged eye-rolls and then turned away to make their purchases.

Afterwards, they headed for the door and Hannah's heartbeat quickened again when one of them suddenly came towards her. But she merely said, 'My word, aren't you a bonny lad?' to Simon and went on her way.

Hannah bought a loaf and then went to the post office, and the greengrocer's for carrots. She had a small vegetable patch behind the cottage but, with tall trees looming over it, the vegetables saw little sun and were neither plentiful nor luscious.

Again, there was nothing of interest to hear. Emerging back into the street, Hannah stared along Churchwood Way in the direction of Foxfield, but she had no excuse for going that way and would need all her strength for the walk home.

Tramping slowly back along the Barton Road, she wondered what it meant that no one was talking about

Rose. That Miss Page had honoured Hannah's wishes and was looking after Rose, perhaps in the hope that her mother would soon make herself known? Or that Rose had already been handed over to the authorities?

A chill passed through Hannah as a third possibility suddenly occurred to her. Could someone else have taken Rose as she lay in her box in the Foxfield porch? No, that was ridiculous. Hannah had been careful to place the box out of sight of the road. But what if Rose had cried and someone had approached the porch to investigate?

Surely that was ridiculous, too. Who'd be passing by so early in the morning? The answer came back at her. The milkman. The postman. A fox . . .

Horror engulfed her but Hannah struggled against it. Far from sneaking off with Rose, the milkman or the postman was more likely to have raised the alarm. As for a fox, it was highly unlikely that it could take Rose and leave nothing behind to trigger questions about what had happened – the box, the blankets, the note . . .

Hannah needed to keep a tight rein on her emotions, since giving way to anxiety would only attract attention and make it all the harder to keep Rose a secret. And once the secret was out, Hannah and Mattie might have no chance of keeping her with them in their own little family. Exhaustion wasn't helping. It was making her imagination take flight in all directions, however fanciful. She needed to rest so she could be strong in both mind and body. Tonight she'd go to bed early.

Reaching the cottage, she took the children inside and looked out of the kitchen window at the washing she'd hung on the line that morning after soaking it in cold salted water and putting it through the mangle to squeeze out some of the wet. Nightdress, sheet, towel, rags . . . It was a relief to see that the bloodstains had gone.

But then another anxious thought slid into her head.

Mrs Harrington was friendly with Alice Irvine, whose father was a doctor. What if Mrs Harrington mentioned Rose to Alice who, in turn, mentioned the baby to her father? He was a kindly man as far as Hannah knew and might worry that the baby's mother could need medical attention after giving birth. If he launched a hue and cry to find her, Hannah's hopes of buying time for Mattie to come home would be blown to pieces.

Why hadn't she thought of this before and mentioned that she was perfectly well in the note she'd left? She'd have to leave another note. Tonight. When she was exhausted already.

Tears welled up in her eyes and spilled down her cheeks.

'Hungry!' Susie tugged at Hannah's skirt.

Wiping her eyes on the backs of her hands, Hannah turned to Susie with a smile. 'Food soon, I promise,' she said.

But as Susie toddled off again, more tears came into Hannah's eyes. Head bowed, she sobbed.

CHAPTER TWELVE

Victoria

The envelope was on the doormat when Victoria came downstairs for her early-morning walk. Realizing it must have been delivered by hand, she wondered if it was from Rose's mother and hastened towards it.

The writing was just the same: awkward, as though it had been written by someone who'd set out deliberately to disguise their usual style. As before, it was addressed to *Miss Page*.

Tearing it open, Victoria drew out the note.

Dear Miss Page,

I hope you didn't mind me leaving Rose with you but I was desperate. I hope she's well and I hope you're well too. I also hope you haven't sent her away. Please don't think she isn't loved. She is, but I need more time.

In case you're worried about me (instead of just hating me for what I did) let me tell you that I'm in good health. I know this because I know about having babies and what to expect.

Thank you from the bottom of my heart for looking after Rose. If I had money to give for something for her to wear, I'd give it. But I haven't any money just now. Sorry.

Victoria read it for a second time, trying to draw some conclusions from it. Clearly, the writer loved Rose and hoped to reclaim her. She had a conscience, too. Victoria was less convinced by the writer's assurance that she knew about having babies. Surely she'd have backed up the claim by stating that she'd given birth before, if that were the case? More likely, she was basing the claim on things she'd heard, which was worrying since hearsay could be inaccurate and might not apply in this mother's case anyway.

Also worrying was the mention of having no money, since it meant the writer hadn't the means to seek medical help should she find she needed it despite her expectations. On the other hand, she'd found the strength to come to Foxfield. Twice. Unless someone else had delivered the baby and notes on her behalf? A trusted friend or sister, perhaps?

Victoria thought about the clothes Rose had been wearing when found. Nightdress, cardigan, nappy and blanket had all been old, worn and ill-fitting, as had the spare nightdress and nappy that had been tucked under the blanket. Hand-me-downs from someone, but who? A well-wisher? Or had they been taken from the mother's own family's store of baby items? There was no way of knowing.

Sighing, Victoria returned the note to the envelope and pushed it into the pocket of her trousers. She made her way through the house to the kitchen door and, unlocking it, stepped into the morning.

She was tired because Rose had needed feeding and changing twice during the night. Victoria hadn't resented her disturbed sleep, though. Rose was a sweet little thing and deserved as much care and love as Victoria could lavish on her.

Rose was sleeping now and it would do Victoria good to have a breath of morning air before the day began to rush forward.

She walked down the garden, leaving a trail of foot-prints in the silvery dew. Anyone who needed her in a hurry would be able to find her by following them. A thrush dug into the lawn for breakfast and emerged triumphantly with a worm. A rabbit hopped across the grass, paused to sniff the air, and hopped on again.

Were their lives as uncomplicated as Victoria imagined? Driven only by instinct and the need to find food instead of navigating the more complex – and often conflicting – yearnings, duties and obligations that made a boiling pot of human emotions? The thought brought Sergeant Paul Scarletti into her mind. Again.

She'd thought about him often since they'd met yesterday morning, though she'd tried to resist it since she could never have the sort of romantic life he represented, so there was no point in dwelling on it. Her happiness was surely better served by concentrating on what she *did* have in her life. Unfortunately, the thoughts kept creeping back.

Dismissing them again, Victoria returned her mind to Rose's mother. Clearly, she was in turmoil and hoping her circumstances would change with time. But in which way might they change and how much time would she need? Already, another day and night had passed since she'd given birth and they were no closer to identifying her.

Naomi had gone along to May Janicki's talk on fashion at the bookshop last night but she'd shaken her head on her return. 'If the baby's mother was there, she did an excellent job of hiding the fact that she was troubled,' she'd reported.

Victoria wanted to allow the mother at least a few more days to get back in touch, but the decision wasn't only Victoria's to make.

She breathed in deeply and then set off back to the house to learn what the others thought should be Rose's fate.

CHAPTER THIRTEEN

Naomi

'So you're giving the girl another day to come forward?' Bert said, when he called at Foxfield to learn how matters stood with Rose.

'Certainly today. Possibly longer, but we'll take it one day at a time,' Naomi confirmed. She'd talked to Victoria, Ivy and Alice and they'd all been of the same mind. 'You called the mother a girl just then, Bert. We all suspect that she's young but we need to keep open minds.'

'Indeed we do.'

'Archibald Lovell is still worried about her, of course. He fears she may not know as much about childbirth and what to expect afterwards as she thinks she does.'

'Especially if she's just a slip of a girl,' Bert agreed. He paused thoughtfully then asked, 'I assume no one has turned up at the bookshop looking scared or under the weather?'

'No, but we've only had the children's club and May's talk on fashion since Rose appeared. We've a more general session today. You're thinking the baby's mother might come along to pretend all is well and divert suspicion away from her?'

'It's possible.'

'We should certainly watch out for anyone who looks unwell or nervy,' Naomi said.

'Or unusually cheerful,' Bert advised. 'They could be putting on an act and overdoing it.'

'True.'

'Of course, she might not come to the bookshop often so won't be missed,' Bert said. 'Not soon, anyway.'

'We can't hold on to Rose indefinitely.'

'Agreed, so we need to take action. I was over in Barton earlier and the people there were talking about all the colds and chills that seem to be going around. If we use that as a conversation opener at the bookshop and when we're out and about, we might hear of people who are looking peaky or keeping to their homes. Rose's mother might be one of them.'

'It's worth trying,' Naomi said. 'I'll suggest it to Victoria, Alice and the rest of the bookshop team.'

She paused then added, 'There's something else.'

She showed him William's note. 'I can only imagine he's warning me that Alexander has found out about our engagement.'

'Looks like it,' Bert agreed. 'You think he'll try to use it against you?'

'It would be a miracle if he didn't. I expect he'll try to renegotiate the settlement.'

'Drag the divorce out so you can't marry me unless you accept a lower figure, you mean?'

'Exactly.'

'If William didn't spill the beans about our engagement, who did?' Bert wondered.

Naomi shrugged. 'It's no secret here in Churchwood, though Alexander had no friends here. The only person who thought well of him was Marjorie, but he couldn't bear the sight or sound of her.'

'Maybe the icicle set a private detective on you.'

'Maybe he did.' After all, she'd once set a private

detective on to Alexander when she wanted to be sure of her ground before confronting him with his bigamy. 'I haven't seen any strangers about the village, though, and I haven't heard that anyone has been asking questions about me.'

'You're known outside of Churchwood, too,' Bert pointed out. 'All it would take would be a chat with someone in a shop in somewhere like Barton.'

Naomi pictured an investigator calling into the grocer's there and mentioning that he was on his way to Churchwood. 'I hear Naomi Harrington is going through some changes,' he might have said.

And the grocer might have answered, 'A divorce, poor woman, but she'll soon have happiness knocking on her door again now she's engaged to Bert Makepiece.'

'I don't suppose it actually matters how Alexander got to hear about our engagement,' Naomi said. 'It's what he plans to do with the information that worries me.'

'The man is a bigamist. There's not much he *can* do without putting his reputation at risk, though I agree he might try to drag out the divorce until you accept a lower settlement. Whatever he does, you've got me by your side. We're more than equal to anything the icicle can throw at us.'

Naomi smiled up at him. 'Of course, there's one way anyone could have realized that we're more than just friends, even if they were just passing on the bus or in a car.'

'My habit of doing this?' he said, drawing her to him and bending his head to kiss her. Bert had no inhibitions about kissing her in public.

'Precisely,' Naomi confirmed. 'It rather signals our engagement to the world.'

'It isn't going to stop me from kissing you in the future.'

He kissed her again. Rather thoroughly. And Naomi was conscious of a blush rising to her cheeks.

'You're incorrigible,' she scolded.

'I'm a man in love. That's what I am.'

It was good to hear. Through anxious times, through unhappy times, Bert was her rock.

Naomi walked to the bookshop with Alice that afternoon. 'May and Janet have both been briefed to talk about the people who are falling sick in Barton,' Naomi said. 'I don't suppose Kate will be coming?'

'Not in the middle of a working day, but she knows about Rose and she'll let us know if she hears anything that might lead us to the mother. She might pick something up while out and about, or from Timmy when he gets home from school.'

They joined Bert, May and Janet in setting out tables and chairs. Kate and Leo had been extraordinarily generous in donating all the money that had been collected for them as a wedding gift towards replacing some of the books and equipment that had been destroyed when the plane crashed into the original bookshop, but more was still needed. 'We should start thinking about a fundraising event,' Alice said.

'We should,' Naomi agreed, wishing for the hundredth time that her settlement would come through and give her enough funds to make a sizeable personal donation. Until then she needed to keep a tight rein on her expenses. 'Let's talk about it at our next team meeting.'

There wasn't time now as they could hear people waiting outside. Naomi went to let them in, holding the door open as they bustled by with the usual enthusiastic calls of, 'Afternoon, Naomi,' and, 'I've been looking forward to this,' and, 'It's my turn to make the tea today.'

Naomi was about to close the door again when she noticed a girl out in the street, pushing two small children in an ancient pram. 'Hannah, isn't it?' Naomi asked.

The girl didn't live in Churchwood but came here occasionally, probably to give herself a change from the Barton shops because her life was an unvaried drudge as far as Naomi was aware. She couldn't be much more than fifteen or sixteen, but her mother was sick so caring for the large family of younger children fell on Hannah's slim shoulders. It couldn't help that her father had a reputation as a curt, unpleasant man.

'Coming to join us?' Naomi asked. 'We'll be having story time for little ones soon.'

The girl shrank back. 'I need to get home.'

'You can't spare even five minutes to sit down and enjoy a cup of tea?'

That appeared to tempt her, and no wonder. Naomi doubted the girl ever had any company or time to herself, either.

'Just five minutes,' Naomi repeated. 'It won't cost anything.'

'All right.'

Naomi lifted the little girl from the pram and Hannah took the baby. 'It's probably healthier for you to be here than in Barton,' Naomi said, leading the way inside. 'I've heard quite a few people there have come down with colds and chills.'

Hannah looked as though she'd heard nothing like that. The poor girl probably hadn't time to chat with anyone.

'Where would you like to sit?' Naomi asked, as Hannah sent a nervous-looking gaze around the room.

Naomi was about to suggest a chair near May Janicki

when Hannah pointed to a different one. 'There,' she said, moving towards it.

Oh dear. The chair Hannah had chosen was within earshot of Aggie Hamilton, who rarely had a good word to say for anyone. How that woman had produced a son as nice as Mattie was a mystery. Hopefully, Hannah would be too busy entertaining her little brother and sister to pay heed to that unpleasant woman, otherwise they might never see the girl in the bookshop again.

She was pleased to see Janet walk over to speak to Hannah. Janet's words would be kind.

Edna Hall called to Naomi and they were talking about knitting when the door was thrown open and the entire room fell silent.

CHAPTER FOURTEEN

Naomi

A small boy spoke into the quietness. 'Who's that lady, Mummy?'

'Ssh,' his mother said, sounding embarrassed.

The lady had struck a pose as though expecting to make an impact and she'd certainly succeeded.

She was young – around twenty – and beautiful, too, but looked more like a film star than a visitor to a village bookshop. She had a voluptuous body which she displayed to advantage in a racy scarlet dress that hugged her hips and bosom. Matching lipstick drew attention to her pouting mouth, while her long, dark hair was arranged in artful waves with one side almost covering an eye. The effect was sultry, teasing and alluring.

'Blimey,' old Jonah Kerrigan muttered.

Blimey, indeed. Wondering if the girl had found herself in the wrong place, Naomi went to greet her. 'Good afternoon. I'm Naomi Harrington, and this is the Churchwood bookshop.' She offered a handshake. 'Have you come to pay us a visit?'

'Yes, I thought I'd look you up.' The girl took Naomi's hand and shook it languidly. Her fingers were long and soft, and her nails were painted with immaculate red varnish.

'You're very welcome. You're not from Churchwood,

are you? I'm sure I'd have remembered if I'd seen you before.'

The notion that she was unforgettable clearly gratified the young woman. 'I'm staying with my uncle in Barton while I recover from an operation.'

This information sent Naomi's thoughts into a spin. Operation? Or a pregnancy and delivery? Was this girl Rose's mother? A glance around showed Naomi that Bert and Alice were wondering the same thing, since they'd both raised their eyebrows questioningly. But after a moment's consideration, Naomi shook her head at them.

She couldn't see this siren as Rose's mother. The girl was too sophisticated to have written those heart-felt notes and, besides, no girdle in the world could make a post-pregnancy stomach as flat as this young woman's.

'I'm sorry to hear you've been ill,' Naomi said. 'Come in and I'll introduce you to some people.'

The young woman sashayed into the room, her cat-like smile suggesting she was pleased by the fact that so many people were staring at her.

'This is Alice Irvine. She helps to organize the book-shop,' Naomi said. 'In fact, Alice is the brains behind it.'

'Fancy,' the young woman said without interest.

'I'm afraid we haven't many books at present but you're welcome to take a look at what we have,' Alice told her. 'We lost most of our stock when a plane crashed in the village but we'll be fundraising for more soon.'

'Fundraising?' The young woman's interest perked up. 'Fundraising how?'

'We haven't arranged anything yet, but we might have a social evening with a raffle.'

'Perhaps I can help,' the young woman said.

'You'd like to sell raffle tickets?' Naomi asked. The girl didn't look the type.

Sure enough, she gave a little laugh. 'Heavens, no. The thing is . . . I sing.' She made it sound momentous.

'What sort of singing?' Naomi doubted a church choir would feature in the answer.

'Popular music. I have a manager who has great plans for my career. Have you heard of Vera Lynn and Gracie Fields?'

'Of course.'

'He's going to make me just as famous as them. Vera Lynn even has her own radio show, you know. *Sincerely Yours*. I'd like my own radio show, too, one day. My manager wants me to sing for our troops as well. I'd like that.'

Naomi wasn't surprised. An audience of men would probably suit this girl perfectly. 'I don't think you mentioned your name,' Naomi said.

'How silly of me.' The girl spoke as though it wouldn't be long before everyone knew her name because it would be up in lights in London's West End and announced over the airwaves, far and wide. 'I . . .' Again she paused for maximum impact. '. . . am Margueritte Moore.'

'It's a pleasure to meet you, Margueritte,' Naomi said.

'Indeed,' Alice seconded. 'Why don't you two sit down and talk about the fundraising idea? I'll fetch cups of tea and join you.'

Naomi saw that Alice's eyes were twinkling with amusement at the way Margueritte had brought the bookshop to a standstill. When she returned, she had Bert with her and his eyes were twinkling, too. Sitting down, he sent Naomi a wink, which relieved her since beautiful young women tended to make her feel insecure. Naomi had never been pretty.

'What's this I hear about you wanting to sing for us?' he asked Margueritte.

'I'm a professional singer,' she told him smugly.

'I imagine that means you get paid for it.'

'Oh, yes.' Her manner suggested she was worth her weight in gold.

'Congratulations. But we're looking to raise money rather than spend it. I'm afraid we've none to spare for fees,' Bert pointed out. 'Of course, if you're offering your services for free, that's different.'

'My manager sorts out the business side of things but he's away at the moment. This performance would be . . . Well, it would just be for fun.'

'That's very generous of you,' Naomi said. 'What sort of songs do you like to sing? You mentioned Vera Lynn and Gracie Fields . . .'

'Would you like to hear me?' Without waiting for an answer, Margueritte got to her feet and smiled around at her audience, pausing until all eyes were upon her. Then, without the slightest sign of nervousness, she began to sing.

'*Wish me luck as you wave me goodbye . . .*'

There was no doubt that she had a great voice. Margueritte belted out the song.

'A little more . . . provocative in the delivery than wholesome Gracie Fields,' Bert whispered to Naomi, because Margueritte was a tease.

Still, everyone was watching and listening, some people with their mouths wide open in surprise. And when Margueritte finished, there was a round of applause.

'You see?' she said, sitting down with a self-satisfied smirk.

'You have a wonderful voice,' Naomi told her.

'So you want me at the fundraiser.' It didn't appear to cross Margueritte's mind that anyone might *not* want her.

'What about music?' Alice asked.

'Usually I sing with a band,' Margueritte said. 'I love the big band sound, don't you?'

'I do,' Alice said. 'But there's no band here, big or small.'

'Is there a piano?'

'Not one that's owned by the bookshop, but it might be possible to borrow one from the local hospital. I'm not sure who could play your sort of music, though.'

'I know a pianist. Sidney Sweetman. He'll be delighted to support me. Shall we say Saturday for the concert?' Margueritte asked.

'This Saturday coming? That doesn't give us much time for making arrangements,' Naomi answered. 'Would you be available the Saturday after? April the twenty-fifth? Mr Sweetman, too?'

'My manager won't be back from Scotland before then so I'll be available. And Sidney will do whatever I ask.'

'Best to check with him, though,' Alice advised. 'Are you on the telephone? Perhaps we might talk again in a day or two?'

'Unfortunately, my uncle doesn't have a telephone.' Margueritte made it sound as though he lived in the Dark Ages. 'How he thinks my manager will be able to stay in touch with me, I just don't know.'

'Perhaps he wouldn't normally need a telephone,' Naomi said.

'Humph.'

'You could telephone me from the Barton post office,' Naomi suggested and Margueritte agreed to do so.

'The hospital I mentioned is the military sort,' Alice said, and Margueritte's eyes lit up, probably at the thought of handsome young soldiers. 'Some of them may want to come and hear you sing.'

'I'd like that. It'll be good practice for entertaining the troops.'

With nothing more to be said about the concert for the moment, Naomi offered to introduce Margueritte to some others.

The girl looked around the room and appeared to find no one of interest. After all, they were mostly women, ageing men and children. 'I should get home. My uncle may need me.'

Naomi knew an excuse when she heard one but took no offence.

'Is there anyone who might take me home?' Margueritte asked.

'There's the bus,' Alice pointed out. 'Did you come on the bus?'

'I did, but . . .' Margueritte shuddered. 'I'm used to cars. My manager has a Rolls-Royce, you know.'

'Fancy that,' Naomi said. 'We've no Rolls-Royces in Churchwood, I'm afraid.'

'And with petrol rationing . . .' Bert added.

'Hmm.' Margueritte got to her feet.

'Thank you for coming and for offering to sing,' Alice said. 'It's much appreciated.'

Margueritte preened at the praise and set off towards the door, walking quickly despite her heels.

'I'll see you out,' Naomi said, hastening after her on much less stylish shoes.

'Lovely singing,' Edna Hall said as Margueritte drew near her.

'I'm a professional,' Margueritte informed her.

'You can belt them out with the best of them,' Jonah Kerrigan said.

Margueritte smiled at that. Jonah was a man, even if he was an old one. She patted his shoulder. 'How sweet of you to say so.'

Outside, she headed for the bus stop, sashaying along

the pavement. When a truck came along she minced into the road and flagged it down. It didn't require telepathic powers to guess that she planned to ask for a lift.

Naomi couldn't help smiling at the rebuff Margueritte would receive, for the driver was Alec Mead, the married and miserable farmer.

Returning to the bookshop, Naomi saw that Aggie Hamilton was on her feet. 'Well, I for one think that sort of singing is disgusting,' Aggie said.

'It was a Gracie Fields song,' Edna Hall pointed out. 'About a soldier asking his sweetheart to wish him luck. I should have thought you'd be in favour of a song like that, seeing as your Mattie is in the army.'

'I don't object to the song but to the way it was sung. Indecent, it was.'

'Hardly that,' Naomi said. 'A little flirtatious, perhaps, but—'

'That girl is a hussy and I don't think your bookshop should be encouraging her. Especially not with the vicar on the organizing team.'

Adam had just walked in. 'Did someone mention me?' he asked.

'I did,' Aggie told him. 'It's a pity you weren't here a few minutes earlier.'

'Oh?'

'A young woman who's staying with an uncle in Barton called in,' Naomi said. 'She's a professional singer and she's offered to sing for free in a fundraising concert.'

'How splendid!' Adam declared.

'You didn't see her,' Aggie pointed out. 'Or watch her . . . perform.'

'She isn't very good?'

'She's . . . Lewd behaviour, I'd call it.'

'Lewd?' Adam looked startled.

'Slightly flirtatious,' Naomi corrected. 'But we can liaise with her on a programme of songs to be sure nothing is inappropriate.'

'That girl would make a Christmas carol sound inappropriate,' Aggie argued.

Adam exchanged sympathetic looks with Naomi. They both knew that Aggie Hamilton was a difficult woman. Fortunately, she lived on the outskirts of Churchwood and wasn't seen in the bookshop often.

'A concert is something to consider,' he said soothingly and then, ignoring the daggers Aggie was glaring at him, he changed the subject by asking, 'Any news of your Mattie?'

'He's a dutiful lad and he doesn't neglect his mother,' Aggie reported. 'But he's said nothing about being granted leave soon.'

'Maybe he'll turn up unexpectedly, just in time for the concert,' Edna Hall said mischievously.

'My Mattie wouldn't see anything appealing in a young female like that,' Aggie said, offended. 'He's a good boy and he'll settle down with a good, wholesome girl when the time is right. You mark my words.'

Naomi saw that Hannah was leaving and went over to speak to her. 'Going already, Hannah?'

'I can't leave my mother for long.' She seemed upset, as though she'd done wrong in resting for even a few minutes.

'Do you have anyone to help you at home?' Naomi asked.

'Help me?'

'To look after your mother and the children? The house, too?'

Hannah's pale cheeks flushed pink. 'I'm managing perfectly well, thank you.'

'I don't doubt it. But a little help now and then doesn't

hurt. A break is good for all of us, whether we spend it reading, walking or seeing friends. Do you manage to see friends, Hannah?'

The flush deepened and Naomi guessed the answer was no because poor Hannah hadn't any friends. How could she have built up friendships with such a wretched home life and so little time to herself? It wasn't right that she should be worn down by a heavy workload of domesticity at such a young age.

'I know you live outside Churchwood but we don't have borders on our community spirit,' Naomi said. 'Please do ask for help now and then.'

'Thanks, but I really must go . . .'

She gathered the children together and went on her way, the heavy pram looking too much for her slender body to cope with, especially since it was old and didn't seem to run smoothly. It was good for a girl to have pride but Naomi worried that there was more to Hannah's independence than that. Given her sick mother and coarse father, perhaps the girl feared that the children would be taken away if she couldn't cope. Naomi decided to keep a lookout for Hannah in future.

Returning inside, she became aware that Margueritte was still under discussion. 'Your Abel may want to come to a concert once he's heard about the singer,' Mrs Hutchings was saying to Mrs Hayes.

'That's what I'm afraid of. I've no wish to see Abel looking like a lovesick swain, thank you very much.'

'I've no wish to pick my Bill's jaw off the floor when that girl comes out in another dress that shows all the advantages nature has given her,' Mrs Hutchings said. 'But if it means we can have more books in the bookshop, I'll grin and bear it. Especially books like *Sunset Kiss*. That was my favourite.'

'I liked *The Count of Adoline*. Count Raoul was so dreamy!'

'Maybe our menfolk will be picking *our* jaws off the floor if we get books with handsome men on the covers,' Phyllis Hutchings joked, and the two women cackled.

Adam sidled up to Naomi, bringing Alice and Bert. 'You think the concert is a good idea?' he asked.

'If it raises funds for more books and equipment, then yes, I do,' Naomi said.

'I agree,' Alice said. 'I'll talk to Matron at the hospital since there's an old piano up there. I'll also find out what she thinks about patients being included.'

May and Janet joined them and were in full agreement. 'I reckon our songbird will stir Churchwood up a bit, but there's nothing wrong with that,' May said.

'And we need funds urgently,' Janet added. 'The handle fell off one of our cups this morning and another two were smashed when a toddler banged into a table. We need crockery, toys, books . . . everything!'

'Let's meet in a couple of days' time to talk about the concert some more,' Naomi said.

'At Foxfield?' May asked.

'Why not come to the vicarage?' Adam offered. 'That way Victoria won't need to worry about keeping you-know-who quiet.'

'Talking of you-know-who . . .' Janet slipped a tin of condensed milk into Naomi's bag. 'How is she doing?'

'Well, I think.'

'But we still need to find whoever left her,' Janet said. 'I'm listening out for clues but I've heard nothing remotely useful so far.'

'Me neither,' said May.

'But we'll keep going,' Janet said.

She and May left to circle the room again. Alice headed

for the books to choose a story to read out loud to the children, leaving Bert at Naomi's side. 'I hope you're not still worrying about the icicle,' he said. 'You can take him on and win, whatever he's got planned, woman.'

Naomi hoped it would prove to be that simple.

CHAPTER FIFTEEN

Hannah

Discipline held the tears in check while Hannah was still in Churchwood, but as soon as she reached the outskirts they spilled over her cheeks like a river bursting its banks, flooding her with helplessness.

How Aggie Hamilton could be Mattie's mother was a mystery. Aggie was all fault-finding dark eyes and a mean mouth, while Mattie was all tender softness. But why, oh why, hadn't he come home? He might not have received the letter telling him of Rose's birth yet, but surely he'd received the letter telling him that a baby was on the way and realized that this was the sort of emergency that called for a reply?

Had his senior officer refused him leave on the grounds that compassion should be reserved for those who behaved well instead of those with loose morals like Hannah? Not that she had loose morals, exactly. What happened hadn't been planned and, while it shouldn't have happened at all, it had been a consequence of love. Deep love. But perhaps that didn't count for much in the army.

What was Hannah to do if he didn't return soon or even send word to her? Her mother was in no condition to help and the news of Rose's birth might even quicken her decline. Appealing to her father was out of the question. He'd take his belt off to give Hannah a whipping as punishment for her behaviour. He'd also banish Rose from the house.

Aggie Hamilton was equally out of the question as a confidante. She'd be vicious in blaming Hannah for Mattie's fall from grace. There was Mattie's father, but he was henpecked and would never go against his wife.

There was no one to whom Hannah could turn.

So far Miss Page and Mrs Harrington appeared to be keeping Rose's birth a secret, but for how long would they or could they do so?

At least Mrs Harrington had given no sign of suspecting that Hannah might be Rose's mother. Probably, it was because Hannah looked young for her age and was never seen with anyone apart from her brothers and sisters. No one had ever seen her with Mattie.

Mattie. Maybe a letter had arrived from him today.

There was no reason to think her father would be at home to notice any letters on the doormat but, just in case he'd called in, Hannah pushed the ancient pram as fast as she could manage. The damaged wheel hit a rut and it took all her strength to straighten it again. It was strange how worry and exhaustion were taking turns to swamp each other.

And how was darling Rose faring? Was she thriving? Hannah had milk for her – in fact, she was hurting from the milk – but had no way of giving her daughter its nourishment. How sad that was! It was even sadder that Rose was living without her mother's kisses and cuddles. Hannah prayed she wasn't feeling abandoned. It wasn't even as though Hannah could be nearby, since it would look suspicious if she went to Churchwood again tomorrow because she rarely went more than once a week in normal circumstances. A change of behaviour now might have people putting two and two together. Hannah couldn't risk it.

CHAPTER SIXTEEN

Ruby

Timmy's eyes were wide when he burst into the farm-house kitchen after school. 'You'll never guess what I heard today.'

Ruby's stomach turned sickly somersaults. Had word got out about the abandoned baby?

Kate was in the kitchen, too. 'What's that, Timmy?' she asked with a wariness which told Ruby that the child was still at Foxfield and that Kate, too, feared that its secret existence had somehow been exposed.

'Adam is arranging a football match between the book-shop team and a team from St John's at Barton.' Adam ran the children's club at the bookshop.

Relief made Ruby feel as though her legs were being scooped out from under her. Thank goodness!

'That's wonderful news,' Kate said.

'I'm hoping to be chosen as our team's centre forward but Adam says we should play our best whatever position we're put in.'

'Quite right,' Ruby said, finding her voice at last. 'It's important to be sporting.'

'Though we'll still keep our fingers crossed for you to be centre forward,' Kate said, winking at Timmy who grinned back.

How settled and carefree he was these days. And how

well he deserved it after his difficult early years. Ruby wondered again if she should take him aside and warn him that unpleasant gossip might be on the horizon. But once again, she was reluctant to spoil his enjoyment in life.

'May I take a carrot to Pete?' he asked. Pete was the ageing pony who pulled the cart, though the truck was used for heavy loads now. Timmy adored the placid old thing.

'Just one carrot,' Ruby told him.

He took one from the basket and bounced out of the kitchen with another delicious grin.

Ruby picked up a tea towel to dry some dishes. Of course, she could find out more about this secret baby simply by asking Kate about it. But Kate might be mortified to learn that Ruby had overheard Alice divulging a confidence and discourage Alice from sharing any more. That could mean Kate missing out because it was difficult for her to visit the village often due to the farm's heavy workload, and it was usually Alice who brought news on her walks to and from the hospital.

No, it was best to keep quiet at present, though it was frustrating to be in the dark.

'You're not still worrying about your parents?' Kate asked.

Ruby roused herself. 'I still haven't decided whether to invite them to the wedding, if that's what you mean.'

Kate knew something of Ruby's difficult relationship with her parents. 'Just do what feels right to you,' she suggested.

Sound advice, but what did feel right to her? Her parents might only have to show their usual coldness to the boy who was supposed to be their son to arouse suspicions about the circumstances of his birth. If the village

110

was already abuzz with talk over the little foundling, the danger was surely increased.

Problems, problems . . .

'I'm going into the village,' Kate announced. 'Is there anything you'd like to add to the shopping list?'

Was shopping merely an excuse for calling on Alice or Naomi to discuss the hidden baby? Ruby had no way of knowing. 'I don't think so, thanks. Will you be back for tea?'

'I expect so. I shan't be long.'

Ruby stood at the kitchen window, watching Kate collect her bicycle from the barn and cycle across the farmyard towards the drive. But, as always, there was work to be done. Ruby set about the ironing. Forty-five minutes passed. An hour. Kate's long slender legs and general fitness made her a fast cyclist, so it was unusual for her to take so long over a few errands. Of course, there might be queues at the shops or she might be chatting to fellow shoppers, but Ruby wondered . . .

With the ironing finished, Ruby put the kettle on the stove for tea, catching her reflection in the small mirror that hung from the kitchen window on wire. Was she looking wan? Probably, since she hadn't been sleeping well. Taking a lipstick from her apron pocket, she applied it to her mouth.

She'd first taken an interest in cosmetics as a young girl who loved fashion and style, and nursed ambitions to become a hairdresser. When life had taken a turn into trouble, they'd become Ruby's way of showing defiance, and she'd accompanied them with bold stares that announced to her parents and the world, 'You might despise me, but you're not going to defeat me.'

This lipstick was new. It had been a Christmas gift from Kate, but Ruby had been determined to finish every scrap of her previous lipstick first. Waste was never good, but it was especially bad in wartime. She also wanted to save money, not only for the wedding but also because she hoped to take Timmy to the seaside one day. He hadn't seen the sea yet – Ruby herself had only seen it once – but she knew he'd love it.

She was thinking that Kate had chosen well with the lipstick when Pearl entered the kitchen. 'What do you think?' Ruby asked, turning towards her.

'About what?'

'This lipstick. It's the one Kate gave me for Christmas.'

'It looks nice,' Pearl said. It was the sort of bland comment she automatically made when asked about things she considered to be something of a mystery. She was more interested in fertilizer. But then she peered closer. 'Really. It looks nice.'

Surprised by her friend's unexpected attention, Ruby gave her a curious look. Was there wistfulness in Pearl's expression? A wish that she too could look nicer, perhaps as a way of making Fred notice her? After all, the atmosphere between them had been noticeably cooler since Fred had declared wedding talk to be dull. 'Want to try it?' Ruby asked, holding out the lipstick.

'Me?' Pearl put her hands up and backed away. 'Don't be daft.'

'You might surprise yourself.'

'I'd feel a fool,' Pearl insisted, but she'd begun shifting from one large foot to the other with the awkwardness that always signalled when lack of confidence was holding her back.

'If you don't like it, you can wash it off.'

'I don't know,' Pearl said bashfully, but Ruby steered her into a chair.

'I'm going to tidy you up first,' Ruby announced.

'What does that mean?' Pearl was wary.

'I'm going to shape your eyebrows so they don't look like hairy caterpillars.'

'Nothing wrong with caterpillars,' Pearl said. 'Except when they're eating the crops.'

'And except when they're wriggling over your face.'

'My eyebrows don't wriggle.'

'That's what you think.'

Ruby got to work.

'Ow! That hurts!' Pearl protested. 'You're not plucking a chicken for the oven.'

'Don't be a baby, Pearl.'

'Ouch! Ruby, stop! I don't like it.'

'I'll stop if that's what you really want. But are you sure?'

'Of course I'm sure.'

'You might want to take a look in this mirror first.'

Ruby held the mirror so Pearl could see her reflection.

Pearl shrieked. 'What have you done?'

'I've only plucked one eyebrow so far. That's why you look lopsided. A caterpillar on one side and a sleek curve on the other.'

'Do something!'

'No whining, then.'

Ruby plucked Pearl's other eyebrow, ignoring the mutters and winces that escaped from Pearl's lips every second or two.

'Much better,' she declared. 'Now for the lipstick.'

'No, you've done enough.' Pearl tried to get up but Ruby pushed her back.

'Don't you want to look feminine?'

'I never look feminine,' Pearl said, but, again, there was longing in her voice.

Kate arrived just as Ruby was applying the lipstick. Nothing in Kate's expression gave any hint that she might have been at a meeting about the secret baby, but Kate was no fool and would hide it well. 'Doesn't Pearl look feminine?' Ruby asked.

'Pretty,' Kate said, which was probably overstating it but brought a blush of pleasure to Pearl's plain face.

The blush deepened when Fred came in. He looked at her. Stared at her, in fact. And for a glorious moment Ruby was pleased to read admiration in his expression. But then he grinned. Nastily. 'Are you practising to be a clown at a fancy-dress party?' he asked.

Ruby gasped. Kate, too. Because they both saw hurt cross their friend's face. Pearl got up and took a none-too-clean handkerchief from the pocket of her breeches, dragging it across her mouth as she headed for the door. 'Going to see the chickens,' she said, stepping outside.

'Tea's nearly ready!' Ruby called after her. Then she rounded on Fred. 'You're an idiot, Fred Fletcher.'

'What did I do?'

'You know what you did. You hurt Pearl's feelings.'

'I was only having a laugh.'

'Do you see us laughing? Did you see Pearl laughing?' Kate demanded.

'Some people can't take a joke.'

'You *know* it wasn't a joke,' Ruby said.

'Turned into mind readers, have you? You're wasted on a farm. You should be at the seaside telling people you'll read crystal balls for them if they cross your palms with silver.'

'Crystal balls are for telling the future, not reading minds,' Ruby snapped.

Fred flapped a hand dismissively, as though the distinction were petty.

'What you said was spiteful,' Ruby added. 'Mean.'

Fred turned his wheelchair around. 'I'm not staying

here to be insulted by people who don't know a joke when they hear one.'

He retreated into the downstairs room where he'd slept ever since he'd come home injured. 'Good riddance!' Ruby called after him.

'He's actually mortified by what he said,' Kate suggested, once he'd closed the door behind him. Doubtless, he'd have liked to slam it shut but the wheelchair made angry gestures tricky.

'Why did he say it, then?' Ruby asked.

Kate supplied the answer though Ruby knew it anyway, her question having been more of a wail of frustration than a genuine enquiry. 'Because he loves Pearl but doesn't want her or anyone else to know it,' Kate said. 'Heck, I suspect he can barely admit it to himself.'

Ruby agreed. 'He's afraid she might reject him. Or that people might think she's only courting him out of pity.'

'Fred's made great progress since he was first injured but he still feels like a wreck of the man he used to be. He can't believe anyone would look at him twice in the romantic sense.'

'Pearl's just as bad,' Ruby said. 'If they're not careful, they'll lose their chance of happiness, because neither will risk saying how they really feel.' She hesitated then added ruefully, 'And I've just made things worse.'

Kate patted her arm. 'Fred should be bringing his false legs home soon. Alice says the hospital is pleased with the progress he's making with them. Maybe he'll feel more like the man of old when he's walking again. Let's hope so, anyway.'

She began to unpack the shopping and Ruby moved to help her, trying to appear casual as she asked, 'Any news from the village?'

'Marjorie is still insisting she saw a ghost,' Kate reported. 'Otherwise, it seems to be business as usual.'

Except that it wasn't business as usual. There was nothing about Kate that spoke of obvious tension. She was smiling and her face was as smooth and clear as ever. But Ruby was sure there'd have been a new lightness about her if the secret baby and her mother had been reunited and all was well. No, the baby was still at Foxfield, and the mother . . . Who knew where the mother was?

Amid the worry of her own situation, Ruby felt another rush of sympathy for that woman – or, more likely, that girl – and wished there were something she could do to help. But unless she discovered the mother's identity, Ruby could do nothing. It was frustrating, waiting around for news, but if there was an alternative, Ruby couldn't think of it. Not yet, anyway.

CHAPTER SEVENTEEN

Victoria

Victoria picked the early-morning post off the doormat and flicked through the names on the envelopes. Naomi, Ivy, Naomi again . . . but what was this? The envelope was addressed to *The girl with the honey-colored hair*. Reading it, Victoria felt a jolt of surprise. Of excitement, too. For she was pretty sure that she was the girl in question. And pretty sure of the sender's identity.

She pushed the envelope into her pocket, paused to ensure she'd look calm, and then went into the dining room where the others were gathered for breakfast. 'Two for you, Naomi,' she said, handing over the envelopes, 'and one for Ivy.'

Naomi's letters looked like bills and Victoria hoped they wouldn't be too much of a worry. Ivy's letter looked personal. Despite sleeping at Edna Hall's house, Ivy and Flower spent their days and took their meals at Foxfield, so it made sense for Ivy's post to be delivered here. 'This is from Mary Becker, judging from the handwriting,' Ivy said. 'You may want to hear what she has to say, Victoria.'

Mary had been their neighbour in London. Ivy tore open the envelope and ran her gaze over the note she took from inside. 'It seems our old house has finally been demolished,' she said. 'Not before time. I was glad to have a roof over my head but it was a nasty, damp place.

Mary's granddaughter is having nightmares because an unexploded bomb was found not far from where she lives, poor little thing. And little Peter Pritchard – remember him? – cut his hand scrambling over a bombsite and it turned septic. He's all right now, but his family were desperately worried.'

Ivy looked at Naomi. 'I've said it before but I'll say it again: I speak for all of us evacuees when I say we couldn't be more grateful to you for taking us in and keeping us safe. We're so happy here and it's wonderful to see the children enjoying the fresh air and countryside. My little Flower, especially, since she was always so unwell before with that bad chest of hers. She hardly coughs at all now she's away from the damp and the smoke and the smog. The school is wonderful, too, and as for the village . . . there's a real community here and we love being a part of it.'

'You're truly a saint, Naomi,' Mags said, and the other London women agreed.

'It's my pleasure,' Naomi assured them.

Victoria stole from the room and went upstairs to make the beds – but also to read her own letter.

She studied the envelope again: *The girl with the honey-colored hair*. That described Victoria's shoulder-length waves well enough, though now those waves were pinned back so they wouldn't get in the way as she went about her day's work.

The note inside was from Paul.

Dear girl with the honey-colored hair,
    Or should I salute you as a young lady? Forgive any clumsiness on my part and believe that my intentions are good.
    If you're hoping this letter is from my comrade, Corporal Brady, and that you're set fair for a lot of flowery language,

I'm afraid I'm going to disappoint you. My description of your beautiful hair is all the flowery language I have in me, since I'm the quieter one of the two American soldiers who had the pleasure of meeting you in Churchwood a few days ago. Paul Scarletti is my name, in case you need reminding (though I hope you don't!).

Why am I writing? As a plain-speaking man, I'll explain plainly that I'd like to see you again, if you'd permit that? I don't know how long I'm likely to be in the area but I'd be honored if you'd grant me the pleasure of an hour or two of your time. A dinner, a cup of the tea you English folk like so much, a walk . . . Whatever you like.

I warmed to you when I saw you. I'd like to get to know you better and I hope the feeling is mutual.

Best wishes,

Paul Scarletti

The letter had been written from a new American base a few miles from Churchwood.

Victoria thought about the letter for a moment and then read it again before thinking about it some more. She felt as though her emotions had been launched into a choppy sea where they were being thrown about by the waves. It was lovely to be considered attractive and to have her company sought. But that sort of attraction – mutual attraction, in this case – could go nowhere.

Impatience rose up in her. Only a fool would torture herself over what could never be, and Victoria hoped she wasn't a fool. She'd never been a frivolous, flirting sort of person. She'd lived a serious life because seriousness had been necessary after her parents had run out of money. She'd needed to grow up fast and provide for them as well as maintain herself. After their deaths had come housekeeping work followed by war work in the wireless factory, and then poor Joan's death and the need to look after Arthur and Jenny. So much seriousness!

Which made it ridiculous that she should allow herself to be catapulted into such a maelstrom of emotion by a chance encounter and a letter. It wasn't as though walking out with an American soldier could ever be more than fleeting fun. Doubtless, Paul Scarletti would soon be deployed overseas or moved to some other part of the country.

Not that it could be the man himself who was bothering her so much as the reminder of what she'd sacrificed. Nothing else made sense, because Paul was a stranger. And yet those brown eyes had affected her more than any other eyes she'd seen in her entire life . . .

Enough brooding.

Victoria returned the letter to its envelope and stuffed it back into her pocket. She wouldn't reply. Instead, she'd continue with her life here and Paul Scarletti would soon find another girl.

She returned to the children, helping them to get ready to go out – to school in the case of the older children and for a walk to the shops in the case of the younger ones.

'Remember,' she urged them, 'not a word about baby Rose.'

'We know!' the children chorused. 'She's a secret.'

'That's right,' Victoria approved. 'And secrets mean . . .?'

The children mimed fastening their mouths.

'Exactly.'

Victoria threw herself into the day's work, determined to keep Paul Scarletti from her mind, but later, when Victoria was rocking Rose in her arms, Naomi said, 'You're very good with her. Maybe you'll have your own baby one day.'

Victoria swallowed and managed a smile. 'I've got my hands full with Arthur and Jenny.'

'But in the future . . .'

'I doubt it. Now, unless I'm much mistaken, this young lady needs changing . . .'

CHAPTER EIGHTEEN

Beth

'I'd like a word in my office, please,' Matron said.

Beth's stomach crumpled with unease. *A word in my office* sounded ominous. She wasn't aware of having done anything wrong but perhaps someone had complained about her. She followed Matron out of the ward and along the corridor, too embarrassed to make eye contact with other nurses or patients in case their expressions showed that they, too, were wondering if she was in trouble.

'Take a seat,' Matron instructed when they reached her office.

Beth sat on the visitor's chair, back straight and hands clasped in front of her nervously. Matron sat behind the desk. 'This is your fourth day with us, Nurse Ellis. How do you feel you're getting on?'

Beth's thoughts flailed. Was this a trick question to test her honesty about a wrongdoing? 'I'm trying my best,' she said. 'Has someone complained about me?'

'Why should you think that?'

'I . . . don't know.'

'Perhaps your conscience is stirring?'

'No.' Well, yes. In a way. Beth was trying hard to be cheerful around the patients but she knew she wasn't on her best form.

Had patients made comments to Matron? 'Bit

miserable, that new girl,' or, 'It's dreary enough being in hospital without a chap's nurse looking like a wet weekend.' That sort of thing.

Matron appeared to take pity on her. 'I always like a chat with new staff members. I find it helps to identify potential problems and head them off before they become unfixable. Not that there's been a complaint in your case. Based on what I've seen so far, you're a capable nurse. Hard-working, too.'

Thank goodness! Beth swallowed hard as relief sank through her body.

'However,' Matron said, and Beth's nerves sharpened again, 'I need to know how *you* feel. Are you happy here?'

Oh, heavens. 'I don't regret coming to Stratton House, Matron. Not for a moment.'

Matron smiled wryly. 'I'm glad to hear it, but you haven't told me if you're happy or not.'

Beth felt herself blush. To her horror, she also felt tears prickle in her eyes. 'I'm perfectly content,' she said, blinking them away. It was true – as far as her work was concerned. 'I'm glad to be learning new things and I'm trying hard to help the patients.'

Matron subjected her to another long stare. 'Please remember I'm here to support you, Nurse Ellis,' she finally said. 'Now, I have a favour to ask.'

'Oh?'

'I assume you've heard about the village bookshop?'

'It's been mentioned. I've also seen Alice Irvine here with books.'

'Mrs Irvine is a great asset to the hospital and patients. To the village, too. It's mostly due to her efforts that the bookshop exists. We're like a branch of the bookshop here at the hospital. We share books with the village and we're welcome at social events, too.'

'That's . . . nice,' Beth said, only to regret her luke-warm tone almost immediately since she'd witnessed at first hand how much the patients enjoyed Alice's visits, whether she was bringing books, reading stories out loud or chatting with them about how they were feeling and any news they'd received from home.

Alice was kind and sensitive. She'd smiled at Beth and said, 'Nice to see you again,' but hadn't forced a conversation.

'I understand there's to be a concert at the bookshop in the near future. I'd like you to be the hospital's liaison with the bookshop team,' Matron said. 'Take a walk down there. Get to know the people and report back with information about the concert.'

'That's to be part of my duties?' Beth was puzzled. She was a nurse, not a social events organizer, even if those social events did benefit the patients. And didn't the hospital already have someone to liaise with the bookshop in the person of Alice, who was capable and efficient as far as Beth could see? Clever, even.

'I suppose I could talk to Alice about it,' Beth said, but Matron clearly disapproved of that idea.

'Alice is a volunteer and I'd prefer her time here to be spent chatting with the patients instead of talking to the staff,' she said firmly.

Yes, but surely a conversation lasting just a minute or two wouldn't . . .

Matron's hard stare withered Beth's protest before it reached her lips. Perhaps Matron was concerned for Alice's health.

Beth had been in the sluice room when she'd overheard them talking in the corridor. 'How are you, Alice? Keeping well?' Matron had asked.

'Very well, thank you, though I felt well last time, too.'

'You were unlucky. There's no reason to expect you won't carry this baby to term.'

'I know. I'm staying optimistic.'

'That's good to hear.'

So Alice was pregnant again after having had a miscarriage. It was understandable that Matron would want her treated gently and Beth wouldn't dream of treating her any other way. But it still seemed excessive to ban a mere conversation about the bookshop, especially since Alice talked about it often to patients. Matron's word was law, though.

'It's to be in addition to your duties,' she said, 'undertaken in your own time, if you're willing? I can't compel you, of course, which is why I described my request as a favour.'

Beth could summon no enthusiasm for the project but Matron was watching her with clear, all-seeing eyes and it would be foolish to get on the wrong side of her. 'If you think I can help . . .?' Beth finally muttered.

'Thank you. Now back to work, please.'

Beth jumped up since Matron had no time for shirkers. Should Beth say thank you in return? For what? Lumbering her with a job she didn't want? Good manners seemed to require it. 'Thank you, Matron,' she said and left the room, feeling disgruntled.

How vexing this liaising business was going to be. If Matron wanted to spare Alice, why hadn't she picked one of Alice's friends for the job? Babs Carter or Pauline Evans? Both were far more outgoing than Beth. Matron might excel at organizing the nurses and the wards, but it didn't follow that she was a good judge of character. In fact, Beth decided, she'd rarely met a worse one.

CHAPTER NINETEEN

Hannah

Hannah was only a couple of minutes into a journey to the Barton shops when she heard her name being called by someone behind her.

Fear rippled through her. Was she about to be confronted by someone who'd realized she was the mother of baby Rose? Or by the police or the authorities if someone had reported her?

She took a deep breath and turned, relieved to see Mr Makepiece approaching on foot with a toolbox in hand, having left his truck some distance from the cottage.

'Away with the fairies?' he asked.

Hannah didn't understand.

'Daydreaming,' he explained. 'I called to you from the truck but you didn't hear.'

Daydreaming hardly described the sick worry that occupied her thoughts these days, but she wasn't going to admit to having troubles even to a man as kind as Mr Makepiece. 'Sorry,' she said, but then she began to wonder why he wanted to speak with her and felt another jolt of panic. If he – or someone close to him, like Mrs Harrington – had guessed her connection to Rose, he might be here to take her back to Churchwood to be questioned about it. 'Is something wrong?' she asked, anxiously.

'What's wrong is that old pram you're pushing,' he said. 'Naomi Harrington reported that one of the wheels wasn't running straight and I can see she's right. Shall I take a look at it for you?'

More relief weakened Hannah's limbs but she clung to the ancient pram's handle and managed to stay upright. When she spoke, her face felt so stiff and drained that it seemed to be cracking. 'That was nice of her.'

'Naomi *is* nice. That's why I'm marrying her.' He grinned and Hannah summoned an echo of a smile in return.

But what if her father happened to drive past and saw a stranger talking to her? Jed Powell didn't welcome interference in his family life.

'Let's get off the road so we'll be safer from passing traffic,' Mr Makepiece suggested.

Since passing traffic was light, Hannah guessed that he'd understood her concerns and was using safety as an excuse for helping her out of sight of her father. Was he also wondering why her father hadn't fixed the wheel himself? Hannah had mentioned it to him long ago but he hadn't bothered to do anything about it. Probably, he'd forgotten, but she couldn't remind him without seeming to criticize him, and that might rouse his anger. It stung her pride to appear pitiable to Mr Makepiece, but if he could mend the wheel it would ease her life considerably.

He touched her arm. 'Come on, young Hannah. Let's see what can be done.'

He nudged her towards a space behind some trees and took the pram from her to push it over the rougher ground. Once there, he bent to inspect the wheel. 'It's buckled,' he said. 'Can we lift the little ones down so I can have a proper look?'

Hannah lifted Susie and Mr Makepiece lifted Simon, making him laugh by pulling a silly face.

Was Mr Makepiece a father? If he'd had children, they'd be grown up by now, since he had to be at least fifty, but they'd have been lucky to have him as their dad. He was a big bear-like man but with a steadiness of temper and quiet sympathy that made a person feel safe in his company. He was as unlike Hannah's father as it was possible to be, and she couldn't help wondering how her life would have turned out if she'd had Mr Makepiece for her father instead. Certainly, he wouldn't have ruined her mother's health with his demands, and neither would he have made his children tiptoe around the house like pale wraiths when he was present. Instead, he'd have loved and valued them. Talked to them, too. With Mr Makepiece as her father, Hannah might even have found the courage to tell him about Rose and ask for his help.

But he wasn't her father and he had other loyalties, so Hannah needed to stay on her guard.

'Mind if I take these blankets out so I can turn the pram upside down?' he asked.

Hannah helped to carry the blankets and pillow to a dry log and watched as he upended the pram, removed the wheel and bashed it with a hammer taken from his toolbox. Finally, he reattached the wheel to the pram, turned it the right way up and pushed it back and forth experimentally. 'I'd be exaggerating if I said it's as good as new, but it's as good as I can get it and a lot better than it was before.'

Hannah could see the improvement. 'Thank you,' she said, meaning it wholeheartedly. 'Would you thank Mrs Harrington for me, too? For asking you to help, I mean.'

'You can thank her yourself next time you're in

Churchwood,' he told her. 'I hope that'll be soon. I'm not saying there's anything wrong with Barton – there are some good people here – but, as you know, we have the bookshop in Churchwood. It's the place we can all find company and a friendly smile – little 'uns, old 'uns and folk who are in between.'

'I'll come back if I can,' Hannah said. 'It's just difficult with the children.'

'Difficult, maybe. But worth the trouble. And it doesn't cost a penny.'

Hannah nodded, growing thoughtful. With Mrs Harrington and now Mr Makepiece encouraging her to visit the bookshop, she had a good excuse for going to Churchwood more often. But, desperate as she was for news of Mattie and Rose, she still thought she'd risk suspicion if she went daily. It was horribly frustrating.

CHAPTER TWENTY

Naomi

Shopping for the household was Victoria's job, technically speaking, but Naomi often shopped herself. It got her out and about, seeing people and taking the pulse of the village. The exercise didn't hurt, either.

Today she was keen to see as many people as possible in the ongoing quest to learn the identity of Rose's mother. Three days had now passed since Rose had been found in the Foxfield porch, and they were still no closer to locating her mother. Naomi visited the cobbler's and the baker's, and was leaving the grocer's when she almost bumped into Edith Mead, who was trying to enter.

'Sorry,' Naomi said. 'I didn't see you there. How are—'

'No matter.' Mrs Mead swept into the shop, cutting off Naomi's words as the door swung shut behind her.

Edith Mead was one of those people who'd lived in Churchwood for years but on the edge of the community, in that she never came to the bookshop or to church, or even visited anyone as far as Naomi knew. She wasn't an unpleasant woman – unlike the Aggie Hamiltons of the world – but she was married to Alec Mead, who farmed the land opposite Foxfield, and that fact alone probably accounted for Edith's frown and harassed air. Alec Mead was a curt man who ruled his boys with rigid discipline. Perhaps he ruled his wife the same way.

Naomi would never expect to encounter a smiling Edith, but had she imagined that Edith's frown had been cutting even deeper than usual just then? That she'd been looking seriously unhappy?

A question came into Naomi's mind. Could Edith be baby Rose's mother? Almost immediately, the answer came back that this was highly unlikely. Alec Mead might well be the sort of man who'd react badly to an unexpected pregnancy, but Naomi thought back ten years or so to when Edith had been expecting her boys. Naomi had been grieving her own childless state at the time – something she was finally over now she had William and so many other children in her life – so she'd tended to avert her gaze from the curving middles of luckier women. Even so, she could recall Edith's slender body swelling in her pregnancies, but when she'd seen Edith out in the fields recently she'd looked thinner than ever.

Something else might be wrong in Edith's life, though.

Concerned, Naomi took her time over posting a letter to William so she could fall into step with Edith when she emerged from the grocer's and set off homewards along Churchwood Way. Keeping pace with her was no mean feat, since Edith was tall and long-legged while Naomi was short and dumpy with bad feet, but, wincing, she pressed on.

'How are you, Edith?' she asked.

'Fine, thank you. How are you?'

Naomi's welfare was clearly far from Edith's mind, but the question had to be asked.

'I'm fine, too.'

'Good.' Edith accelerated as though to leave Naomi behind but, gritting her teeth, Naomi set off in pursuit and managed to draw level again.

Edith wasn't pleased. 'Is there something you want from me?' she asked, obviously irritated.

'Forgive me,' Naomi said. 'I've no wish to intrude on your private business but you seem a little . . . troubled.'

'There's nothing wrong with *me*.' Was that bitterness twisting Edith's mouth?

'Someone in the family, then? Is one of the children sick? Your husband . . .?'

'My husband isn't sick. He's as fit as a fiddle.' Another twist of bitterness was followed by a muttered, 'He thinks he's twenty-five again.'

Before Naomi could answer, Edith withdrew back into herself. 'I appreciate your kindness in asking, Mrs Harrington, but you've no need to concern yourself in my affairs.'

'I understand,' Naomi said. What she understood was that something *was* wrong, but Edith didn't wish to talk about it. She looked to be in need of a friend, though. 'It would be nice to see you at the bookshop one day.'

'I don't think so.'

'We have all sorts of activities. Talks about practical things like wartime recipes and making clothes as well as chatting over cups of tea.'

'My husband doesn't approve of chatter. He especially doesn't approve of gossip.'

Alec Mead didn't approve of much at all as far as Naomi could see.

'Though what right he has to dictate the rules when—' Edith broke off abruptly, mouth tightening as though she wished she hadn't mentioned him.

Sensing that she'd only alienate Edith by asking more questions, Naomi said merely, 'You're always welcome at the bookshop if you change your mind. You don't have to stay long if you're needed back at home. A few minutes in good company can lift the spirits even if it's spent complaining about the weather.'

Getting Edith through the door and feeling less alone would be the first step. Confidences could come later if the problem persisted.

'I'm busy,' Edith said, clearly intending it to be the final word on the subject. She gave a brusque nod by way of a farewell and walked off at speed.

Misery was coming off her in waves, though, so Naomi decided to keep an eye on Edith as best she could.

She walked on through the Foxfield gateposts and up to the house, letting herself in using her key instead of disturbing Suki or Victoria, though Suki must have been listening out for her since she emerged from the kitchen and presented her employer with a silver tray.

'The post, madam,' she said.

Her voice was neutral but carefully so, and her expression was wary, as though she'd seen something in the post that was likely to trouble Naomi. What now?

'Thank you, Suki.' Naomi picked up the envelopes and carried them into the sitting room where she could be alone, the London families tending to use the drawing room which was bigger and able to hold them all.

The top envelope was obviously a bill. Ditto the second. It was the third envelope that must have bothered Suki, and no wonder. It was addressed in Alexander's sharp, spiky handwriting. Setting the bills aside for the moment, Naomi opened Alexander's letter. Unsurprisingly for a man who insisted on having the best things in life and looked down on anything else, both envelope and notepaper were of a quality that could only be described as luxurious.

Dear Naomi,

I understand you're engaged to be married once our divorce has come through. Congratulations. I'm glad to know that you're looking forward to happiness.

Congratulations? Glad? Naomi wasn't fooled. Alexander hadn't written to promote her happiness. He had something else in mind. She read on to learn exactly what that was.

I'm also glad to hear from William that he's happy at his new school and enjoying spending time with you as well as at home with his family.

Glad this, glad that . . . She was more convinced than ever that Alexander was simply working up to something, laying the groundwork by holding out the lures of an early marriage to Bert and a continued relationship with William before delivering . . . what? The price of his cooperation, Naomi guessed.

With regard to the financial settlement we agreed . . .

Yes, here it came.

. . . I find myself in difficulties in raising the full sum you demanded, since my investments haven't performed as well as I'd hoped. Wartime presents challenges to all sorts of businesses and, unfortunately, some of the stocks and shares in my personal portfolio have suffered losses.
    In the interest of us both moving forward in our lives – you with your forthcoming marriage, me with my need to provide for William and his sister – I wonder if we might review the financial settlement to something more manageable? Without a review, I fear it may take me a very long time to raise sufficient funds. It may also mean cutting back on family expenditure.

In other words, he'd drag the financial settlement out as long as possible to keep her from marrying Bert, and he'd ensure that William was kept short of money, too.

The alternative arrangement I have in mind is . . .

Naomi sputtered when she read the figure he suggested he pay her. It was precisely half of the agreed amount.

She went in search of Suki. 'I'm going out again,' she said.

'Hmm,' Bert said, when Naomi approached him in his market garden. 'I think you'd be excited if you had news of baby Rose's mother. Instead, you've got a face like thunder. You've heard from the icicle?'

She showed him Alexander's letter and watched disgust embed itself in his features.

'It's blackmail, pure and simple,' he said.

Naomi's thoughts exactly. 'It isn't as though the settlement we agreed was unreasonable, since it was for less than half of the trust fund money Alexander fleeced from me. If I agree to his current demand, he'll be returning less than a quarter of that fund. And it was money my father worked hard all his life to save for me.'

'You're not going to agree?' Bert asked.

'Certainly not, though it may mean the divorce is dragged out for years.'

Naomi felt tears pool in her eyes. She wanted to marry Bert – her soulmate – as soon as possible, not at some distant time in the future. Bert gathered her close. 'If I know you, beloved, you won't let that happen.'

'No.' She drew in a deep breath and summoned her fighting spirit. 'I won't.'

CHAPTER TWENTY-ONE

Beth

Having been saddled with the job of bookshop liaison, Beth wanted to get it over with as soon as possible. Once she had information about the forthcoming concert she could report it to Matron and then lapse back into her own private world instead of simmering with resentment.

Approaching the bookshop, she heard chatter and children's merry laughter drifting out of the open windows. They made a joyful sound like distant church bells and for a moment the contrast with her own feelings was painfully apparent. But she straightened her shoulders and headed for the door. Should she simply march straight in? No one had said anything about needing to book a place in advance, but then she hadn't been interested enough to ask any questions. Would she need to book a place anyway? Surely not when she was here only to ask a few questions.

She opened the door and stood on the threshold, taking in the scene. The room was crowded with women of all ages, mostly sitting on chairs while small children sat on laps or rugs or played with their friends. As Beth watched, a large, bear-like man in his middle years leaned over the banisters. 'Any chance of tea before we faint from thirst up here?' he asked.

'Less of your cheek, Bert Makepiece,' someone called back. 'It'll be two minutes.'

Beth realized the man called Bert had spotted her. 'Good afternoon,' he called. 'Come in and make yourself comfortable.'

Other people noticed her then – which made Beth feel awkward. She was almost glad when Alice Irvine got up and came to greet her. 'It's lovely to see you, Beth. You've timed your arrival perfectly.'

'That's because tea is on the way,' someone called out, joking.

'Actually, I'm only here for information about the concert,' Beth said. 'Matron sent me.' An errand that still seemed ridiculous, given that Alice was clearly fighting fit and would doubtless be visiting the hospital again soon, when she could pass on all the information Matron could possibly want to know.

'You can still have a cup of tea,' Alice pointed out.

'You certainly can,' Bert said, joining them. 'You probably need one after that long walk from the hospital. I'm Bert Makepiece, by the way, and this . . .' He gestured to a woman who'd approached. She looked familiar, and Beth realized it was the woman who'd required Alice's help with some sort of emergency the day Beth had arrived in Churchwood. 'This is my beloved, Naomi Harrington. Soon to be Naomi Makepiece.'

Not another happy romance to tug painfully on Beth's lonely state!

'It's good to meet you, Beth,' Bert said, 'but you'll excuse me if I return to my woodworking class? One of the chaps might drive a nail through their finger if I'm not there to supervise and I'm sure you'd rather relax than administer first aid.'

Bert moved away and Naomi sent Beth a smile. 'It's

nice to meet you properly. I'm afraid I was a little distracted the first time we met.'

She didn't explain the nature of her emergency but perhaps it had passed into history.

'You're welcome to borrow a book if you enjoy reading,' Alice said. She gestured to a table where a selection of books was laid out. 'We lost most of our books when the plane crashed last year.'

'There was a plane crash?' Surprise had the words tumbling out of Beth's mouth before she could call them back. The last thing she wanted was to show interest. It was too late now, though.

'A German plane came down on the Sunday School Hall where the bookshop used to be held.'

That explained the gap between the buildings around the village green.

'It destroyed almost all of our books and equipment, from chairs to play rugs,' Alice continued. 'Fortunately, Naomi is buying this house to give us a permanent base and we're building up a new stock of books.'

'Helped by the generosity of supporters like Kate Kinsella,' Naomi said, as though keen to share the credit. 'Have you met Kate, Beth?'

'She's one of the land girls?' The one with the lovely face and chestnut hair, if Beth's memory served her correctly.

'Actually, she's the daughter of the farmer who employs two land girls, but she works on the farm as well. She got married a few weeks ago and she and her husband donated all the money that was collected as wedding gifts.'

'How kind,' Beth murmured. It *was* kind. Beth was impressed by both Kate Kinsella's generosity and the way these Churchwood people seemed to be pulling together. But it didn't change the fact that she had no wish to be one of them. 'I'm afraid I really must . . .' she began but Naomi had started talking, too.

'I'll fetch some tea,' she said.

'Meanwhile, I'll introduce you to a few others,' Alice said. Linking Beth's arm with a friendliness that came naturally to her, Alice drew her further into the room.

Names washed over Beth. May Janicki was the stylish woman Babs Carter had mentioned, and she certainly was fashionable in her beautifully cut skirt and jacket in forest green. Beside her, Beth felt dowdy, though May was friendly. A woman called Janet Collins was apparently another bookshop helper. She was older and it was easy to picture her as the sort of mother and grandmother who offered warmth and comfort to her family.

Another older woman was called Ivy. She and her little granddaughter, Flower, had moved out from London a few months earlier along with several other evacuees and found a welcome in Churchwood. Once again, Beth was struck by how much kindness was to be found in this village. Poor Ivy had the bowed legs that resulted from rickets, a childhood weakness caused by poor nutrition and too little exposure to sunlight, perhaps because London was often filled with smog. Fending for herself and a small granddaughter must have been hard.

'Excuse me a moment,' Alice said when someone called her over, and Beth found a baby was suddenly being thrust towards her by a younger woman.

'Hold Robbie for me, will you? I need to wipe his brother's nose.'

The baby was in her arms before Beth had a chance to protest. She held him stiffly, more used to injured soldiers than infants, but he smiled up at her anyway as his mother used a handkerchief on the face of a boy aged about two or three.

'Thanks,' she told Beth, reclaiming Robbie.

Naomi returned with tea and Beth felt obliged to take a cup. As Naomi hastened off to deal with a spillage of some sort, Beth felt a tug on her sleeve. 'Sit down and keep me company,' an elderly woman said.

'I'm not staying long,' Beth told her.

'You can sit while you drink your tea.'

Beth sat reluctantly.

'I'm Edna Hall,' the woman announced. 'You nurses do a wonderful job at that hospital. I'm sure your pretty faces buck the men up no end.'

Pretty? Cassandra Carlisle was pretty. Beth was ordinary. Doubtless the comment had been well meant, though, so she forced a smile.

'You've heard there's going to be a concert?' Edna asked.

'That's why I'm here. To get information about it for Matron.'

'We're all looking forward to it. Well, most of us. Some – and I'm mentioning no names here – disapprove of the singer.' She nodded towards a tight-lipped woman who looked as though she disapproved of many people and many things.

'I know nothing about the singer,' Beth admitted.

'She has a good voice. I'll say that for her. But I suspect she's rather a minx, if you take my meaning? Not like you, dear. You look like a good girl.'

Was that shorthand for a plain girl? A boring girl? Beth smiled thinly but it didn't matter because Edna was looking at someone else. 'Oh dear. I'm afraid you need to brace yourself, Beth.'

Glancing round, Beth saw that the unhinged woman who thought she'd seen a ghost was approaching them. 'Marjorie isn't malicious,' Edna whispered, 'but she does enjoy sticking her nose into other people's business.'

'I need to speak to Alice,' Beth said, excusing herself before Marjorie could pounce.

'Very wise, dear,' Edna approved.

'About the concert?' Beth reminded Alice, who smiled.

'What would you like to know?'

'I'm . . . not sure. Matron asked me to come for information and report back to her.'

'I see.' Alice looked thoughtful for a moment before saying, 'She's a wise woman, is Matron.'

She was certainly an annoying one. But enough of that. Beth needed information if she was to avoid the need to return. 'The date would be useful, I suppose. The starting time, too. Then there's ticket price, cost of refreshments, any restrictions on numbers attending . . .'

'The date is Saturday the twenty-fifth of April, and we'll probably start around seven. There's been a lot of interest, though, so we may have both matinee and evening performances. Bookshop events don't have fixed prices. We ask for donations so people only pay what they can afford. The same applies to refreshments. As for numbers attending . . .'

'You won't know until you've decided on the number of performances,' Beth guessed. 'Perhaps you could let me know the next time you come to the hospital?' Surely Matron couldn't object to Alice simply passing on just one detail?

'I could,' Alice agreed. 'Or you could come to the bookshop again. You might enjoy yourself.'

'We'll see,' Beth answered, only to be distracted by a minor commotion as the door opened and two people stepped in.

One of them was Kate Kinsella. The other was an RAF flight lieutenant, presumably her husband. Amid the cries of welcome and the surge of people going to greet them, Beth noticed again how glowing Kate looked despite her shabby breeches and the ancient jumper that had a hole in the elbow. As for her husband . . . goodness! He wasn't handsome in the golden-haired way of Oliver Lytton, but he had his own style of attractiveness. Tall, well built and very upright in his uniform, he had laughing blue eyes and the sort of energy that spoke of enthusiasm for life. His face bore some scarring, probably from burns, but far from diminishing his attractions, it added character.

He had his arm around Kate, who glanced up at him with loving eyes. The sight carved a hollow inside Beth. It was definitely time to leave.

She headed for the door, only for someone to catch hold of her arm. It was Kate. 'It's lovely to see you here,' she said.

'I'm only here on an errand.'

'Maybe so, but I hope our bookshop works its magic on you and makes you want to visit again.'

'I doubt I'll have time,' Beth fibbed.

'Making time can be difficult,' Kate conceded. 'Sometimes we just have to barrel through our workloads and hope things fall into place.' She spoke as though from experience.

Kate's husband offered a handshake. 'Leo Kinsella. Welcome to Churchwood. It's the best place on earth.'

'It's a pleasure to meet you,' Beth said politely, but the radiance emanating from this couple was too much to bear. 'Excuse me.' She slipped past them and through the doors into the outside world.

Job done, though it was a pity she hadn't come away with a book since she might have returned it via Alice on one of her visits to the hospital. She'd noticed a Daphne du Maurier book on the table. *Rebecca*. Having heard good things about it, she'd thought it might have been useful for taking her mind off her own woes. But perhaps it was for the best that she'd come away empty-handed. At least this way, she wouldn't be sucked into further involvement with the bookshop.

Now to report to Matron and return to the peace and quiet of her room. The quiet, anyway. It would be a while before time lived up to its healing reputation so she could feel at peace again.

CHAPTER TWENTY-TWO

Naomi

'Books!' Heading home from the bookshop with Alice, the word suddenly burst out of Naomi's mouth.

'What about books?' Alice asked.

'Sorry,' Naomi said. 'I didn't mean to startle you. I was thinking out loud.'

'About books?'

'About books in relation to Edith Mead. I'm concerned for her.'

'She never looks happy.'

'I think she's particularly *un*happy at the moment.'

'Do you know why?'

'I suspect it's something to do with her husband. I know he's miserable at the best of times, and I'm sure his word is law at home, but that's been the case for years. I feel something might have changed.'

'She'll be a difficult woman to help,' Alice said.

'I've encouraged her to come to the bookshop, but I doubt she'll do it. I was thinking of how else I might get through to her and came up with the idea of—'

'Books,' Alice finished. 'If Edith won't come to the bookshop, the bookshop can go to her?'

'In a manner of speaking. Alec Mead would run us off the farm if we turned up there, and he might well take his anger out on his wife. There's something of Ernie Fletcher about Alec Mead.'

'He's a little more presentable than Ernie but just as bad-tempered and inclined to consider himself master of all he surveys,' Alice agreed. 'Though at least his children are clean and well dressed and they go to school, which is more than Kate's father ever managed for his children, Kate especially. But you're right. Visiting Edith at home is out of the question.'

'Which is why I thought I'd keep a book in my bag and lend it to her the next time I see her. It may be the first step towards getting her over the bookshop threshold and making friends but, even if it isn't, I hope it'll make her feel less isolated. Besides, books offer escapism and entertainment. And I imagine Edith is in need of both.'

'It's a lovely idea,' Alice said. 'I'll look out for her and have a book ready in my bag, too.'

'I know you'll be discreet.'

'Marjorie will never hear of it from my lips,' Alice said, smiling. Then she looked over her shoulder as though checking that no one was close enough to overhear what they were saying. 'No news from Rose's mother, I suppose?'

'Nothing at all.'

'Do you think it means she's given up on trying to get her daughter back?'

'Who knows? Perhaps it was always unrealistic of her to expect her circumstances to change.'

'You'll give her a little longer, though? Just in case?'

'We all want to give her as much time as possible. But . . .'

'The clock is ticking,' Alice finished.

'Rose's birth needs to be registered, and if her mother can't look after her . . .'

'The sooner she's given to adoptive parents, the better.'

'Always supposing adoption is possible. I imagine there are fewer adoptive parents stepping forward while so many men are away at the war,' Naomi said. 'I hate the thought of the little thing going to an orphanage, though.'

'Let's hope that won't be necessary.'

They'd reached The Linnets. 'Are you coming to the bookshop tomorrow?' Alice asked.

'I may give Victoria time off to go in my place. She needs a break and it'll do her good to relax for a couple of hours.'

Alice nodded.

'I must say, Alice, you're looking very well,' Naomi observed then. 'Radiant.'

Alice patted the slight curve of her stomach. 'I'm feeling well. And I'm hopeful of a happier outcome this time.'

Last year's miscarriage had hit Alice hard. 'I couldn't be more pleased,' Naomi said.

Alice's baby would be born into a loving home with loving parents, even if the baby's father was away at the war just now. The circumstances of the foundling baby were clearly more challenging, but Naomi would do what she could to help.

She parted from Alice with a hug.

CHAPTER TWENTY-THREE

Victoria

Victoria hastened into the sitting room to answer the telephone. 'Good afternoon,' she began when the call was put through.

'Mrs Harrington?'

'I'm her housekeeper. Mrs Harrington isn't here, I'm afraid.' Naomi had returned from the bookshop only to go out to see Bert. 'But—'

'She's out?' The voice tutted. 'But I need to speak to her.'

'Was she expecting you to call?'

'She knows I need to speak to her.'

But not right now. 'May I take a message, Miss Moore?' Victoria smiled as she guessed the caller's identity. Naomi had warned her that Margueritte was 'quite a character'. She heard an irritated sigh and could picture the petulant look that accompanied it.

'Is the piano in place?' Margueritte asked. 'I want to start practising as soon as possible.'

'I believe steps have been taken to borrow one from the hospital, but I don't think it's in the bookshop yet.'

There was another tut. 'How am I supposed to prepare for a concert without a piano? Mrs Harrington does know I'm a *professional* singer?'

'I believe you told her that.' Margueritte probably told everyone she met. 'Perhaps you could ring back later when Mrs Harrington might be home and have more information for you. I believe you're not on the telephone so she can't ring you.'

'My uncle doesn't have a telephone so I'm calling from one of his neighbours' houses.' What an inconvenience! 'I suppose I'll have to ring back. But tell her I need the piano soon.'

'I'll remind her,' Victoria promised. 'About the piano and also the fact that you're a professional.'

'One more thing. My pianist has an engagement for the night we originally agreed. I told him to cancel it, of course, but there's some nonsense about a contract. It's highly annoying. Anyway, it means that the concert will need to be on May the ninth.'

'I'll pass that on, too,' Victoria promised. 'And let's hope the new date is convenient.'

Margueritte had already rung off.

Victoria joined the others in the drawing room. The children had returned from school and the children's club, and their mothers had returned from the aircraft factory. Stroking Jenny's hair from her forehead, Victoria dropped a kiss on it and asked Arthur how he'd enjoyed the club.

'It was good,' he reported. 'Adam got us playing a game. He stood with his back to us and we had to creep up on him and tap his shoulder. He was allowed to keep looking round, though, and if he caught us moving, we were out of the game.'

'Did anyone win?'

'No one won the first time we played. I won the second time.'

'Well done, Arthur!'

'We played skittles, too. I was on a team with Lewis and Timmy Turner. We didn't win but it was fun.'

Victoria was pleased. Arthur had struggled on first moving to Churchwood and got himself into trouble. Not because he had a bad bone in his body – he hadn't – but through a combination of trying to entertain the other London children and bad luck. It was lovely to see him so settled and happy, and it made her more convinced than ever that she'd made the right decision in putting the children's best interests before her own, even if she couldn't suppress the pang of loss that came into her heart every time she thought of Paul Scarletti.

A burst of laughter reached her. Mags, Sheila and Pat were huddled in a corner. Mags saw Victoria watching and beckoned her over. 'We're just teasing Pat,' she said.

'About what?'

'They're being ridiculous,' Pat said.

'Not at all,' Mags denied. 'Mr Bartlett has a crush on you, so he has.'

'Rubbish.'

'Mr Bartlett is your supervisor?' Victoria asked.

'He is,' Mags confirmed. 'And Pat is his teacher's pet.'

Pat rolled her eyes.

'He's a man of sense if he's attracted to you, Pat,' Victoria said, 'and he'll be a lucky man if you return his interest.'

'Don't you start,' Pat said.

Victoria squeezed her shoulder and went to see to dinner. It would be lovely for Pat if she found a new man. Of course, Pat had two children already so she'd need to be sure he'd take them on as stepchildren and treat them kindly. But why not? Pat's circumstances were different from Victoria's. Pat's children were her own and secure in her love, so they'd never feel they were obstacles in her path.

Victoria really needed to throw Paul's letter away.

CHAPTER TWENTY-FOUR

Ruby

'You want to borrow the bicycle?' Kate sounded surprised, and no wonder. Ruby hated the bicycle.

'The exercise will do me good,' she reasoned. 'I've put on a bit of weight despite rationing and I'd like to be trimmer when I walk down the aisle.'

'Does this mean you're ready to arrange the wedding?' Kate's eyes had brightened. She was radiantly happy with her Leo and made no secret of wanting everyone else to be happy, too, though the coolness between Pearl and Fred was continuing.

'Not quite. But it won't hurt me to start slimming down now.'

'You have a lovely figure already, Ruby. But if you want more exercise, then of course you can borrow the bicycle.'

Ruby cursed the bike later when she got on it and wobbled through the farmyard. She cursed it for a second time when she hit a rut as she rode down the drive to Brimbles Lane, and for a third time when a rock in the ground caught the front wheel and threatened to launch her over the handlebars. How Kate and Pearl managed to speed along on this uncomfortable machine was a mystery. Ruby supposed it was because they were both long-legged, Kate's slender athleticism and Pearl's strength enabling them to stand up and pump the pedals at speed over the rougher ground. They were more used to facing the great outdoors than Ruby, too. Not that she was blind to the beauty of the countryside. She liked to see open skies with glorious sunrises, sunsets and scudding, pearl-like clouds. She also liked the greenery that was showing on trees and bushes and in the flowers that were peeping under the hedgerows – dusky bluebells and delicate primroses.

After all, the East End of London hadn't offered much in the way of wildflowers and freshness. It had offered soot-filled air instead, the dankness of the river down by the docks and sometimes other smells, too, as ships were unloaded of spices and other cargoes they'd carried from thousands of miles away for distribution around the country.

On the other hand, she preferred to huddle indoors when it was cold or raining, and as for this bone-shaking torture . . .

Oomph! Ruby hit another rut and a shudder racked her entire body. She was looking out for hazards but her steering was less than accurate and she often hit the very hazard she was trying to avoid. She was going to ache after this cycle ride and doubted she'd gain anything by way of compensation.

Certainly not a trimmer figure, since that had just been an excuse for taking up cycling. Ruby had simply grown restless waiting for news of the abandoned baby. Every time anyone called at the farm – even the postman and the milkman – she'd feel tension squeeze her body in case she heard that the baby was a secret no longer. Every day Timmy left the farm she'd fret about what he might be hearing and how he might respond. On his return, she'd search his face anxiously for clues.

She'd decided it was better to try to find out for herself what was being said in the village. It might give her more time to decide what to do, especially about Timmy. As well, she couldn't get little Rose's mother out of her head. Visiting the village shops might give Ruby a chance to see or hear something that could help to identify the troubled girl. Or woman. Ruby was trying to keep an open mind about that but couldn't help feeling that the mother was likely to be young.

As well as visiting the shops she could cycle up and down some of the side streets. Probably, there'd be little to gain since it was highly unlikely to lead her to the baby's mother but, as an unmarried mum herself, Ruby thought she might have a stronger instinct than most people for recognizing the mother's fear and anxiety if their paths happened to cross. Besides, wild goose chase or not, trying to do *something* was better than doing nothing.

Eight years had passed since her own pregnancy, but Ruby had forgotten nothing of that time. How starry-eyed and naive she'd been, and how excited to be taken on as a trainee hairdresser in the salon on Keifer Street. Most people she knew had their hair cut by friends or family members since they hadn't the money to pay for anything else. As a child, Ruby's own hair had been cut by her mother, but Joan Turner was a straight-laced and miserable woman whose only goals were neatness and modesty. Notions of style, attractiveness and fun were not only beyond her but disapproved of by her.

From the age of twelve, Ruby had managed her hair herself, trimming and teasing it into waves like those of some of the film stars she saw in *Film Weekly*, the magazine her neighbour Iris brought home from the house where she worked as a charwoman. Vivien Leigh, Greta Garbo, Joan Fontaine, Marlene Dietrich . . .

'Vanity is a sin,' Ruby's dour mother told her, not hiding her distaste whenever Iris handed over a magazine with a smiling, 'Another one for you, Ruby, rescued from the bin.'

Ruby's father was equally disapproving. 'Learning how to keep house will be far more useful when you have a husband than all that film-star nonsense.'

Hairdressing wasn't Ruby's first job on leaving school. To please her parents, she took work in a mackintosh factory. 'A sensible, steady job to see you through until you're married,' they approved.

But it was dreadfully dull and, whenever she had the chance, she called at salons to ask if there might be any opportunities for her. She was delighted when Mr Chapman of Estella Beauty looked at her thoughtfully after she'd raced there from the factory one Saturday afternoon. 'You want to train, you say?'

'Yes, please!'

'We might have an opening here,' he said, before adding, 'for someone who's eager to please.'

'I'm very eager,' she assured him, too enthusiastic and innocent to pick up on what he might mean beneath the surface.

His wife entered the office. 'Who's this?' she demanded.

'A young woman who's looking for employment,' Mr Chapman told her in businesslike tones. 'We have an opening now Jane is no longer with us.'

The mention of Jane had Mrs Chapman's lips pursing. 'That girl left us in the lurch.'

'Indeed, Stella. But now we have another girl willing to step into the vacancy.'

Mrs Chapman looked Ruby up and down, not

appearing to like what she saw but giving in to necessity. 'You'll start by sweeping the floors, cleaning the salon and washing hair. You won't get near a pair of scissors until you've proved yourself.'

'I'm keen to get on so I won't disappoint you,' Ruby promised.

'You can start, on trial. I won't keep you if I'm not satisfied.'

'It's all vanity,' her mother said, when she heard about Ruby's new job.

Her father agreed. 'Ideas above your station – that's your problem, Ruby.'

It was a pity they couldn't be pleased for her but she'd never been the sort of daughter they wanted – an imitation of her mother. If they had to have a daughter at all, that was. They'd made no secret of the fact that they'd have preferred their only child to be a son. At the salon she set to work willingly, not once complaining about the never-ending hair she had to sweep from the floor or the way the constant washing of customers' hair, brushes, combs and such roughened her hands. She was efficient about keeping a tally of the towels that were sent to and from the laundry. She polished basins and mirrors until they sparkled and even looked after the yapping dogs some customers brought to the salon.

Mrs Chapman spoke to her only to issue commands, but Mr Chapman was generous with his praise. 'You're doing a fine job, little Ruby,' he told her on her second day.

He'd startled her by coming up behind her as she was polishing a mirror, so close that she could sense the waft of his breath across her cheek.

A few days later he startled her again, so much that she almost fell off the stool she was using to stack towels on a shelf. 'Careful,' he said, taking hold of her hips to steady her.

Ruby felt a fool. 'Sorry,' she said, blushing.

'You've nothing to apologize for, dear girl,' he told her. 'Accidents happen.'

'Let me,' he said another time when she dropped some hairpins. He helped her to return them to their box and then closed his hand around hers, keeping it there as they rose to their feet.

'Thank you,' Ruby said, beginning to feel awkward. 'I'd better get those towels ready for the laundry.'

'Of course, dear child.'

It was the friendly-uncle approach that lulled her into a false sense of security.

The night it happened, Mrs Chapman left promptly to visit her mother. Ruby was leaving just after her when Mr Chapman stepped out of the office. 'Could I have a word, please, Ruby?'

Trepidation trickled through her. Anxiously, she followed him into the office, passing close by him as he held the door open and then closed it behind her. 'Am I in trouble?' she asked. After all, she was still on trial and perhaps Mrs Chapman felt she hadn't performed her work to a satisfactory standard.

'On the contrary, little Ruby. We're very pleased with you.'

'That's a relief.'

'You're a hard worker and you're eager to please. That's what you said at the interview, isn't it? Eager to please?'

'It is. I want to get on and become a hairdresser.'

'You certainly please me, little girl.' He moved closer.

Ruby took a step back only to come up hard against a wall. 'I need to get home now, Mr Chapman,' she said, feeling wary, though not quite understanding the reason why.

'All in good time, my dear. All in good time.' He reached up to touch her cheek. 'So pretty!'

Ruby wanted to move away but he was blocking her in. 'Mr Chapman, I don't think this is—'

'Don't you like me?' he asked.

'Of course I like you. But—'

'If I like you and you like me, there isn't a problem, is there?' With that, he moved in on her.

Ruby pushed against him. Told him to stop. But it made no difference and it was all over quickly. Ruby wasn't sure exactly what had happened, but she knew it was horrible. She was certain it had been wrong, too. Terribly wrong.

Mr Chapman stepped away, tidying himself and then reaching into his pocket for his wallet. 'A little treat for you, my dear,' he said, holding out a one-pound note. 'A little extra to thank you for your friendliness.'

Ruby burst into tears. Ignoring the money, she finally got to the door.

'Don't be like that, little Ruby,' Mr Chapman chided. 'I didn't do anything you didn't want. You told me you liked me.'

Ruby simply fled.

'You're late,' her mother grumbled dourly when Ruby arrived home.

She was very late, having paced the streets, crying in distress. But she couldn't face telling her parents what had happened, knowing they'd blame it on her vanity and her discontent in not settling for work in the factory.

That night she lay awake, wondering what she could have done to stop Mr Chapman from thinking that she wanted . . . *that*. Had there been something in her words, her look, her manner, that had misled him?

But he was a married man, for goodness' sake! More than twice her age. And she'd told him to stop . . .

Whatever the rights and wrongs of it, Ruby couldn't continue working there. But what if Mrs Chapman came round to the Turners' house to complain that Ruby hadn't turned up? What would happen then?

She returned to the salon the next day, hiding in an alley until Mr Chapman left to go wherever it was his habit to go on a Wednesday morning. Running to the door, Ruby pushed through it, relieved to see there were no customers yet. 'You're late,' Mrs Chapman pointed out, mouth pinched with annoyance.

'I'm sorry, but I don't wish to work here any more,' Ruby told her.

'Why not?'

'I don't feel . . . comfortable.'

'Comfortable? What does that . . . Oh, I see. You as well.' Mrs Chapman tutted, then said, 'You young girls shouldn't encourage him.'

Ruby gasped. 'I didn't encourage him!' she said, but Mrs Chapman wasn't interested.

'Go on, then. Get out,' she ordered.

'What about my wages?'

'You'll need to see my husband about those.' Mrs Chapman's smile was nasty.

'I can't see him.'

'Then you'll have to go without, won't you?' Mrs Chapman stepped away as a customer entered. 'Alicia! How lovely to see you!' She looked over her shoulder and gave Ruby a sharp nod towards the door. '*Go.*'

For a few weeks, as she returned to working at the

mackintosh factory, Ruby went about her daily business feeling upset and bewildered because she still couldn't fathom how Mr Chapman could have interpreted her friendliness as being more than that. Neither was she able to understand how his wife could have regarded the whole episode as no more than a nuisance.

Only gradually did it dawn on Ruby that she had an even bigger problem to face. Terrified of how her parents would react, she disguised her changing body under looser clothes. Handing her wage packet to her mother each week and receiving only a few shillings in return meant she could save little, but she still saved everything she could, not knowing exactly how things would turn out but guessing instinctively that she'd need every penny she could pull together.

When she finally confessed to her parents that she was expecting a child, they were furious. Her mother called her unkind names and her father demanded to know the identity of the child's father. Ruby refused to share it, knowing the Chapmans would only conspire together to call her a liar. They might even accuse her of trying to extort money from them.

'Some married man, was it?' her father sneered.

They wanted to send Ruby away to give birth out of sight of the neighbours and have the child adopted so no one need ever know it existed. But none of what had happened was the baby's fault. Ruby was growing a new and innocent little person and, feeling flutters of movement inside her, she knew she'd love her baby for its own sake.

'I'm going to look for lodgings,' she told her parents, but they decided it would only make people talk and, worse, she might be seen out and about with a child born outside wedlock.

They decided the baby should be passed off as her

mother's. It certainly saved face outside the home, but inside it was different. Ruby wasn't forgiven and, when Timmy was born, he was treated as a shameful inconvenience.

In Ruby's eyes, though, Timmy was the bringer of joy.

'Are you my mum?' he asked her one day. 'My real mum, I mean?'

Ruby was shocked. 'What makes you think that?'

'I heard Mother and Father talking.'

'Do you mind?'

'No, I'm glad. I like you better than them, and they don't like me at all.'

She put her arm around him and squeezed him. 'I'm glad to be your mum. But it needs to be a secret. You can't tell anyone.'

'Why not?'

'Because . . . because I don't have a husband.'

'Is that bad?'

'To some people.'

He nodded thoughtfully. 'All right. It's a secret.'

She wondered if he'd be able to keep it, but he never once slipped up.

Ruby neared the end of Brimbles Lane at last, only to discover that nothing happened when she squeezed the bicycle's brakes. No wonder Kate and Pearl brought it to a halt by slamming their feet to the ground. Ruby's halt took longer and was far less elegant, a mad scuffling as her feet sought purchase on the rough ground. She winced at the soreness in her legs and rear end when she finally got off. Propping the bicycle against a bush, she crept into the woods behind Foxfield, wondering if she might chance upon the mother watching the house in the hope of seeing her child. But if she was there, she was well hidden.

Returning to the bicycle, Ruby got back on, grimacing at the thought of even more aches and pains, and continued into the village. She cycled up and down several side streets, hoping she wouldn't need to stop quickly. A few people were out and about, but her instincts didn't stir. She stole searching looks at the people in the bakery, where she went to buy bread, and in the grocer's, where she went to buy Timmy a copy of the *Beano* comic. But no one mentioned the abandoned baby and no one made her instincts quiver.

Kenny was in the farmyard when Ruby returned home. 'What's this?' he said, nodding at the bicycle.

'I'm trying to get fitter,' Ruby told him.

'Kate said you're getting trim for the wedding. Don't overdo it, though.' He glanced around as though to be sure Ernie wasn't nearby then wrapped his arms around her and nuzzled her neck. 'I like your figure as it is. Does this mean you want the wedding to be soon? Because I can't wait.'

Oh, heck. It was lovely that Kenny was keen for them to be man and wife, but there was no way Ruby wanted to marry while there was a danger of the village hearing about the secret baby and starting gossip circulating. 'I still need to think about a few things first,' she said.

'What things?'

'Like who to invite. My parents, for two.'

'That's easy,' Kenny said. 'You don't like them and, from what you've said, they don't like you. *Or* Timmy. You don't need to invite them to the wedding.'

It wasn't as simple as that, though. What Kenny said was true, but her parents had allowed her to keep Timmy. Even if they'd resented doing so, Ruby wondered if she owed them something for that.

'I'll think about it,' she said.

'Just set the date,' Kenny answered, and then he laughed. 'Otherwise I'll start thinking you're going cool on me.'

With all her other worries, it was the last thing Ruby needed to hear.

CHAPTER TWENTY-FIVE

Victoria

'I insist,' Naomi said. 'It's time you had a relaxing couple of hours at the bookshop.'

'But it's Saturday. A working day,' Victoria pointed out.

'Victoria, you're working seven days a week.'

'Only to make up for the time I spend with Arthur and Jenny.'

'I'm not keeping a tally. I know how hard you work, especially now we have Rose with us. I'll look after her for a few hours. Ivy and Suki will help, if needed.'

Victoria opened her mouth to object only for Naomi to cut across her.

'Besides,' Naomi said, 'people might think it odd if you stay at home most of the time. You'd started to make friends before Rose arrived. We don't want people suspecting something is wrong here.'

'Put like that . . .' Victoria conceded.

'You'll be doing me a favour as well,' Naomi said, smiling ruefully. 'The piano is being delivered today and Margueritte said she may come to supervise its installation. It might be helpful if you do the supervising instead. There'll be a knitting and sewing club session going on and we don't want anyone there getting upset or provoked into an argument.'

'Especially not with knitting needles in their hands to use as weapons.'

'Ouch,' Naomi said.

'All right,' Victoria agreed. 'I'll admit to being curious about Margueritte Moore.'

'Just keep her in check. If you can.'

'Careful!' Margueritte cried.

Bert paused to sigh and exchange looks with Victoria. 'We're being careful,' he pointed out.

He'd brought the piano on the truck. Now he was unloading it, assisted by Victoria and May and using planks of wood as a makeshift ramp.

The piano reached the pavement. 'Wait!' Margueritte commanded.

They waited, and she came to inspect the instrument. Her pouting mouth turned downwards when she saw how scuffed and scratched it was. 'Is this really the best piano you can find?'

So much for gratitude. 'We're lucky to have it,' Victoria told her.

'Hmm,' Margueritte replied dourly. Then she looked towards the young man she'd brought along. 'Sidney!'

He scurried forward, a short and slightly built man with a jacket that flapped off his shoulders, a large nose and black spectacles which he pushed up his nose even when they hadn't slipped down it.

'Try it,' Margueritte ordered.

He raised the lid and ran his fingers over the keys. 'It's a little flat but I can tune it,' he said.

Margueritte nodded and then, as though Bert, Victoria and May had taken a tea break to which they weren't entitled, said, 'You should get it inside.'

Victoria was tempted to salute but shared more amused looks with Bert and May.

They wheeled the piano into the bookshop with

Margueritte giving the sort of guidance that meant she simply got in the way. 'Over there,' she ordered, pointing to a wall.

'Not today,' Bert said. 'As you can see, we have knitters and sewers here. We'll have the children's club later and the little 'uns will be running around. We're putting the piano in a corner out of the way. You can always move it when you practise – as long as you move it back afterwards.'

'I need to practise now,' Margueritte argued. 'It's the reason Sidney is here.'

Bert was firm. 'Not possible, I'm afraid. But if you wait half an hour for our knitters and sewers to finish . . .?'

Margueritte was outraged. 'Don't you realize I'm a professional singer, not some . . . amateur?'

'And it's a fine voice you've got,' Bert conceded, mild but immoveable. 'You could always fill the time by making cups of tea for you and your friend. Lubricate the vocal cords so you're ready to sing in half an hour.'

'Humph!' Margueritte stormed down the room to a vacant chair, Sidney hastening after her. He opened the music case he'd brought and took out several sheets of music for her to consider.

'Not that one,' she told him, making no effort to lower her voice. 'Perhaps this one . . .'

May was called away to give advice to the sewing women and Victoria sent Bert an approving smile. 'Margueritte doesn't stand a chance against you.'

'It doesn't do to let talent go to the head. Anyway, it's nice to see you out and about and not just at the shops.'

'Naomi insisted.'

'That's my woman.'

'I suppose I'd better circulate.'

'I'd better be off home. Don't be tempted to make tea

for everyone. Leave that job to someone else. You work hard enough.'

Bert left and Victoria went over to Margueritte. 'I'm sorry to interrupt, but I have a copy of the bookshop programme for you.' She handed it over. 'You'll see when we're open so you can work around those times for your rehearsals. Assuming you'll wish to rehearse again after today?'

'Of course. I'm—'

'A professional,' Victoria finished. 'You can collect the key from Mr Atkinson who lives next door. If he isn't at home, Naomi Harrington keeps a key at Foxfield and Alice Irvine keeps one at The Linnets. You'll need to return the key after each rehearsal.'

'It won't be convenient to go searching for a key every time I want to rehearse,' Margueritte complained.

'The conditions of our insurance mean we can't let people hold on to keys,' Victoria said. She wasn't sure that was true but it felt more tactful than explaining that Margueritte wasn't to be trusted with a key of her own.

Leaving Margueritte to stew about it, Victoria went to join some knitters who wanted help with winding wool.

'Hold your arms up and I'll pop the wool over your hands, dear,' Molly Lloyd instructed. 'You've got younger, stronger arms than most of us, but I'll still be quick. I remember having to do this for my mother when I was young and my arms ached horribly.'

'My Jim has finished reading *The ABC Murders*,' Mrs Larkin said. 'Might we have the book cupboard open so I can change it for something else?'

'I don't see why not,' Victoria said. 'This is the bookshop, after all.'

'I need to return *In the Name of Love*,' Mrs Hayes said.

'I'd like to read that one,' Mrs Hutchings told her.

The door opened and a young girl looked in nervously. Victoria went to greet her, realizing this must be Hannah, whose pram wheel Bert had fixed. She looked little more than a child herself, far too young to be a drudge to her family. 'Hannah, isn't it? Do come in.'

The girl looked alarmed, perhaps because she thought she was interrupting something serious since the knitters and sewers appeared to be so industrious. 'I haven't really got time,' she said, embarrassment colouring her face.

'You needn't stay long. You could have a cup of tea and I could look out some books for the children.' Hannah had the two smallest children with her.

'No, thank you. I just thought . . . I need to get home.'

With that she backed away, but as she turned the little girl tumbled and began to cry. Victoria scooped her up and took her outside as Hannah carried her brother. 'There, there, darling,' Victoria soothed, rocking the little girl. 'What's your name? Something pretty, I'll guess.'

'It's Susie,' Hannah said, her face anxious as though she wanted to snatch her sister from Victoria's arms.

'Pretty indeed,' Victoria said. 'I'd have liked brothers and sisters, though I'm sure they make for a lot of hard work when they're as young as these. Did you have to leave school to look after them? I had to leave school early, too. I needed a job because my parents had run out of money, and when they died young, I was left alone in the world. That's when I discovered the importance of friends. I hope you'll make friends with the people here in Churchwood.'

Hannah simply stared back uncertainly, but Victoria wasn't expecting an answer. She was merely trying to establish common ground so Hannah could feel less alone with her situation and more willing to open up. When she was ready.

Victoria placed Susie in the pram. Hannah tucked the boy in beside her and then turned, saying, 'Bye.'

'I hope we'll see you again,' Victoria said.

She waved as Hannah moved away then gave herself a shake. The world was full of people with far worse problems than wistfulness for a life that couldn't be hers. People like Hannah who seemed to have so little while Victoria had so much – a good job, friends and, best of all, the care of two children who loved her. It really was time Victoria pulled herself together. Ceasing to think of Paul Scarletti would be a good first step . . .

CHAPTER TWENTY-SIX

Hannah

Hannah didn't know what to make of Victoria being out socializing at the bookshop yesterday. Did it mean that she'd handed Rose over to the authorities, so had more time to spare for relaxing? If so, Hannah might never be allowed to see her daughter again.

But other people at Foxfield might have been taking care of Rose to give Victoria a break: Mrs Harrington, for one, since Hannah hadn't seen her in the bookshop. Her maid, Suki, for another. Then there were the London women. The evacuees. Hannah believed most of them had jobs, but there was an older one among them with sadly bowed legs who seemed to spend most of her time looking after the children.

Guilt swamped Hannah at the thought of Victoria needing a break. It hadn't been fair to burden her with the care of a newborn when she was already looking after two orphans and working as Mrs Harrington's house-keeper. But she looked so kind and there really hadn't been anyone else.

Besides, Hannah had only intended to leave Rose for a couple of days until Mattie came home, but there was still no word from him.

If only she could find out what was happening at Foxfield. She couldn't see a way of doing that but, just in case Rose was still there, Hannah decided to post another note through the Foxfield door that night, begging Victoria to keep Rose with her for a few days longer.

CHAPTER TWENTY-SEVEN

Naomi

'Is that another note from Rose's mother?' Naomi asked, seeing Victoria pick something white and rectangular off the doormat. 'Sorry, I didn't mean to startle you.'

Victoria had gasped at the sound of Naomi's voice. 'No, it's . . . just an ordinary letter,' she said, stuffing the envelope into the pocket of her skirt.

'I wish Rose's mother would write,' Naomi said. 'It would be helpful to know how she's getting on. It's been a whole week since she left the baby with us.'

'It certainly would,' Victoria agreed.

'I'll be shopping this morning,' Naomi announced. 'Perhaps you could give me a list of anything we need?'

'I'll go and write one now.'

Victoria returned as Naomi was putting on her coat and hat. 'We don't need vegetables since Bert kindly left a basket with us yesterday, but we need flour and sugar. And bread, of course. And if you can get condensed milk for Rose . . .'

Naomi walked into the village and bought bread. She was emerging from the baker's when she saw the very person she wanted to see walking away at speed.

It was at times like this that Naomi wished she'd been blessed with longer legs and more comfortable feet. 'Edith!' she called, chasing after her quarry.

Edith turned and saw her.

'What is it?' she asked. 'I'm in rather a hurry.'

Naomi heaved air into her lungs. 'I just thought that, since you can't come to the bookshop, I could lend you a book informally.' She took a P. G. Wodehouse comedy from her bag and passed it over.

Edith looked bemused, as though Naomi had offered her a gift from the moon.

'I find light-hearted books like this cheer me up,' Naomi said. 'At the very least they take me out of myself for a while.'

'Mrs Harrington. Naomi. I appreciate your kindness but I haven't time for reading.'

'Keep it as long as you like,' Naomi urged. 'It won't be in your way since books take up little space.' Being small, they could also be hidden from a disapproving husband.

'I really don't . . .'

But Naomi was backing away.

Edith sighed and stuffed the book into the canvas bag she was carrying alongside her shopping basket. She turned and walked on, and Naomi did likewise in the opposite direction.

Seconds later she heard a cry. Whirling around, Naomi saw that Edith had dropped the bag and some of the contents were rolling across the pavement and into the road. There were tins and what looked like apples.

Naomi hastened back to help. 'It's all right,' Edith said, crouching down to retrieve her shopping. 'I can manage.'

Naomi blew dust off two tins she'd picked up from the gutter. 'No harm done,' she said, passing them over.

'Thank you.' Edith took them and looked away swiftly. Not swiftly enough to hide the shimmer of tears, though.

'Edith, you're obviously upset and I can't believe that dropping your shopping is the cause,' Naomi said.

'I'm fine,' Edith insisted, but her shoulders shook as she began to sob.

Naomi drew the woman into her arms and let her cry, stroking her back to give comfort.

But Edith soon got a grip on herself. 'I'm sorry,' she said, stepping away in obvious embarrassment.

'Edith, I'd like to help.'

'You can't.' Edith shook her head firmly. 'The kindest thing you can do is leave me alone.'

With that, she walked away.

Poor woman.

Naomi turned away, too, to return to the shops. She was almost there when a truck drew up ahead of her and Alec Mead sprang out jauntily. Jaunty wasn't a word she'd normally have used to describe Alec Mead, since dour had always suited him better. But jaunty he was. And looking something of the dandy in a smart shirt and jacket, and with his hair newly cut.

She watched as he walked into the grocer's. Walked? No, he strutted, looking not only smart but highly pleased with himself.

Following him, she even caught a whiff of cologne.

He headed straight for the counter. 'A packet of Woodbines, please,' he said.

The cigarettes were duly handed over, as were money and change. Then the farmer swaggered from the shop.

He'd gone by the time Naomi had made her own purchases and returned outside, but she was pleased to see Bert's truck approaching. Moments later, Bert climbed out. There was nothing jaunty about him. Bert was big and steady, dry land in a stormy ocean. 'It's lovely to see you, beloved,' he said.

'I'm glad to see you.'

'Oh?' He wasn't surprised that she was pleased to

see him. He'd read something in her expression. Bert's shrewd wits saved a lot of time.

Naomi told him about the Meads. 'I'd never have marked Alec Mead down as a philanderer, but all things are possible,' he said.

'Edith may be upset about something else,' Naomi pointed out.

'True. As ever, we must keep open minds. Of course, meddling in other people's marriages may be pushing our noses in where they're not wanted.'

'I'm not suggesting we meddle. I just want to be ready to help if Edith decides she needs a friend after all.'

'Forewarned is forearmed,' Bert agreed. 'Let's try to learn how things stand and take it from there.' He stiffened suddenly. 'Well, beloved, I'd better be on my way. Lots to do!'

Naomi glanced around and saw Marjorie approaching. 'You're just trying to avoid her,' she hissed at Bert.

'Guilty as charged.' With that, he winked and walked away.

'Marjorie, how nice to see you,' Naomi lied.

'You too, Naomi. We never seem to spend much time together these days. Not like the old days.'

'Life is so busy, isn't it?'

Naomi tuned Marjorie out, murmuring an occasional 'Mmm' but her thoughts were elsewhere, remembering the day Margueritte Moore had first come to Churchwood. Naomi had seen her waving at Alec Mead's truck as though to ask for a lift to Barton.

The chances of miserable Alec Mead giving a lift to anyone had seemed so remote that Naomi had smiled, picturing his curt refusal, and given the matter no more thought. But now she wondered if Margueritte did in fact account for a new peacock-strutting Mr Mead and his tearful wife. Margueritte had to be fifteen years his junior and he was hardly an Adonis. But Naomi supposed he wouldn't be the first man to lose his head over a young and beautiful siren, and she might be flattered by the attention.

'I'll come with you now, shall I?' Marjorie asked.

Roused from her thoughts, Naomi felt foreboding creep over her. 'I'm sorry?'

'I'll come to Foxfield now, shall I? You just agreed we should have a cup of tea together.'

'What I meant was . . .' Naomi scratched around in her head for an excuse for putting Marjorie off. It would be a disaster if she came to Foxfield and saw baby Rose. 'What I meant was that I'd love to come to your house for a cup of tea.'

Marjorie's expression slid downwards. 'I haven't been to Foxfield in an age.'

'I know. And we'll put that right soon. But you'd be doing me such a favour by letting me come to you. There are so many people living at Foxfield now that it's hard for me to have a minute's peace. Sitting in your house for half an hour will be blissful, Marjorie.'

'Well, of course, Naomi. I'll be glad to help.' Marjorie's expression brightened.

As they set off for Marjorie's shabby little house to drink weak tea and be swallowed up by the sagging sofa, Naomi considered it a salutary lesson in the need to pay attention.

It was particularly annoying considering there was something Naomi wished to do at home – something that had been forming in her mind ever since receiving Alexander's letter. 'It's been lovely, but I won't impose on you any longer,' she finally told Marjorie.

'You're not imposing. I could put the kettle on for more tea and—'

'Kind of you, but I'm expected back at Foxfield.' Naomi got to her feet to signal that she wasn't to be talked round, though it still took her more than five minutes to get away.

Hastening home, she picked up the telephone in the sitting room and asked the girl at the exchange to put her through to the office of Sir Ambrose Goodison, the solicitor who was representing Naomi in her divorce.

Had he been a good choice of solicitor? Naomi had chosen him to show Alexander that she had a heavyweight fighting in her corner, since Sir Ambrose's reputation was well known. Unfortunately, the Great Man of Law also had a Great Way with Billing. His fees were extortionate.

Naomi winced every time she received a bill from him, but changing lawyers might look like weakness to Alexander and he was certain to try to exploit it.

'May I speak with Sir Ambrose?' she asked when she was connected to his office. 'My name is Naomi Harrington and I'm a client.'

'Mrs Harrington!' the Great Man said, coming on the line. He always greeted her as though they'd been close friends for years. 'How are you, my dear? The weather hasn't been kind, has it?'

Naomi wasn't bothered about the weather and, with time being money, she was unwilling to talk about it. 'I'm calling to check the progress of my divorce,' she said instead.

'Coming along, Mrs Harrington. Coming along. These things take time.'

It had already taken months. 'And the financial settlement?'

'Coming along with the divorce.'

'Is there no way of hurrying it along? The terms have long been agreed.'

'Would you like me to ask Mr Harrington to meet some of your day-to-day expenses? It would be perfectly usual in a divorce case. As I believe I've mentioned before.'

Naomi could picture him wagging his finger as though she were a naughty schoolgirl who hadn't listened to advice, but the last thing she wanted was to extend a begging bowl to Alexander. He'd love the power it gave him. The sense of doling out charity. Naomi would rather starve.

'I don't want a penny from him except for the agreed settlement,' she said. 'Is there any reason in law why the settlement can't be paid before the divorce is finalized? If both parties agree?'

'None at all. Would you like me to ask if Mr Harrington is agreeable?'

'No, thank you. I just want to know the legal position.'

'Understood, dear lady.'

'Thank you for your advice.'

'It's always a pleasure to speak to you, Mrs Harrington. Always a—'

'Goodbye, Sir Ambrose.' Naomi put down the phone before the bill could mount higher.

CHAPTER TWENTY-EIGHT

Ruby

Hopeless as she knew the mission was, Ruby had been out on the bicycle again, riding around Churchwood in the hope of seeing something that would lead her to baby Rose's mother. Cycling wasn't getting any easier. In fact, Ruby had hit a rut and it was only by a miracle that she'd managed not to fall. She'd still banged her shin, and got off to hop away the pain while calling the bike horrid names. But then she'd got back on and resumed her ride, seeing and hearing nothing of interest in the streets or in the shops.

Back at the farm, Fred had just returned from the hospital where he'd been practising on his new legs. 'How do they feel?' Ruby asked.

'Weird.'

'I suppose they must. At first. Can you walk on them?'

'Not like a normal person. I can't bend the false knee so I lurch from side to side like a drunken bear.' He scowled at the memory.

He'd hoped for better, Ruby guessed. And his pride was hurt.

'I imagine it'll get easier over time,' Ruby suggested.

Fred sighed. 'That's what they tell me. But it'll never be like having two good legs.'

'Even so, lurching must be better than not walking at all?'

'I suppose.'

'Are the new legs painful?'

'Yes.'

'Will that improve over time, too?'

'So they say.'

Pain was manly to Fred, Ruby imagined. It was the lurching he hated, probably because it signalled to the world that he was disabled now.

The session at the hospital had worn him out; he looked exhausted. Hopefully, his spirits would improve after a decent night's sleep. 'Things are looking up for you, Fred,' she said. 'New legs, an income from your carvings . . . Who knows what the future holds for you now?' Ruby paused then added, 'Maybe even marriage.'

Fred made a scoffing sound. 'Now you're being ridiculous.'

'Don't you want to get married?'

'I don't bother thinking about it since it's never going to happen.'

'Because . . .?'

His expression accused her of being an idiot. 'Look at the state of me.'

'You're still—'

'What? The same person inside? That's rubbish, too. I'm not nearly the man I was. I'm a cripple. And instead of doing a man's job, I'm scratching around for a few shillings here and there from people who buy my carvings out of pity.'

Ruby felt frustration rise inside her. 'You're the one who's talking rubbish, Fred Fletcher. Losing your legs doesn't make you less of a man and no one is buying your carvings out of pity. You may not be earning a lot of money yet but you're only just beginning to build the business.'

'It's not a *business*. It's a bit of whittling!'

'It can be more than that, if you let it.'

'Haven't you got anything better to be doing with your time than spouting nonsense at me?'

'Fred, I only want—' Ruby broke off as Fred began to sing to drown out her words.

'Tipperary Pete had the smelliest feet,
One sniff would have you fainting . . .
The science boffins went to work,
A stink bomb for creating . . .'

'Be sensible for once, Fred,' Ruby urged, but he closed his eyes to shut out even the sight of her. Ruby sighed, but she wasn't fooled. Fred was hurting.

Pearl entered just as Fred was reaching the song's climax.

'So Hitler and his wicked folk
Were all around collapsing.
While Tipperary Pete and his terrible feet
Were heroes up and dancing!'

She gave him the merest glance but said nothing. It was worrying. In the past she'd have asked Fred what he'd done to cause an upset and then ticked him off for being pessimistic, rude and objectionable until he'd cried out for mercy.

Now she simply washed her hands and sat down at the table, reaching for the newspaper that lay there.

The situation was getting serious. Pearl wasn't just withdrawing from Fred. She seemed to be pulling back from all of them. Untroubled by the awful weather and ramshackle living conditions, Pearl had loved working

179

on Brimbles Farm and feeling valued for the first time in her life. But perhaps the hurt Fred was inflicting on her was making her question whether it was too high a price to pay for remaining here. Perhaps she was wondering if she might be just as useful and valued on another farm, where Fred's presence wouldn't be a constant reminder of that hurt.

Ruby felt a pang of loss at the thought of her friend moving away. 'All right, Pearl?' she asked tentatively.

Pearl didn't even look up. 'Never better,' she said, but it was a lie.

Kenny entered then and Ruby rushed to peel potatoes before he could nag her about the wedding.

CHAPTER TWENTY-NINE

Victoria

'It's children's club at the bookshop later,' Arthur reminded Victoria after they'd come home from school for lunch.

She ruffled his hair. 'I haven't forgotten.'

'We're going to make more skittles – one set from old tin cans and the other set from wood. Mr Makepiece is helping with the wooden set.'

'Just as long as you don't cut your fingers,' Victoria said.

Arthur grinned. 'I won't.'

'When can I go to children's club?' Jenny asked.

'You already go to story time and children's crafts, as well as those getting-ready-for-school mornings,' Victoria pointed out.

'I know. And I love them. But all the rest of it . . . Children's club sounds exciting!'

'You can start when you're five. Which isn't far away.'

Victoria hugged Arthur and then stepped aside so the other older children could pass outside with him. 'Take care,' she called. 'And no dawdling on the way. I don't want to hear that you made yourselves late.'

They set off chattering happily and Jenny ran back inside to see how Naomi's dog, Basil, was faring today. She was trying to make him a coat out of scraps of fabric and Basil seemed resigned to the venture. He was a long-suffering dog.

Victoria closed the door and as she turned to follow Jenny she noticed a small piece of folded paper caught in the narrow space between the wall and the umbrella stand that was shaped like an elephant's foot. Bending, she picked it up and recognized the awkward handwriting of Rose's mother spelling out *Miss Page*. It must have been dropped through the letterbox last night and glided where it couldn't easily be seen. Not that it would be the first item of post to glide there. Victoria normally had a thorough look around when she picked the post off the doormat, but she'd forgotten to do so this morning after being seen by Naomi holding a very different sort of letter. Feeling like a naughty schoolgirl caught out in mischief, she'd stuffed that envelope in her pocket, anxious to keep it private though she wasn't sure why. It wasn't as though there was anything shameful about it.

> *To the girl with the ravishing smile,*
>
> *Well, I haven't heard from you in reply to my last letter. I don't like to think that it means you've decided against replying but only that you haven't had time or are thinking about what to say. Perhaps you're even working out a date for when I might see you? I'm sure you understand that soldiers don't always get to choose their free time, but rest assured I'll do my best to fit in with your schedule. I know you work, too, in that beautiful house, though I don't know what you do there. You're intelligent and quick-witted so perhaps you're a secretary to an important person. You can gather from this that I'm thinking about you. Often.*
>
> *Duty calls me now, so I'll finish with the hope that I'll hear from you soon.*
>
> *Best wishes,*
> *Paul Scarletti*

Reading it had triggered what was beginning to feel like a daily maelstrom of conflicting – and exasperating – emotions in Victoria. So much for pulling herself together and ceasing to think of him! But, once again, she'd stuffed the letter into her pocket, knowing she wouldn't reply.

Now guilt swamped her at having missed the note from Rose's mother, especially after telling Naomi that no such note had been received. She opened it without further delay.

Dear Miss Page,

I'm sorry I haven't been able to claim Rose back but I still hope to do it. Soon. Please, please look after her for a while longer. I know it's a lot to ask but I've no one else to turn to. I can't lose my baby and she shouldn't lose the mother who loves her. Please, please be kind!

Victoria took the letter to Naomi in the sitting room, apologizing for having missed it before.

'No need to apologize,' Naomi told her, as understanding as ever. 'These things happen at the best of times and you're so very busy at the moment.'

Workload had little to do with it, but Victoria let it pass, waiting as Naomi read the note.

'At least we know Rose's mother still hopes to take Rose back,' Naomi said, when she'd finished.

'True. Do you want to give her more time to make whatever arrangements she has in mind?'

'What do you think, Victoria? You're taking on most of the responsibility for Rose.'

'I'm worried that her mother may be hopelessly out of her depth and dreaming of arrangements she has no real prospect of making.'

'So am I. We may only be delaying the inevitable.'

'On the other hand . . .'

'Quite,' Naomi said. 'On the other hand . . .'

'It would be cruel to deprive the girl of a chance to at least try to make a home for Rose.'

'We're of one mind, Victoria. For the moment.'

'How much longer do you think we should allow her?'

'Goodness, I don't know. Let's take it one day at a time.'

They exchanged smiles and moved into the drawing room where Jenny was holding bits of fabric to Basil's face. 'Which do you like best?' she was asking him. 'The blue one or the red one?'

Basil simply sat and endured.

'I think the red one suits you best,' Jenny said.

She turned and saw Victoria. Jumping up, she ran to wrap her arms around Victoria's legs. 'Basil wants a red coat. Will you help me to make it?'

'Of course I will, poppet.'

Jenny was all smiles and Victoria's heart gave a little squeeze of love for this child she'd taken on. Of love for Arthur, too. She could never regret it.

She really must throw Paul's letters away. She was a fool for hanging on to them at all.

'Basil is going to look beautiful in his new coat, Mrs Harrington,' Jenny said.

'Of course he will.' Naomi exchanged amused glances with Victoria, and both turned to Basil, who simply looked stoic.

CHAPTER THIRTY

Hannah

Staring sightlessly out of the parlour window, Hannah wished for the hundredth time that she could see and hear what was happening at Foxfield. Had the note she'd left last night been found? Had it persuaded Miss Page and Mrs Harrington to hold on to Rose a little longer?

Hannah's heart skittered suddenly as her father drove the Edmundson's van on to the forlorn patch of ground in front of the cottage. He was back from work earlier than usual. Had he somehow heard about Rose?

Sick with trepidation, she stood to the side of the window, half hidden behind the curtain, and watched as he got out, a tall, strong man who dwarfed his fragile wife and his children, too. Did he look angry? Intent on punishing her? He glanced up at the sky as though assessing the weather and frowned. But frowns were hardly strangers to Jed Powell's face, and he looked no more annoyed than on a typical day.

Clinging to the hope that her secret was still safe from him, Hannah glided away from the window to light the stove beneath the kettle so she could make him tea. She began to dry the dishes she'd washed earlier, too, wanting to look busy when he entered because it always seemed to annoy him if she was ever idle.

Her stomach flipped when he opened the door and

stepped into the room, but no onslaught came as it surely would have done if he'd known about Rose. 'I want food soon,' he announced, as though she could magic a meal in moments. It would have to be a hot meal, too. He wouldn't settle for less.

'Kidneys,' he said, tossing a bloodied package on to the table.

Hannah scrambled for the frying pan to start cooking them without delay. She already had what she called a vegetable pie in the oven: chopped carrots, onions and turnips topped with a layer of sliced potatoes, still in their skins because Ma had told her once that there was good-ness in them and nothing should be wasted.

Her father sat at the table with a newspaper he'd picked up from somewhere. He didn't ask after Ma. He didn't ask how Hannah was and he ignored the children. When the tea was made, she placed a cup beside him. 'I want a clean shirt,' he said.

Since when did he want to change just to go to the Wheatsheaf? She glanced at the shirt he was wearing. It was a little grubby but it bore no obvious bloodstains from the meat he delivered. Oh well. It was no bad thing if he wanted to smarten himself up. Hannah only wished he'd improve his standards as a husband and father.

'There's a shirt hanging up,' Hannah told him.

He drank his tea and then got up to go to the sink. 'How am I supposed to wash with this mess everywhere?' he demanded.

The sink was cluttered with the pots and pans Hannah was using for her cooking. 'Sorry,' she said, beginning to move them out of his way, though he never usually both-ered with a wash at this time.

He sighed irritably and, unwilling to wait, went out to the water pump that was just outside the kitchen door.

There, he peeled off his shirt and washed his face and upper body, drying himself on the old shirt. Returning, he climbed the stairs to the bedroom he shared with Ma.

Hannah could hear the low murmur of voices but no actual words reached her, and only a couple of minutes passed before he clomped back down the uncarpeted stairs, buttoning the clean shirt and pushing the tails down under his trousers. He'd brushed his hair, Hannah noticed. Usually, he brushed it only once a day, before he left for work. Had someone criticized his rough and ready ways down at the Wheatsheaf? As far as Hannah knew, the pub was frequented by a rough and ready crowd, but perhaps that was changing.

He looked towards the frying kidneys, his frown impatient. Hoping the pie was ready, Hannah bent to the oven with a fork and stabbed the vegetables. They were soft enough.

'Everyone wash their hands and sit down,' she told her brothers and sisters, dampening a cloth so she could wipe the hands of Susie and Simon.

No one played up in their father's presence. They all took their places around the table and sat quietly, sneaking glances at their father from time to time to be sure no wrath was about to head in their directions.

Hannah served up the dinner, wishing she could give more kidney to the children but allowing each of them only a small amount so their father could have more. She prepared a plate of food for Ma but put it in the oven to keep warm, not liking to leave their father alone with the children in case one of them forgot themselves and made him shout.

After he'd finished eating, he got up and unhooked his jacket from the pegs by the door. 'I'm going out,' he announced, though his intention was obvious.

He didn't say where he was going – he rarely did – but perhaps he thought it wasn't worth explaining that he was going to the Wheatsheaf because where else could he go?

This time he took the van, though, which worried Hannah because she strongly suspected he wasn't allowed to use the van – and its petrol supply – for his personal benefit. Maybe he wanted to keep his shirt fresh by avoiding the sweat he'd work up by walking, but if Edmundson's got to hear of it, her father might even lose his job and then where would the family be?

Was there no end to their troubles? There was certainly no sign of an end to Hannah's trouble, no word having come from Mattie. Not wanting to worry Ma, Hannah set her cares aside as she took the plate of food upstairs. 'Your dinner, Ma,' she said, pretending to a cheerfulness she didn't feel.

She sat on Ma's bed, spread a rag over Ma's lap to catch any food that fell, and encouraged her to eat. It was heartbreaking to see how much Ma struggled. Her appetite was poor but it would only get worse if she didn't force herself to eat. 'You cook well, Hannah,' Ma said.

'You taught me well.'

'I'm sorry I've let you down, sweetheart.'

'You haven't let me down!'

'It isn't right that you should be tied to the house and to the children, too. You should be having fun at this time in your life. Seeing friends, meeting nice young men . . .'

Tears formed in Hannah's eyes at the thought of Mattie – the only nice young man she could imagine ever wanting – but she blinked them away. 'I like my life, Ma.'

'You're a good girl,' Ma said, squeezing Hannah's hand. 'But you look tired.'

'Only because the light in this room is dim now the sun has moved to the other side of the house.'

Afterwards, as Hannah washed the dishes and stared at the rough ground behind the cottage, she let the tears fall at last and for the first time allowed an awful question to come into her mind. What if Mattie had no intention of writing to her? No intention of accepting Rose as his own? And no intention of supporting them?

The Mattie she knew and loved would never turn his back on them. But what if he wasn't the Mattie she knew and loved any more? War could change people. Hannah knew that because she'd heard stories of men who'd survived the 1914 war but never been the same again, even if they bore no outward sign of injury. Mr Walton, a man who lived in Barton, was one of those men. He was notorious for shouting at people but Hannah had heard him described as, 'A lovely chap before he went to war. Never got over the shell shock.'

Was it possible that Mattie's nerves might have been shredded by his wartime experiences? Or might going to war simply have broadened his horizons by showing him that there were places and people beyond their small pocket of Hertfordshire? Places to see and people to enjoy spending time with – flirting with, perhaps – before settling down as a husband and father. Mattie was only eighteen, after all.

Fear gripped Hannah at the thought of losing him. She wouldn't be able to bear it. And losing Mattie would also mean losing any chance of keeping Rose . . .

CHAPTER THIRTY-ONE

Beth

'A moment of your time!'

Not more demands? Hearing Dr Harrison's voice, Beth glanced up at the galleried landing of the hospital's main entrance hall only to realize he wasn't calling to her but to Dr Thomas, who was making his way down the stairs. Relieved, Beth walked on, aware that Dr Thomas had turned to wait for his colleague but taking little notice as Dr Harrison jogged down the steps towards him.

She didn't see precisely what happened – a trip, she supposed later – but Dr Harrison suddenly cried out and fell, knocking into Dr Thomas, who then fell with him in a tangle of white coats and flailing limbs.

Beth was the first to reach them as they landed at the bottom of the staircase. Tom, the porter, was close behind her. 'Could you fetch help?' Beth asked Tom.

'Of course.'

He hastened away and Beth made a rapid assessment of the scene. Dr Harrison was sprawled over the lower steps and groaning. 'Try to keep still, Dr Harrison,' Beth told him. 'It looks like you've broken a leg and you don't want to cause more damage by moving.'

Her priority was Dr Thomas, who was out cold. Blood was welling from a cut on his temple, but was he breathing? No. Beth moved him just enough to open his airway and was relieved when he began to breathe again. What next? She took a clean handkerchief from her pocket and applied it to the wound.

It felt like an age before Matron and Dr Marwood rushed up, though it could only have been a couple of minutes. Beth explained about the fall and what she'd done.

'Congratulations, Nurse,' Dr Marwood said. 'You might just have saved Dr Thomas's life, or at least prevented oxygen deprivation from damaging his brain.'

Matron gave Beth an approving nod.

More help arrived in the form of porters bearing stretchers and, to everyone's relief, Dr Thomas began to murmur as he resurfaced from unconsciousness.

'You were on your way out, Nurse Ellis?' Matron asked then.

'I was.' She'd intended to walk through the woods. 'But if I can be useful here . . .?'

'I think we can manage now, thank you.'

'Very well.' Beth headed for the door, encountering another approving nod from Tom the porter.

'Oh, Nurse Ellis?' Matron called.

Beth walked back. 'Yes, Matron?'

'You haven't forgotten about the bookshop?'

Oh, for pity's sake! 'There's nothing more to report. Not since I told you that the date had changed.' Beth had heard of the change from Alice but there was no need to mention that.

'You'll keep in touch with Mrs Harrington in case there are more changes?'

Beth swallowed down irritation. 'Certainly.'

Matron's smile looked triumphant.

Fortunately, Beth was saved from having to fake an answering smile because Matron's attention was recaptured by the crisis when a porter handled Dr Harrison with less precision than she'd have liked. 'Careful, there!' she chided, and, sighing, Beth went on her way.

Every cloud had a silver lining. Not for anything would Beth have wanted the doctors to be hurt but, with two of them out of commission temporarily, life at the hospital was likely to become even busier than usual. With luck, Matron would have more important things on her mind than nagging Beth about matters that fell outside her duties, and Beth would be too busy to think about her bruised heart.

CHAPTER THIRTY-TWO

Naomi

Victoria was looking worried when she returned from the shops.

'What's wrong?' Naomi asked, concerned. 'None of the children are in trouble?'

'No, no. It's just . . . I hope you won't think I'm gossiping?'

'You're hardly a Marjorie, Victoria.'

'No. Well, it was just a little strange. I saw the singer – Miss Moore – getting into a van.'

'Not Alec Mead's truck?'

'No. It was definitely a van, though I only saw the back of it from a distance. It was the way she behaved that caught my attention. She seemed . . . furtive, as though she had something to hide.'

'I see,' Naomi said.

'You don't sound surprised.'

'I've been wondering if she might be having a little dalliance with someone.'

'Alec Mead,' Victoria said, clearly putting two and two together to make four.

'Perhaps he borrowed a different vehicle.'

Victoria shook her head. 'Mr Mead was driving his tractor across one of his fields when I walked past just now.'

Naomi was surprised. 'You're sure you saw him and not one of his sons?'

'It was definitely him.'

'Then perhaps I was wrong to suspect him.' Naomi would be glad for Edith's sake if he were innocent, though clearly something was wrong in Edith's life. And if the driver wasn't Alec Mead, who was he?

It wasn't Naomi's business, of course, but it was worrying if Margueritte was behaving with stealth and secrecy. It suggested she knew she was doing wrong. The only vans in Churchwood belonged to Mr Miles the grocer and Wally Prince who swept chimneys and washed windows. Both men were unlikely candidates for Margueritte's attentions. Perhaps the van belonged to someone in Barton or one of the other nearby villages. Naomi could only hope Margueritte didn't bring grief to one of the area's families. Trouble might lead to cancellation of the concert, too.

'I'll let you know if I see or hear anything else,' Victoria said.

'Thank you. In the meantime, I'll tell Alice and Bert what you saw so they can keep an eye on the situation, too.'

Naomi caught Alice just as she was setting off for the hospital.

'So we have two possible problems in the village,' Alice concluded. 'The Meads for one and Margueritte for another. Of course, Alec Mead could simply be going through a minor crisis. You know the sort of thing. People reach a certain age, decide they're in a rut and want to smarten themselves up so they can feel young again. He might not actually be seeing another woman.'

'Would smartening himself up account for Edith's tearfulness?' Naomi asked.

'It might, if Alec told her she looks old and needs to smarten herself up, too.'

'It's possible,' Naomi conceded. 'Let's hope his crisis passes soon. All we can do for Edith in the meantime is be kind to her.'

'Agreed,' Alice said.

'What are your thoughts about Margueritte?' Naomi asked.

'That she may be a Barton problem rather than a Churchwood one. I hope we manage to hold the concert before she causes any real trouble. She may be off soon anyway once her manager returns from Scotland.'

'Let's keep our fingers crossed,' Naomi said wryly.

They parted with a hug, Alice walking on towards the hospital and Naomi heading for Bert's market garden where she could talk to him in private – something that could be difficult at busy, bustling Foxfield.

'Behold the Churchwood herald of news,' he said, smiling when he saw her. 'Have you glad tidings to report? Or more problems?' He studied her expression then said, 'Problems, then. Out with them, woman.'

'The first thing is bad in some ways but good in others.' Naomi told him about the latest note from Rose's mother. 'It's good that she still hopes to reclaim Rose.'

'But it leaves you and Victoria not only looking after Rose but trying to keep her a secret, too.'

'She's a dear little thing so looking after her isn't a problem, but the longer the situation drags on, the more likely it is her mother's hopes of getting her back will turn out to be fantasies. And the more likely it is that we'll get into trouble for delaying handing Rose over to the proper authorities.'

'Still, you're going to keep looking after her,' Bert guessed. 'Of course you are. You're a kind woman and so is Victoria. Now for the second problem.'

Naomi filled him in on the Meads and Margueritte. She told him what Alice had said, too.

'Alice could be right,' Bert said. 'I could have a word with Alec Mead, but I don't think it would help. In fact, I think interference would stoke his temper and I wouldn't want him to take his fury out on his wife.'

'Heavens, no,' Naomi agreed.

'I'll keep an eye out for whatever Alec may be up to and I'll leave Edith in your capable hands, beloved. Any more doom and gloom to darken my day?' His grin robbed the words of any offence.

'No, but I'd like your opinion on something.'

'Fire away.'

She told him about her conversation with the Great Man of Law. And then she told him what she planned to do about it. 'I think I need to discuss it with William first, since it might affect him. Rather badly. And I don't want to do it in a letter or even a telephone call in case he simply tells me what he thinks I want to hear. I'd prefer to look him in the eye and gauge how he really feels about it.'

'Then it's lucky he's coming to stay soon, isn't it?'

CHAPTER THIRTY-THREE

Beth

'Just the person I'm looking for,' Matron said.

She was smiling but Beth thought it was the smile of a cat that had a small mouse trapped in its sights, the mouse being her. What now?

'Matron,' Beth acknowledged, standing straight since Matron had no tolerance for sloppiness.

'About the concert. Do you have any more news for me?'

'Not since the last time we spoke about it.' Only two days earlier, for goodness' sake!

'You've seen the bookshop, Nurse Ellis. The premises aren't large and we'll only be able to take a limited number of patients, even if there's a matinee performance as well as an evening one. That means other patients – even those fit enough to be included – will be disappointed.'

'It's a shame,' Beth ventured.

'I'd like you to explore a solution.'

'A solution?' Beth was puzzled.

'We can't make the bookshop bigger and we can't ask village residents to stay away to make room for our patients. What we need is a performance here at the hospital. Even the least able-bodied patients will be able to attend then. Perhaps the matinee could be held here.'

'I see,' Beth said.

'I suggest you walk into the village and talk to Mrs Harrington. You've no objection, Nurse Ellis?'

Of course she had. Once again, she was being asked to use her off-duty time for Matron's errands when all Beth wanted was to be left alone. But she couldn't refuse, and besides, the concert really might cheer the patients. 'No objection at all,' she said, with as good a grace as she could muster.

Matron beamed. 'Then I'll leave the mission in your capable hands.'

Wonderful. Beth turned to walk away.

'Oh, and Nurse Ellis?'

Beth turned back.

'Make it soon, hmm?'

Beth saw Alice in Ward One a little later. She was reading a story and the patients were rapt, not least Private Eddie Henderson. Beth sidled up to him and kept her voice low. 'I'm sorry to interrupt, but it's time for your medication.'

He took the tablets she offered and washed them down with water.

'You have your therapy soon and the medication should help with the discomfort,' she told him.

'That it will, Nurse. Thank you.'

The story came to an end and a round of applause went up, patients calling out about how good the story – and Alice's reading of it – had been. Private Henderson turned to Beth. 'That was grand, wasn't it, Nurse?'

'Mrs Irvine reads well.'

'She writes well, too. She's having a story published in *Tales of Adventure* magazine soon. Here, Alice!'

She came over.

'I was just telling Nurse Ellis here about your literary career.'

'I'm not sure I'd call one story sale a career, exactly,' Alice said, smiling.

'But you're writing more?' Private Henderson asked.

'I am writing more, but whether I manage to *sell* more remains to be seen.'

'Congratulations on the one you've sold,' Beth said.

A book slipped from Alice's hands. She'd been carrying several. Beth stooped to pick it up and offered it back only to realize that Alice's hand bore the scars of an old injury that might have weakened it. 'You've got a lot of books there,' Beth said. 'Let me help. Are you heading for Ward Two?'

'I am.' They set off in that direction. 'I had an accident a couple of years ago,' Alice explained as they walked, and Beth flushed, fearing that she'd embarrassed her over the injury.

'You didn't stare,' Alice assured her. 'But there's no reason you shouldn't know about it.'

'I'm sorry,' Beth said.

'I'm used to it now. Most of the time. It still frustrates me when it slows me down or makes me drop things. And I've found it hard to adjust to being unable to get office work. I used to organize my father's medical practice but I'm a terribly slow typist now and no employer wants that.'

Beth must have looked surprised. Few married women went out to work, and Alice's time appeared to be fully committed to the hospital and bookshop. 'I may be married but I want to earn money to put by for the future,' Alice explained.

Beth could understand that, on reflection. The war had torn many men from their jobs with no guarantee that those jobs would be waiting for them when peace finally came. In fact, with so many men likely to return all at once, it might be difficult for them to obtain any sort of job for a while, particularly if the women who were covering their employment were reluctant to stand aside. Not that they'd necessarily have a choice. Men still had the upper hand in the world. 'Is that why you're writing stories?' Beth asked.

'To earn money? Partly,' Alice admitted. 'But I love reading and I'm beginning to love writing. I like to achieve things, too. To make the best of my talents, however modest they may be, and to make the best use of my time. You look as though you understand that.'

'I do,' Beth said, though she felt a pang of distress as she remembered how she'd thought Oliver would respect and admire her professional skills.

'I'm also expecting a baby so that'll be another expense,' Alice confided.

'Congratulations.'

Matron emerged from her office and Beth felt like a naughty schoolgirl again, caught talking about a forbidden subject, though the prohibition on talking to Alice about the concert while she was on hospital premises seemed as ridiculous as ever.

'I couldn't manage the books so Nurse Ellis is helping me carry them,' Alice said.

'I see. Once you've done that, Nurse Ellis, I'd like you to fetch clean bedding and make up the bed Private Ogden has just vacated.'

'Yes, Matron.'

They continued to Ward Two. 'Where would you like me to put the books?' Beth asked Alice.

'On that table there,' Alice said, pointing. 'Don't rush off, though. I've something for you.'

She produced a copy of Daphne du Maurier's *Rebecca* from her bag. 'I thought you might like to borrow it.'

Beth was surprised. Touched, even.

'Just let me have it back when you've finished with it,' Alice said. 'You can give it to me here or drop it into the bookshop.'

Reluctance to visit the bookshop must have shown in Beth's face.

'We all need friends in our lives,' Alice said.

Her tone was gentle but Beth felt stung. Did Alice consider her to be an object of pity? Beth's pride recoiled in horror.

'I'm quite contented with my life, thank you,' she said.

Alice's kind face softened even more but it only increased the stinging sensation. 'I'm sorry. I didn't mean to add to your hurt,' she said.

Add to it? Had Alice guessed that Beth was already nursing unhappiness? Clearly she had, and it was mortifying.

'There's no shame in feeling lonely sometimes,' Alice said. 'I've felt that way myself. Opening ourselves up to friendship can feel scary but the rewards can be wonderful.'

A thought struck Beth suddenly, scalding her with even more humiliation. 'Is that why Matron keeps sending me into the village for information about the concert? She thinks I need *friends*?' Beth's bitterness made friendship sound like a disease.

'People want you to be happy, Beth.'

'I take responsibility for my own happiness, thank you. I don't appreciate interference.'

Alice reached out a sympathetic hand but Beth stepped away. 'I need to get back to work.'

She set off to return to Ward One and was almost there when she realized she was still holding *Rebecca*. She felt an urge to turn tail to thrust it back at Alice but knew such behaviour would only look petulant. Instead, she took the book into the sluice room and placed it at the back of a cupboard from where she could collect it when she went off duty.

There'd be more dignity in reading it and returning it with thanks afterwards, making no mention of their awkward conversation. Behaving well would be the best way of persuading Alice that Beth wasn't an object of pity, after all.

She went to the linen cupboard and found Pauline Evans there. Pauline greeted her with a smile, looking oddly excited. 'Have you seen him yet?' she asked.

'Seen who?'

'That means you haven't seen him, because you'd know about it if you had.'

It wasn't hard to work out what had brought the sparkle to Pauline's eyes. There was a handsome man on the premises. Beth wasn't interested. She'd had her fill of handsomeness with Oliver Lytton back in London.

'I take it there's no rush for that bed linen,' Matron said from behind them.

'Sorry, Matron,' Beth and Pauline said in unison. Arms full of sheets and pillowcases, they parted to go about their duties.

Was the handsome newcomer a patient? If Beth were required to nurse him, she'd treat him no better – and no worse – than anyone else. Good looks were superficial, after all.

She set about making the vacated bed with practised efficiency. The bed next to it was occupied by Private Tomlinson who'd lost some fingers but was doing well. He woke from a doze just as she gave the neighbouring pillows one last plump.

'I must have nodded off,' he said.

'Hopefully, it did you some good.'

'I haven't missed Alice's visit, have I? I need something new to read and help with writing a letter.'

'I'm afraid she's moved on to another ward now,' Beth told him. 'I can help you with your letter if it's urgent, though I'll have to finish my shift first.' A cup of cocoa would have to wait.

'That's kind of you, Nurse. I want to write to Elspeth. She's my girl back at home.'

'Lovely,' Beth said, thinking that there seemed to be no escaping happy romances in Churchwood.

Still, keeping busy was a good thing. With luck, it would help her through the stinging humiliation until she could feel calmer again. Alice had meant well. Beth was in no doubt about that. Alice had obviously been through difficult times herself with that injured hand and a miscarriage. But she also had a warmth and appeal that must have brought friendships to her door all her life. People might sympathize with her misfortunes, but they didn't pity her as a person the way they seemed to be pitying Beth. It wounded her pride, but all she could think to do was to summon her dignity to prove that no pity was required.

CHAPTER THIRTY-FOUR

Victoria

'Good morning.'

The voice came from behind her as Victoria stood in the grocer's shop. Rich, deep and unmistakably American, it sent shivers all over her skin, even though it seemed to be directed at all the occupants of the shop instead of Victoria personally.

'Good morning,' Mr Miles the shopkeeper replied and other voices murmured good mornings, too. Naomi's was one of them.

Victoria stood rigid, afraid to turn because she knew she must be blushing. As subtly as she could manage, she breathed in deeply and willed the heat in her face to recede.

'May I help you?' Mr Miles asked the newcomer.

'I wouldn't want to push in front of this young lady,' Paul Scarletti said, and now Victoria sensed he was gesturing towards her. 'Miss . . . er . . .?'

'Page,' Naomi supplied.

'I wouldn't want to push in front of Miss Page,' Paul repeated.

'Victoria won't mind if you're in a hurry,' Naomi told him.

'Victoria Page,' he said, as though trying the name on for size. 'Pretty name.'

Enough nonsense. Victoria took another deep breath

and turned, meeting those dark eyes with what she hoped was an unconcerned smile. 'Please go ahead, if you're in a hurry,' she told him.

'I wouldn't say I was in a hurry.' His smile held warmth and humour, and now he wasn't sitting in a vehicle she could see that he was tall and trim. 'I was passing by and just thought I'd stop for a look around this village. It sure is pretty here.' A twinkle in his eye told Victoria that he considered her to be the prettiest thing.

'Passing by?' she questioned sceptically, and he grinned. He'd been passing by in the hope of seeing her.

Aware that other people might be watching – not least Naomi – Victoria said, 'Please feel free to go ahead of me anyway,' and turned her attention to the rack where newspapers, magazines and comics were displayed.

Their pages swam before her. She couldn't concentrate. Gritting her teeth, she forced herself to focus.

Behind her Naomi introduced herself to the American. 'I'm Naomi Harrington, a resident of Churchwood. On behalf of all of us I'd like to say you're very welcome in our village and in our war.'

'It's a privilege to serve our countries, ma'am.'

'And a challenge.'

'I think of it as both a duty and an adventure but, yes, it's a challenge, too.'

'You're far from your home and family but, as I said, you're welcome in Churchwood. If you come again, we'll be delighted to get to know you better.'

'That's mighty kind, ma'am.'

Victoria selected the *Beano* for the children – it was their favourite – and glided discreetly back to the counter to pay for it. Turning to leave, she saw that Paul had been cornered by Marjorie Plym. 'You must tell me all about America,' she said.

Poor man, but at least he was too busy to pay Victoria any more attention.

'I'll see you at home,' she said to Naomi, but she hadn't quite reached the door before Paul called, 'It was nice to see you, Miss Page.'

'I hope you enjoy your time in England,' Victoria called back, barely glancing at him before she stepped outside.

A few steps on she paused, chiding herself for a fool. Enjoy his time in England? She'd made it sound like a holiday, not a war. Still, she was free of him now and that was a good thing. Victoria walked on.

She was feeding Rose when Naomi returned. Victoria was aware of warmth in her cheeks and hoped Naomi would say nothing of the encounter in the shop. She didn't, but Victoria sensed her employer watching her thoughtfully.

It was later when they were alone in the sitting room that Naomi finally said, 'You know, Victoria, you've done a splendid thing in taking on Arthur and Jenny.'

'It's a privilege. They're wonderful kids.'

'Indeed. But I feel you'll be making a mistake if you decide that looking after them means depriving yourself of romance and children of your own.'

'They've been through a lot.'

'Even so. Not having children is my biggest regret in life. Oh, I've come to terms with it now and I've learned to love other people's children instead. But I've also learned that our supply of love isn't limited. It expands to take in as many people as need it. You're a loving person, Victoria. Loving children of your own needn't weaken your love for Arthur and Jenny.'

'Maybe,' Victoria said, not wanting to argue.

'Besides,' Naomi continued, 'Arthur and Jenny might

benefit from having a father figure in their lives. It would need to be the right man, of course, but the only way to find the right one is to give men a chance. Discreetly, I mean. I'm not suggesting disrupting the children's lives for a succession of romances, but only that, if you meet a man you like, you don't dismiss him on principle. I saw how that American looked at you and I saw you blush. You're blushing now.'

'I hardly know the man.'

'You'd met that American sergeant before today, though.'

'Not by design!' Victoria assured Naomi.

'But you'd met him. That's what matters.'

'It was a chance meeting on Churchwood Way early one morning. He asked for directions and we spoke for a few minutes. I didn't even tell him my name.'

'Even so, a spark was lit between you. And there's more to the story, I suspect.'

Oh, heck. 'He wrote to me. Twice,' Victoria admitted. 'But I never wrote back.'

'Only because you have this idea that you need to stay single for Arthur and Jenny's sakes.'

Victoria didn't answer because what could she say? Naomi was right.

'All I'm suggesting is that you should explore that spark,' Naomi said.

'It would unsettle the children,' Victoria insisted. 'Anyway, Paul could be sent away to fight at any time.'

'None of us knows what the future holds, my dear. Just give yourself a chance to get to know him a little better. He's a stranger in our country who deserves to be offered hospitality, so invite him to tea. With all of us. Tell him the invitation is from me if that feels more comfortable. Do you really want to move through the future, wondering what might have happened? Or do you want to see if that spark survives an hour or two in his company? If it doesn't, you'll know for sure that there could never be anything between you and you can put him behind you.'

Did Naomi have a point? Perhaps. If the spark died, Victoria would indeed be able to move on from Paul. But what if it burned brightly? What then? Arthur and Jenny had to come first.

'Do you know his address?' Naomi asked.

'Yes.'

'Because you didn't throw his letters away.'

'I never got around to it,' Victoria said, but Naomi was no fool. She knew Victoria still had the letters because they meant something to her.

'Write to him now and I'll post the letter when I call on Molly Lloyd,' Naomi suggested. 'She hasn't been well and I want to check on her.'

'When do you want him to come?'

'I rather suspect we'll have to fit around his duties.'

Victoria nodded and got to her feet, heading for the door.

'Oh, and Victoria . . .' Naomi said.

Victoria paused.

'You'll let me see the letter, won't you? Given that you're offering hospitality in my name.'

Clever Naomi. She knew Victoria might sabotage it.

Victoria went up to her room and took out pen and paper. She made several attempts at the letter before she was satisfied with what she'd written. She took it down to Naomi who read it.

Dear Sergeant Scarletti,

I'm writing at the request of my employer, Mrs Harrington, whom you met in the shop today. Having told you that you're welcome in our village, she'd like to invite you to take tea with us on a date that's convenient to you. If you'd like to accept this invitation, please telephone to the number above.

Yours sincerely,

Victoria Page

It was hardly the most gushing invitation, as Naomi's wry expression testified when she read it, but she gave it a nod anyway. 'That'll do the trick, I expect,' she said.

But Victoria had one more card to play. 'There's Rose,' she reminded her employer. 'We aren't allowing visitors while she's here.'

'I think we can make an exception. It'll only be for an hour or so and Ivy or Suki can take Rose up to the attic floor so he'll neither see nor hear her.'

Victoria nodded, defeated, but amid her worry there was a frisson of excitement.

CHAPTER THIRTY-FIVE

Hannah

Hannah had got up early to make time for a visit to Churchwood. She spent the morning on laundry and general cleaning as well as changing Ma and Pa's sheets so Ma could feel fresh. After washing up the lunch dishes she set out with Susie and Simon in the pram. It would need to be a quick visit, but Hannah was desperate to pick up any news that she could.

She'd just reached Churchwood when she saw Aggie Hamilton walking in her direction. Hannah's heart tapped rapidly against her chest. She breathed deeply in an effort to steady herself and reduce the flush of colour that had risen to her cheeks. Then she fixed a friendly smile to her face.

She needn't have bothered. Frowning sourly as usual, Mattie's mother swept by without acknowledging Hannah with as much as a nod. What an unpleasant woman she was. It was to Mattie's credit that he was such a lovely person despite his parentage.

At least, Hannah had always *thought* he was lovely. The doubts that had infiltrated her mind crept back into its nooks and crannies, taunting her with questions. *What if he's changed? What if his love has withered like a neglected plant? What if the thought of being a father to Rose appals him so much that he refuses to acknowledge her as his own?*

No! Mattie wasn't like that.

She was disappointed to find that the bookshop was closed this afternoon although a poster on the door announced that it would open its doors later for an evening session. There was another poster in the window, advertising the forthcoming concert that would feature professional singer Margueritte Moore and raise funds for the bookshop. Hannah could hear Miss Moore practising in there now. What a lovely voice she had, though she broke off suddenly to bark, 'Not so fast, Sidney.'

Hannah assumed Sidney must be the pianist.

'I need to hold that note so the audience can appreciate the power of my voice,' Miss Moore continued.

The music started up again but poor Sidney came in for more criticism almost immediately. 'Sidney, for goodness' sake! You're drowning out my voice . . .'

Hannah walked on but slowed when she neared Foxfield. How she longed to go closer to try to catch a peek at baby Rose, but she feared looking odd. Suspicious, even. She turned away instead, and began heading back up Churchwood Way. Noticing that Susie's socks had slipped to her ankles, Hannah crouched down to pull them up. They were limp with age and had already been darned several times but there was no money for new socks.

Hearing the swish of wheels, Hannah looked up to see a girl cycling past. A young woman, rather. Hannah believed she was one of the land girls who worked on Brimbles Farm where Kate Fletcher lived. Kate Kinsella, rather. This was the glamorous one with hair like a film star's and a mouth coloured bright red with lipstick. Hannah couldn't imagine being glamorous. Right now she felt downtrodden and dowdy and still not terribly well. Mattie had always said she looked like a princess to him even if her clothes were old and her fingers chapped. Would he think she looked like a princess now?

Hannah continued walking. Up ahead of her two people emerged from the bookshop – Margueritte Moore and a young man. Sidney the pianist, presumably. He was small and his jacket looked too big for him, but Margueritte Moore . . . Goodness, she was even more glamorous than the land girl. She had artfully waved dark hair, a pouting red mouth, a tight-fitting red dress that showed her curves and red shoes with high heels. Hannah had never seen red shoes before and she certainly hadn't seen such high heels. Men must flock to a girl like this and there was something about her that suggested she enjoyed their attention, teasing and flirting with them and perhaps even turning them into rivals for her affections. Hannah wanted only Mattie and hoped one day to be blissfully happy with him, the way Alice Irvine and Kate Kinsella seemed to be with their husbands.

Sidney spoke but Hannah wasn't close enough to hear his words. Margueritte's voice carried, though. 'You'll have to catch the bus by yourself, Sidney. I have errands here so I'll make my way home later.'

The man looked disappointed but rallied himself. 'You sang well today, Margueritte.'

'Thank you.' Margueritte didn't tell him that he'd played the piano well. Perhaps she thought he'd played badly or perhaps she simply had no space in her head for other people's feelings.

Sidney walked on towards the village green. Margueritte let him get ahead and then set off in the same direction, tossing her hair over her shoulder and swinging her hips. But then she slowed her pace and looked around as though to check if anyone was watching her. She looked to be the sort of girl who usually liked to be noticed, but something furtive in that glance suggested that this time she wanted *not* to be seen.

Hannah was in plain sight, but Susie had put up her arms and cried, 'Down!' so perhaps Margueritte thought Hannah was too occupied with the children to be watchful of anyone else.

Hannah lifted Susie down from the pram but looked up again just in time to see Margueritte scoot around a corner into a side road. Filmer Street, Hannah thought it was called. How odd.

Walking on, Hannah reached the side road which was indeed Filmer Street. Margueritte was moving along it as fast as she could manage in her heels.

She neared a van and Hannah realized with dismay that it was the van her father drove. Was he delivering meat here? Usually, he delivered to shops, but perhaps he delivered to houses, too. It wasn't as though he talked much at home about his work or anything else except for ordering the family about and scolding. Then again, he might simply have parked here to slack off work and smoke a cigarette.

Either way, she didn't want him to see her. 'Stay close,' she told Susie, intending to cross Filmer Street quickly. But then she saw her father get out of the van. For a moment she was unsure whether to scurry onwards or acknowledge him. But her dismay turned to horror as, smiling, he opened his arms and Margueritte Moore walked straight into them. Seconds later they kissed. What on earth . . .?

A sudden shriek sliced into her musings.

'Look out!'

CHAPTER THIRTY-SIX

Ruby

Ruby had gasped and called out a warning the moment she saw the child running into the road. She'd also tried urgently to come to a halt but between the failing brakes and her short legs – doubtless, her incompetence as a cyclist, too – she struggled to stop and couldn't even steer to safety since the child had taken fright and didn't seem to know which way to run.

Then someone – an older girl – swooped down in front of Ruby, moving fast enough to push the child out of the way but not fast enough to escape herself. The bicycle crashed into her and both she and Ruby fell to the ground with the bicycle caught between them.

For a moment Ruby's pain drowned out all other thoughts but then, still feeling battered and bruised all over, she staggered to her feet, aware that amid the overall discomfort, her left knee was throbbing and her hands were stinging from grazes. Ignoring the soreness, she picked up the child who'd begun to wail and said, 'There, there.'

Then she reached down with her free hand to try to pull the bicycle off the older girl, whose injuries were clearly worse than Ruby's because a low moan was escaping her lips.

'Let me help,' someone said, and Ruby saw that it was

the new nurse from the hospital. The one called Beth or something similar.

With the bicycle out of the way, Beth crouched down beside the older girl who looked frighteningly pale to Ruby. Not that she was unconscious, but she was obviously suffering.

'Don't rush to get up,' Beth told her. 'Take your time and, when you're ready, tell me where it hurts. I'm Beth Ellis, a nurse from Stratton House. You are . . .?' When the girl didn't answer, Beth looked at Ruby.

'I think she may be called Hannah,' Ruby said.

'Is that right?' Beth asked the girl.

'Yes, but I'm fine.' Making a visible effort to get on top of the situation, Hannah attempted to sit up only for Beth to ease her down again, saying, 'Just rest for a moment.'

'I can't . . . I need . . . Susie . . .'

'She's here,' Ruby said, assuming Hannah meant her little sister. 'Look, I've got her.'

Ruby stepped into Hannah's line of vision and held Susie out. 'You're not hurt, are you, sweetheart?' she said, smiling at the child whose wide eyes still showed alarm but who managed to give a tentative smile in return. Ruby looked back at Hannah. 'See? I'll fetch the pram so you've no need to worry about that, either.'

Ruby brought the pram over, limping a little but feeling her strength returning. 'Pram and baby boy undamaged,' she reported.

Hannah looked relieved momentarily but then she gritted her teeth and made another attempt to sit up.

'Steady,' Beth urged. 'Moving may cause more damage.'

But Hannah wouldn't be stopped. She sat up at last with Beth supporting her shoulders. 'I need to get home,' she said, but the poor girl looked drained.

'It was quite a nasty collision,' Ruby said, worried about her.

Beth nodded. 'I saw it.' She bent closer to Hannah again. 'Are you able to tell me where it hurts yet?'

'I'm just a bit winded,' Hannah insisted, though she winced when she tried to push herself to her feet.

'You're in pain,' Beth pointed out.

Hannah simply shook her head but as she got to her feet she grimaced and leaned forward, an arm cradling her stomach.

'I think she may have been bashed in the middle by the handlebars,' Ruby said. 'There's a retired doctor further along the road. Dr Lovell. He's very kind and I'm sure he won't mind checking Hannah over.'

'I don't need a doctor,' Hannah said, but the denial was clearly based on wishful thinking rather than reality.

'I'm afraid I have to insist,' Beth said.

'I'll lead the way,' Ruby said.

'No!' Hannah cried. 'No doctor. Please, I really don't want to see anyone.'

But since she obviously wasn't thinking straight, Ruby put Susie into the pram with her younger brother, propped the bike up against a garden wall for collection later and then wheeled the pram towards The Linnets.

Beth put an arm around a still-protesting Hannah to help her on the walk. 'Let Dr Lovell give you the all-clear. You'll soon be on your way.'

'I need to go *now*. Please. I need to get home.' Hannah was close to tears.

'Dr Lovell won't expect to be paid for seeing you,' Ruby assured her, in case Hannah was afraid of landing her parents with a bill.

It didn't seem to help.

'You needn't fear he'll tell your parents what happened,

either,' Ruby said. 'Not if you're as fine as you think. He's very understanding.'

That didn't seem to help, either. Was Hannah afraid that being even a few minutes late home might get her into trouble? If her parents were tyrants, it would explain why Hannah looked like a drudge trailing her brothers and sisters around. At her age she should be having fun.

Ruby hated the idea of Hannah getting into trouble but they couldn't let her go on her way only to have her collapse halfway home.

Reaching The Linnets, Ruby put the brake on the pram, took the children out and stepped through the cottage gate to rap on the door. With luck, Alice would be home, because if anyone could settle Hannah, it would be her. Alice might be fiery in the face of injustice but mostly she was kind and gentle, and always kept a calm head in a crisis.

But the door was opened by Dr Lovell himself. 'Goodness, what's this?' he asked, seeing the small crowd on his doorstep.

'Hannah had an accident with a bicycle,' Ruby explained. 'I was riding it.'

'It wasn't your fault,' Hannah said. 'It was mine. I took my eye off Susie and she ran into the road.'

'There was a cat on the opposite pavement,' Beth said. 'Susie must have seen it and run towards it.'

Hannah nodded as though it made sense that Susie would be attracted by a cat. But then she said, 'I'm sorry to have troubled you, Dr Lovell. I was shaken up but now I'm better so I'll just be on my—'

'An accident with a bicycle sounds nasty and I can see you're in pain. Come in, all of you. Don't worry, Hannah. Hopefully, you've come to no serious harm, but I'd like to be sure.'

'No!' Hannah sounded desperate now.

'It'll only take a few minutes,' Beth said firmly and between her and Dr Lovell, they got the protesting girl inside and into a room that had probably been intended as a drawing room but instead was being used as some sort of study, judging from the books and paperwork that filled the shelves and every surface, including the floor. Ruby had heard that Dr Lovell was spending his retirement studying ancient civilizations. Ruby found their own civilization complicated enough.

'I'm sorry you don't want to be examined, Hannah, but I can't in good conscience let a young girl like you go on her way unless I'm sure you're in reasonable shape,' Dr Lovell said, shifting papers from a sofa, 'especially not when you're responsible for two young children.'

Hannah burst into tears.

'Don't be frightened, my dear,' he soothed as he laid her down and placed his hands on her middle. 'I'm just going to—'

To what? Ruby wondered, for he'd broken off suddenly, and though he was no longer touching her, Hannah's cries had increased to broken-hearted wails.

Dr Lovell and Beth exchanged stunned looks. Which meant what, exactly? Ruby felt impatient to know but then understanding rushed in.

She, too, felt winded.

CHAPTER THIRTY-SEVEN

Hannah

Hannah didn't need to open her eyes to know that the people around her were shocked. She could sense it because it was as though all the air had suddenly been sucked from the room. Hands over her face, she sobbed, knowing hope was all over now.

With her secret exposed and Mattie still absent, she had no chance of reclaiming Rose. Miss Page might have held on to Rose while she thought there was a realistic prospect of her mother providing a home for her, but once she knew Hannah was that mother – a young girl with nowhere to take the child and no means of supporting her – she'd hand the baby over to the authorities and Rose would be adopted or placed in an orphanage.

Hannah's parents would doubtless hear about Rose, too. Ma would be anxious and disappointed. Pa would be furious. And her little brothers and sisters would be caught up in the shame of Hannah's disgrace. Despair racked her, body and soul.

'Weep as much as you need and then we'll talk,' Dr Lovell said. His voice was gentle. Kind. But it wouldn't change anything.

In time the sobs subsided, as sobs always do even though the heart still bleeds. Dr Lovell passed Hannah a handkerchief so she could dry her eyes and blow her nose. Then he glanced at Beth and the land girl. 'Perhaps some tea, if one of you wouldn't mind? A little milk for the children, too?'

'I'll go,' Ruby said, and she headed for the kitchen.

Dr Lovell and Beth helped Hannah to sit up and settled her back against the cushions. 'You gave birth alone?' Dr Lovell asked.

'I had no choice,' Hannah admitted.

'You were brave.'

Beth snorted, clearly thinking Hannah had also been foolish. Which was true. Hannah knew that childbirth could be dangerous, but even so . . .

'You must have been frightened,' Dr Lovell said.

Terrified, but what else could she have done? 'I'd helped my mother when she gave birth to Susie and Simon,' Hannah said, not wishing to appear totally ignorant. 'I knew what to expect. What to do.'

'You were still lucky there were no complications,' Dr Lovell said, and Hannah shuddered at the thought of what might have happened. Luck had been on her side that night.

It had deserted her now, though. 'What are you going to do?' she asked, feeling sick with dread.

'First of all, I'm going to finish examining you, and then I'm going to tell you about your daughter,' Dr Lovell said.

His examination was careful but quick. 'I don't think you've suffered any serious damage, but expect some soreness and bruising, and let me know if the discomfort continues. Now, on to your daughter. I imagine you've been worried about her?'

'So worried!' Hannah confirmed, eager for news.

'Rose is doing well. Very well. You chose wisely in leaving her with Miss Page and Mrs Harrington. She's getting the best of care and she's thriving on it.'

'Is she . . .?'

'Unhappy? She shows no sign of it. She's rather captured the hearts of everyone at Foxfield, so she hasn't been short of love. Which isn't to say that she wouldn't benefit from seeing her mother.'

'I'd love to see her,' Hannah said fervently. If Rose was to be sent away, Hannah wanted to say goodbye at least, even if she'd feel like her heart was being torn from her body. Grief at the thought of losing Rose brought more tears to her eyes. 'Can I see her soon?' she asked.

'If you're up to it, I suggest we walk over to Foxfield and talk to Miss Page and Mrs Harrington shortly.'

'Will they be angry with me?'

'They'll be relieved that Rose's mother has been found, and they'll be concerned for you as well as your baby. They're good people. Which is why you left your daughter with them, of course. Why don't I go over there in a moment to check that they're home and, all being well, I'll come back for you?'

'People might see me,' Hannah pointed out. She'd grown used to secrecy, and even though she knew her secret was certain to ripple through Churchwood sooner or later – reaching Barton, too – she hoped for a little time in which to brace herself.

'My dear, people come and go at Foxfield all the time,' Dr Lovell said. 'No one will think it strange if they see you going there. And I think we really need to talk to Miss Page and Mrs Harrington about the future.'

Hannah nodded, miserable at the thought of the shape the future was likely to take.

'Here comes the tea,' Dr Lovell announced as Ruby returned with a tray. 'Thank you, Ruby.'

The land girl set it down on a pile of books near Hannah.

'Would anyone else like a cup?' Ruby asked.

'Perhaps you could all have a cup,' Dr Lovell suggested.

He was being sensitive, Hannah realized. She'd feel less conspicuous if they were all drinking. Declining tea for himself, Dr Lovell left and Hannah's stomach plunged with dread again. How was she going to face the disgust she was sure to see on the faces of Mrs Harrington and Miss Page? Every minute Dr Lovell was away felt like an hour. Five minutes passed. Six. Seven. Was he struggling to persuade the Foxfield women to let Hannah over the threshold? Beth and Ruby tried to help the time pass by entertaining the children and talking commonplaces, but their words barely registered with Hannah.

When the clock on the mantelpiece showed that ten minutes had passed, she heard the cottage door open and close, and her heartbeat quickened again. But he was smiling when he entered the room. 'Ready?' he asked.

Hannah got to her feet only to sway as weakness overtook her again. 'Careful,' Beth said, catching hold of her. 'Perhaps you should rest a little longer.'

'I'll be fine,' Hannah insisted. A deep breath steadied her a little.

'All right, but hold on to my arm,' Beth said.

Hannah was glad to do just that as they all walked over to Foxfield. Hannah steeled herself to face revulsion as the door was opened by Mrs Harrington.

But the older woman simply drew Hannah into her arms. 'Oh, you poor child.'

The relief brought another gush of tears into Hannah's eyes. She sobbed for a little while and then Mrs Harrington guided her into a room while the maid took Susie and Simon off to the kitchen. When Hannah could see through the shimmer of tears, she realized it was a sitting room. 'Sit down, my dear,' Mrs Harrington encouraged, but Hannah had something to say first.

'I'm so sorry,' she began. 'So sorry I brought trouble to your door. Inconvenience and expense as well.'

'Rose is a darling,' Mrs Harrington said, as though that fact cancelled out any trouble. Any inconvenience and cost as well.

She steered Hannah into a chair and the others took seats as well. Then Mrs Harrington opened the sitting room door again and Miss Page walked in, carrying a bundle wrapped in a white shawl.

'Here's your beautiful little daughter,' she said, smiling warmly.

'Oh!' Hannah took Rose from her and gazed down at the tiny face. At the rosebud mouth. At the eyelashes fanning the soft cheeks in sleep. At the tiny snub nose and the delicate eyebrows . . .

Overwhelmed by love, she kissed Rose's forehead. Then she gathered her close and breathed in the scent of her.

'As you can see, she's thriving,' Miss Page said.

Hannah swallowed down emotion and nodded. 'Thank you. I didn't want to leave her. I love her so much!'

'We can all see that you love her dearly,' Mrs Harrington said.

But what was to be done? That was what they all wanted to know.

'You suggested in your notes that you needed more time,' Mrs Harrington said. Her voice was gentle but probing. Which was understandable. 'Can you tell us what you're waiting for?'

Hannah hesitated. She wanted to be honest with these kind people but she couldn't tell them about Mattie. Not yet. He deserved a chance to make arrangements for their future before anyone judged him unfairly for going away and leaving a pregnant young girl behind. A chance, too, to tell his awful mother about Rose so she didn't hear it from someone else.

'Hannah, no one forced themselves on you, did they?' Mrs Harrington said, clearly misinterpreting her hesitation. 'You've no need to feel ashamed if—'

'It wasn't like that!' Hannah sprang to Mattie's defence.

'But Rose's father . . .?'

'I love him! And he loves me.'

'He's away from home, though?' Mrs Harrington guessed. 'Perhaps serving in the forces?'

Hannah hesitated again, needing to be careful. 'Something like that.'

'He knows about Rose?'

'I've written to tell him. And to ask him to come home.'

'Has he replied?'

'Not yet,' Hannah admitted, and while no one exchanged looks with anyone else, it felt as though they were avoiding each other's gazes deliberately to hide the fact that they weren't half as confident in Mattie's love as Hannah. 'He'll come, though,' she insisted. 'When he can.'

'Getting leave can be difficult,' Miss Page acknowledged. But did she really believe that was the problem here, or was she merely trying to comfort Hannah?

'What do you hope will happen when Rose's father returns?' Mrs Harrington asked next.

'I hope we'll get married,' Hannah said. 'I know I'm only sixteen, but in the circumstances . . .'

'You think your father will give his consent?'

'I don't think he'll like the alternative.' Which was shame. Even the thought of the word made Hannah wince, since shame had no place anywhere near darling Rose. She was pure and beautiful.

There was a moment of quietness, but what was everyone thinking? That Hannah was deluded? 'Please,' she urged. 'Whether you trust in Rose's father or not, please give me more time.'

'How much time?' Mrs Harrington asked.

Hannah had no answer because she had no way of knowing when Mattie would return.

'Rose's birth needs to be registered,' Mrs Harrington pointed out.

'Now?'

'Maybe not quite yet. But soon.'

'Will you give me until then?' Hannah pleaded.

Mrs Harrington looked at Victoria and then at Dr Lovell. She looked at Beth and the land girl, too, as though trying to divine their opinions even though they had no involvement in Rose's care. She must have encountered no opposition because she sighed. 'Very well. We'll do our best, but we can't promise to keep Rose a secret for much longer. That doesn't mean that any of *us* will let slip about her deliberately . . .'

'I certainly won't,' the land girl said.

Beth looked less certain but finally shrugged agreement.

'But things have a way of slipping out anyway, particularly from the mouths of children,' Mrs Harrington said. 'With nine children living here, some as young as four, it's a wonder word hasn't got out already.'

'I understand.' Hannah would just have to hope that the secret stayed hidden long enough for Mattie to get home, but it felt like a clock might be ticking down to disaster. Tick, tock . . .

There was something else Hannah needed to say. 'I'm afraid I don't have any money to pay for Rose's milk and

225

anything else she needs. Not at the moment. When her father comes home . . .' Hannah was horribly aware that a lot depended on Rose's father coming home.

'Money is the least of our concerns,' Mrs Harrington said. 'Is there any other way in which we can help you? By speaking to the family of Rose's father, perhaps?'

'No!' Seeing Mrs Harrington's eyebrows rise in shock at the vehemence, Hannah attempted to soften her reply. 'I mean no, thank you. It wouldn't . . . Rose's father needs to speak to his family himself.'

It was obvious from their faces that they all thought this didn't bode well for the future, but there was nothing Hannah could do to make them understand about Mattie's home situation. Not without giving his identity away.

'Sometimes people can be kinder and more understanding than expected,' Mrs Harrington ventured.

Perhaps that was true of some people. It wouldn't be true of Aggie Hamilton.

'Is Rose's father a Barton boy?' Mrs Harrington asked then.

Hannah looked down at Rose so no one could read the answer in her expression. Mattie was a Churchwood boy, but if that became known it would be a stepping stone on the way to identifying him. Hannah hated misleading this generous woman who'd taken Rose into her home, but for Mattie's sake it was better that they thought he was indeed a Barton boy.

'We're taking no decisions about the long-term future today, but we should consider what's going to happen over the next week or two,' Mrs Harrington said, 'assuming we manage to keep Rose's existence secret.'

What did she mean? Hannah was fearful.

'I'm thinking about how we're going to help you to see

Rose,' Mrs Harrington explained. 'I presume you wish to see Rose while she's here?'

'Oh! Yes!' Hannah was desperate to see her.

'We need a cover story,' Miss Page suggested. 'Perhaps we could say that Hannah is coming here so I can teach her to cook some of my favourite recipes. After all, there's a lot of recipe swapping in the village with rationing making meals so unvaried.'

'That's an excellent idea,' Mrs Harrington approved. 'Hannah?'

'It is,' Hannah agreed. 'I'll come as often as I can, if that's all right? It won't be every day, and it won't be for long. Not with my mother at home and the other children needing to be looked after.'

'Just come whenever you can,' Miss Page said.

'Meanwhile, we'll spread the word about the cooking lessons so no one becomes curious,' Mrs Harrington said, adding with a murmur, 'Especially not Marjorie.'

How nice they all were. 'Thank you,' Hannah told them. 'Thank you so much.'

She held Rose close again, breathing in the scent of her and not wishing to let her go but knowing she had no choice. 'I need to go home now,' she said, with regret.

'Are you sure you're well enough?' Mrs Harrington asked. 'You live quite some distance along the road to Barton, I believe.'

'I'm sure,' Hannah insisted.

'I'll walk with her,' Beth offered. 'I can cut across country to return to the hospital.'

'Thank you. I'll feel more at ease knowing Hannah will have you beside her,' Mrs Harrington said.

The land girl spoke to Hannah then. 'I'm Ruby, in case you don't already know. I'm sorry I hurt you with the bicycle, but perhaps it's worked out for the best now you have people willing to help you.'

Perhaps it had. It felt good to have people like these on her side. But the clock was still ticking down to the moment Rose might have to be sent away.

Hannah gave Rose one final kiss before handing her back to Miss Page. Then the children were brought back from the kitchen and Hannah, Dr Lovell, Beth and Ruby made their way outside, Beth carrying Susie and Ruby carrying Simon. The children were settled in the pram and, with Miss Page and Mrs Harrington waving farewell, the little group walked towards the gateposts over the crunching gravel that Hannah had avoided the night she'd left Rose here.

Once through them, Ruby said, 'Come here,' and folded Hannah into a quick hug. 'I'm at Brimbles Farm if you ever need me. Don't worry that you'll make a nuisance of yourself if you ask me for help. I *want* to help.'

With that she sprinted off to retrieve the bicycle, leaving the rest of them to cross the lane to Dr Lovell's cottage. 'Promise me you'll seek my help if you or anyone else in the family is ever unwell, Hannah,' he said, when they reached it. 'There won't be a bill so you needn't worry about that.'

'Thank you.' The oft-repeated words felt inadequate.

'Good luck.' He patted her arm and headed for his door.

Hannah walked on with Beth and the children. 'I'll push the pram,' Beth said. 'You take it easy.'

Beth hadn't said much at Mrs Harrington's house but Hannah suspected she hadn't missed a thing. There was something intelligent and watchful about the nurse. 'You should do as Dr Lovell said,' she told Hannah. 'If you or anyone else is ill . . . Even if it's just a sniffle, it's best to get checked over.'

Hannah nodded, and quietness descended. Should Hannah try to make conversation? She could ask how Beth was getting on at Stratton House. She could . . .

Hannah realized that Churchwood's gossipy woman was approaching. Marjorie Plym. Oh, heck. Should she warn Beth about her? A glance at the nurse told Hannah that Beth had already taken the woman's measure and was preparing to deal with her swiftly.

'What's this?' Marjorie asked, eyes darting between them excitedly. 'New friends out for a stroll?' Doubtless, she thought it would be a strange sort of friendship and hoped there was a story attached.

'I'm a nurse and I'm helping Hannah because one of the children nearly had an accident with a bike,' Beth explained. Her tone was dry and unemotional as though to dampen Miss Plym's hopes of a tale to tell.

The gossipy woman wasn't to be so easily thwarted. 'A bicycle? They can be dangerous machines when they're ridden recklessly. Was it ridden recklessly?'

'No recklessness was involved. No one was negligent. And no one was badly injured,' Beth said. 'Now, if you don't mind, I'd like to get Hannah and the children home.'

Miss Plym was blocking the way.

'Sooner rather than later,' Beth added, and Miss Plym stepped aside.

'I hope we'll see you both at the bookshop,' she called, but Beth was already marching onwards.

A few paces on, Hannah noticed that Beth's cheeks had grown pink.

'I hope I wasn't rude?' Beth asked. 'Only I can't abide tittle-tattle.'

'You weren't rude,' Hannah assured her, though she thought Beth had been rather starchy.

Was she starchy by nature? Or because her nursing required it? Or was there some other reason Beth was a little brusque? Not liking to question this efficient and self-contained young woman, Hannah turned her thoughts back to Mattie only to jump in surprise when a vehicle passed them.

It wasn't her father's van — it was the Churchwood grocer's — but it still put Hannah in mind of something she needed to say. It was going to be awkward, though. 'My father drives a butcher's van,' she finally said. 'If he should happen to pass by and stop, would you mind telling him . . . or rather not telling him . . .'

'I'll tell him the accident was caused by a person on a bicycle wobbling out of control,' Beth said. 'I won't mention Ruby's name.'

Goodness, she didn't need things spelling out to her. It was Hannah's turn to flush, embarrassed at having given the nurse a hint that Jed Powell wasn't a nice man. She felt guilty, too, because while Ruby hadn't been the most proficient cyclist, it was Hannah who'd neglected to keep an eye on Susie.

'It wasn't really Ruby's fault,' Hannah said.

Beth glanced across at her. 'Will your father hunt her down to give her a piece of his mind?'

'I don't think so.' He might curse the cyclist in the heat of the moment but he wouldn't be interested enough to follow up on the incident.

'Then there's nothing to worry about, is there?' Beth said. 'Besides, I imagine Ruby can give as good as she gets in an argument.'

How practical Beth was! She'd shown kindness and concern today but not the sort of spontaneous warmth that had been shown by the others. Once again, Hannah was intrigued.

'Are you feeling all right?' Beth asked, and Hannah realized she must have slowed her pace.

'I'm fine,' Hannah said, though she was still feeling exhausted and sore. She made an effort to walk faster but Beth showed more of that understated kindness by slowing her own steps.

'I'm sure I can manage from here,' Hannah finally said. 'I must be taking you miles out of your way. I think that cart track along there will lead you to the hospital.'

'I'll see you all the way home,' Beth insisted.

It wasn't the answer Hannah wanted. Not only did she feel guilty about the long walk home that Beth faced, she also dreaded the thought of the nurse seeing the dilapidated building the Powells called home. Something brisk about Beth suggested it would be a waste of time trying to change her mind, though.

Hannah's tension mounted as they neared the cottage, though that was too picturesque a word for the Powells' house. Cottages were pretty, like Dr Lovell's home, which had a lovely name, too: The Linnets. This house was called Fenton's End and it looked as though its original owner – perhaps the Mr Fenton who'd named it – had met his end here. In fact, it looked like the house at the end of the world – the roof covered in moss and the windows mismatched with flaking brown paint on the frames. The nearby woods looked like predators threatening to swallow the place up, and there were weeds everywhere. Rubbish, too, for the space that might have been a front garden, given care, had been used as a dumping ground for a broken chair, a tin bath with a hole in the bottom, empty beer bottles . . .

Beth looked the house up and down but made no comment. Hannah's shame was still acute and she was sure her cheeks were flaming. 'Thanks for your help,' she said again. 'I really can manage now.'

She was relieved when Beth stood aside and let Hannah take control of the children, but the nurse hadn't finished with Hannah yet. 'I hope you'll take the advice and offers of help you were given today,' Beth said, 'whether that's for medical care or anything else.'

'Yes, I . . . I'm grateful,' Hannah murmured, burying her face in little Simon's neck.

'Being grateful is all very well,' Beth pointed out. 'But you need to accept support, Hannah. Not just for your sake, but for the sake of your family, too.' She paused, and then, as though she'd guessed that Hannah was feeling embarrassed about her home, added, 'I was brought up in a house that was even smaller than this.'

Hannah's head came up in surprise. 'But you're a nurse. You're educated.'

Beth's mouth twisted. 'I'm from far humbler beginnings than most of my nursing colleagues but I don't believe the circumstances of our births should hold us back. I still have a lot to learn as a nurse, but I see no reason why I can't learn as easily as anyone else. Just because someone owns money and property, it doesn't mean that they're cleverer or kinder or better in any other way. Be proud of the person you are, Hannah. Many a weaker girl would have folded up and collapsed under the burdens you're carrying.'

With that she nodded goodbye and went on her way.

Goodness. Beth had left her with a lot to think about. But nothing could drive out the fear that Rose would be taken away.

Where was Mattie? Was he on his way home to her? 'Please come soon,' she murmured.

CHAPTER THIRTY-EIGHT

Beth

Urgh! Beth tugged her shoe out of a deep patch of mud that had been camouflaged by twigs and leaves. Although still new to the area, she'd come to know much of it by studying maps to aid her while out on her solitary walks, and she'd reckoned that by taking this shortcut through the woods she'd reduce her journey back to the hospital by at least fifteen minutes. She'd underestimated the mud, though. Likewise, the density of the undergrowth which had torn at her hair and clothes and left a scratch across her cheek.

She wiped her shoes on a tussock of grass and pressed onwards, thinking about Hannah and comparing their lives. Without a doubt Beth had been the luckier of the two. Even if her parents didn't understand her and would have preferred her to take a different path, she was in no doubt that they loved her and had done what they could to support her in her choices.

By the sound of things, Hannah had been given no choice about how she lived her life, having been required to abandon any wishes of her own to look after her family. Her mother's illness couldn't have helped, of course, but Beth suspected that Hannah's father wouldn't have been interested in her wishes in any circumstances.

Beth had been brought up in a home that was always

neat and clean, too. As she'd mentioned to Hannah, it had been a small house but her parents had taken a pride in it.

But perhaps Hannah would be luckier in love and her mystery man would step up to marry her and help her. Beth hoped so, anyway. Hannah was so young. So vulnerable. Which was probably how she'd let herself get carried away with Rose's father.

Beth couldn't imagine allowing herself to get carried away. Not even with Oliver. But who knew what might have happened if they'd met in different circumstances – when she was only sixteen and he was going off to risk his life in the war? Whatever the rights and wrongs of the situation, Hannah was a brave young girl who was doing her best for her child. Beth wouldn't judge her. She only wished she could do more to help.

A thought slid into her mind. Hadn't Beth been rather hypocritical in preaching at Hannah to accept help when she herself had rejected Alice's advice so frostily and resented Matron's attempts to integrate her into the community, too?

Beth had sought Alice out that morning in an attempt to smooth over any bad feeling, but her approach had been more in the way of proving Alice wrong than accepting support. 'I've started reading *Rebecca* and I'm enjoying it,' she'd said.

Alice had given one of her lovely smiles. 'I'm glad. I'm sorry I upset you last time I spoke.'

'Think nothing of it,' Beth had told her bracingly. 'I'm fine.'

With that, she'd walked off with her head held high. But she'd thought about what Alice had said a lot.

Beth's pride still rebelled at the idea of Alice and Matron regarding her as lonely and unhappy, but in truth she was both of those things. And she wasn't doing a very good job of improving her situation on her own.

Tom the porter smiled at her dishevelment when Beth finally reached Stratton House. 'Been dragged through a hedge backwards, Nurse Ellis?'

'Something like that.'

'May I?' He reached out to her hair and removed a leaf. 'Thank you.'

'Hold up. There's something else . . .' This time he removed a twig.

'Ah, Nurse Ellis,' Matron announced, happening to pass by. 'Have you been to the village to enquire about the concert matinee?'

Beth had clean forgotten that she'd gone into Churchwood for that purpose. 'I haven't managed to discuss it with anyone yet.'

'But you'll do so soon?'

A part of Beth wanted to tell Matron that she knew what was going on with all this manipulation. Another part of her was afraid to do anything of the sort. She had thoughts to process first. Feelings, too. She simply nodded.

Matron smiled. 'I suggest you get yourself cleaned up, Nurse. You look less than pristine.'

'Quite a character, our Matron,' Tom said, as Matron walked away.

'Hmm,' Beth said dourly. 'I do need to clean up, though. I'm on duty shortly.'

'Put your feet up for a few minutes first. That's the ticket.'

If only unrequited love and hurt pride could be so easily cured.

*

'Sorry, Nurse,' Private Underwood said for about the seventh time as Beth helped him into a clean pyjama top a little later.

'You've nothing to apologize for,' she told him.

'Spilling my tea down myself makes me feel like a clumsy child.'

'Accidents happen to all of us,' Beth assured him. 'Besides, you're unwell.'

Her ears picked up the sound of footsteps approaching along the corridor that led to the ward. Two sets, she thought, the lightness of one suggesting it belonged to a nurse and the crisp heaviness of the other suggesting it belonged to a man – a doctor, perhaps. 'This could be the doctor coming now,' she told her patient.

She made haste to fasten his buttons and straighten his pillows.

Laughter joined the sound of the footsteps. 'Thank you, darling,' a male voice said.

It was followed by a female voice, breathy with apparent excitement. 'My pleasure, Doctor.'

A chill ran its icy fingers along Beth's spine. She couldn't identify the second voice, but the first . . . It couldn't be . . .

But there was no mistaking that silky intimacy wrapped up in a package of humour and charm. It belonged to a snake.

Of all the rotten luck! Unable to escape, Beth stood with her hands clasped in front of her and her gaze cast down at the floor while her heart thumped painfully in her chest. The doctor reached her side and asked amiably, 'What seems to be the trouble here, Nurse?'

'Private Underwood is complaining of pain and his temperature is high.'

'A possible infection, then. All right, Private Underwood.

I'll take a look at you. In case you're wondering who I am, I'm Dr Lytton. I'm here temporarily to cover for one of the doctors who is off due to an accident.'

Beth stepped aside and at that moment Oliver Lytton noticed who she was. 'Good heavens! Fancy both of us fetching up here in the depths of Hertfordshire.'

Obviously, he'd forgotten that she'd told him she was transferring here. His thoughts had been too full of Cassandra Carlisle.

He turned to Teddy Underwood. 'This nurse and I worked together in London.'

Worked together? Beth hadn't expected him to describe her as a former sweetheart or even as someone he'd walked out with for a while. Not to a patient. But he'd spoken as though she really was no more significant in his memory than someone he'd worked with once or twice.

'Small world,' Private Underwood observed.

'Isn't it? Now about this pain . . .'

Beth stood miserably by as the patient was examined and Oliver prescribed medication. 'I hope to see you looking sprightlier soon,' he told him.

He nodded at Beth to indicate that she could help Private Underwood to fasten his pyjama top again and then sauntered away as though he hadn't a care in the world. Probably he hadn't.

'He's a charmer, ain't he?' Teddy Underwood said.

Beth smiled tightly.

'My ma tells my sisters never to trust the good-looking ones. Too full of themselves, she says.'

Private Underwood's mother sounded like a sensible woman.

CHAPTER THIRTY-NINE

Ruby

It had taken Ruby a long time to reach Brimbles Farm after leaving Foxfield. For a while Hannah's situation had driven out awareness of her own woes and she'd assured Dr Lovell that she only had a scrape or two. But as she'd set off to return home, the minor injuries she'd sustained reminded her of their presence in a chorus of aches, throbs and stings. She'd skinned a knee, grazed both hands, banged an elbow, walloped a shin and generally felt as though she'd been rolled over by a train. Several times.

Getting off the bicycle, she'd decided to push it instead. Trudging onwards, her thoughts had returned to poor Hannah and, in turn, to those frightening days when she herself had realized she had a baby on the way. That fear had changed into something else over time. Anger.

Partly it was over her parents' attitude, since they'd never stopped condemning her for what happened. Partly, it was over the treatment she saw meted out to other girls who'd fallen pregnant outside of marriage. Acid comments, disgusted looks, disapproving whispers . . . Ruby had witnessed them all. But mostly it was over the way the children of unmarried mothers were regarded as dirty and disgusting when they were shining stars of innocence and joy.

Ruby understood Hannah's determination to hold on to Rose, but was it likely that she'd be able to do so? Hannah's mystery man *could* come home soon and make things regular, but would he? If he was a serving soldier, he'd need permission to return home and that might not be forthcoming for some time. But it boded ill that he hadn't even sent word to say he'd return as soon as it could be arranged. Nor had he sent money or even re-assurance of his love.

Ruby had reached the farm at last and locked the bike up in the barn. Inside the farmhouse, she'd inspected her wounds, but apart from dabbing at the grazes with a damp cloth she'd covered them back up and tried to put them from her mind, wishing she could be more like Pearl and Kate who took the small injuries that came from working on a farm in their stride. She allowed herself the rare treat of an early cup of tea and a few minutes of rest to give her battered body a chance to recover, but time was marching on and she needed to make tea for everyone else. She got to her feet, grimacing at her stiff-ness, but determined not to make a fuss.

She had the tea ready when everyone came in for their break. 'May I have a word afterwards?' Ruby whispered in Kate's ear.

Kate looked curious but then hid her interest and talked about the carrot crop instead. As everyone else filed out after the break, Kate lingered. 'Well?' she asked. 'Are you about to confess that you've smashed up my bicycle? Buckled a wheel? Torn a tyre? Wrecked the chain? Frankly, I'm more concerned about you. I've noticed you're moving slowly and keeping your hands hidden.'

'The bicycle is fine, though I did have . . .'

Ruby broke off as someone knocked on the kitchen door. It was Alice, who walked in only to come to an abrupt halt. 'Have I arrived at an awkward moment?' she asked, obviously sensing that she was interrupting something. 'It would be no trouble for me to come back another day. I was just passing on my way home from the hospital.'

'It's good that you're here,' Ruby told her. 'You need to hear this, too. Let's sit down and—'

'Forgot the twine,' Pearl announced, barging in only to halt as Alice had done. 'What?' she asked. Pearl wasn't especially sensitive to atmosphere but she'd picked up on this one, and doubtless she suspected that she'd been the topic of conversation because her mouth took a truculent downturn. 'Should I go back out?'

'No.' Ruby didn't want to make things worse for Pearl by offending her. 'You might be able to help.' She was relieved to see that Pearl looked less aggrieved. Perhaps including her in the secret might even draw her closer to them again.

'Help with what?'

'I'm about to explain but first you have to promise to keep it secret.'

'Blimey,' Pearl said, looking at Kate and Alice, who simply looked back with serious expressions. Had they guessed that what Ruby had to say concerned the secret baby? Probably.

'Promise, Pearl?' Ruby urged.

'All right. I promise.'

Ruby took a deep breath and told them about Hannah.

'Poor lamb,' Alice said.

'She must be terrified,' agreed Kate.

'A foundling baby,' Pearl said, her amazement clear. 'Gosh.' Then she thought about it and added, 'That Hannah girl looks as though a puff of wind could blow her over. I'm not surprised she hasn't been able to tell her father about the baby if he's a bully.'

'I believe a bully perfectly describes him,' Alice said, 'and Hannah's mother is too sick to stand up to him on her daughter's behalf.'

'Is there anything we can do to help?' Kate asked.

'Keep the secret, just as you've been keeping it ever since Hannah left Rose at Foxfield,' Ruby answered. 'And if anyone wonders why Hannah has started visiting there, keep up the story that she's going for cooking lessons. Make it sound ordinary. Dull, so not even Marjorie Plym will sniff out that there's more to her visits than that. As for anything else . . . I only wish I knew how we could help.'

'I suppose it's a question of waiting a while longer to see if the baby's father turns up,' Alice said. 'If he doesn't . . .'

'We'll have to cross that bridge when we get to it,' Kate finished.

Ruby looked out of the kitchen window. 'We'd better get back to work or Ernie will storm in and accuse us of taking wages under false pretences.'

No one spoke but the words *miserable old skinflint* hung in the air.

'Talking of work,' Alice said, 'I've got something for Fred.'

'What's that?' Pearl asked.

'Here comes Fred now,' Ruby announced, seeing him approaching from the barn in his wheelchair.

'Why are you all staring at me?' he asked when he entered the kitchen.

Alice handed him a small piece of paper.

'What's this?'

'Read it.'

'*Chess set, sparrowhawk, kingfisher* . . . It's just a list of some of my animals and stuff.'

'It's a list of items I left with a gift shop in St Albans. They haven't bought them yet, but they've taken them on a sale-or-return basis.'

'Did you hear that, Fred?' Ruby exclaimed. 'A gift shop wants your carvings!'

Fred's eyes had lit up with excitement – but he dampened it swiftly as though afraid that excitement now would only set him up for disappointment later. 'Sale or return means they can give them back?' he asked.

'If they don't sell,' Alice admitted. 'But in case they *do* sell, you need to be ready to supply the shop with more items. How are you getting on with the new legs, by the way?'

'They're nothing like the old legs.'

'But better than nothing – once you get used to them.'

'Humph,' Fred said.

Not so long ago Pearl would have yelled at him for being negative, but she ignored him now, picking up the twine and leaving the kitchen without another word.

Ruby swapped looks with Kate and Alice and they all shrugged helplessly, both at Fred's sourness and Pearl's retreat. Then Alice left, Fred wheeled himself into his bedroom – probably to sulk and feel sorry for himself – and Kate asked the question that was tormenting Ruby's mind. 'Are you going to tell Timmy about Hannah?'

In other words, was she going to warn him to brace himself in case news leaked out about Rose and unpleasant things were said about unmarried mothers and their offspring?

'I don't know,' Ruby admitted.

The minutes ticked slowly down to the time Timmy was due home from school. Would the news have reached him already?

Ruby heard him coming before she saw him. His

laughter danced in the air and warmed her heart. When he entered the kitchen, his eyes were merry. 'What's so funny?' Ruby asked.

'I was telling Pearl about what happened at school.'

'Which was?'

'We were asked to draw something that could be produced with flour. Albie Barnabus drew a garden.'

'He thought Mrs Gregson said flowers?'

'He did.'

'I hope no one was unkind about it.'

'We all laughed but so did Albie. He likes a joke. Is tea nearly ready? I'm starving.'

'When aren't you?'

'I'm a growing boy. That's what Pearl says.'

'Pearl is right.' About Timmy, anyway, even if she was wrong in her handling of Fred.

Ruby watched Timmy as he ate his bread and jam, clearly enjoying it and equally clearly enjoying life.

'You're not going to tell him?' Kate said afterwards.

'Not yet. I can't spoil things for him. Not unless it becomes unavoidable.'

'I'll let you know the moment I hear if word gets out about Hannah's baby,' Kate promised, 'though living so far from the village means we may be the last to hear the news.'

Was Ruby taking a risk in not warning him? Time would tell.

CHAPTER FORTY

Ruby

'You won't mind if I call at Foxfield?' Ruby asked Kate, the following morning. 'I'd like to keep abreast of any gossip and see Hannah, if possible. Just to give her some moral support. I'll do the shopping while I'm in the village and I'll try to be quick.'

'Of course. You must go,' Kate agreed.

The door to the grocer's had been left open when Ruby arrived in the village. She could hear the murmur of voices inside. Approaching slowly, she neared the door and crouched down, pretending to remove a stone from her shoe as she listened to what was being said.

'I'm disappointed,' Maggie Larkin was saying. 'I saved my coupons and my pennies and what did I get? Inferior goods.'

'I heard they need all the rubber for the war effort so there's little to spare for women's girdles,' Edna Hall told her.

'There's no point in having girdles if they don't hold us in where we need a bit of help with our figures,' Maggie argued.

Girdles, not babies. Ruby judged it safe to enter. She was greeted with pleasant smiles. 'You're lucky,' Maggie told her. 'Young things like you don't need foundation garments like us older folk.'

'My time will come,' Ruby said.

Maggie nodded. 'Age and gravity. They come to us all. But the war should be over by the time you need a girdle and there may be rubber aplenty.'

'I hope so,' Ruby said.

She bought custard powder and, noticing a tin of condensed milk, bought that, too, intending it for baby Rose. Then she headed for the baker's. The talk there was of the National Loaf that had recently been made compulsory. Some people liked the wholemeal bread but others didn't. Ada Hayes was one of them. 'I'm trying to get used to it but it just doesn't agree with me,' she complained.

'It uses less flour and can be cut thinner,' her crony Phyllis Hutchings explained.

'I understand about the shortages but . . .' Ada lowered her voice. 'It gives me the runs.'

Poor Ada.

Satisfied Hannah's secret was still safe – for the moment – Ruby bought a loaf and headed for Foxfield. Naomi opened the door and invited her inside. 'I've been to the shops,' Ruby reported. 'No one was talking about Hannah or her baby.'

'That's good to hear. Victoria was at the shops earlier, too, letting it be known that she'd be teaching Hannah some simple wartime recipes.'

'Have you seen anything of Hannah?'

'She's here now and so is our new nurse, Beth. Go and join them,' Naomi invited. 'They're in the kitchen. Suki has the children in the sitting room.'

Ruby found Hannah sitting in a chair, cradling Rose. Beth sat beside her while Victoria rolled pastry.

Hannah looked at Ruby warily. 'It's all right,' Ruby soothed. 'I'm only here to see how you are. And to hand over this.' She took the tin of condensed milk from her bag.

245

'Oh!' Tears shimmered in Hannah's eyes. 'You're all being so kind!'

'No one should ever be *un*kind,' Ruby replied, but plenty of people were unkind at times and Hannah would be judged harshly if her secret were to be exposed. The thought of it made Ruby feel guilty.

Here was Hannah – young, raw and vulnerable – while Ruby sat in front of her, guarding her own secret with lies and leaving poor Hannah thinking she was the only one living under a cloud of shame. Ruby wasn't concerned with protecting herself, though. It was darling Timmy who needed shielding.

She touched a finger to Rose's cheek. 'She looks well.'

'She's getting the best care here,' Hannah said. 'Victoria, Mrs Harrington . . . They're wonderful.'

'Rose looks contented in your arms, too. She knows she's loved.'

'Do you really think so?' Hannah looked desperate for approval.

'I really do,' Ruby confirmed.

'I've always loved babies and children,' Hannah said. 'I had hopes of becoming a teacher but it wasn't to be.'

'You were needed at home?' Ruby guessed.

Hannah nodded. 'I missed a lot of school.'

Rose did indeed look well but Hannah looked strained. She was pale. Trembling slightly. And much too thin. Presumably, there was no news of Rose's father. Perhaps there never would be news and Rose would need to be handed over to the authorities. Poor Hannah. Ruby would be bereft without Timmy.

Beth had got quietly to her feet and glided over to Victoria. Ruby saw her take a florin from her purse and put it on the table. 'A small contribution to your extra costs,' Beth explained.

'It's very generous of you, Beth, but there's no need,' Victoria told her.

'I want to help,' Beth insisted.

Ruby supposed Beth was thinking not only of the cost of maintaining Rose but also of the food Hannah would be taking home – like the rhubarb tart Victoria was making now. Perhaps Ruby, too, could help by supplying Hannah with produce from the farm. Skinflint Ernie needn't know if a few vegetables were smuggled out and Kate would be all in favour of it. Vegetables were hardly the answer to Hannah's problems but they might help to ease the pressure on her to feed her family on what was doubtless a tight budget. With luck, plentiful good food might even mellow her father's temper.

Hannah was overcome with gratitude when Ruby explained what she had in mind.

Beth clearly approved of the offer, too. She gestured towards Rose. 'May I?'

'Of course.' Hannah handed the baby over.

'Hello, beautiful girl,' Beth said, and her rather solemn face broke into a smile that put Ruby in mind of the sun suddenly blazing from behind passing clouds. She was a good person, Ruby decided.

Beth handed the baby back and then Ruby took a turn in holding the infant. How sweet she was! The embrace carried Ruby back through the years to Timmy's first days on earth. He'd been beautiful, too. He still was, in his own urchin-like way. It angered Ruby to think of the names some people would call both these children just because they'd been born outside wedlock.

'I need to get back to the hospital,' Beth said.

'I need to get back to the farm,' Ruby said.

They both promised to look in again when they were able.

Naomi showed them to the door. 'As I said before, Beth, I'll speak to Miss Moore about the concert as soon as possible, but she isn't on the telephone so it's a case of catching her when she's rehearsing in the bookshop.'

'I understand.'

Ruby must have looked puzzled. 'Matron wants the concert matinee to be held at the hospital, if possible,' Beth explained. 'That way more patients will be able to enjoy it.'

Ruby nodded. It was a good idea.

'If I don't catch Miss Moore soon, I'll drop her a note,' Naomi promised.

Setting out together, Ruby and Beth walked up Brimbles Lane side by side, Beth carrying Ruby's shopping while Ruby wheeled the bicycle.

'I didn't like to ask, but I assume I'd have been told if there was news of Rose's father,' Ruby said.

'I didn't like to ask either, and I assumed the same,' Beth told her, and they shared sympathetic looks because if the chap didn't step forward soon, Hannah was likely to lose her baby.

They continued onwards in thoughtful silence for a while, then Ruby roused herself to ask, 'How are you settling in?' There was something about Beth Ellis that made Ruby wonder if she might be lonely.

'At Stratton House? I like the work and hope I'm going to be useful to the patients.'

'And in Churchwood?'

Beth paused before answering. 'There are some nice people here. Very nice people.' She sounded surprised by it.

'The village has its share of narrow-minded residents but it also has a way of taking strangers into its bosom,' Ruby said. 'Me, for one.'

'You're an outsider?' Ruby imagined Beth was merely being polite since she must have picked up on the cockney accent that underpinned Ruby's speech.

'I'm from London. The east side, near the docks. I came to work as a land girl and the village has welcomed me with open arms. I'm not the only one.'

Ruby mentioned other newcomers who'd found happiness here, even if it had taken time before they felt accepted: May Janicki, Evelyn Gregson who taught at the school, Victoria and the other evacuees . . . 'And Alice Irvine, of course. You probably know her from the hospital.'

'I do.'

'It can be tricky, living so far from the village, but it's worth making the effort to visit,' Ruby continued. 'I find that even a few minutes passing the time of day with people at the shops can boost my mood. And the bookshop is a wonderful place for fun and friendships.'

Beth nodded, looking thoughtful.

'You should also call at the farm if you ever want company,' Ruby said. 'We're always busy but that won't stop us from making you welcome. Most of us, anyway. The farmer is a miserable old so-and-so, but we don't take much notice of him. I'm not the only female there. Kate, the farmer's daughter, still lives at home though she's married now, and there's also Pearl, another land girl.'

'I believe I've met them. Briefly.'

'You can trust Kate and Pearl. Alice, too. She often passes on news when she's walking to and from the hospital. She can help us to keep each other up to date with Hannah's situation. And it's nice to chat over a cup of tea.'

Beth nodded again, and when they parted at the drive to the farm she gave Ruby a smile.

Ruby got on the bike – cursing it as always – and rode up to the farm to report on her visit. Both Kate and Pearl were sympathetic to Hannah, but when Fred came in Pearl clamped her jaw shut and ignored him. In turn, Fred ignored her, though Ruby intercepted him giving Pearl a wary look. Kate saw it, too. 'I feel like banging their heads together,' she told Ruby.

'Me too,' Ruby said. 'Me too.'

It was evening when Ruby stepped outside to take in some air and clear her head since problems were circulating around it endlessly. Hannah and Rose, Timmy and the wedding, Pearl and Fred . . .

She'd walked to the drive so didn't hear the kitchen door open and close behind her. Neither did she hear Kenny's footsteps until he spoke. 'Who is he?' he said.

Ruby turned, not understanding. 'Who's who?'

'This man you're seeing.'

Ruby's mouth dropped open. 'I'm not seeing any man.'

'Don't lie, Ruby. It's obvious. You keep sneaking away from the farm, you won't set a date for the wedding, your thoughts are miles away . . .'

Ruby sighed but she could see that Kenny was genuinely worried and genuinely hurt. 'It's you I love,' she assured him. 'You I want to marry. No one else.'

'Then why—'

'I've a lot on my mind,' she admitted. 'There's a secret, but it isn't mine to share. You need to trust me, Kenny.'

She took a step towards him and reached out to touch his face. 'Will you, Kenny? Trust me? Just for a little while longer?'

He groaned, took her into his arms and kissed her. 'I'll try,' he murmured. 'I'll try.'

And with that she had to be content.

CHAPTER FORTY-ONE

Beth

'Lovely day, isn't it?' Oliver asked, falling into step beside her.

Beth felt a painful twist of anguish. It was impossible to avoid him in the hospital – though she never lingered by him if she could help it – but it seemed unfair that she should be ambushed by him as she took an early-morning walk in the hospital grounds.

'It is,' she said, knowing she sounded stiff but hoping she came across as simply uninterested. She had no wish to add to his conceit by letting him know that he'd hurt her, and neither did she wish to show that she was still vulnerable to his charms.

'It's strange how the fates have thrown us together again,' he said. 'Perhaps it means something. After all, I enjoyed your company back in London.'

'Only for a little while.' Again, she hoped she sounded as though she was merely pointing out a fact rather than stirring a grievance.

'Perhaps I made a mistake in letting you go,' he said.

Beth stared at him. Was he serious?

'I always liked you, Beth.' He smiled, and despite her resistance Beth felt her bones weaken.

'I have my motorbike here,' Oliver continued. 'Maybe we could ride out into one of the nearby towns for a meal. What do you say, Beth?'

'I . . .' She was saved from having to answer by Tom, the porter, coming out on to the hospital steps and shouting, 'Telephone call for you, Doctor.'

Oliver gave Beth an apologetic grimace. 'Sorry, I must dash. But a meal would be nice, yes?'

He jogged away and Beth was left cursing her own weakness for him. She'd be a fool to risk letting him bruise her heart further – unless he really did regret having let her go? He'd looked at her with so much softness in those blue eyes . . .

Urgh! She turned her mind elsewhere. To poor Hannah Powell. It was a pity she lived so far away because Beth would love to do more to help her.

Perhaps she should look into buying a bicycle to make it easier to travel between Stratton House and Hannah's cottage. Between those places and Churchwood, too. Beth doubted she could afford one by herself but other nurses like Babs and Pauline might be willing to invest in one they could share. That would involve cracking open the door to becoming friends, though, and Beth wasn't sure she was ready for that. On the other hand, wasn't that door being cracked open already? By Beth's interest in Hannah? By sharing that interest with Alice, Victoria and Ruby? Beth had never felt more confused.

CHAPTER FORTY-TWO

Naomi

'So far, so good,' Bert whispered in Naomi's ear as they made their way out of church after the Sunday morning service.

'Let's hope it stays that way,' Naomi murmured back.

No gossip about Hannah. No gossip about Rose. Marjorie was up ahead of them, her nose raised as though searching for a whiff of scandal, but she didn't appear to be finding any.

'Lovely service,' Naomi told Adam, shaking the vicar's hand when they reached him at the door.

'I'm glad it went well,' he said, which was code for *I'm glad Hannah's secret is safe*.

The fewer people who knew about it, the better, of course, but Naomi hadn't hesitated to share it with Adam. Not only could he be trusted, but as an active sort of vicar who was out and about in the parish every day, he was also likely to be among the first to pick up any chatter and be able to give early notice of it. He'd also help Hannah if he could.

Walking through the village, Naomi and Bert heard music coming from the bookshop. 'I'd like a word with Margueritte,' Naomi said.

She knocked on the door to warn of her arrival and walked inside, glancing around to see if there was anyone

253

there who shouldn't be. The owner of the van Victoria had seen, for one. But as far as Naomi could see, only Margueritte and Sidney were there.

'Yes?' Margueritte demanded as though she owned the place.

'I was passing and thought I'd ask how you're getting on?'

'Very well, of course. Didn't you hear me singing?'

'I did, and yes, you sounded excellent.'

Margueritte preened.

'I've been hoping to see you because I have a favour to ask,' Naomi said.

'Oh?'

'The matron at the hospital has requested that the matinee be held there so more patients can watch it. Would that be agreeable?'

Margueritte's eyes had lit up. 'Certainly. I'm sure the men there would enjoy my performance.'

If it didn't give them all heart attacks. 'Thank you,' Naomi said. 'I won't disturb you further.'

'All right?' Bert asked, outside.

'It seems so. But I really hope she won't bring trouble to Churchwood.'

'We've got enough trouble already,' Bert agreed.

They walked on towards Foxfield and were almost there when Edith suddenly darted out from the drive that led to the Meads' farm. She looked even thinner, if that were possible, but perhaps that was merely an impression created by her obvious agitation. 'I need to return your book,' she told Naomi, holding it out.

Naomi took it with a smile. 'Did you enjoy it?'

Edith was already turning away. She glanced back over her shoulder. 'To be honest, I didn't manage to read it.'

'Then keep it a little longer.'

'Thank you, but no. I don't have time for reading.'

'But . . .'

Too late. Edith was gone.

'At least you tried to help her,' Bert said.

'Tried but failed.'

'You haven't failed yet because you haven't given up on her yet. The important thing is that Edith knows you care about her and she knows where to find you if she wants your help. That's as far as you can take things at the moment, my love. Come on. Let's get inside and have a glass of my home-made wine.'

Bert poured wine for all the grown-ups, taking a glass to Victoria who was in the kitchen cooking lunch. Suki was enjoying a day off with her family but Naomi had no fear of her spilling the beans about Rose and Hannah. Suki was loyal and discreet beyond her years.

Hearing the telephone ring, Naomi went to answer it.

The caller was Paul Scarletti. 'Mrs Harrington? I hope I'm not disturbing you? I wouldn't normally ring on a Sunday, but—'

'You're not disturbing me, Sergeant, and it's fine to call me on any day of the week.'

'I'm mighty relieved to hear it. The thing is, I have some time off tomorrow.'

'You'd like to accept our invitation to come and take tea?'

'I'd love to accept it. If that's all right? I know I'm not giving you much notice.'

'There's a war on. You have your duties and need to snatch your free time where you can.'

'That's exactly right. I can be with you at around four, if that suits? I've been promised the use of a motorcycle.'

'We'll look forward to seeing you. Please don't expect a feast, though. The war that's limiting your free time is also limiting our food supplies.'

'It's the company I want.'

'I'm sure we can stretch to a sandwich,' Naomi told him, pleased by the eagerness in his voice. It boded well for Victoria – if she allowed herself the freedom to enjoy it and discover where it might lead. She'd been on edge ever since the invitation had been sent.

In the background she heard someone complaining that Paul should stop hogging the phone.

'Until tomorrow, Sergeant,' Naomi said, bringing the call to an end.

She headed for the kitchen. 'Sergeant Scarletti just rang,' Naomi told Victoria. 'He's coming to tea tomorrow.'

Victoria blushed.

CHAPTER FORTY-THREE

Victoria

'We're simply giving hospitality to a soldier who's far from home,' Naomi told the children. 'I hope you'll all make him welcome and be on your best behaviour.'

'We will,' Arthur promised, speaking for all of them as the eldest – just – and their natural leader. 'It's what you gave us, isn't it? Hospi . . .'

'Hospitality,' Naomi confirmed.

Victoria's stomach squeezed with nerves when a knock sounded on the door. She went out into the hall, took a deep breath and opened it.

Paul greeted her with a smile. 'I'm delighted to be here,' he said, presenting her with a bouquet of flowers.

'They're lovely!' Victoria said, taking them. 'But I'm sure you won't mind if I pass them on to Mrs Harrington. She owns this house, after all, and she's the hostess for this tea. You're a guest of the entire household.'

'Understood,' Paul confirmed. He smiled again. 'Here's hoping I don't disgrace myself.'

Victoria led the way into the drawing room, where a sea of curious faces studied him openly. 'This is Sergeant Paul Scarletti,' Victoria announced. 'Look at these beautiful flowers he's brought for us all.'

'How kind,' Naomi said, and the children nodded,

though there was no doubt that they'd have preferred a gift of sweets or chocolate. 'Do sit down, Sergeant.'

'Please. Call me Paul,' he told her, sitting in an armchair.

'We've got egg sandwiches,' Flower announced, gesturing to a tray.

'Egg sandwiches are wonderful, aren't they? I imagine they're a treat, seeing as rationing is making things tough for you over here.'

'Isn't it tough for you, too?' Arthur asked.

'America is a big country with a lot of space for growing food so we're not suffering as much over there. And we soldiers are being fed pretty well.' He laughed suddenly. 'Which makes me think I shouldn't eat your precious egg sandwiches.'

'You're a guest,' Jenny pointed out. 'We should treat guests nicely. That's what Victoria says.'

Paul glanced up at Victoria and the warm appreciation in his dark eyes sent a frisson skittering over her skin. 'I'll put these flowers in water and give Suki a hand,' she said, heading for the door.

'Tea's ready,' Suki told her when she reached the kitchen.

'Thank you. I can take one of the trays. May I leave these flowers here? They're for Naomi.'

A knowing look in Suki's eyes told Victoria that the maid knew full well who the flowers were for, but she simply said, 'Of course you can.'

They carried the trays into the sitting room – tea things on one and glasses of watered-down milk on the other.

'This is my first English tea-drinking ceremony,' Paul said as they put down the trays and handed round cups and glasses. Plates, too, for the sandwiches and scones.

'Don't you have tea at home?' Arthur enquired.

'Coffee, mostly, but I'm liking everything I've seen of England so far and I'm looking forward to trying tea.'

Naomi gave Victoria a smile. It suggested that liking everything he'd seen of England included Victoria herself.

Feeling the warmth of a blush bloom in her cheeks, Victoria was glad that the children kept Paul talking. 'How far away is America?' Lewis asked. 'When we came here, we had to take a bus and then a train and then another bus. We travelled more than twenty miles!'

'That must have been an adventure,' Paul said. 'America is a little further away than that.'

'Thirty miles? Forty miles? A hundred miles?'

'More like three thousand miles to the east coast. Even further to the west coast.'

'Cor! How did you get here? Not on a bus?'

'I travelled on a ship across the Atlantic Ocean. It took more than a week as we moved in convoy.'

'You slept on the ship?' Arthur asked.

'I sure did.'

'Do they have elephants in America?' Flower asked.

'And giraffes?' Jenny added.

'Lions and tigers, too?' Lewis said, making a roaring sound.

'Only in the zoos,' Paul told them. 'But we do have animals you folks don't have. Let me think . . . Yes, there's mountain lions, bears, buffalo, skunks . . . They're smelly little critters.'

The children laughed. 'What else is different?' Arthur wondered.

'The buildings. In places like New York, they're taller than anything. The Empire State Building has a hundred and two floors.'

'Cor!' Lewis cried.

'That's a lot of stairs,' Ivy said, smiling. 'I wouldn't want to reach the top only to remember I'd left something at the bottom. But I suppose there must be lifts.'

'Elevators? There sure are. Oh, and money is different, too.' He dug in his pocket and brought out a small bag. 'I can't spend this here but I brought it to remind me of home.' He emptied the bag into his palm. 'This here is a penny.'

'We have pennies, too,' Arthur said. 'There are twelve pennies in a shilling and twenty shillings in a pound.'

'Our pennies are also called cents. One hundred cents make a dollar. This here's a nickel. It's worth five cents. This is a dime, worth ten cents. And this here's a quarter, worth twenty-five cents.'

'We have names for coins, too,' Arthur said. 'Tanners, threepenny bits, shillings, florins, half crowns . . . Is a dollar equal to a pound?'

'I believe a dollar is worth about a quarter of one of your pounds.'

'Five shillings?' Arthur asked, and Victoria was pleased by his swift arithmetic.

'That's right,' Paul said. 'Here. Take a coin, each of you. The value doesn't matter since you can't spend it. Just choose one you like the look of.'

'Are you sure?' Victoria asked. 'If the coins remind you of home . . .'

'I still have plenty.'

Another half-hour passed quickly with Paul having no chance to talk to Victoria. Not that she minded. She was happy simply to observe how good he was with the children and with the adults, too. He was polite, considerate, good-humoured . . .

Naomi thought so too, judging from the knowing look she gave Victoria. It was the sort of look that said *I told you so*.

'It's been a wonderful afternoon, but now I must get back to base,' Paul said. 'First, let me test myself on all your names. Mrs Harrington . . .'

'Naomi.'

He nodded and continued. 'Victoria, Jenny, Arthur, Flower . . .' He named each child and adult in turn and was correct in every case.

'You must come again,' Naomi said, getting up to allow Paul to do the same. 'There's a concert in the village a week on Saturday if you're free?'

'It'll depend on my duties.'

'Of course.'

He shook hands with everyone, even the children, and Naomi said, 'Victoria will show you to the door.'

'I hope you didn't feel overwhelmed by the children,' she said as they stood in the hall.

'They're great. All of them. I had a swell time.'

'I'm glad.'

'I'd like to see you again, if you'd like it, too? At that concert, if not before.'

'Perhaps,' Victoria said.

'The children come first. I understand that. But I could visit here again. Or take you out, with or without the children.'

'Let's see.'

With that he had to be content.

He put on his cap, kissed her cheek and stepped outside to where the motorbike awaited him. He sketched a wave as he mounted it and Victoria waved back, feeling a pang as he passed through the gateposts and touching a hand to the place he'd kissed.

Back inside, everyone was talking about him. How nice he was. How interesting. How well-mannered. Victoria was aware of Naomi's eyes on her now and then but was grateful when nothing was said to embarrass her publicly. Something needed to be said privately, though, and later, when Naomi was in her sitting room looking over some

261

bookshop business, Victoria went to her. 'I like him,' she admitted. 'Perhaps I will see him again.'

'The children needn't know if you see him sometimes. We can make an excuse for your absence. I don't like dishonesty in general, but little fibs can be helpful.'

'I don't want to rush anything.'

'Of course not. Just take things slowly and see what develops.'

CHAPTER FORTY-FOUR

Ruby

Hannah wasn't there when Ruby called at Foxfield early on Tuesday but it was a relief to know that her secret was still safe. 'Bert can take those vegetables to her, if you like,' Naomi told her, for Ruby had brought a small bagful with her.

'That would be wonderful, if it's no trouble.'

'He's donating vegetables from his market garden, too.'

'Hannah won't mind them being delivered?'

'Bert understands that visitors might arouse her father's suspicions so he won't go to her house. We've agreed a hiding place with her, in nearby bushes.'

'That makes sense.'

'Beth visited again,' Naomi said then. 'She mentioned that you'd been kind to her.'

'Just friendly.'

'You think she needs friends. I agree.'

'We all need friends,' Ruby said.

'Indeed we do. Can I offer you some tea? I hope you won't mind if I say you're looking tired.'

Ruby could hardly deny it.

'I expect you're worried about Timmy.'

Ruby couldn't deny that, either. Naomi knew all about his situation. 'Thanks for the offer but I need to get back to the farm.'

Naomi smiled. 'How many times have I heard Kate say the same thing? Still, it's farmworkers who keep us from starving so I won't complain. I'll tell Hannah you visited. She needs to know we're all on her side.'

Ruby returned to the farm. Seeing Kenny working in a field, she headed towards him. 'You've been out again,' he said.

'But I haven't been seeing another man. Remember, Kenny, it's you I love.' She kissed him before saying, 'I should get out of this field before Ernie shouts at me for standing on the crops.'

She left him with a smile but was sure he still had his suspicions. The sooner Hannah's man came home, the better for everyone.

Kate was in the kitchen, having brought in some vegetables for lunch, when Ruby entered the farmhouse. She glanced around to be sure no one else was there and said, 'I didn't see Hannah but her secret is still safe. So far.'

'That's good,' Kate said, but she looked troubled.

'What is it?' Ruby asked.

'Pearl. I saw her looking at some papers. Women's Land Army papers.'

Ruby felt her eyes widen in dismay. 'Do you think she may be thinking of asking for a transfer to a different farm?'

'She wouldn't talk about it, but that's what I suspect.'

'I still feel like banging her and Fred's heads together,' Ruby said.

'Me too,' Kate told her. 'Let's hope things change when he brings his new legs home.'

Ruby agreed, but she felt as though a storm was looming on Churchwood's horizon and would soon be rushing in on them.

CHAPTER FORTY-FIVE

Victoria

'I like Paul,' Jenny had declared after the sergeant's visit on Monday.

'Do you, poppet?' Victoria had asked.

'So do I,' Arthur had said.

'I'm sure he liked you, too. I'm sure he liked all of us.'

Mags and the other women had given Victoria sly looks after he'd left, guessing that he liked her best of all. But the children didn't appear to have picked up on any suggestion of romance and for that she was grateful.

Two letters had come from him since then – a letter for Naomi thanking her for her hospitality and another for Victoria telling her she just had to say the word and he'd be along to see her again, duties permitting.

But I'll understand if you want to take things slowly. Arthur and Jenny are terrific kids and deserve to come first in your attentions . . .

Beginning to mewl, Rose cut into Victoria's thoughts.

'Hungry?' Victoria asked her. She prepared a bottle and fed her, and then walked her around, patting her back to wind her.

Someone knocked on the front door. 'I'll go, if you

can hold Rose?' Victoria said to Ivy, knowing Suki was busy in the kitchen and wanting to save Ivy's poor legs.

'I'll be glad to hold her,' Ivy said, smiling because Rose was loved by everyone at Foxfield.

'You'll—'

'Keep her quiet? Of course I will. Won't I, precious?' Ivy touched a finger to Rose's cheek.

Keeping the baby quiet when anyone came to the house was crucial.

Victoria closed the door to the drawing room to reduce the chance of noise escaping, and went to answer the knock.

She found Marjorie Plym outside. Miss Plym was definitely not party to Hannah's secret. 'How nice to see you, Miss Plym,' Victoria said, forcing a smile. 'I'm afraid Naomi isn't in. She's at the bookshop. Perhaps you'll see her there?'

'She wasn't there when I popped my head in on my way past.'

'I think she intended to call in at the post office first. I expect she's arrived at the bookshop now.'

At that moment Rose let out a wail.

'What was that?' Marjorie asked.

'What was what?' Victoria questioned, hoping she managed to pull off an innocent look.

'That wail? It sounded like a baby.'

'Just the younger children playing. I'll be sure to tell Naomi you called.'

'I'm sure it was a baby.'

'Just the children playing,' Victoria repeated. 'Good day to you, Miss Plym.' She closed the door before Marjorie could utter another word.

'Sorry about the wail,' Ivy said, when Victoria returned to the drawing room.

'It wasn't your fault. Babies cry. Unfortunately, it was Marjorie Plym at the door.'

'That old gossip! She didn't hear anything, I hope?'

'She did, but I told her the noise was made by the children playing.'

'Good thinking.'

Rose began to wail again. Victoria took her from Ivy and walked about the room, rocking her. When Rose didn't settle, she carried her out into the hall and on into the study, wanting Ivy to have some peace. 'What's the matter, darling?' Victoria murmured. 'Didn't I wind you properly?'

She lifted Rose over her shoulder and patted the little back. And then – horror of horrors – she saw Marjorie's face at the window, looking in with a mixture of surprise and gratification at having been proved right about there being a baby in the house.

No, no, no . . .

Marjorie turned away and hastened off, doubtless to tell the whole of Churchwood what she'd seen.

Victoria returned to the drawing room. 'Disaster,' she told Ivy. 'Marjorie saw Rose through the study window. I need to go after her.'

'Quick as you can,' Ivy urged, taking Rose again.

Victoria kicked off her slippers, shoved her feet into shoes and raced out of the house. Reaching the gateposts, she was appalled to see that Marjorie was already far ahead, almost running down the street. It wasn't often that she had gossip to impart that was as exciting as a secret baby. 'Miss Plym!' Victoria called but the woman didn't hear her – or chose not to hear her.

Victoria broke into a run, too, but Marjorie was on a mission and didn't slow.

'Miss Plym! Stop!' Victoria called again, seeing that

Marjorie was drawing perilously close to the bookshop. 'Please stop!'

Marjorie didn't stop, and although Victoria was gaining on her – her feet pounding the ground and heart pounding in her chest – she feared she might be too late to avert disaster . . .

CHAPTER FORTY-SIX

Hannah

Hannah could understand why the bookshop was so popular. She was here hoping for news of Mattie but it was
also nice to sit Susie and Simon on a rug to play with
decent toys instead of the chipped and mostly broken few
they had at home. To be given tea and a biscuit. And to
receive smiles and comments such as, 'They're a handful
at that age, aren't they?' accompanied by understanding
nods at the children.

She could see how it helped other people, too. One
elderly lady had been welcomed back after being unwell.
She'd been ushered to a chair away from draughts and
people had gone over to ask how she was doing. 'It's so
nice to be here again,' she'd said. 'Thank you all for rally-
ing round when I was confined to bed. It was such a relief
to have you coming in to check on me as well as light my
fire, feed me soup and wash my dishes.'

Alice Irvine had announced that someone else was ill
now. An elderly gentleman called Humphrey Guscott.
'I'm drawing up a rota so we can be sure one of us checks
on him every day,' she'd said. 'Please come and have a
word if you're able to help.'

Hannah could have enjoyed it here if she hadn't been
so sick with worry about Rose, not to mention her father
kissing Margueritte Moore. She'd been straining her ears

to hear what Mattie's mother had to say but, so far, Aggie had said nothing about Mattie. She'd merely complained that . . .

The door flew open and Marjorie Plym burst in, looking feverish with excitement.

She came to a halt just inside the room, her thin chest heaving from her rush. 'I've seen it, Naomi!' she cried. 'I've seen the baby at Foxfield. Why have you been keeping it secret, even from me?'

Every head turned to her and there was silence.

'What baby?' someone asked then.

'Probably just Marjorie's imagination taking flight again,' another woman answered.

Hannah's gaze fixed on Mrs Harrington imploringly. *Please do something.* Mrs Harrington appeared to flounder for a moment, but then made a visible effort to pull her wits together. 'Nice to see you, Marjorie. I'm glad you're here because the book you wanted is here, too, and I've set it aside for you.'

'There *is* a baby at Foxfield,' Miss Plym insisted, still standing by the door and shouting to Naomi across the room so everyone could hear. 'I saw it with my own eyes. I thought it odd when Victoria told me I'd only heard children playing so I crept round to the study window and there the baby was, in Victoria's arms. I know it wasn't a doll because I saw its arms moving. I couldn't tell if it was a boy or a girl, though, since it was wrapped up in a shawl.'

Hannah groaned inside. A silent groan of despair.

'Marjorie, I think you're straying into business that doesn't concern you,' Naomi warned, walking over as though to shut Miss Plym up physically.

No one else moved. A mother shushed her child so she could watch the scene that was playing out along with everyone else.

'Is it Victoria's baby?' Marjorie asked, still abuzz with the sort of bright-eyed excitement that threw caution to the wind.

'No, she isn't my baby,' Victoria said, walking into the room behind her, looking vexed. 'She's simply been entrusted to my care temporarily.'

'It's a girl, then!' Marjorie said, as though she'd uncovered another delicious secret. 'But why are you keeping her hidden?'

'It's none of your business,' Naomi said, sharply now, but Marjorie seemed to be riding too high on the wave of a possible scandal even to notice.

'There must be a reason for keeping the baby hidden,' she persisted. 'If she isn't yours, Victoria, perhaps she belongs to one of those London women who wants to keep her existence quiet because the father isn't her husband. Or maybe she's Suki's baby.'

Was there no one this woman wouldn't smear in her quest for attention? Hannah could bear it no longer. She leaped to her feet. 'Stop it, Miss Plym!' she cried. 'Just stop it! The baby isn't Miss Page's. She doesn't belong to any of the evacuee women, either. Or to Suki. She . . . She's mine!'

Hannah's cheeks felt scalded with heat. Her heart thudded in her chest, and tears of frustration and near-despair welled up in her eyes.

For a moment the room was silent. Then Susie began to cry, upset by Hannah's distress. Simon started wailing, too.

Hannah bent to them. 'We need to go,' she said, scooping up Simon and gesturing to Susie to get up quickly, too.

'Hannah, wait,' Mrs Harrington urged, hastening to her side, but Hannah couldn't stay a moment longer. Tears had burst out over her cheeks.

Alice had come over, too. 'Let's go to The Linnets,' she

suggested. 'We can talk there about the best way to deal with this situation.'

But Hannah shook her head. There was no good way forward now the secret was out. It was only a matter of time before it came t o her father's ears and then there'd be hell to pay.

Already scandalized whispers and murmurs had begun to race around the room.

'What I'd like to know is who's the baby's father?' Hilda Bates said to Mattie's mother.

'It wouldn't surprise me if that girl doesn't even know,' Aggie Hamilton replied. 'The Powells are a ramshackle family and that girl probably has ramshackle morals, too.'

More tears tumbled out of Hannah's eyes.

'Come back to The Linnets even if you're not ready to talk,' Alice urged. 'Just until you're a little calmer.'

'Yes, do,' Mrs Harrington agreed.

But once again Hannah shook her head, so Mrs Harrington, Alice and Miss Page ushered her and the children outside, where Hannah lifted Susie and Simon into the pram.

'Marjorie did a terrible thing in there but it needn't mean the end of the world,' Alice soothed. 'People may talk about you for a while, but it doesn't mean your parents are certain to hear about Rose. Not with your mother staying indoors, and as for your father . . . I've never spoken to him but I've seen him around and he doesn't strike me as particularly approachable.'

Alice meant well but, approachable or not, Hannah's father was certain to hear about Rose sooner or later. 'I need to go home,' Hannah insisted.

'If not The Linnets, come back to Foxfield,' Mrs Harrington said. 'A cuddle with your daughter may be just the thing you need to steady you.'

The idea of holding Rose tugged hard at Hannah's heart. She *longed* to hold her little daughter in her arms. But she'd already upset Susie and Simon with her tears. She didn't want to do the same to Rose. Besides, if she went to Foxfield, she'd need to walk through the entire village on her return to Barton. People would be spilling out of the bookshop by then and word about Rose would be spreading. There'd be judgemental stares. Whispered condemnations . . . Hannah couldn't put Susie and Simon through that.

'I have to get home anyway,' Hannah said, between sobs. She never liked to leave her mother alone for long.

'We can't force you to stay,' Alice said. 'But please don't give up hope.'

They were words of comfort but they couldn't comfort Hannah now. Alice was all kindness, but she inhabited a different world from Hannah. She couldn't know what it was like to live in fear of her father and feel weighed down by guilt at the shame she was bringing to her family's door. Alice had a father who loved her and a handsome husband who appeared to do the same, and when she had her baby it would bring joy to all concerned.

'Rose's father may arrive home any day,' Victoria said, adding her voice to the attempts to console Hannah, but Mattie had never felt more distant.

'You've been kind,' Hannah told the three women, and with that she set off towards Barton.

She hadn't gone far before she heard Marjorie's voice again. 'Naomi, I really didn't mean—'

'Not now!' Naomi barked, and with a wail Marjorie ran off, presumably to feel sorry for herself at home.

Hannah's handkerchief was wet from the children's tears so she dried her own eyes on her sleeve and attempted a smile of reassurance for Susie and Simon.

Neither seemed reassured and both continued to stare at her with large, wary eyes, whimpering occasionally.

Trudging onwards, Hannah thought about what lay in store for her, and the thoughts felt as hot and painful as flames. It was true that her mother was unlikely to hear about Rose and it was also true that her father wasn't an approachable man. But he was often at the Wheatsheaf for a pint and his job took him to Barton, Churchwood and other towns and villages where he might pick up rumours and tittle-tattle. Gossip had a way of sneaking through cracks and crevices to reach daylight.

What should Hannah do? Come clean and tell him herself that she'd given birth to a child? Hannah shuddered at the thought.

Of course, her father was hardly free from fault himself. Not after kissing Margueritte Moore. For a moment Hannah considered telling him that she'd seen the kiss so he had no right to criticize her behaviour when his own was terrible, too. But she feared she might only double his anger or – worse still – trigger him into walking out on Ma and the children. What would happen to the family then?

Reaching the shabby cottage, she lifted Susie and Simon from the pram and went inside, entering by the back door into the kitchen and pausing there to splash water over her face to try to disguise the ravages her tears must have left behind. Then she fixed a smile on her face and went up to her mother, carrying Simon and holding Susie's hand, not only to keep them safe but also in the hope that Ma would be too busy with them to pay much attention to her eldest daughter.

She was alarmed to see her mother looking even paler than usual. 'What is it?' Hannah asked. 'Are you in pain?'

'It's only a headache. Sorry, Hannah. I hate to be such a worry to you.'

'I'll make you some tea and fetch a flannel.'

Hannah returned downstairs with the children and set the kettle to boil. Waiting for it, she prepared the teapot and set an ancient wooden tray with a cup, saucer, bowl of warm water and rags that would do service as flannels. Stepping outside, she snipped a few of the bluebells that grew by the kitchen door, dropping them into another cup since there wasn't a vase and hoping their fragrance would help to ease Ma's head. When the kettle boiled she allowed a couple of minutes for the tea to brew, since the tea leaves had been used several times before due to both rationing and a tiny household budget.

Deciding the children would be safe in the parlour for a few minutes since no fire was burning in there, she shut them inside and carried the tray upstairs, where she was rewarded with one of her mother's grateful smiles.

Dipping a rag into the bowl, Hannah smoothed it across her mother's forehead. 'Is that better?' she asked.

'Much better, darling. Thank you.'

Ma drank some tea and then lay back against the pillows, managing to smile despite her frailness. 'You're a good girl, Hannah.'

But she wasn't. She'd brought shame and disgrace on her family and there was almost certainly going to be trouble.

Hannah had never felt more desolate.

CHAPTER FORTY-SEVEN

Naomi

Depressed, Naomi went about the routine of the bookshop, forcing herself to smile and chatter when all the time she was worrying about Hannah and aware that people were whispering about her. She was glad when the session ended. She helped to tidy up the toys and books and then set off home, on feet that always felt more troublesome when her spirits were low.

She neared the Foxfield gateposts and Marjorie stepped out from behind one of them. She must have been awaiting Naomi's return and now she approached, crab-like with hesitation, her face showing patches of puce due to her awkwardness.

'I hope I haven't caused an upset?' she said.

'Of course you've caused an upset!' Naomi roared, unable to hold back on the fury. 'Will you *never* learn to keep your nose out of other people's business?'

'I didn't mean any harm,' Marjorie protested.

'So you always say. But you *cause* harm with your gossiping, Marjorie. Time and again you cause harm. You say you won't do it again but you always do and I'm sick of it.'

'Naomi, please!'

'*Go*, Marjorie. I'm in no mood to talk to you.'

'But—'

'Just go!'

Marjorie burst into tears and ran up the road towards home. Which was the best place for her since Naomi could hardly bear to look at her.

CHAPTER FORTY-EIGHT

Hannah

Hannah felt sicker with every hour that took her closer to her father's return from work. When she heard the butcher's van pull up on to the scrubby patch of land in front of the cottage, she thought she might actually vomit, but she took a deep breath, ushered all the children into the parlour and waited in the kitchen so she could face her father's anger alone. He flung open the kitchen door and she braced herself for his fury, but he simply threw a paper-wrapped parcel on to the table and said, 'Be quick. I'm going out.'

Hannah drew some rapid conclusions. He couldn't have heard about Rose yet. He'd brought meat home for their dinner. And he wanted the dinner served soon since he had plans for the evening.

Hannah's first feeling was relief that Rose was still a secret. But concern soon followed. Plans for the evening meant what exactly? Not the Wheatsheaf, she guessed. Margueritte Moore? Was he in love with her, in so far as Jed Powell could love anyone? Would he leave his family for her? Hannah was in no doubt that destitution would follow for the family if he did. He wasn't the man to sacrifice his own pleasures for theirs and if he went away, they'd be out of his thoughts as well as out of his sight.

'Hot water,' he demanded, and Hannah snapped to attention.

Having already boiled the kettle, she poured warm water into a bowl and placed it on the table with a towel. Her father scooped water over his face and then dunked his head in the bowl, before giving it a shake and towelling it dry. Water had splattered all over the kitchen but Hannah knew better than to complain. She simply used the towel to mop up the spillages and made her father a cup of tea as he sat down and dug in his pocket for a Woodbine. He lit the cigarette, sucked on it and then slowly blew out smoke. He didn't ask about Ma or the children.

Hannah was relieved to discover that the package contained sausages. How her father managed it she didn't know, but meat extra to their rations appeared in the cottage kitchen once or twice a week. Perhaps Edmundson's gave it to him because it wouldn't survive overnight without going off, but there were the other possibilities – her father might have cheated Edmundson's customers or bought the meat on the black market.

There was nothing suspicious about unrationed sausages, though, and they'd be quick to cook. Her father grew impatient when he brought home other meat, not understanding that it was often tough and needed to be cooked slowly.

There were four sausages in all. Two would go to her father and the remaining two would be shared between the rest of them, bulked out by potatoes and vegetables. Hannah set the big heavy frying pan on the stove and got to work frying the sausages with the potatoes. Carrots and cabbage were already simmering.

She set the table and called the children in, speaking quietly as she helped them to wash their hands and sit at the table.

After the meal her father pushed himself to his feet and clomped up the uncarpeted stairs. The low murmur of voices reached her. Probably, Ma was asking about his day and trying to be cheerful, but all Hannah heard from her father were grunts and occasional curt replies. He came down wearing another clean shirt. Sitting back at the table, he smoked his way through another couple of cigarettes then got up and went out. Once again, he took the van.

Hannah carried her mother's food upstairs. Ma did her best to eat it but soon declared she could manage no more. 'You eat it, Hannah. You're looking peaky – and no wonder, with all you do. I'm sorry your life has come to this, my darling.'

Hannah had to blink back more tears. 'I'm fine,' she insisted.

She took the plate back downstairs and gathered the children round so they could each have a spoonful of Ma's leftovers. Then she washed the dishes and allowed herself a rare few minutes alone at the kitchen table. Her father hadn't heard about baby Rose yet, but he might hear about her tonight. And when he came home with a belly full of beer . . .

Hannah felt like a prisoner awaiting execution.

CHAPTER FORTY-NINE

Ruby

Ruby was standing at the kitchen window when she saw Alice approaching the farmhouse. It was obvious from Alice's face that something was wrong. Ruby hastened to open the door and beckon her inside. 'I hope you're not here to tell us that—'

'Hannah's secret is out? I'm afraid I am.' Alice stepped into the kitchen. 'Is it safe to talk?'

'There's just the two of us here,' Ruby confirmed, gesturing to Kate and herself.

'What happened?' Kate asked as they sat at the table.

Alice told them about Marjorie's appearance in the bookshop.

'That woman!' Ruby declared, seething.

'What's to be done?' Kate wondered.

'There's a question!' Alice gave a helpless shrug. 'Hannah is still hoping her chap will come along and save the day, but no one has the heart to tell her she's dreaming so it's a case of trying to support her while hoping her parents don't get to hear about Rose.'

'I can understand Hannah needing to see for herself that she's been let down by her chap,' Kate said. 'I'm worried about what her father might do if he hears about the baby, though.'

'We're all worried about that,' Alice said. 'We've told

281

her to come to Foxfield or The Linnets if she needs to escape. We've also told her you'll be willing to help – and Beth, too. I'm hoping to see her at the hospital later.'

An anxious silence descended. Gradually, Ruby realized that attention had shifted to her. 'You're wondering if the time has come to tell Timmy what's going on,' she guessed. 'Unfortunately, I think it has.'

'I'm sorry,' Alice said, getting to her feet. 'Timmy deserves to be happy.'

She patted Ruby's shoulder in passing as she headed for the door.

'Was that Alice I saw?' Pearl asked, appearing a few minutes later.

Ruby told her the news.

'What rotten luck!' Pearl declared.

'Poor Hannah and poor Timmy, too,' Kate agreed. 'But we'll do all we can to help and I hope you will, too.'

'Of course,' Pearl said, but without much commitment behind it.

'Meaning you'll help for as long as you're here but then you'll leave?' Ruby asked. 'You used to be happy here.'

'I was happy. But now . . .'

'Tell Fred you love him,' Ruby urged.

'I don't love Fred!' Pearl scoffed but it was a sham, obviously intended to save face since she was sure any such declaration would only lead to rejection and perhaps even howls of laughter from Fred.

'We're not going to argue with you,' Kate said. 'But we care for you, Pearl. We'd hate to see your pride getting in the way of your happiness.'

'Pride? You're talking nonsense,' Pearl said. 'I only came in to hear what Alice wanted. I'll go back to work now.'

She headed for the door only to pause and look back.

'I'm truly sorry about Hannah. About Rose and Timmy, too.'

With that, she went out.

'There's just no talking to her,' Ruby said, frustrated.

Then her thoughts turned to the conversation she needed to have with Timmy and dread haunted her for the rest of the afternoon. 'Go and meet him from school,' Kate suggested. 'If you bring him straight home, he'll have less chance of hearing the gossip from anyone else.'

It was sound advice. 'You don't mind?'

'Of course not. Ernie will complain, but leave him to me.'

Ruby rode the bicycle to the school gates, arriving just as the children began to emerge. Timmy grinned when he saw her. 'I wasn't expecting you,' he said.

'I hope it's a nice surprise. Be quick, though. I can't be away from the farm for long. You know what Ernie's like.'

'Miserable,' Timmy said.

She noticed several groups of people whispering together but simply waved to a few acquaintances and concentrated on hurrying Timmy away from the school. 'Good day?' she asked, when they were clear.

He told her about his lessons and what he'd done during playtime.

Ruby smiled in the right places but Timmy was no fool despite his tender years. 'Is something wrong?' he finally asked as they neared the farm.

'There's nothing wrong with you, me or anyone at the farm,' she assured him, 'but there's something we need to talk about. Let's go into the orchard.'

There was a log there where they could sit with little risk of being disturbed. Timmy's eyes were wary as they sat down. His apprehension made Ruby feel as though her heart was bleeding. 'Do you know Hannah Powell?'

she asked, reaching for his hand and trying to squeeze comfort into it.

'The girl who's always looking after her brothers and sisters?'

'Yes, that's her. It seems she's had a baby . . .' Ruby told him the story. 'So you understand the problem?' she asked, when she'd finished.

'I mustn't do or say anything if people are mean.'

'Sort of. I don't want you joining in if people are mean about Hannah – certainly not – but you mustn't do or say anything that'll make them wonder about *our* situation. You've nothing to be ashamed of, Tim. You're a wonderful boy and I couldn't be prouder of you. But some people . . . They might judge us unfairly. So keep your chin high and your mouth zipped, and if you feel yourself getting annoyed . . .'

'Take some deep breaths and walk away.'

'Excellent.' Ruby rewarded him with an approving smile but, oh, how she hated to see his little face looking so burdened with care.

They made their way to the farmyard, where Ruby locked the bike in the barn. 'Go into the kitchen and I'll join you in a moment,' she told Timmy and then went in search of Kenny. 'You know that secret I mentioned?' she asked.

Kenny nodded.

'It isn't a secret any more.'

'Does that mean you're going to tell me about it?'

'Do you know Hannah Powell?'

'Is she related to Jed Powell?'

'His daughter.'

'Bad lot, Jed Powell. Aggressive. Mean.'

'Hannah has had a baby and she isn't saying who the father is.'

Kenny let out a whistle and ran a hand through his thick auburn hair, leaving it standing on end. 'Jed'll be livid about that.'

'He doesn't know. Not yet. The secret is out in the village but the Powells live near Barton and haven't heard about it. Not yet, anyway. Mrs Powell stays in bed most of the time and Jed Powell isn't exactly Mr Life-and-Soul-of-the-Party in Churchwood. Hannah still wants to give the father of her baby the chance to step forward and put things right, but we think he's in the army or one of the other services and it may take a while. So the longer Jed Powell is kept in the dark, the better. I'm trusting you, Kenny. I'm trusting you to say nothing to anyone about Hannah.'

'I won't go blabbing about it.'

'Good. Because not blabbing is important to Hannah and to Timmy, too. His birth is still a secret and I need it to stay that way. People are already being horrible about Hannah and her baby. I don't want them being horrible about Timmy.'

'If anyone is horrible about you and the boy, they'll have me to answer to,' Kenny said, his chin rising and his hands tightening into fists.

'I don't want you to fight. I want your silence. Promise me you'll respect that, Kenny.'

'You know I will.'

She knew he'd *try* to respect it, but would he succeed?

CHAPTER FIFTY

Beth

'We must go for that meal soon,' Oliver told Beth as she was leaving Stratton House to walk into Churchwood before starting a later shift.

He smiled and Beth felt the old attraction rising. But she managed to give only a non-committal smile in return, unsure yet if she was prepared to give him a second chance. Had he really decided that Cassandra Carlisle wouldn't suit him despite her beauty? Had he really come to value Beth's worth instead?

She walked briskly down Brimbles Lane, glad that the days were long at this time of year. Victoria answered her knock on the Foxfield door and looked relieved that the caller was Beth. 'It's nice to see you again,' she said.

Beth stepped inside. 'How are . . . things?'

'Rose is still with us but I'm afraid Miss Plym found out about her.'

Oh no. 'Miss Plym? She's the woman who . . .'

'Likes to gossip, yes.'

'It sounds as though she's caused trouble.'

Victoria took Beth into the sitting room and told her the sorry story. Beth's heart squeezed at the thought of what Hannah must have gone through. How brave of her to admit to being Rose's mother like that. But what would happen when her parents learned about Rose, her father especially?

'I suppose there's still no sign of Rose's father?' Beth said.

'Not as far as I'm aware.'

Which meant that Hannah was facing public disgrace all alone. 'Poor girl,' Beth said.

'Indeed.' Victoria looked up at the sound of footsteps crunching over the gravel drive. 'Here comes Naomi.'

Moments later Naomi entered the sitting room.

'Shall I make tea?' Victoria asked.

'Not for me, thank you,' Beth said. 'I need to get back to the hospital while it's still light. I only came to see if there's anything I can do for Hannah and Rose.'

'Victoria told you what happened?' Naomi asked.

'She did, and I couldn't be sorrier. So . . .?'

'Hannah needs support, though giving it to her is likely to prove tricky,' Naomi said, with obvious regret. 'I'm hoping she'll still come to Churchwood to see Rose but she may be too scared of feeding the gossip in case it increases the chances of her father hearing about the situation. She doesn't want us calling on her, either.'

'Are people being nasty?'

'Some. Others are more sympathetic. I'm afraid it's a case of waiting to see what happens next. If we manage to see Hannah, we'll certainly tell her that you've been asking about her.'

'Thank you.' Beth rose to her feet. She'd call at the post office before leaving the village.

She got there to find it was busy. Choosing a box of writing paper, she joined the queue at the counter and became aware that two women ahead of her were talking. 'I don't know what Naomi was thinking, taking in that girl's illegitimate baby,' one said.

'I'm sure she meant well, but it'll have to be sent away now. There's no way the Powells can look after it properly, even if Jed Powell allowed it in his house. Not with Jane Powell so ill and that daughter getting up to who knows what with any man who happens to spare her skinny self a look.'

'Hannah Powell is a sweet girl and a brave one, too,' Beth said, unable to keep quiet.

Both women turned to her. 'You're entitled to your opinion, young lady, but we've known the Powells far longer than you,' one of them said.

'You tell her, Aggie,' her friend encouraged.

'If you've known the Powells for longer, why haven't you stepped in to help Hannah and her mother?' Beth demanded, and when they simply stared at her in surprise added, 'Well?'

The women continued to stare, their mouths opening and closing without finding words.

'You've no answer, it seems,' Beth concluded. '*Decent* women would have taken Hannah under their wings and helped. You didn't help, so what does that make you?'

From behind her came the sound of clapping. Beth whirled around to see Kate Kinsella applauding her. 'Well said!'

The women only pursed their lips. 'I'm not staying here to be insulted,' one said.

'Neither am I,' said the other.

Noses high, they flounced from the shop.

'Good riddance to them,' Kate said, moving to Beth's side. 'I think you're going to fit into Churchwood just fine, Nurse Ellis. Into the nicer part of it, anyway.'

'I spoke out of turn,' Beth told her, thinking that if Matron got to hear of her haranguing the locals, there might be trouble ahead.

'You spoke the truth,' Kate insisted. She looked around at the remaining customers. 'Anyone care to argue with that?'

Those other customers suddenly found themselves engrossed by the ceiling or the floor.

Kate grinned. 'I used to be the only rebel around here. Then Alice came – much more tactful than me but a real fighter against unfairness and unkindness – and now we have you speaking up, too. Well done.'

Beth didn't know what to say and was glad to be spared having to say anything because, with the nasty women gone, she was at the front of the queue. She paid for her notepaper and left, encountering a wink from Kate as she went.

She walked back to Stratton House and entered by a side door, intending to go up to her room. The sound of laughter reached her suddenly. It was quiet laughter but there was something intimate about it that suggested two people flirting. Beth's footsteps slowed and then stopped. She heard the murmur of voices followed by a giggle, and a heavy feeling came over her as she recognized the male voice. For a moment she was torn between retreating and walking on but decided to press onwards since her shoes were rubber-soled and her footsteps probably hadn't been heard. The voices came from an office. She glanced in as she passed and it was just as she'd imagined.

Babs Carter was leaning back against a wall. Smiling down on her, an arm resting on the wall above her head, was Oliver Lytton.

'So you'll come out with me?' Beth heard him say.

'Perhaps,' Babs answered, but the teasing note in her voice suggested she was playing games, because of course she'd go out with him.

289

Beth hastened onwards. It was stupid to feel hurt again since she already knew Oliver had a wandering eye for women. But hurt she felt. Foolish, too. At least she had the comfort of knowing she hadn't actually agreed to have a meal with him. It would spare her from the humiliation of being fobbed off with an excuse for cancelling the plan because he'd found a prettier girl.

Up in her room, she spent a few minutes staring out of the window and taking in deep breaths to steady herself. Then she changed into uniform and went down to Ward One.

Babs Carter was on duty there, too. Beth tried not to judge her. After all, Babs probably had no idea that Beth shared a history with Oliver and no idea that he'd asked her, too, to go out with him.

After Matron had given them a short update on how the patients were faring, Beth set about stripping the bed that was being vacated by Private Ollerenshaw. 'Well, Nurse,' he said, 'I'm looking forward to being at home with my family again, but I've been treated well here. You doctors and nurses have made me comfortable, and Alice – Mrs Irvine, I should say – has got me reading books. Who'd have thought it? I was never minded to read books before the war but now I love 'em. You'll tell her thanks from me?'

'I'll be sure to,' Beth promised.

She wished him good luck and waved as he made his way to the door. 'Nurse!' someone else called. It was Corporal Ron Barton. 'I need . . .'

Too late. He vomited over his bedclothes.

Babs Carter got to him first.

'I'm so sorry,' he said, and vomited again.

Babs took it in her stride. 'No need to apologize. We'll have you cleaned up in no time.'

She was a good nurse. A kind nurse. A decent colleague, too, since she always seemed willing to do more than her fair share of work. With her curving figure, smiling dark eyes and air of good cheer, it was no wonder that Oliver was attracted to her.

'I'll fetch clean bedding,' Beth offered, and Babs smiled, saying, 'Do you hear that, Corporal Barton? We'll soon have you shipshape again. Are you still feeling sick? No? Perhaps I should fetch you a bowl anyway . . .'

'How are you getting on with that Daphne du Maurier book?' Alice Irvine appeared at Beth's side by the linen cupboard, dressed for her walk home.

'Very well,' Beth said, rousing herself.

Oliver swept past. 'It's good to see you, Alice,' he said.

'It's good to be here.'

'You're looking as lovely as ever.'

'If I'm looking happy, it's because I've received a letter from my husband,' Alice replied and, with a small kick of shock, Beth realized that Alice hadn't warmed to the handsome doctor.

Oliver walked on, oblivious, but Alice lingered by Beth, saying, 'I always feel happy when Daniel writes. He's a loving, faithful man. Full of fun, too.'

'How . . . nice.' Had Beth imagined that Alice had stressed the word *faithful*? Was it a way of warning her about Oliver's wandering eye? Or of advising her that a man like that wasn't worth wasting emotion on? Beth wasn't sure whether to feel mortified at having given away her weakness for the man or grateful for the advice. She decided she felt both.

'I'll see you again soon,' Alice said, patting Beth's arm.

Beth went about her duties, but time and again her thoughts returned to Alice's comments. Alice was right about it not being worth squandering emotion on such a man as Oliver, and Beth determined to get over him sooner rather than later.

But what should she do about Babs? Warn her about Oliver's roving eye? Or mind her own business?

CHAPTER FIFTY-ONE

Victoria

Victoria hadn't written back to Paul yet. She wanted to take things slowly with him and feel confident that Arthur and Jenny were happy to have him in their lives even as an occasional visitor. She'd been delighted when they'd told her they liked him, but everyone at Foxfield had said the same thing. Victoria was keen to learn if Arthur and Jenny had any private thoughts and feelings about him but didn't wish to put them on the spot by asking them directly. She'd seen them playing with the coins Paul had given them – Arthur had a dime and Jenny a nickel – but so far she hadn't heard them saying anything about him.

Now Jenny had got into bed and Arthur had come up to wish his sister goodnight, Victoria crept along the landing to hear what they had to say to each other.

'Do you think Victoria will read me a story?' Jenny asked her brother.

'She might not have time,' Arthur told her. 'Not with the baby to look after.'

'Victoria is always looking after the baby.' Jenny sounded sad.

'Yes, but she knows I can read you a story if she can't. You won't miss out, Jen.'

It tore at Victoria's heart to realize that Jenny was

feeling pushed to the sidelines. Neglected, even. And Arthur probably felt the same.

She stood for a moment on the landing, aghast at letting them down and feeling tears prickle her eyes. But then she swallowed hard and entered the room with a smile. 'I'm here to read you a story,' she announced, vowing always to make time for reading in future.

Sitting on Jenny's bed, Victoria wrapped an arm around her. 'Which story would you like?'

They settled on *The Velveteen Rabbit*, one of Jenny's favourites.

Arthur stayed to listen, which was unusual but hardly surprising if he too felt he had to grab the crumbs that fell from the table of Victoria's attention.

Afterwards, she tucked Jenny in for the night, bending to kiss her and feeling Jenny's arms suddenly thrown around her neck. 'You do still love *us*?' Jenny asked.

'Of course I do! I need to spend time with Rose because she's small and needs help, but she won't be here for ever.'

'I like Rose,' Jenny said, 'but it'll be nice to have you to ourselves again.'

'We're a big household here. I can't ignore the other children,' Victoria warned.

'We're your special children, though,' Jenny said with obvious satisfaction, and Arthur also looked relieved.

Jenny snuggled down and Arthur ran back to the drawing room to finish a jigsaw. Victoria moved on to her own room, sitting on her bed and thinking over what Jenny had said.

Naomi had meant well in encouraging Victoria to see more of Paul but she hadn't understood how insecure the children were after losing both their parents and being uprooted by the war. They needed to know that Victoria loved them and wanted them so much that she'd never let anyone else come between them – not a baby and not a man. Victoria had sworn to their mother that she'd always put the children first and she'd meant it, too – whatever it might cost her personally. She might have lost sight of that recently but it was time to remember it now and do the right thing. Which was to ease Paul out of her life and focus on the children.

She said nothing about it to Naomi or anyone else during the rest of the evening but lay in bed later thinking it over and seeing no alternative.

Had any doubts remained, they would have been quashed the following morning when she heard Arthur and Jenny talking again.

'Come on, Jenny. You don't want to be late for Nearly School, do you?' Not being quite five, Jenny hadn't started proper school, but Evelyn Gregson, one of the teachers, had suggested that the bookshop open to four-year-olds on a couple of mornings each week for stories, drawing and play to prepare them for proper school. Naomi was one of the volunteers who helped on these mornings, which they called Nearly School.

'Of course not. I love Nearly School,' Jenny told him. 'I love everything about living here. This house, the book-shop . . . They make me happy.'

'Me too,' Arthur agreed.

'I hope we can stay here for ever.'

'So do I. I missed London when we first came but not any more. Now I wouldn't want to live anywhere else.'

Clearly, they were desperate for security.

Victoria never liked to put off painful things, reason-ing that the sooner they were behind her, the sooner she could start to recover. As soon as the children left, Victoria returned to her room to write a letter.

295

Dear Paul,

This is a difficult letter to write, since I fear that what I have to say won't be welcome. I like you, Paul. I like you very much. I enjoy your company and I know that everyone else here enjoyed your company when you came to tea.

But I'm afraid I think it's best if we don't see each other again. In fact, I must insist upon it. My other commitments need all of my attention. I thought that was the case at the beginning and now I'm more convinced of it than ever.

I'm sorry. Please believe that I wish you well.

Kindest regards,

Victoria Page.

She read it through but couldn't improve on it, so she tucked it into an envelope, wrote Paul's address on the front and added a stamp. There. Now to post it.

Her gaze fell on the coins Paul had so kindly given Arthur and Jenny and her face crumpled.

Dashing away tears, she told herself she was being ridiculous. She hardly knew Paul.

And yet . . . She supposed it must be the promise of what might have been that was oversetting her.

Fighting to get a grip on herself, she went downstairs, but between Rose's needs and Victoria's regular duties, it was a while before she was free to go into the village. Telling Suki and Ivy that she was popping out for a few minutes, she headed for the pillar box outside the post office. She lifted the envelope to the slot, only to pause as a wave of grief rippled through her.

'Are you all right?'

Startled, Victoria looked round to see Naomi. Why wasn't she at Nearly School? Perhaps she'd left the children with other volunteers while she called at the bakery in the hope of buying them buns. 'I'm . . . fine,' Victoria said, but it was obvious that Naomi saw that there was no truth in the words.

Her gaze moved to Victoria's letter and a mix of frustration and compassion showed on her face. 'I hope you're not writing to Paul to break things off between you?'

'I can hardly break off something that hasn't really begun.'

'Please don't post it,' Naomi urged. 'Give yourself more time before you do anything so drastic.'

Should she? Victoria hesitated again. She was exhausted after a largely sleepless night. Maybe she was overreacting to what she'd heard the children say. And she liked Paul so very much . . .

But no. She dropped the letter through the slot. 'It had to be done,' she insisted, only for tears to burst over her cheeks. 'Excuse me,' she said. 'I need . . . I'm sorry.'

Unable to say more, she ran back towards Foxfield.

CHAPTER FIFTY-TWO

Ruby

Ruby raised her eyebrows when Kate returned from the village shops but Kate only shook her head. There was still no news of Hannah's mystery man. It didn't bode well, but at least Hannah's father hadn't heard about Rose yet. As far as they knew.

In turn, Kate raised her eyebrows at Ruby, but a small shake of her head was all Ruby had to offer, too. It meant she'd got nowhere with trying to talk to Fred about Pearl. 'He just wheeled himself away the moment I mentioned her.'

Kate sighed, having apparently had the same experience when she'd tried to talk to Fred. 'Let's see what happens when he brings his new legs home this afternoon. I know he says he doesn't like them, but he may start to feel differently if he's able to walk into the house, even if he does sway like a drunken sailor.'

When Kate brought Fred back from the hospital, he managed to walk through the door on his new legs and, even though he moved awkwardly, Kate and Ruby clapped their hands and cried, 'Well done, Fred!'

'Glad to see you're making progress,' Pearl told him, but her manner was as stiff as his false legs and she went straight out again, mumbling something about oiling shears.

'Cup of tea, Fred?' Ruby offered, the effort of walking clearly having worn him out.

'Or maybe a beer to celebrate?' Kate suggested.

'Don't care which,' Fred said morosely. Far from looking triumphant, he looked depressed.

Kate fetched him a bottle of beer but it did nothing to lift his mood.

Neither did the news that Kate passed on from Alice. The gift shop in St Albans had sold three of Fred's woodcarvings and wanted to extend the range.

'I think Pearl is considering leaving us,' Ruby told him.

She was watching him carefully so saw his eyes flare momentarily but all he did was shrug. 'That's up to her, isn't it?'

Ruby hadn't realized that Timmy was on the stairs. 'I don't want Pearl to leave,' he told Ruby.

'Neither do I, Tim, but we might not be able to stop her.'

Timmy looked downcast. Life wasn't being kind to her boy just now and it was breaking Ruby's heart.

CHAPTER FIFTY-THREE

Hannah

He found out.

It had taken two days for the news to reach him but the moment her father slammed the van door so hard it almost burst off its hinges, Hannah guessed that he'd heard about Rose.

She bundled the children into the parlour. 'Stay there until I come and fetch you,' she told them.

'Why?' Milly asked. 'What's going on, Hannah? Why is Pa so angry?'

She'd heard that slam, too. Judging from their wary expressions, so had Simon and Susie.

'I haven't time to explain now,' Hannah told them. 'Just stay in here no matter what you hear.' Hannah had a beating in mind and, from the look on Milly's face, so did she.

Hannah closed the door and returned to the kitchen just as her father threw open the kitchen door and stepped inside with his fists clenched and anger blazing in his eyes. 'You little—'

He made a grab for her but Hannah jumped out of his reach, using the table as a barrier between them. 'How dare you bring shame on this family?' he roared. 'I'll tan your hide for this!'

He lunged for her again but Hannah moved swiftly away, circling the table.

She heard Michael speak in the parlour. 'Is Dad hurting Hannah?'

'Shush,' Milly told him, and Hannah caught the sound of a sob.

Then a creak overhead suggested that Ma was stirring. Hannah couldn't decide what to do. Evade her father for as long as possible in the hope that it would tire him at least a little before he beat her? Or surrender now and get the beating over with, out of sight of Ma and the children even though they'd be certain to hear it?

She sidestepped again as her father tried another grab. Missing her, he banged on the table in frustration. 'Don't you dare . . .'

The door to the stairs opened and Ma appeared, still in her nightgown. 'What on earth's the matter?' she asked.

'*She's* the matter,' her husband said, pointing towards Hannah. 'That little—'

'Jed, please!' Ma protested, but Hannah didn't want her mother involved.

'Go back to bed, Ma,' she urged, trying to be gentle.

A sneer twisted her father's face. 'You don't want your mother hearing what you've done? Is that it?'

'She isn't well.'

'She's going to feel a lot sicker when she knows what you've been up to.'

'Hannah, what's this about?' Ma asked, and it grieved Hannah's heart to see that Ma's frailty meant she had to hold on to the doorframe for support.

'She's been lying with some man, that's what it is,' Hannah's father announced.

Ma looked bewildered. 'Hannah?'

'That's not the worst of it,' Pa said. 'She's had his kid.'

'No, Jed! She wouldn't. She couldn't have. You've got it wrong.'

Pa only sneered again. 'What do you know of anything when you spend all day in bed? She could have had ten kids and you wouldn't have noticed.'

Ma looked at Hannah and must have seen the truth in her eyes. The shock on Ma's face made Hannah want to weep. 'Ma, I'm sorry.'

Ma's hand went to her mouth. She shook her head in confused distress.

Hannah took a step towards her only to spring back as Pa lunged forward again.

'Stop, Jed!' Ma cried. 'Hurting Hannah won't help.'

'It's what she deserves for bringing shame on this family. Who's the father? That's what I'd like to know. He deserves a good hiding, too.'

Ma looked back at Hannah, her expression perplexed and no wonder. She'd had no idea that there was a boy in her daughter's life.

Hannah simply shook her head. She wasn't telling.

A thought must have occurred to Ma because she suddenly burst out with, 'Did someone *force* himself on you, darling?'

'Eh?' Pa said, the possibility not having occurred to him.

'Hannah's a good girl,' Ma insisted. 'She would never have . . . She wouldn't have . . . Not without being forced.'

'Who did it?' Pa roared.

Hannah hated having to disappoint her mother but she wasn't going to lie. 'No one forced himself on me.'

'Thank goodness,' Ma said, though relief would doubtless be followed by the realization that Hannah had given herself willingly.

Pa was faster to understand. 'That means you wanted what he did, you little—'

'Just tell us who he is,' Ma said, quietly now. She looked

302

horribly tired. 'Maybe he can be persuaded to marry you.'

'Unless he's already wed,' Pa said.

'I'm sorry, but I'm not going to talk about my daughter's father,' Hannah said.

'Your daughter? The baby is a girl?' Another thought struck Ma, her fatigue making her reactions slow. 'Where *is* the baby?'

'Someone – a kind person – is looking after her for me,' Hannah explained.

'Someone's looking after it *for you*?' Pa scoffed. 'Until you can bring it here, is that what you think? Well, you're mistaken, girl. No child born on the wrong side of the blanket is going to be welcome here and neither is its slut of a mother.'

'You want me to leave?' Hannah asked.

'You think you deserve to stay after what you've done?'

'Jed, no!' Ma cried.

'Very well,' Hannah said. 'I'll leave you to look after Ma and the children. It means getting them all up in the mornings, of course. Serving them breakfast. Feeding them their lunches and their dinners, too. Washing sheets, towels and clothes. Ironing those that need ironing. Mending any that need mending. Cleaning the house. Doing the shopping . . .'

'We need Hannah,' Ma pleaded.

Pa's anger had undergone a check as Hannah listed all the responsibilities that would fall on his shoulders. He looked frustrated, as though he wished he could throw her out on the street there and then but a glimmer of common sense must have told him he'd never manage.

'All right,' he said. 'I'll not make you leave *now*.' He was saving face by suggesting he could change his mind at any moment. 'But you'll be out on your ear if you so much

303

as look at a man again. As for that ill-gotten baby, you can tell your friend that she won't be looking after it any more. Not *for you*. Because you'll be having nothing to do with it. Tell her she's to send it to an orphanage or wherever else unwanted kids are sent. And tell her tomorrow.'

Retorts bubbled up in Hannah's throat. *Hypocrite! I'm not the only one who's let the family down. You're letting us down with your behaviour, too. A grown man playing around with a woman who's young enough to be your daughter . . .*

But she looked at Ma, so weak as she clung to the doorframe, and thought of the wide-eyed children waiting in the next room. And she swallowed the words down, hating to do it but feeling she hadn't a choice. Ma would be devastated if she knew about Margueritte Moore and, for all that Jed Powell was a horrible man, the family needed him. Without him they'd have no money for food or fuel or Ma's medicines. They'd have nothing.

CHAPTER FIFTY-FOUR

Victoria

'There, there, darling.' Victoria held a sobbing Hannah in her arms. The girl was distraught and no wonder, since she believed she was losing her much-loved daughter.

Not that Victoria had been surprised to hear that Jed Powell was refusing to offer a home to baby Rose. It was understandable that he was feeling anger and shame over Hannah's fall from grace. It was also understandable that taking in a new baby might seem dauntingly impractical given Mrs Powell's illness and the fact that there were already six children straining both the available living space and household budget. But had he really needed to be so cruel in his treatment of Hannah? Jed Powell sounded a brute.

It wouldn't help matters to say so, though. Hannah's heart was breaking at the thought of losing her child and the best thing Victoria could do was simply hold her and let her cry.

Perhaps later Victoria would mention that children who were adopted by others could be loved and happy. She had her own experience to draw on there, having taken on Arthur and Jenny. They missed their real parents, of course, but they had Victoria to love them and fight for them now.

Not that the circumstances of Hannah's child were identical. Victoria had never known Arthur and Jenny's father but she'd come to know their mother well. The children, too, so she was hardly a stranger when she took them under her wing. Even so, many children were adopted by strangers and enjoyed the security and affection of being very much wanted.

With no word having come from Rose's father, Victoria could see no alternative to the baby being sent away from Churchwood. It wasn't as though Victoria could look after her indefinitely. As a temporary cook-housekeeper, Victoria's job – and therefore her home and income – was far from guaranteed into the future, and finding an alternative position was already likely to be difficult with an eight-year-old boy and four-year-old girl in tow. With a baby as well, it would surely be nigh on impossible.

Besides, Jed Powell might insist on his unwanted granddaughter being sent miles away from Hertfordshire if he considered that having her living nearby would be awkward and embarrassing to him and a distraction to Hannah, too. Victoria had little knowledge of the law but she imagined that Hannah's age would mean all the power lay in Jed Powell's hands and it would be his decision that counted with the authorities.

Poor Hannah. Victoria exchanged sympathetic looks with Naomi but both stayed silent so Hannah could work through her grief undisturbed. And surely that grief was far more profound than the lowness Victoria was feeling after writing to Paul? Again and again, she'd reminded herself that she barely knew the man so it was ridiculous to feel so upset.

'You could always write back to him to say you made a mistake,' Naomi had suggested, but Victoria had shaken her head and said, 'I didn't make a mistake.'

She was still sure of that. But, oh, it hurt!

In time Hannah's sobs eased, though they left her with

her breath juddering and catching in her throat. 'M—Rose's father will be so upset if Rose is sent away,' she said.

M? Did the man's name begin with a letter M? Victoria looked at Naomi enquiringly, but Naomi only shrugged, probably because she knew of no young men in Barton whose names began with that letter.

'You still haven't heard from him?' Naomi asked gently.

'No,' Hannah said.

Victoria and Naomi exchanged more looks. Their faith in Rose's father was weakening by the day.

After a moment Naomi sighed and asked, 'Is your father likely to come here to check that Rose has been sent away?'

Hannah wiped her face on a handkerchief Victoria had supplied. 'I don't think so. He wouldn't be *comfortable* here, and I don't think he'd go to the bother.'

'Perhaps we'll hold on to Rose for a little longer, then,' Naomi said.

'You will?' Hannah launched herself off the sofa to throw herself on the floor at Naomi's feet and clutch her lap. 'Thank you!'

Naomi stroked Hannah's curls. 'We can't keep her for much longer, though. Her birth needs to be registered and it wouldn't do for her to get too attached to us. It wouldn't be fair to her.'

'Her father will come soon. I'm sure of it.'

'Let's hope so,' Naomi said, but her voice lacked conviction.

Victoria cleared her throat. 'We need to talk about what you're going to tell *your* father, Hannah. I suggest you tell him you passed on his instructions but don't mention that we're going to ignore them for the time being. We want your father to stay away, and if he thinks we're ignoring his wishes . . .'

'He might come and be horrid to you and Mrs Harrington,' Hannah finished.

'He might also have Rose taken away by force,' Victoria said.

Hannah looked horrified.

'We're not suggesting that you *lie* to your father,' Naomi said. 'Just that you're selective in what you tell him.'

'I shouldn't need to lie,' Hannah said. 'I'll tell him you understand his instructions. That should be enough to keep him away.'

Would it, though? They'd need to be careful if they were to avoid arousing his suspicions. And that might involve more heartache for Hannah. 'Your father drives a butcher's van, doesn't he?' Victoria asked her.

Hannah nodded.

'He might grow suspicious if he sees you coming to Foxfield when he's driving through the village. I know we have the cover story of cooking lessons, but that was before he knew about Rose.'

'You think I shouldn't come any more?' Hannah looked woebegone.

'Not for a few days, anyway,' Victoria said. 'I think you'd be taking a big risk.'

'Victoria's right,' Naomi agreed. 'I know it'll be hard for you to stay away but—'

'I'll do it,' Hannah said, though her bottom lip trembled and more tears shimmered in her eyes.

'Might there be a way of getting messages to you?' Victoria asked. 'Messages about Rose, letting you know how she's getting on? A way of you getting messages to us, too, if there are any developments or you need our help?'

'That's a good idea,' Naomi said. 'I assume we shouldn't post notes through your door.'

Hannah shook her head vigorously to confirm that might only cause more trouble. She thought for a moment then said, 'There's a row of three sycamore trees on the Barton Road before you reach our cottage. Perhaps messages could be nailed to the back of one of those trees?'

'They might be destroyed by wind or rain,' Naomi pointed out. 'I have a small tin we can use to hold messages and I can ask Bert to wedge it between a couple of large stones. He has some white rockery stones at his market garden; I'm sure he won't object to those being used since they'll be easy to spot.'

'You're quite a way out of Churchwood so I don't feel we can promise to leave messages or collect them every day,' Victoria said. 'But we'll try our best to let you know how Rose is getting on.'

Naomi nodded. 'Don't be alarmed if you hear a rumour that Rose has been sent away. We need to circulate such a rumour and keep Rose hidden again so no one tells your father she's still here. We'll leave a message for you if she really needs to be sent away.'

'I understand,' Hannah said.

'That's settled, then,' Naomi continued. 'Now I suggest you give Rose one more cuddle and then go home. You don't want your father to come looking for you.'

'No, I don't.' Hannah shuddered.

She cradled Rose and dropped a kiss on her head, then bundled Susie and Simon into the pram and went on her way.

She was sobbing again, which tore at Victoria's sympathies, but at least tears might convince Jed Powell that Hannah had followed his instructions and was crying because she'd never see her child again.

Victoria only hoped the day wouldn't come when that happened for real. It all turned on Rose's father.

CHAPTER FIFTY-FIVE

Naomi

There were many good men in the world. Naomi knew that. There were men she admired and liked – Archibald Lovell, Adam Potts, Alice's Daniel, Kate's Leo, May's Marek, Janet's Caleb . . . And there was one man she loved as well as admired. Bert, of course.

But there were other men who were far from good and she'd met a few of them in her years on earth. Jed Powell was one. So was Alexander. Both were bullies in their different ways.

Alexander might not use his fists to dominate but he used words of anger and intimidation. Naomi couldn't wait to get rid of him in the divorce. Thankfully, his son, William, was due any time now.

Bert was the first to notice when William walked between the Foxfield gateposts. 'Here comes young spider-legs,' he announced.

Naomi joined him at the sitting room window. William was a tall, thin boy with awkward spindly limbs that had inspired his nickname. Noticing them at the window, he waved and gave a grin that suggested he was glad to be here. That grin warmed Naomi's heart. Who'd have thought Alexander's secret son could have become so precious to her? But so it was, and she'd have to take care to ensure he could decline the request she was going to make of him without feeling guilty or ungrateful.

'I'll leave you alone with him for a while,' Bert said. 'It might increase the pressure on the lad if I'm here, too.'

Naomi nodded. Bert's proposal was both sensible and sensitive. 'You won't go far?'

'Only into the drawing room.'

He kissed her, wished her luck, and left, Naomi following as far as the hall where she opened the door to William. He wrapped his skinny arms around her but, when he drew back, his eyes – as clear and blue as Alexander's but so much gentler! – showed concern. 'I hope my father hasn't—'

He broke off as Suki entered the hall from the kitchen. 'Tea?' she asked, smiling at William, who'd become a friend.

'Yes, please, Suki,' Naomi said.

William took off his coat and dumped his bag in a corner then followed Naomi into the sitting room. 'I hope he hasn't caused trouble for you?' he said, finishing the question he'd begun.

'We'll talk about your father in a moment. Tell me about your journey first. You're here in good time so I assume it was easy.'

'It was,' William confirmed. He was at school near St Albans, a mere bus ride away. But he was keener to talk about Alexander. 'I really didn't tell him about your engagement.'

'I believe you.'

William looked relieved. Clearly, it had been preying on his mind. 'I don't know who did tell him, though.'

'I'm not sure that matters. Bert and I haven't kept it hidden, so your father could have heard about it from any of many sources.'

Suki knocked on the door and entered with a tray of tea things and a large sandwich she must have had ready. 'I expect you're hungry,' she told William.

'I'm always hungry.'

Naomi thanked Suki and invited William to eat. He did so with gusto since his appetite was good, though he never seemed to get any fatter. Afterwards, he picked up his teacup. 'There was something . . . triumphant about my father when he told me he knew of the engagement. Is he trying to use it against you somehow?'

Naomi passed over the letter Alexander had written. William read it through and looked ashamed. 'You're not going to give in to him?'

'Certainly not. I have an idea for how to respond but it could affect you, William, and I need to know how you feel before I act.'

William's expression turned wary. 'What is it?'

'First, let me assure you that I'll understand if you don't like the sound of it. I wouldn't hurt you for the world and I hope you know that. Promise me you'll tell me if it makes you feel uneasy. I shan't hold it against you.'

'All right.'

Naomi took a deep breath and told him what she had in mind.

'Yes,' he said. 'Do it.'

'Take some time to think about it.'

She didn't want him agreeing to the plan to please her, only to come to regret it.

'But—'

'Later, William. Now I'd like to take you into the drawing room to meet someone.'

'Not another waif and stray?' he asked. He considered himself to be one of them.

'Well . . .'

'You're the kindest woman on earth,' he told her fervently.

Bert was playing horses with Jenny and Flower when they entered the drawing room. With a little girl on each of his large knees, he was jigging them up and down in a pretend race. 'Faster, faster!' Jenny yelled.

'Yes, faster!' Flower echoed.

But when the girls saw William they slid off Bert's knees to hug the new arrival. William was a favourite with the evacuee families. He swung the girls around, greeted the others and chatted for a while before looking about and asking, 'Where's the newcomer?'

Victoria turned from the window. She had Rose in her arms. 'A baby?' William said, amazed. 'Whose is she?'

'She's a secret,' Jenny told him.

'Yes, but William is one of us so he can share it,' Victoria said. It crumpled Naomi's heart to see how wan and forlorn she looked, but, always dignified in adversity, Victoria was making an effort to hide it.

She told him about Rose and Hannah. 'Hannah sounds very brave,' William said, for she was younger even than him.

'May I?' He gestured to the baby and Victoria transferred Rose into his arms.

For a moment he was quiet. But then he looked up at Naomi. 'She's beautiful,' he said. 'And innocent. Just as I'm innocent of the circumstances of my birth. If people can't see that, they're . . . Well, they're not worth bothering about.'

Naomi guessed where he was heading. 'William, I meant it when I said you should take time to think about what we just discussed. Take the weekend.'

Even if, for Naomi, the suspense would be hard to bear.

CHAPTER FIFTY-SIX

Beth

Poor Hannah! Beth had heard the news from Alice, who often volunteered at the hospital on Saturday mornings.

'What can I do?' Beth had asked.

'It's difficult to know what any of us can do except be kind to Hannah if we see her and leave a note or two for her in the tin I just mentioned. And keep hoping that Rose's father will appear.'

The likelihood of Beth seeing Hannah by chance had to be tiny. Unless Beth walked over to see her, of course, but if she couldn't knock on the door, she'd be wasting her time. Perhaps she'd write a note, though, and leave it in the tin to show Hannah that she had friends who cared about her.

Friends. Beth had been thinking about that word often. Babs wasn't her friend exactly, but Beth liked her and hated the thought of her being made unhappy by Oliver. Would an almost-friend warn her about him? Beth still couldn't decide.

In the hope of clearing her mind, she went out to walk among the trees during her break. Hearing voices up ahead, she paused. Were Oliver and Babs sneaking some time together out here? Beth turned to walk in a different direction but then laughter reached her. It wasn't the full-bodied giggle of Babs. It was a lighter sound.

'You look as fresh as a daisy, Pauline,' Beth heard Oliver say.

Pauline? Pauline Evans?

Beth scanned the wood in disbelief but there they were, Oliver leaning back against a tree and holding Pauline's waist as she stood in front of him.

'I look no different from usual,' Pauline told him teasingly.

'Then your usual is delightful,' he said. 'You must gladden the patients' eyes.'

Just as she was gladdening his eyes – or so Oliver implied.

'Now, are you going to put me out of my misery by agreeing to come out with me on the motorbike?' he asked. 'We can go for a meal . . .'

Beth walked away, with her heart racing.

Babs Carter and Pauline Evans were the best of friends. They couldn't know that Oliver was showing an interest in both of them, and it didn't bode well for their friendship if they found out about each other.

Beth's dilemma was even more complicated now.

CHAPTER FIFTY-SEVEN

Ruby

Alice had delivered the sad news about Hannah to
Brimbles Farm on her way to the hospital on Saturday
morning. Ruby had been brooding about it ever since.

Would Jed Powell hurt his daughter? Would he learn
that Rose remained at Foxfield and have her taken away
by the authorities?

And how was Hannah feeling, stuck out on the Barton
Road without friends and protectors, abandoned by the
man she loved and probably knowing that Rose's days in
Churchwood must be coming to an end?

By Sunday morning Ruby was out of patience with
waiting for further news. Alice had told them about the
message tin and they'd all offered to use the bicycle to
help to collect and deliver messages. Ruby wrote one now:

> *Sorry to hear the news but remember you have friends you can*
> *call on if you need help or just want to chat. I'm one of those*
> *friends. So are Kate and Pearl. Love from Ruby x*
> *PS The vegetables near this tin are for you.*

She'd collected a small bag of them.

Ruby told Kate that she was going out and cycled
towards Hannah's tumbledown cottage, hating the bike as
much as ever but huffing and puffing with determination.

It was Ruby's intention to cycle past the cottage in the hope that Hannah might see her and come out to talk if the coast was clear of Jed Powell, though it was a Sunday so he was likely to be at home. There was no sign of the butcher's van on the patch of scrubby land outside the house when Ruby reached it, but perhaps he didn't have the van on days he didn't work.

She resisted even glancing towards the cottage as she passed, for fear of raising his suspicions. Instead, she rode on for a hundred yards or so, waited for a few minutes to give the impression that she had other business near Barton and then turned and cycled back. Again, she avoided looking at the cottage but brought the bike to a halt about fifty feet beyond it at the place Alice had described as the home for the message tin. Dragging the bike into the bushes, Ruby found the tin and placed her note inside.

She didn't rush off, waiting to give Hannah a chance to come out. A moment later, nearby bushes rustled and Hannah appeared.

'How are you?' Ruby asked, though she could see the girl looked frail and anxious.

'Missing Rose.'

Touched by Hannah's woebegone face, Ruby hugged her and Hannah cried in her arms.

'Sorry,' Hannah eventually said, drawing back to wipe her eyes.

'It's fine to cry,' Ruby assured her. 'You're not visiting Churchwood any more, I believe?'

'I daren't risk it in case it makes my father realize Rose is still there. I can imagine what the people there are saying about me, though. The gossip has already spread to Barton. A gaggle of women were whispering together when I went to the grocer's but broke off suddenly when

317

I walked in. One of them glared at me and another one sniffed. She muttered something that sounded like *strumpet*. I don't know that word but I can guess what it means.'

'I'm sorry,' Ruby said. She wanted to tell Hannah that she understood exactly how it felt to have a child out of wedlock, but how could she? She couldn't. Not without exposing Timmy's situation. Even so, guilt at her silence clawed at her.

'I'm going to lose Rose, aren't I?' Hannah said.

'You still haven't heard from her father?' Ruby's voice was gentle.

Hannah shook her head. 'I haven't lost faith in him, but time is running out.' Tears were shimmering in her eyes again.

Ruby cradled the sobbing girl for a second time.

'Remember you have friends and there are places where you'll always be welcome,' she said. 'Foxfield, The Linnets, Brimbles Farm . . . I'm sure Beth will be concerned about you, too, when she hears what's happened. You're not alone, Hannah.'

As comfort it still felt inadequate.

Hannah glanced over her shoulder as though fearing her father might appear at any moment. 'I should go, but thanks for coming.'

She took the note from the tin, nodded an acknowledgement of the vegetables and left.

Ruby cycled home and found Kenny in the farmyard. 'I've been to see Hannah Powell,' she said. 'Her father knows about the baby.'

'I didn't tell him!'

'I'm not suggesting you did. Word was bound to reach him sooner or later. But he doesn't know yet that Rose is still at Naomi's house. He thinks she's been sent away.'

'Why hasn't she?'

'Because Hannah still hopes Rose's father will appear.'

'Doesn't sound likely. Not if he hasn't even written.'

'I think Hannah is coming round to realizing that, but until then we need to keep her secret. We need to keep our own secret, too. About Timmy, I mean.'

She was conscious of that feeling of shame again. Of guilt in letting Hannah think that she alone had to bear the stigma of being an unmarried mother in the area. But as always when the guilt came, pictures of Timmy swam before Ruby's mind's eye. He was her first responsibility. And Ruby had to protect him above all others.

CHAPTER FIFTY-EIGHT

Naomi

Bert and William rushed away the moment the church service ended so William could spend a few more hours in the market garden before he returned to school the following morning. With her short legs and bad feet, Naomi intended to walk home at a more leisurely pace.

She spoke to a few people as she made her way through the churchyard and nodded to several others. Doubtless, some of them were gossiping about Hannah but, having made it plain that she wouldn't hear a bad word against the girl, no one did so in Naomi's hearing. Not even Marjorie.

Guessing that Marjorie had shut herself up at home and was likely to be too upset to set foot in the village for a while, Naomi had called round to see her yesterday. Marjorie had answered her knock by opening the door only a couple of inches and peeping through the tiny space.

'I'm not here to apologize for the way I spoke to you,' Naomi had said, to avoid any misunderstanding on that point. 'But I do care about you, and I want to know that you're all right.'

Marjorie had opened the door a little wider, enough to show that her eyes were red-rimmed and her nose bright pink. The handkerchief she was holding also gave testimony to the fact that she was tearful still. 'You've never spoken so harshly to me before, Naomi.'

'Perhaps I should have done. Are you going to leave me standing here or let me inside?'

Marjorie stood back so Naomi could enter but more tears formed in her eyes. 'I hope you're not going to berate me all over again.'

'Not unless I need to. But I want some assurance that you've learned your lesson at last. Gossip causes harm. Real harm. We were keeping baby Rose a secret to give Hannah and her child's father a chance to plan a future together. Thanks to you, that chance may have been lost.'

'I'm sorry. I didn't think . . .'

'That's the problem, Marjorie. You never do think. You let your excitement run away with you instead. So here are some words of advice. The next time you scent a whiff of gossip, *wait* before doing anything about it. And ask yourself an important question. Which is this: might you cause distress if you spread the gossip? If in doubt, don't do it.'

'I'll try, Naomi. I promise.'

Marjorie's words hadn't filled Naomi with confidence but they'd been a start. And if Naomi kept repeating the advice, maybe – just maybe – Marjorie could reform. 'Perhaps you'd like to put the kettle on now,' Naomi had said, and Marjorie had jumped up in heartfelt relief that at least some of her disgrace had been lifted from her shoulders.

Trudging homewards now, Naomi's thoughts turned to Victoria. How selfless and brave that young woman was! But Naomi still believed Victoria had made a mistake in dismissing Paul Scarletti. Of course, the children had to come first, but perhaps a way could have been found of reconciling the children's interests with a little romance for the woman who cared for them.

Just then, Naomi realized Edith Mead was cutting back some early growth from the hedgerow that bordered their drive.

'Edith,' she said, only for Edith to gasp and clutch at her heart.

'Sorry. I didn't mean to startle you,' Naomi told her. 'I just wanted to ask if you're aware of our bookshop concert next Saturday.'

'I'm aware of it, but I shan't be going.'

'It's on a Saturday evening. Surely, you won't be busy then?'

'Work on a farm is never done. Good day to you, Mrs Harrington.' With that, Edith walked away up her drive, even though some straggles of hedgerow remained to be cut.

Oh dear. Naomi hadn't meant to hound the poor woman. With Hannah doubtless suffering out on the Barton Road, this wasn't proving to be the best of days.

But hours later, William and Bert returned from the market garden and William said, 'I haven't changed my mind about what we discussed on Friday. You told me to think about your plan and I've thought about it a lot. I want you to go ahead with it.'

'Are you sure? If you need more time . . .'

'I don't. Obviously, I'm hoping my father will give in to you, but if he doesn't, I'm prepared to take the consequences.'

'Those consequences could affect your sister as well as you,' Naomi pointed out.

'But my father will decide whether to let those consequences loose or not, so the responsibility will be his. I'll make sure my sister knows it. My mother, too.'

Bert patted William's arm approvingly. 'Good lad,' he said.

'William, play with us!' Jenny cried, and, as the boy got down on the floor to do just that, Bert moved to Naomi's side.

'A fine boy, that, despite his parentage.'

'He is.'

'So you're going ahead?'

'I am. But I don't know when.'

'Do it tomorrow. Get it over with.'

'But what if something happens with Hannah and Rose?'

'You'll only be away for a few hours and there'll be other people here to fight Hannah's corner, if needed. Victoria . . . Alice . . .'

'All right,' Naomi said. 'I'll go tomorrow. Could you spare the time to come with me?'

She'd always thought of him as bear-like, but now there was something of the wolf about him as he smiled and said, 'I wouldn't miss it for a hundred pounds.'

CHAPTER FIFTY-NINE

Victoria

'Look, Victoria!' Jenny said, waving a sheet of paper. 'Do you remember I told you that we learned about Noah and his ark in Sunday School this morning?'

'I do remember.'

'I've drawn a picture of them.'

Victoria took the sheet of paper. 'Wonderful elephants,' she praised. 'I like the tiger, too. Its stripes are lovely. This is a cow, isn't it? And a sheep?'

'A pig, too. And a dog and a cat and a zebra . . . I know the animals went into the ark two by two, but I didn't have enough room for two of each animal so I'm pretending some of them are in the ark already.'

'That makes perfect sense. Have you drawn anything, Arthur?'

'I helped Jenny with her drawing.'

'Arthur drew the elephants,' Jenny admitted and, grinning, Arthur ruffled her hair.

'I only helped a little bit,' he said, which was probably a fib, but this was how they were with each other: kind and generous.

'Can we play catch now?' Jenny asked her brother.

'We can,' he confirmed.

'Can I play?' little Flower asked him.

'Course you can,' he said, and she gave him one of her hero-worshipping smiles.

They ran off into the garden and Victoria stood at a window watching them play for a while. How happy they were. How secure and settled.

How worth her sacrifice. A bleak feeling passed through her but she straightened her shoulders and went about her day. There was no place for self-pity in this life she'd chosen, even if her smiles felt weighted with lead and even if she did feel the prickle of tears sometimes.

CHAPTER SIXTY

Beth

Beth felt as though a carousel were turning in her head – round and round and round again – but in place of cheerful wooden horses there were problems. Babs Carter's hopes for her romance with Oliver Lytton, for one. Ditto Pauline Evans's hopes. Hannah Powell and baby Rose . . .

Besides these problems, Beth's romantic disappointment was beginning to feel like old news which had grown stale and lost its urgency. In fact, when Oliver had said, 'You're looking pretty, Beth,' she'd stared at him in astonishment and then almost rolled her eyes.

And when he'd said, 'About that meal . . .' she'd said, 'No, thank you,' and walked away to see to a patient.

There was little she could do about Hannah – she'd passed the girl's cottage on a walk to Barton but hadn't seen her – but when it came to Babs and Pauline, responsibility sat like a squat goblin on Beth's shoulders. The trouble was that she couldn't decide on the direction that responsibility should take.

Should she warn the girls that Oliver was playing games with them? Or should she keep quiet about what she knew and leave them to discover Oliver's games by themselves, sparing them the additional pain of going through their humiliation in front of her?

It wasn't hard to imagine that Oliver had told them the same thing he'd told Beth back in London when he wanted their relationship to be kept secret: 'I think we should be discreet about the fact that we're seeing each other. At least until I'm more settled here. I don't want Matron to think I'm distracting you from your work.'

Had each girl wondered why the other was going around sparkling with excitement only to meet with evasion when they'd questioned it? Or were they each so occupied in floating on their respective clouds of elation that they'd barely noticed that the other was floating happily, too?

There was an alternative to speaking to them or keeping quiet: Beth could involve Alice, who might know the best way to approach the problem. But Babs and Pauline might then assume that Beth had been gossiping about them. Perhaps even spying on them. If only she could decide what to do! Standing at the window of her small room, she looked out as twilight descended, wishing it would bring her some wisdom.

A knock sounded on her door. Now what? Beth blushed and felt the guilt goblin prod her conscience when she opened the door to find Babs Carter outside. 'I wonder if I might borrow a hair clip?' Babs asked. 'Two, if you've got them? I seem to have lost one and I'm guaranteed to lose another.'

'Erm . . . Yes. I'll just . . .' Beth headed for the small tin in which she kept her clips.

She expected her visitor to wait at the door but instead Babs followed her inside, glancing out of the window and then looking around the room. 'Settled in?' she asked.

'Yes, thank you.'

'It's lovely to overlook trees, isn't it? I like that about

Churchwood – it's fresh and green, but it isn't boring. Not with the bookshop and the friendly people in the village.'

'It's a nice place,' Beth agreed. She handed over the clips. 'Well,' she added in the sort of tone that signalled the conversation was at an end – or so she hoped.

But Babs sat down on the bed and gestured to a photograph that stood on the window ledge. 'Is that your family?'

'My parents, yes.'

'They look to be good people.'

'They are.'

Babs still showed no sign of wanting to leave. Beth didn't wish to be rude but . . .

'He hurt you, didn't he?' Babs said suddenly.

What? Hot colour scorched Beth's cheeks and her heartbeat quickened painfully. 'I'm not sure I understand what you—'

'Our handsome doctor, Oliver Lytton.'

For a moment Beth was too flustered to answer. It was mortifying that Babs had guessed how Beth felt about him. Had other nurses guessed, too? 'I don't talk about personal matters,' she finally got out. 'And it would hardly be appropriate for me to talk about a man you're . . .' Oh, what was the right phrase? 'A man you're involved with.'

Babs raised an eyebrow. 'You don't really believe I'm serious about him?'

Wasn't she? 'I don't know,' Beth said, surprised. 'It isn't my business anyway.'

'I'm not a fool and neither is Pauline.'

The mention of Pauline's name must have made Beth's eyes flare in shock because Babs laughed. 'Pauline and I . . . We got the measure of handsome Oliver as soon as we realized he was pursuing both of us. In secret, of course. We're not supposed to know about each other but, of course, we do.'

Goodness. 'I'm glad neither of you are being taken in by him,' Beth said. But why were the nurses still encouraging him?

'I'll bet he's set about making the hearts of nurses flutter at every hospital he's served in,' Babs said.

Beth shrugged but the comment reminded her of Cassandra Carlisle and cost her a pang.

'Pauline and I know what he's like because we're best friends and tell each other things,' Babs explained. 'Perhaps you weren't as lucky.'

Had Beth been fooled into thinking Oliver really cared for her because she had no close friends to warn her that he only wanted secrecy so he could play the field? It certainly hadn't helped.

'Oliver still likes you,' Babs suggested now.

Oh, heavens. She wasn't angry, was she? 'I haven't encouraged him,' Beth said. 'If he wants me at all, it's only as backup for when no one more exciting is available.'

'It's the same for all of us,' Babs said, waving away any need for Beth to apologize. 'Oliver Lytton needs taking down a peg or two. Pauline and I wonder if you'd like to help us to do it?'

'Help how?' Beth asked.

Babs patted the space next to her to invite Beth to join her on the bed. It was as though she was also inviting her to become a friend. A proper friend.

Beth breathed in deeply, straightened her shoulders and sat.

'Well,' Babs began. 'What we're thinking is this . . .'

CHAPTER SIXTY-ONE

Hannah

Hearing something drop through the letterbox, Hannah ran to see what it was, hope swelling in her heart. But she found just a single envelope addressed to Pa. A bill. Not a letter from Mattie.

It meant she'd have nothing to report when she went to the tin Bert had left behind the sycamores, except for the fact that her father still seemed unaware that Rose remained at Foxfield.

'Well?' he'd demanded when she'd returned from Foxfield, three days ago now.

'I told them what you said.'

'And?'

'They said they understood your instructions.'

He'd nodded and then his lip had curled. 'Let that be a lesson to you in behaving like a . . .'

Hannah had banged a pan on the stove to drown out the word but it had hurt her even so. What she felt for Mattie was love. Pure love. And the pain of being away from him – from Rose also – was intense.

Several notes had been left in the tin for Hannah so far. From Victoria, Mrs Harrington, Alice, Ruby and Beth, all wishing her well. How kind they were.

But Rose couldn't stay at Foxfield for ever. Not only was she making more work for the household, she was also putting strain on everyone by needing to be kept secret. Churchwood might know of Rose's birth but no one could know that she remained at Foxfield in case word of it reached Hannah's father. Mrs Harrington had apparently set about creating the impression in the village that Rose had been given up, but all it would take for that impression to crumble was a slip of the tongue from one of the Foxfield children. Besides, there was the law and all that registration business . . .

Would Hannah go to the tin today to find a note saying Rose was being sent away?

Gathering Simon and Susie together, she hastened to see if a new message had been left for her. There was nothing. Was that a good thing or a bad thing? Hannah only wished she knew.

CHAPTER SIXTY-TWO

Naomi

'Ready?' Bert asked when he called for Naomi on Monday morning.

'Ready,' she confirmed. 'Alexander needs to learn once and for all that I'm not to be browbeaten.'

'What he needs is to be thrown down a lift shaft and left there, but let's content ourselves with a verbal confrontation. I'm rather looking forward to it.' Bert sent her a grin.

William accompanied them as far as St Albans where he was at school. 'I wish I could come back to Churchwood for the concert next weekend,' he said, hugging Naomi.

'It's your mother's birthday and you can't miss that,' she answered, 'but we'll see you soon.'

Bert hugged him, too, and he loped away on his long, spidery legs.

Naomi and Bert headed for the station to catch the train into London.

'Good morning,' the receptionist said when they arrived at Alexander's office. The girl was new and clearly had no clue as to Naomi's identity. 'Do you have an appointment?'

'I don't need an appointment to see my husband,' Naomi told her.

'I'm sorry. I didn't realize. If I could just . . .'

But Naomi didn't stop to listen. With Bert beside her, she walked past the reception desk into the corridor behind it, hearing the girl calling out, 'I say! If you wouldn't mind . . .'

They kept on walking until they reached a familiar door. After a cursory rap, Naomi opened it and they stepped into the anteroom to Alexander's office. Here his secretary held court. Miss Seymour was a beautiful young woman with fair hair like spun silver but as much warmth as an ice carving. Their abrupt entry brought a frown to the smooth forehead. 'Mrs Harrington,' she said, getting to her feet. 'I wasn't expecting you today.'

'Why would you expect me when I didn't tell you I was coming?'

'If you're hoping to see Mr Harrington, I'm afraid he has a full diary so he may be unable . . .'

Naomi simply stepped past her.

'Really, Mrs Harrington, I must insist that—'

'Insist away,' Bert told Miss Seymour as he too stepped past her. 'It won't make any difference.'

Naomi gave the inner door another cursory rap and walked into Alexander's private sanctum with Bert following behind her.

Alexander was on the telephone. He broke off, surprised. Then a cunning sort of hope rippled across his angular features. He spoke into the telephone again. 'Might I ring you back shortly, Julian? I just need a few minutes . . . No, I shan't keep you waiting long.'

He returned the handset to its cradle and rose to his feet, holding out his arms in a gesture of magnanimity. 'Naomi. Mr – er – Makepiece. What a pleasure this is.'

'Hmm,' Bert said. 'You may be getting a little ahead of yourself with your pleasure.'

Alexander's smile wobbled but he took a deep breath and fixed it back in place. 'You received my letter, Naomi?'

'I did.' She pulled it from her bag and slapped it down on top of his elegant desk. 'The answer is no. I don't want to review how much of my trust fund you're to repay. We agreed terms months ago. I expect you to stick to them.'

'But my investments . . .'

'I don't actually believe they've fallen in value but, even if they have, I don't care.'

Alexander's glittering eyes hardened. 'Well, I can't force you to agree to a review, but it may mean delaying the divorce. As for my children . . .'

'Oh, no,' Naomi told him. 'Don't think you can keep me waiting out of spite. What's going to happen is this. Number one: you're going to cooperate so the divorce goes through as soon as possible. Number two: you're going to pay the agreed settlement within the next week. That's right, Alexander. One week. And number three: you're not going to take your frustrations out on William. An angry word to him, a sulky silence, an act of spite and I'll shout out loud about your bigamy. That's a promise. Is that all understood?'

'I can't magic money out of the air, Naomi.'

'I don't want a penny of *your* money. I just want you to return some of *mine*. Agree to my terms or I'll go back out through your door and tell Miss Seymour and all your other colleagues that you're a bigamist. Right now.'

'You'd be hurting William,' Alexander pointed out, as though that strangled Naomi's threat at birth. For a moment a smirk played on his mouth but he covered it up quickly.

'Actually, we spoke to young William,' Bert said.

Alexander rounded on him in obvious annoyance. 'Mr Makepiece, you're not married to Naomi yet so it's hardly appropriate for you to be meddling in matters while she's still married to me.'

'That's where our views differ,' Bert said, his voice calm but his demeanour about as moveable as Mount Everest. 'I may not be married to Naomi yet, but I'm engaged to her. More importantly, I love her and care about her. And that means stepping in when she needs my support, whether you like it or not. Now, to go back to what I was saying, we spoke to young William and he's given Naomi his blessing to announce your bigamy to all the world if you persist in trying to bully and manipulate her out of the money she's due.'

'William would never have agreed to that.'

'You don't know your son at all well, do you?' Bert said. 'Naturally, he doesn't relish the thought of his illegitimacy becoming known, but still less does he want to see Naomi cheated.'

'You just want to get your own filthy hands on my money,' Alexander accused.

Bert only sighed. 'What a sorry specimen of manhood you are, judging others by your own low standards. I'd love Naomi if she were penniless and, what's more, the woman knows it.' He glanced at Naomi, who smiled. She did know it.

'I can see we haven't persuaded you, Alexander,' Naomi said. 'Very well.'

She marched towards the door, opened it and faced his secretary. 'Miss Seymour. There's something you should . . .'

Chasing after her, Alexander grabbed her arm and tugged her back into his office, kicking the door shut again.

'I suggest you remove your hand from Naomi's arm,' Bert told him. 'Otherwise there might be consequences, and I'm sure you'd rather avoid messing up your well-groomed hair and staining your pristine shirt.'

Alexander released Naomi as though she'd become diseased.

'I take it you agree to my suggestion now?' Naomi demanded.

'Just go,' Alexander said.

'We'll go when you've answered Naomi's question,' Bert said.

'All right! I agree.'

'That wasn't too hard, was it?' Bert asked. 'Any more silly games and nonsense and you know what'll happen. Goodbye, Alexander. I hope never to see you again.'

'One week for the money,' Naomi said warningly.

'Go!' Alexander roared.

It was Bert's turn to take Naomi's arm but he did so respectfully, tapping her hand in a gesture of reassurance.

Together, they sauntered from the room.

'I don't know about you but I'm feeling rather peckish,' Bert said when they got outside. 'What do you say to tea and a bun to celebrate a job well done?'

'I say it sounds perfect.'

They found a small cafe where Bert held up his teacup in a toast. 'Cheers,' he said. 'Mission accomplished.'

'Not quite. Not until the money actually arrives in my account.'

'Do you think he won't pay?'

'I think he probably *will* pay. Grudgingly. But I don't trust Alexander an inch, so I'll still feel better once the payment has been received.'

'He's a slimy customer, all right.' Bert sipped some tea and then grinned. 'You really were magnificent, beloved.'

'The person who was magnificent was William. It was brave of him to give me his blessing. I'm glad I didn't have to expose his father's bigamy, though. William would have been hurt despite what he said about feeling no shame.'

'He's turning out to be a fine young man. That's your influence.'

'Yours, too. And Alice's. And Victoria's . . . But his own good nature should take most of the credit.'

'I won't argue with that,' Bert said.

'I need to tell him how we got on. Come on. Let's go home and I'll telephone his school.'

They returned to Foxfield and Naomi spoke to William's housemaster. 'The message is simply: *It worked*,' she told him. 'William will understand what I mean. Oh, and if you could add the word *thanks*?'

CHAPTER SIXTY-THREE

Beth

He was there, pausing in the corridor as he wrote on a patient's notes. Beth straightened her shoulders and walked towards him, smiling. 'Good morning, Dr Lytton. I hope you're well?'

She saw his interest stir at this show of friendliness. Perhaps he imagined she was having second thoughts about turning down his invitation.

'All the better for seeing you, Nurse Ellis,' he told her, before leaning towards her and adding, 'or should I say, *Beth*. That's much prettier. You're well, too, I hope?'

Beth resisted the temptation to show how increasingly tedious she found his flirting now she knew there was no substance to it with her or anyone else. She tried her best to appeal to his ego by looking dazzled by him, faking a simper, which was no easy task since she'd never been a simpering sort of girl, not even when she'd seen Oliver as a golden-haired prince. 'I'm very well, thank you.'

He smiled to show his perfect teeth, and Beth let her gaze dwell on them as though she thought they were sparkling with diamonds.

'Dr Lytton!' a porter shouted.

'Duty calls,' Oliver told Beth. 'But let's talk again later.'

'I'd like that.' Beth did her best impression of doe eyes but her expression hardened as he walked away.

She went in search of Babs and Pauline, finding them in the nurses' lounge. 'I think the seed is sown,' she reported. 'Now we'll have to wait to see if it takes root.'

CHAPTER SIXTY-FOUR

Hannah

There were two notes in the tin when Hannah opened it on Tuesday morning. She took them out with trembling fingers, her stomach churning with dread in case this was the news she feared.

The first note was from Ruby, reminding Hannah that she had friends who were thinking of her and also advising her to hold her head high since Rose was beautiful and as far from shameful as it was possible to be.

The second note was from Victoria. Hannah's stomach crunched again when she recognized the handwriting. It was a relief to read that she, too, wished Hannah well and assured her that Rose continued to thrive. There was no mention of Rose being sent away yet, but Hannah felt as though a clock were ticking in her ear, counting down to the dreadful moment. Tick, tock . . .

CHAPTER SIXTY-FIVE

Beth

The day after Beth had sown the seeds of interest in Oliver, he came up behind her and laid a hand on her shoulder as she tidied the sluice room. His breath was warm on her neck.

'I looked for you last night but couldn't find you,' he said.

A fib. He'd taken Babs out on his motorcycle.

'That's a pity,' Beth said, pouting with fake disappointment.

'Never mind. I'm looking at you now, and what a lovely sight you are to a tired doctor's eyes.'

Had she really fallen for this sort of nonsense in the past? She must have done. Now she had to struggle to keep up her act. 'Perhaps we could spend some time together this evening?' she suggested. It was a mischievous suggestion because he'd promised to take Pauline for another romantic walk in the woods.

'If only that were possible. I'm dining with Dr Marwood, I'm afraid.' The falsehood dropped from his lips like slippery satin. 'But have you heard that there's to be a fundraising concert for the Churchwood bookshop on Saturday?'

'It's been mentioned. There's a matinee performance here, I believe.'

'Yes, but we'll probably be too busy to attend that. Would you like to come with me to the evening performance in the village?'

Beth widened her eyes in apparent delight. 'I'd love to. As long as I'm not on duty.'

'I'll cross my fingers that you'll be free.'

He glanced over his shoulder as though checking that no one was watching and then drew her to him. He kissed her cheek and moved towards her lips. But then footsteps sounded in the corridor and he released her. 'I've missed you,' he said, leaving her with a wink.

Beth wiped her cheek on a handkerchief. What a liar he was!

'Roots growing nicely,' she told Babs and Pauline later.

CHAPTER SIXTY-SIX

Victoria

Victoria kissed Rose's downy little head. 'Let's give you some fresh air,' she suggested.

She opened the kitchen door and peered into the back garden cautiously. It was early so she wasn't expecting anyone to be about, but even so, she wanted to take no chances in exposing Rose to prying eyes.

The garden was empty apart from a squirrel and some birds. Victoria didn't venture outside but merely stood in the open doorway, ready to duck back inside should the need arise.

'Good morning.'

The voice made Victoria gasp. She shrank back, cradling Rose protectively.

'I didn't mean to startle you,' Paul said.

'I wasn't expecting . . . It's early . . . I didn't think . . .' Victoria knew she was gabbling, but it was as though a tempest were sweeping through her emotions and tossing them into the air – shock, delight at the sight of his kind brown eyes and warm smile, pain because he shouldn't be here. 'I wrote a letter . . .'

'I received it.'

Then why . . .? 'I shan't change my mind,' she told him.

'Maybe you won't. And if you tell me to leave, I'll go. But would you hear me out first?'

'I don't see the point of—'

'Please.'

She hesitated. Ran her tongue over her suddenly dry lips. And finally nodded.

'I like you, Victoria. I think you like me. But while I respect your wish to put the children first, I'm not sure you're on the right track with that line of thinking. Before you fire up, let me explain my reasons for saying that. That little one you have in your arms . . .'

'She isn't mine and doesn't come into . . . my situation.'

'My point is that, even if she did, it wouldn't change how I feel about you. As long as there's no other man in your life. I wouldn't like to tread on toes.'

'I still have Arthur and Jenny, and they must be my priority,' Victoria explained.

'Well, sure. But that doesn't mean nothing else matters. Like your happiness.'

'The children make me happy.'

'I don't doubt it. But there are different kinds of happiness and I don't believe that caring for the children means you have to close the door on . . . let's call it romantic happiness. It needn't weaken how you feel about them.'

'But it might unsettle them.'

'Not if it's approached carefully. I'm not suggesting whisking you away from them to live it up in town or at the shore. I'm suggesting a friendship with you *and* the kids – with everyone else here, too – and that we take it from there. It may go nowhere, and I may be sent to serve overseas anyway, but I'd like to . . . I'd like to see what happens.'

Victoria hesitated.

'There's something else I'd like you to think about. I lost my own pa when I was small. My mom did her best to make up for it, but what turned things around for me was when she married again. My stepfather was – still is – a wonderful man. He took an interest in me. My education. The sports and hobbies I enjoyed . . . And we've had many a man-to-man talk over the years. In short, he's enriched my life and I like to think that his influence has made me a better person.' He let that sink in then added, 'I'm glad my mom has him as her husband, too. If she'd dedicated her life to me at the expense of her own happiness, I'd be carrying a lot of guilt around.'

That jolted Victoria. It hadn't occurred to her that self-sacrifice might burden the children with guilt.

'I'm not trying to complicate things for you and I certainly don't want to worry you,' Paul said. 'I just want to leave you with those thoughts. I need to return to duty now and I'm sure your household will soon be needing your attention. The final thing I want to leave you with is a question. Do you want to spend your life thinking *if only*? If only we'd tried things . . . If only we'd taken a risk . . .'

Victoria had no ready answer. But those words – *if only* – struck her as desperately sad.

'I'll return for the concert if my duties permit,' Paul told her. 'If you haven't changed your mind, I won't say another word to cause you grief. I'll be sorry but I'll always be glad I met you. I admire you, Victoria. I admire your courage and selflessness. I also think you're beautiful.' He nodded at Rose. 'She's beautiful, too.'

With that he nodded farewell and left.

Victoria stood in the open door, her thoughts in a whirl. Paul had made their situation sound simple but people didn't always see things the same way. Children, especially. And Arthur and Jenny had been through so much already.

And yet, those words . . . *If only*. Sad words indeed.

CHAPTER SIXTY-SEVEN

Ruby

'He just isn't himself any more,' Ruby said, watching Timmy through the kitchen window as he wandered around the farmyard before school.

She could see the strain of secrecy weighing down on him and robbing him of his carefree energy. He'd grown watchful and wary.

'It's only temporary,' Kate said. 'Things will settle down eventually.'

Ruby supposed she was right, though she couldn't shake off her feelings of guilt. Guilt over Timmy. And guilt over Hannah, because even if – or rather, when – Rose left Churchwood to be adopted, her young mother would be left behind and would bear the stigma of having borne a child out of wedlock for years to come. Meanwhile, Ruby was sheltering behind lies.

Timmy went off to school and the work of the farm continued. 'I need to go into the village to post a letter,' Pearl announced, after lunch.

'Is this a letter to your parents?' Ruby asked, hoping it was nothing more worrying.

Pearl only shrugged. The letter must be to the Women's Land Army.

'I know you're not happy at the moment, but please

don't leave,' Ruby begged. 'You're needed here. More importantly, you're *wanted* here.'

Kate pleaded with Pearl, too. 'Don't rush into a decision you could come to regret. You might feel differently in a few weeks' time.' Once the edge of her disappointment had been blunted.

'I've enjoyed myself here,' Pearl admitted. 'I've liked having you two as friends. But it's time to go.'

'This is Fred's fault,' Ruby declared furiously, but Pearl merely said, 'I need to borrow the bicycle. If that's all right, Kate?'

'Of course it is. But I wish you weren't borrowing it to get away from us.'

Pearl looked as though she wanted to say something in reply – perhaps to point out that she wasn't trying to get away from *them* – but the task seemed to be too much for her. She shrugged helplessly and went out to fetch the bicycle.

Frustration burst over Ruby and she hammered on Fred's door. 'Get out here, Fred Fletcher. *Now!*'

A few seconds passed. Ruby hammered again. 'Come out or I'm coming in. I don't care if—'

'I'm coming!' Fred bellowed.

The door opened. 'What's the problem?' he asked, wheeling himself into the kitchen because he was still spending most of his time in his chair.

'*You're* the problem! Because of *you*, Pearl's leaving.'

Alarm flared in Fred's eyes but he fell back on disbelief. 'She won't leave. She likes it here and nowhere else would put up with her.' He attempted a laugh but it fell flat.

'Joke away, Fred. You're a fool. Pearl *is* leaving and it's because *you've* made her unhappy.'

'I can't help it if she drives me nuts,' Fred said.

'Have it your way,' Ruby sneered. 'Deny it all you like,

347

but you know the truth and so do we. You love Pearl and she loves you. But you're letting your stupid pride stop you from doing anything about it.'

'Pearl doesn't love me.'

'She *does*!' Ruby and Kate yelled together.

'Think about it, Fred,' Kate appealed. 'You won't let Pearl see that *you* love *her*. So why should she let you see that *she* loves *you*?'

'You're talking nonsense. If you don't get to work, Ernie will be after you, and you can't blame me for that.'

Ruby looked at Kate. 'I could kill him.'

A glance through the window showed Pearl leaving the barn with the bicycle. Grabbing the wheelchair's handles, and ignoring a protesting 'Oi!' from Fred, Ruby pushed it to the kitchen door which she threw wide open.

'There, Fred,' she said, pointing at Pearl. 'There's your chance of a wonderful future about to disappear down the drive. Pearl won't be able to go back on it once she requests a transfer, so she'll move on while you'll be left behind, lonely and bitter for the rest of your days. And all because you're a coward.'

'I'm not a coward! I fought in the war!'

'There are different kinds of cowardice, Fred. Yours is fear of rejection. Not that Pearl will reject you, but you're too lily-livered to take a chance.'

Pearl waved as she set off. Ruby waved back but was scathing to Fred. 'You should wave, too, Fred. Wave your happiness goodbye.'

'You're talking rubbish,' he said, but as Pearl neared the drive, Ruby saw his panic rise. 'Wait!' he called to Pearl.

She glanced around. Put her feet to the ground. 'Why?' she demanded.

Fred didn't appear to know what to say next so Pearl rolled her eyes and prepared to pedal off.

'No, wait, will you?' Fred shouted. He sounded irritable, but that was Fred all over when it came to emotion.

Even across the farmyard, it was possible to see Pearl sigh. 'Wait for what?'

'Just come back,' Fred said.

She brought the bicycle over. 'Well?'

'I'm sorry I said you looked like a clown when Ruby put lipstick on you.'

'Is that it? Apology accepted.' But clearly the hurt remained. She turned the bicycle.

'Wait a moment, for heaven's sake!' Fred cried.

'What for this time?'

Fred took a deep breath. 'You looked nothing like a clown. You looked . . . well, nice.'

'Humph.' Pearl stepped away. Or rather attempted to step away. Fred had grabbed her shirt.

'Stay there if you don't want your shirt to be torn,' he said. 'My hands are strong from using this wheelchair and whittling wood.'

'Bully for you,' Pearl sneered. 'You're a strong man but I'm a strong woman. Get on with whatever you want to say or I'm stepping away, and if you rip my shirt, I'll rip yours so we'll be even. Not that I could care less about—'

'Just give me a chance to speak!' Fred howled.

'I don't have all day to waste on listening to you, Fred Fletcher. It's not as though you can have anything to say that's worth listening to.'

'I'm trying to tell you that I like you.'

'*Like* me? I like lots of things. Boiled eggs, rainbows, the smell of the earth after rain, the—'

'Shut up, Pearl!'

'Oh, charming! I don't see why I should stand here and put up with your nonsense when—'

'I'm trying to tell you I love you!'

349

'*What?*'

Fred glanced back and saw Ruby and Kate watching him. Pink in the face, he returned his gaze to Pearl accusingly. 'Now look what you've done!'

'I've done nothing.' But Pearl had turned pink, too. 'It's your own fault if . . .'

'Do you *want* me to strangle you?'

'Just you try it, Fred Fletcher. You're the one who'll end up dead.'

Ruby rolled her eyes. 'You're making a complete hash of this. Both of you. Pearl, unless I'm much mistaken, Fred is trying to propose to you.'

Pearl turned even pinker and looked down at the ground, tracing an awkward pattern with her boot. 'If that's the case, he isn't doing a very good job.'

Fred looked outraged. 'That's because—'

'Stop talking,' Ruby barked at him. 'Now, then.' She took a hand of each of them and joined them together. 'You go first, Fred. Tell Pearl how you feel and what you want.'

He looked around nervously. Ernie, Kenny and Vinnie had appeared. 'Everyone's watching,' he hissed.

'Then you'd better get it right. All you need to do is tell Pearl you love her and will be honoured if she'll become your wife.'

'I can't say that! It's soppy!'

Ruby clouted him on the head. 'Say it.'

Fred muttered a curse then looked at Pearl. 'What she just said.' He nodded towards Ruby.

'You have to say the actual words, you dolt,' Ruby told him.

'Urgh!' He took a deep breath. 'Pearl, I love you and I want to marry you.'

'You missed out the bit about being honoured,' Pearl said, though she was grinning now.

'You're just trying to make me look stupid,' Fred protested.

'You manage that all by yourself,' Pearl told him.

Fred sighed again. 'I'll be honoured. There. You'd better stop all this mawkish nonsense from now on or we won't suit. Well? What's your answer?'

'I'll think about it,' Pearl said smugly.

'*What?*'

'Pearl,' Ruby warned, not wanting her friend to ruin the moment.

'All right,' Pearl said. 'I've thought about it.'

'And?' Ruby prompted.

'My answer is yes.' With that Pearl launched herself on to Fred in his wheelchair so she was lying across him, enormous boots flailing in the air.

'Gerroff!' he cried, his speech muffled beneath her.

'Not on your life,' Pearl told him. 'We're engaged now and you can't go back on it or I'll sue you for breach of promise.'

'Fred, do you have a ring?' Ruby asked him, thinking it was unlikely.

'Course he hasn't,' Pearl said, sitting up on Fred's lap.

'I haven't got diamonds and stuff, but I've got a ring,' Fred said. He produced a wooden ring from his pocket and showed it to Pearl. 'I made it. You probably think it isn't good enough, but I can't afford—'

'I love it!' Pearl snatched it from him, slid it on to her finger and held her hand up so she could admire it. 'Thanks, Fred.'

She smacked a giant kiss on to his mouth then got up, saying, 'Look at this, everyone. I'm engaged. To be married. Who'd have thought it? Me? Engaged!'

Ruby found Kate at her side. 'Well done,' Kate said. 'I was beginning to think we'd never get them hitched.'

'We haven't got them up the aisle quite yet,' Ruby said.

'But we will,' Kate predicted, 'even if that's a battle for another day. Anyway, you'll be walking up the aisle first. You're going to be happy with Kenny.'

'I think I am. He'll need nagging sometimes and he'll need keeping in his place, but I love him.'

'Did I hear my name mentioned?' Kenny asked, coming over.

'Ruby was just saying how much she loves you.' Winking at Ruby, Kate walked away.

'What you did for Fred,' Kenny said. 'You're quite a woman, Ruby Turner.'

'I'm *your* woman, Kenny Fletcher.'

Ernie made a disgusted sound. 'I'm going back to work,' he said, heading for the fields.

No one rushed to follow him. He'd been a tyrant in his day, apparently, especially to poor Kate. But now he was like a surly cur who still bit when he could but whose fangs had been blunted.

Ruby joined in the celebrations, glad for Pearl and Fred, but despising herself. Quite a woman, Kenny had called her, but she felt like a coward every time she thought of Hannah.

CHAPTER SIXTY-EIGHT

Naomi

'There's a telephone call for you,' Victoria said as Naomi entered the house after giving Basil a turn around the garden.

'Oh? There's nothing wrong with William, I hope?' Had Alexander gone back on his word and upset the boy?

'The caller is Sir Ambrose. I don't know if that's a good thing or a bad thing.'

'Neither do I,' Naomi said. 'But I'm about to find out.'

She hastened to the telephone and greeted the Great Man of Law. 'Hello, Sir Ambrose.'

'Good afternoon, dear lady. It's a pleasure to speak to you, as always. How are you?'

'That rather depends on what you're ringing to tell me,' Naomi said, bluntly. The Great Man's flowery talk could be tedious and the longer he spent on it, the higher his bill would be.

'I have excellent news for you. Mr Harrington has found a way to pay your settlement early. In fact, he's already paid it. In full.'

Relief knocked Naomi back on her heels. She took a deep breath and straightened. 'That really is excellent news.'

'Didn't I say you were in safe hands with me from the beginning?'

'You did.' It was Naomi's own efforts – Bert's and

William's, too – that had brought this settlement about, but she could be generous in her triumph.

'Furthermore, he's anxious for the divorce to proceed as soon as possible.'

'As am I,' Naomi reminded him.

'You should be liberated from the marriage soon, dear lady.'

'The sooner the better. I won't keep you talking now since I know you're a busy man.' An expensive one, too. 'I'll say goodbye. And thank you.'

She put the telephone down before he could spout more flowers.

'Good news?' Victoria asked, when Naomi returned to the drawing room.

'Indeed.' Naomi told Victoria what had happened.

'I'm pleased for you, Naomi. You deserve to be happy. Bert will be delighted for you, too.'

'He will. I'll go round and share the news now.'

Naomi hastened to Bert's market garden, delighting in the fine spring afternoon. The sky was blue and the air was fresh. Buds thickened on trees while yellow celandine and wood anemones grew beneath them. And all around was birdsong.

'Is it spring that's put that bounce in your step or something else?' Bert asked when he saw her approaching.

'Alexander has paid the settlement. In full.'

'Ha! Well done, beloved. You're the one who persuaded him to do it. Not that money-bags lawyer you employed.'

'*We* got him to do it, and so did William.'

'Young spider-legs did well,' Bert acknowledged. 'So, if the divorce is likely to go through soon, we can start thinking about our wedding. We haven't really talked about the sort of occasion we'd like yet.'

'A Churchwood wedding,' Naomi told him. 'One for the whole community. It's a pity the divorce means Adam can't marry us in church, though.'

'The divorce was the icicle's fault. I don't understand why the church wants to punish you, the innocent party, by denying you a church wedding to a man who loves and values you as he ought.'

'That's what Adam says but it's out of his hands,' Naomi said. 'He wants to bless us in church, though, and I think we should make the blessing the focus of the celebrations.'

'Agreed. We can always get wed at a register office in private before then as a nod to the legalities.'

'We're going to be busy,' Naomi said.

'We're always busy. Talking of which . . . Are we all set for tomorrow's concerts?'

'It's just a case of transporting the piano to the hospital for the matinee. Perhaps you could take Margueritte and Sidney, too?'

'Of course, and I can assure you that I'll be impervious to her charms.'

'I'm glad to hear it. Afterwards, it's a case of bringing them all back to the bookshop for the evening. The whole village seems to be excited about it so it's going to be a crush fitting everyone in.'

'We'll manage just the way we did for young Kate's wedding. The weather is forecast to be fine so we can open all the doors and spread into the garden as well as around the bookshop. Upstairs, downstairs and on the stairs themselves. Young Margueritte has a powerful voice. It'll reach all through the bookshop and beyond it.'

'Alice has arranged for Dr Marwood to bring his gramophone and records for dancing afterwards if people are so inclined.'

'I think they probably will be,' Bert said.

But at that moment they both grew more serious. 'No news about young Hannah's young man, I suppose?' Bert asked.

'None at all.'

'Poor girl. And poor Rose. Does the baby mean Victoria won't be coming to the concert?'

'She's coming. Ivy wants to stay at home with Rose. She says the noise of a concert will be too much for her.'

'Or maybe she's just being kind to Victoria.'

Naomi smiled. 'I suspect she is. I'd better be on my way. I need to telephone the school to tell William his father has finally paid the settlement.'

Reaching home, Naomi called the school and managed to speak to William himself, who was delighted. 'I only hope your father doesn't take his anger out on you,' she said.

'He can *try*,' William told her. 'But he won't beat me down.'

How William had come on from the nervous boy she'd first met. He'd been terrified of Alexander then.

Alice called round just as Naomi put down the telephone. She, too, was delighted to hear of Alexander's capitulation.

'I come with more wonderful news,' she said. 'Pearl and Fred are engaged.'

'That is good news,' Naomi said.

'I'm surprised you haven't heard it already, since Pearl's been shouting about it ever since it happened. She's normally a hard worker but she says she's much too excited to work. Naturally, Ernie is apoplectic, but every time he opens his mouth to complain she tells him to close it again because a girl doesn't get engaged every day.'

'That means there are two weddings coming up for Brimbles Farm,' Naomi said.

'Your wedding will make three for Churchwood.'

'Happy times,' Naomi observed but, again, thoughts of Hannah appeared to hit both of them together.

'Life is ever a seesaw,' Alice said. 'As some people ride high with happiness, others are brought down low. I only hope Hannah can take comfort in the thought of Rose going to a loving home. Not that Hannah will ever get over losing Rose. Not completely.'

Was Alice thinking of her own miscarriage last year?

'How are you keeping?' Naomi asked.

Alice patted her middle. 'Very well. I'm staying hopeful.'

'I'm glad to hear it.'

'Have you actually heard from Hannah?' Alice asked then.

'Bert collected a note from the tin this morning but it was pretty much the same as the other notes she's left. Hannah just said that she's grateful to us for looking after Rose and sent her daughter a kiss.'

'Which means she's no closer to being able to reclaim her.'

'Sadly not. Unfortunately, I don't think we can give her any longer. If Rose is to be adopted, the sooner she gets to know her new parents, the better it will be for her.'

'I think you're right,' Alice said. 'You did your best for Hannah.'

'We all did our best for her,' Naomi said, but she still felt terrible for the grief Hannah would suffer.

The clock on the mantelpiece struck six thirty. 'Time is marching on, so I'll leave you in peace,' Alice said. 'I'll see you both tomorrow. The concert has the whole village abuzz.'

But out on the road to Barton there was a young girl whose happiness was in shreds.

357

CHAPTER SIXTY-NINE

Hannah

'Come here, darling.'

Ma held out her arms and Hannah went to her, to be gathered close. 'I'm so sorry I'm not being a better mother to you,' Ma said.

'You're a wonderful mother,' Hannah told her, even as tears were flooding from her eyes.

So many tears these days! A week had passed since her father had learned of Rose's existence and ordered her to be sent away. Ever since then Hannah had striven to put on a brave face in front of her mother, assuring her that, yes, what happened had been upsetting – terribly upsetting – but she was coping.

Clearly, Ma hadn't been fooled and couldn't bear to watch Hannah's suffering in silence any longer. 'If I wasn't so weak, you wouldn't have been burdened with so many cares . . .' Ma said. 'You'd have lived as a girl of your age should live – with a light heart – and needn't have sought solace in the arms of a boy who's let you down.'

'It wasn't like that, Ma.'

'I know you believe that, darling, and I don't blame you for turning to him. A friendly smile can look like sunshine when the rest of life is a gloomy shade of grey. But he let you down and so did I, and now you've lost your baby.'

Perhaps Hannah stiffened or perhaps Ma's instincts

stirred because she drew back a little to look at Hannah's face. 'Your baby *has* been sent away? You told your father—'

'I told him I'd passed on his instructions and I had.'

'But the baby is still in Churchwood?'

Hannah didn't answer.

'Oh, darling!'

'Miss Page and Mrs Harrington . . . They said they'd keep her for a little while longer, just in case.'

'In case this boy of yours reappears?'

Hannah shrugged.

Ma gathered her close again. 'I wish you could keep your child, darling. I'd have been distraught if I'd had to give up any of mine. But I'm worried that you're only making things worse for yourself by delaying the inevitable. The longer this goes on, the harder it will be to part with Rose.'

'I won't let her go until I haven't a choice,' Hannah insisted. 'I haven't been seeing her. Not since Pa found out. I can't go to Foxfield in case he spots me there or gets to hear of me visiting. But I know time will run out any day now and I may never see Rose again. Never even get to say goodbye . . .'

Ma was quiet for a moment, then she drew back again and said, 'I can't see a way for you to keep her, but I can give you a chance to say goodbye. And to say goodbye with pride.'

'How?' Hannah asked.

'You've mentioned a concert.'

'It's tomorrow.'

'I want you to go to it. Ask Mrs Harrington and this nice Miss Page to bring Rose along so you can say goodbye to her in a way that shows the whole world that you're not ashamed of her.'

'I'm not ashamed of her.'

'Let those Churchwood gossips know that by holding your head high. They don't know you, Hannah. They don't know what a good girl you are. To me. To all your brothers and sisters. I couldn't be prouder of you. Go and show that you're proud of your Rose, too.'

'What about the children, though?' Hannah said. 'I can't take them all.'

'I'll look after the children.'

'You're not well enough, Ma.'

'I'll be fine for a few hours. You can help me get downstairs and I'll explain to the older ones that they need to be good while you're away. They're of an age to understand that now, and to help with the little ones, too. As for your father, if he asks, I'll tell him I've insisted on you going to the concert because you've been so unhappy. It's only half a lie because you *have* been so unhappy.'

'I'll need to get a message to Mrs Harrington and Victoria,' Hannah said.

'Will that be possible?'

'I can try.'

'Try now. Do it before your father gets home.' Because then it would be too late.

Hannah wiped her eyes, kissed Ma and ran downstairs to write a note.

Dear Victoria and Mrs Harrington,

I hope to come to the concert tomorrow. Would it be possible for you to bring Rose? I know I have to let her go but I want everyone to see that I love her and I'm not ashamed of her.

She bundled Susie and Simon into the pram and wheeled them down the road towards the tin. There was a note already inside it.

Dear Hannah,

Just a brief line to let you know that Rose continues well.
I imagine we'd have heard if there was good news from you
so I'll just say we're thinking of you.

Victoria x

It was a kind note and Hannah appreciated it, but if it had been left not long ago it probably meant that no one would be coming to check the tin again. Not today, since evening was approaching. Possibly not tomorrow, either, since everyone would be busy with the concert arrangements.

But there was nothing more Hannah could do. She pocketed Victoria's note, put her own note into the tin and prayed it wouldn't be received too late.

CHAPTER SEVENTY

Naomi

'Everything looks to be in order,' Naomi declared to Alice as they surveyed the inside of the bookshop. Everywhere was clean and sparkling and the air smelled divinely of the potted hyacinths and other spring flowers that decorated the window ledges. Chairs and small tables had been arranged upstairs and downstairs wherever possible, and in the kitchen crockery and glassware were laid out for refreshments.

'We're lucky with the weather,' Alice said. 'We'll be able to spill into the garden.'

'Let's just hope there's no accident with the piano when Bert brings it back from the hospital.'

'You're picturing it sliding off the ramp when he loads it on to the truck?'

'Or when he unloads it.'

'Never,' Alice said confidently. 'Bert is Mr Reliability.'

'He is, isn't he?' Naomi agreed.

'I'm so glad you've sorted things out with Alexander. You'll be able to put that horrible man firmly behind you and get on with marrying a much better man now.'

'I'm a lucky woman.'

'As am I,' Alice said.

'You look radiant.'

'Talking of radiance . . .' Alice said, as they made their way outside. 'Here comes another bride-to-be.'

Pearl was cycling towards them along Churchwood Way. Seeing them, she skidded to a halt beside them. Radiance wasn't a word that was normally associated with someone who was dressed so scruffily, but somehow it fitted Pearl's air of being delighted with the world. 'That's lucky,' she said. 'I was just coming to see you, Naomi.'

'Oh?'

'The thing is, I can't seem to keep still since Fred suggested getting spliced so I went out on Kate's bike to use up some energy. I've been all over this morning, cycling miles and miles, and I thought I'd take a look in Hannah's message tin as I was passing that way. There's a note for you.' Digging in her breeches pocket, she pulled out a note which was badly crumpled now and passed it to Naomi.

Naomi read it quickly. 'Hannah's coming to the concert,' she said. 'She wants to see Rose there.'

'In public?' Alice was surprised.

'It seems she accepts that she has to give Rose up but wants the world to see that she isn't ashamed of her.'

'How brave,' Alice said.

'I should say so,' Pearl agreed.

'Thank you for bringing the note, Pearl, and congratulations again on your engagement. You're coming to the concert tonight?'

'I certainly am and Fred's going to squire me. After all, I'm a fiancée now and I expect to be treated like a princess. Me, a fiancée!' She shook her head in wonder and then pedalled away calling, 'Cheerio!' over her shoulder.

Naomi exchanged smiles with Alice. 'It's going to be a strange day, isn't it?'

'Happy for some. Unhappy for Hannah.'

And unhappy for Victoria, too. Naomi couldn't fault how Victoria was showing a brave face to the world but was sure the girl was suffering inside. 'I'd better go and tell Victoria about Hannah's note,' Naomi told Alice, and they parted with a hug.

CHAPTER SEVENTY-ONE

Ruby

'Are you bothering with work today or not?' Ernie said sourly as Pearl burst into the farmhouse kitchen, fresh-faced from her cycle ride.

'Not,' Pearl told him. 'It isn't every day you become a fiancée, you know.'

'That was yesterday's excuse. You did no work then so you need to make up for it today.'

'I'm still celebrating.'

'If you think I'm going to pay your wages for—'

'Oh, shut up, Ernie!' A chorus went up from Pearl, Ruby, Kate, Kenny, Fred and even Vinnie, who was always happy to skive off when an opportunity presented itself.

But when Ernie returned to work so did Kenny, and he beckoned Vinnie to follow him.

'I need more wood for my whittling,' Fred said, leaving the kitchen to go to the barn.

'I picked up a note from Hannah while I was out,' Pearl said when only Ruby and Kate remained.

'Oh?' Ruby asked, exchanging glances with Kate, who was obviously thinking the same thing: there might be news of Rose's father.

'Hannah's coming to the concert tonight. She wants to say goodbye to her baby in public so people can see she isn't ashamed of Rose.'

'She's finally given up hope of Rose's father appearing?' Kate asked.

'It looks that way.'

'Poor Hannah. She must be grief-stricken.'

'Devastated,' Ruby agreed. Her heart would have been torn to shreds if she'd had to give up Timmy.

'But how courageous, too,' Kate added.

'Yes,' Ruby said, but her own cowardice appalled her. Still, she had to protect Timmy . . .

'We must all keep an eye on Hannah at the concert,' Kate said. 'Make sure no one has the chance to attack her to her face, even if they gossip behind her back.'

Fred returned with a supply of wood. Pearl looked at him and frowned. 'You'd better wash your hair before the concert,' she told him. 'It's a pit of grease.'

'Stop nagging,' Fred protested, but it was clear that he'd be washing his hair before the concert.

Needing to be alone for a while, Ruby walked down to the orchard. Ten minutes later, she went to find Kenny. 'What do you think?' she asked, after she'd told him what she was considering. 'It wouldn't embarrass you?'

'I couldn't care less what other people think,' he answered. 'Unless they're mean to you, in which case . . .'

'No fighting,' she instructed, uncurling his fists and kissing him.

She spoke to Timmy next, whispering in his ear. 'Could we have a word? In private?'

His eyes widened. 'What about?'

'Come upstairs and I'll tell you. It's nothing to worry about, though, and I won't do anything unless you agree.'

They went up to their room. Ruby closed the door behind them and sat on her bed, patting the space beside her to signal to Timmy to join her.

He sat but turned saucer eyes towards her.

'I wonder how brave you're feeling?' she asked.

CHAPTER SEVENTY-TWO

Beth

'I'm well enough to go to the concert, aren't I, nurse?'
Corporal Andy Smith asked.

'I believe you've been passed fit,' Beth told him.

'Will you be coming?'

'I have to work.'

'Pity. It sounds as though it's going to be wonderful.'

'I can't wait,' Private Jeffries said.

'Me neither,' Private Willis said.

Matron was bustling around looking pleased.

Ward One occupied the largest room so Matron had
decided to hold the concert in there, moving the sicker
patients to other wards temporarily. Beth was one of
those who had been asked to move them, also bringing
patients from other wards to the concert.

'Cor!' Private Pickles said, when she brought him into
Ward One in his wheelchair.

Beth looked up to see what had struck him and saw that
Margueritte Moore had arrived. And what a siren she was
with her tightly fitting dress, artfully arranged hair and pouting mouth. Other men had been equally struck and Beth
saw that some of them had their mouths open in wonder.

The concert began and Beth lingered for a moment as
Margueritte spoke to the audience. 'Who'd like a song?'
she teased.

'Me!' the men called.

She sent them a smile then turned to the bespectacled young man who was her pianist. 'Sidney?'

He played the introduction to Glenn Miller's 'Boog It' and Margueritte began to sing. What a wonderful voice she had! Beth was pleased that the patients were set for a real treat of an afternoon. Smiling, she headed for the door to continue her duties and saw Oliver looking into the room.

'I'm terribly sorry,' Beth told him. 'I'll have to miss tonight's performance. I've been scheduled to work late today.'

'What? Oh! What a shame,' he said, but Beth could sense his relief because now he had eyes only for Margueritte.

CHAPTER SEVENTY-THREE

Victoria

'He's back! He's here!' Jenny yelled. She ran downstairs to meet a startled Victoria in the hall. 'It's Paul. I think he's coming to the concert.'

She must have spotted him from the landing window.

Paul. Victoria's heart jolted and then cantered in her chest. Her feelings had been in a whirl ever since he'd come to see her on Wednesday. What was she to say to him? She simply didn't know.

Arthur appeared. 'Did you say Paul was here, Jen?'

'He's walking up the drive.'

Arthur opened the door to him. 'I scored at football yesterday, Paul. Two goals.'

'Football? That's soccer to the folks back home,' Paul said stepping into the hall. He didn't look at Victoria but awareness of his closeness skipped along her skin like electricity. 'Two goals, hmm?' he asked. 'That's a mighty fine achievement. Unless the other team scored ten goals?'

Arthur grinned, knowing he was being teased. 'They didn't score any.'

'I've got a picture of a cat to show you,' Jenny told him. 'It's a cat with whiskers and a tail.'

'I can't wait to see that, Jenny Wren.'

Other children appeared. Paul was kind to them all,

lifting up little Flower so she wasn't lost in the crowd around him.

'I'm just here to say hello,' he said.

'Aren't you coming to the concert?' Jenny asked.

'Well now, I'm not sure about that.'

He looked towards Victoria at last. Once again, she was struck by the kindness in his dark eyes, though he didn't raise an eyebrow or do anything else to suggest that the decision was hers. She guessed he was trying to protect her from any backlash from the children if she'd decided against him.

'It would be nice if you came,' she said, conscious that her voice sounded oddly husky.

He breathed in deeply. 'Then I'd love to come.'

'There's going to be dancing afterwards,' Jenny said. 'Maybe you could dance with Victoria.'

'Maybe I could,' he agreed. 'I'd like to dance with you too, Jenny. And Flower, of course. And Mary and Orla. We could all dance together. I could show you a dance from back home, too. It's called the Lindy Hop.'

'Are you a good dancer?' Arthur asked.

'I don't think Fred Astaire is likely to rush to sign me up for one of his dancing films, but I like to dance. It's fun and that's important. We're living in strange times with this war on and I think we need to appreciate the good things life still has to offer. Like friendship. I'd like to be a friend to all of you. It may not be a long friendship, since the US army may decide to send me overseas and I may never have the chance to come back. But not everything lasts for ever and the trick is to enjoy what we have while we have it.'

Victoria guessed he was also thinking of other ways in which the friendship could end. They might realize the spark between them was a mere fleeting thing, though it was blazing inside her like a conflagration just now.

Or – awful thought – the fighting might leave him seriously injured or even worse.

'What do you say to a friendship between us?' he asked the children. 'Even if it's a short one.'

'I'd like to be friends,' Jenny said.

'Me too,' Arthur added, and the others gave eager nods of agreement.

'Then let's enjoy the moment and make it an evening to remember.'

'Time to get ready,' Victoria told the children, and they rushed off to wash and brush up.

Left alone with Victoria, Paul turned to her with sincerity gleaming in those dark eyes. 'Thank you,' he said. 'I really do hope to dance with you tonight.'

'I'd like that.' She felt shy, excited and fizzing with possibilities. But there was something he needed to know. 'Remember the baby I was holding when you came to talk?'

'Uh-huh.'

She explained about Hannah and Rose.

'Brave girl, this Hannah, to come to such a public event,' Paul said. 'I'd like to add my name to those who want to protect her.'

What a lovely man he was!

She led him into the sitting room where Rose slept in a wooden cradle Bert had made for her. Paul went over, smiled down at her and said, 'I'll be happy to keep an eye on her if you want to get ready, too?'

'I shan't be long.'

Victoria changed quickly and went downstairs to find Paul with Rose in his arms. 'I hope you don't mind,' he said. 'She woke and seemed to want attention.'

Rose looked perfectly contented now.

'Well then, young lady,' he told the baby. 'It's almost time to take you to your mom.'

CHAPTER SEVENTY-FOUR

Hannah

'Are you sure you're all right?' Hannah asked her mother, chewing her lip anxiously.

'We're going to be fine,' Ma insisted. 'Aren't we?' She looked round at the other children.

'Yes, Ma,' Milly said, and Michael and Johnnie nodded.

'Off you go, Hannah, or you'll be late,' Ma said. She was sitting on the ancient sofa, swathed in blankets.

Hannah still hesitated. Ma looked so frail yet Hannah's heart ached to hold Rose for what might be one last time.

'Go!' Ma instructed.

Hannah began to move swiftly. 'The stew is simmering on the stove for your dinner,' she said, though she'd already explained that several times, and then she ran to the window to be sure that Pa hadn't arrived home from work.

He hadn't, though he might appear at any moment and forbid her to leave the house. As a precaution, she let herself out by the kitchen door and pushed her way through trees until she reached the road some yards on from the cottage. Here she broke into a trot but kept looking behind her as well as ahead, ready to jump back into the trees at the first sight of a van.

She made it to the outskirts of Churchwood having ducked into the trees twice, but, thankfully, she hadn't seen her father. The quickest route to the bookshop lay straight along Churchwood Way but Hannah made her way behind the buildings instead, climbing a fence into the bookshop's back garden. No one was visible at the rear windows so she crept along the side towards the front. Leaning around the corner and hoping she was hidden by a bush that grew there, Hannah glanced through the nearest window and saw Mrs Harrington and Mr Makepiece positioning the piano.

No one was in the street just then so Hannah walked around to the front door and knocked. She was glad when Mrs Harrington opened it immediately. 'Come in, Hannah,' she invited.

Hannah was relieved to step inside, shivering as though the air outside had been cold and hostile instead of warm and bright. 'Did you see my note?' she asked.

'I did. Victoria will be bringing Rose over soon. In fact, I've finished here so I'll go and hurry her along.'

Did Mrs Harrington think that once the audience started to arrive, Hannah would be unable to bear the censure in their faces and flee? Perhaps she was right. Hannah was dreading the gossip so the sooner she had Rose in her arms, the better.

Mrs Harrington left and Alice walked down the stairs with May Janicki. 'Everything's shipshape upstairs,' she reported to Mr Makepiece. 'Hannah, it's lovely to see you.'

Alice gave Hannah a hug. May and Mr Makepiece sent her winks. How nice they were!

'Would you mind helping now you're here?' Alice asked. 'You could arrange the flowers on the window ledges and polish some glasses.'

Hannah guessed they were trying to keep her busy so her anxiety wouldn't run away with her, but she was glad to help.

Then the door opened and Victoria entered, Rose hidden in a bundle beneath her coat. Hannah's breath caught in her throat.

'Well?' Victoria asked, smiling. 'Do you want to hold her?'

In answer, Hannah simply ran to Victoria and took Rose into her arms, dropping a kiss on to the sweet forehead as tears came into her eyes.

'We thought we'd sit you in this corner,' Alice said, pointing to a chair near the hearth. 'You should expect some surprised looks since people believe Rose was sent away. Maybe some disapproving looks, too. But one of us will be with you all the time so you won't be alone.'

Hannah raised a tear-stained face. 'I don't know what to say except thank you and I've said it so many times already.'

'Repetition doesn't stop it from being sincere,' Alice said.

Hannah sat in the corner and cradled Rose close, drinking in the sight of the soft blue eyes and rosebud mouth and trying to fix them in her memory for all time. 'I love you so much,' she whispered.

Victoria had brought a man with her – an American soldier – as well as several children. 'I'm Paul Scarletti, a friend of the folk at Foxfield and also, I hope, a friend to you and your beautiful daughter.'

How charming he was.

The door opened again and Hannah breathed in deeply, bracing herself as not just Mrs Harrington and the evacuee women arrived, but also other people.

'If anyone is nasty, they'll have me to deal with,' Victoria said. 'All your other friends, too. You're not alone.'

But Hannah still felt that a part of her would soon be torn from her heart, since she'd probably never see Rose again after tonight.

CHAPTER SEVENTY-FIVE

Beth

'Ready?' Babs asked.

'Ready,' Beth and Pauline chorused.

They filed past the mirror in turn. All three girls were dressed smartly, Babs in red, Pauline in green and Beth in the blue dress she'd bought in London for what had turned out to be her final date with Oliver. She'd decided it was ridiculous to think of it as jinxed. It was a pretty dress and she no longer wished to waste it. In fact, she felt good in it.

They'd taken care with their hair, too, teasing it into waves and pinning it back from their faces. As a final touch, they'd added lipstick to their mouths.

Gathering their coats and handbags together, they left the hospital to walk into Churchwood, wearing their comfortable shoes and carrying their best shoes in their bags.

'This is going to be fun,' Babs predicted as they reached the bookshop.

Beth wasn't sure that *fun* was the appropriate word, but if they taught someone a valuable lesson, that would be worthwhile.

'Lovely to see you,' Alice said, hugging each of them as they entered. 'As you can see, it's going to be a squeeze, but we're getting used to squeezes in the bookshop.'

'I like a bit of friendliness,' Babs said.

'Just as well,' Alice said, smiling. More people arrived and she turned to greet them.

Glancing around, Beth noticed Hannah in a corner, holding baby Rose, while Victoria and an American soldier stood guard close by. Did this mean that Rose's father had turned up at last? Hannah's wan face suggested not and Naomi confirmed it, pausing by Beth to explain the situation.

Admiring the young girl's courage, Beth sent Hannah an encouraging smile.

'There he is,' Babs whispered. 'Our quarry. I'll go first, shall I?'

Beth gestured her forward and watched as Babs threaded her way through the revellers until she reached the piano. 'Oliver!' Babs said sweetly.

He turned and Beth couldn't resist a smirk when she saw how surprised – no, how appalled – he looked.

'I managed to get here after all, darling,' Babs said. 'Isn't that nice?' She reached out to stroke his sleeve.

Looking like a siren from the cinema screen with her hair falling over an eye, Margueritte Moore took his other arm and tugged him closer. 'Who's this?' she asked, subjecting Babs to a glitteringly hostile stare that took in her appearance from top to bottom.

'Tell her, Oliver,' Babs encouraged.

'This is – erm – Babs Carter. She's a nurse at the hospital,' he said.

'And the rest, Oliver. And the rest.' Babs offered a handshake to Margueritte. 'I'm walking out with Oliver. I'm his sweetheart. You're the singer, I suppose?'

Babs made singing sound almost indecent.

'Me next,' Pauline whispered to Beth. She sailed forward. 'Oliver, angel. Matron changed her mind and gave me time off work so we can enjoy a lovely evening together. She didn't want to get in the way of true love.'

Margueritte's eyes glowed with even more hostility at this revelation. Taking her cue, Babs stepped back in mock horror. 'Pauline!' she cried. 'You don't mean Oliver and you are . . .?'

'Well, of course I mean Oliver and I are . . . together. We're looking forward to a happy future. Aren't we, Oliver, dearest?'

'Um,' he said.

'Oliver?' Babs demanded. 'Tell me she's making this up. That's it's *me* you want. All those lovely things you said to me . . . All those kisses . . .'

'What about all those kisses you gave me?' Beth asked, sidling into the group.

'Not you as well!' Babs and Pauline chorused.

'Yes, me as well,' Beth confirmed. 'You too, I suppose?' she said, turning to Margueritte.

'Me?' Margueritte drew herself up. 'Oliver didn't fool *me*,' she announced haughtily. 'As if I'd fall for a man who spreads himself around among mere nurses. *I* am a professional singer. An artiste.'

Beth felt a smile twitch on her lips and a quick glance at Babs and Pauline showed they were struggling not to giggle, too.

'Oliver,' Margueritte said. 'You really must move away. I need to look through this music with Sidney. Take your little nurses somewhere else.'

Oliver opened his mouth but stayed silent, obviously having no idea what to say.

'You can forget about taking me somewhere else,' Babs told him, flouncing away.

'And me,' Pauline said, copying the flounce.

'You can also forget about me,' Beth said. 'You're not

a nice person, Dr Lytton. You use people without an ounce of consideration for their feelings. Well, on this occasion you've been found out, so it serves you right if you're embarrassed. And I don't think you'll have much luck with any of the other nurses at Stratton House after we tell them what's happened.'

'It's just a misunderstanding,' he finally said, but Beth only rolled her eyes.

'Dr Lytton!'

It was Matron calling. Oliver hesitated but clearly had nothing reasonable to say to Beth in his defence. He shrugged helplessly and went to meet Matron. 'Trouble, Dr Lytton?' Beth heard Matron ask.

'Not at all,' he lied. 'Let me see you to a chair . . .'

Babs and Pauline drifted back to Beth. 'Mission accomplished, ladies,' Babs announced.

'Well done, us,' Beth agreed.

They'd taught Oliver an important lesson about using people, and her bruised heart had finally healed in the process. Now she knew for sure what sort of man he was, she couldn't like him much. In fact, she couldn't like him at all. He might have angelic good looks that cast her ordinariness into the shade but he no longer dazzled her. Beth was a better person than him and she deserved a better man in her life. When the time was right, that was. Until then, she was determined to have fun and enjoy having friends.

Friends. The thought of it warmed her through and through. She'd come to Churchwood intending to hide her feelings away, but she'd learned to admit to them instead, to show vulnerability and know that others were vulnerable, too. To learn also that friendship wasn't about weakness but about sharing strength.

'Come on,' she said to Babs and Pauline. 'Let's find seats. I'm going to enjoy this concert.'

CHAPTER SEVENTY-SIX

Naomi

The applause was loud and thoroughly deserved because Margueritte Moore had sung well, even if she'd also raised a few eyebrows.

Naomi got to her feet and thanked Margueritte, presenting her with a bouquet of spring flowers cut from Churchwood gardens. 'You've given us a lovely evening,' Naomi told her. 'You really are a true professional, Miss Moore.'

Margueritte looked smug.

Naomi thanked Sidney, too. He got up and bowed, again and again, as though not sure when to stop, until Margueritte suddenly growled 'Sidney!' doubtless because he was stealing her limelight.

The evening grew more informal then, people changing seats and calling out to friends. Naomi looked towards Hannah, glad to see that she had Alice as well as Victoria and Paul around her now. A few people had looked surprised at the sight of the baby given the rumour that she'd left Churchwood, but no one had said anything unpleasant. Not in Naomi's hearing, anyway. Hopefully it would stay that way.

Someone crossed the room with as much speed as the crush allowed. It was Dr Lytton. He reached Margueritte but she tilted her chin and turned away. 'Leave me alone,' she told him. 'I'm going out for some fresh air.'

'Margueritte, angel, those nurses were just making trouble out of spite because I wasn't interested in them. Think about it, Margueritte, why would I look at any of them when you're here? Beautiful, talented . . .'

She didn't stay to listen but stepped outside. Oliver followed and, to Naomi's surprise, so did Alec Mead. Good grief. She hadn't even known he was here but he'd dressed up for the occasion in what she supposed he considered to be a rather natty tweed jacket, though his eyes were hostile now.

What on earth . . .? Sensing trouble, Naomi went outside, too.

'What's this, Margueritte?' Alec Mead was demanding.

Oliver turned to him, frowning. 'I've no wish to be rude, but you're interrupting a private conversation. I suggest you run along just now and speak to Miss Moore later. If she wants to listen to you.' His tone suggested that was unlikely.

Alec Mead stretched his neck forward, a cockerel spoiling for a fight. 'I've no idea who you are, Mr La-di-da, but Margueritte is perfectly happy to talk to me. She's been talking to me for weeks and we've become what you might call close.'

'I doubt that,' Dr Lytton sneered.

'Now, you look here, you stuck-up—'

'Margueritte?' Another voice spoke. Another surprise, for the speaker was Jed Powell, who must have been waiting in the shadows. He, too, was dressed up.

'Who are these men?' Oliver asked Margueritte.

She shrugged. 'Just men.'

'What do you mean by that?' Alec demanded. 'You know you like me, Margueritte. You told me so.'

'Like *you*?' Jed sneered, looking down on the farmer, who was at least three inches shorter. 'She likes *me*.'

'Gentlemen,' Oliver said. 'I think you've mistaken Miss Moore's friendliness for something else. You're both old enough to be her father and, to be honest, I don't think either of you is her type.'

'You think *you're* her type?' Jed Powell scoffed. 'A snob and a weakling? Margueritte, tell him he's wrong. It's my van you've been coming out in. Me who's been taking you for drinks.'

'You gave her lifts and spent money on her? So did I!' Alec looked outraged now.

'She was playing with you both,' Oliver said, with a patronizing drawl. 'I suggest you walk away with dignity instead of becoming bores about it.'

'Margueritte!' Alec implored. He stepped towards her, barging into Oliver, who stumbled and accidentally cracked his head into Jed's face. Jed pushed him away, only for Oliver's head to collide with Alec's face before he fell to the ground and lay sprawling.

'Enough!' declared Bert, who must have been drawn outside by the shouting.

Glancing around, Naomi saw that more people were watching the scene from windows and the open door.

'You're all behaving like fools,' Bert chided. 'That includes you, Miss Moore. It doesn't take a genius to work out that you've been toying with these men for your own entertainment and to see what you could get out of them. Two of them are married with responsibilities. This other one . . . Well, he's been toying with several girls, judging from what I've seen today. You should all be ashamed.'

Paul Scarletti had come out, too. He hauled Dr Lytton to his feet. All three men were bleeding. 'Get in

382

the bookshop,' Bert ordered. 'There's a first-aid kit in there and I'm sure Matron and her nurses can assess the damage.'

'I'll manage by myself, thank you,' Oliver said, clearly trying to summon some dignity.

'Don't make yourself look an even bigger fool,' Bert told him, scathingly. 'You've nothing to gain by crawling away to a hole somewhere.' He gestured around them at the watchers.

Naomi noticed that Edith Mead had appeared. 'I came out for a walk because I thought the village would be quiet with the concert on,' she told Naomi. 'I saw the commotion and realized *he* was involved.' She looked at her husband in disgust. 'To think I let you bully me for years when you're just an addle-headed fool who can't see when a girl is using him,' she sneered.

'Edith, I—' Alec began, shame-faced, but Edith put up a hand to shut him up.

'I don't want to hear your pitiful excuses. You want to have your fun, so I'm going to have mine.'

'Would you care to join us in the bookshop, Edith?' Naomi asked.

'I would. I'll be coming regularly from now on. And if you don't like it' – she pointed an accusing finger at her husband – 'then tough. I've been a worm all my married life but my eyes have been opened and I've turned.'

'Better late than never,' Naomi approved.

'I suggest you get yourself home once you've been cleaned up,' Edith told Alec. 'And if you want to stand a chance of getting into my good books, you can mend the shelf I've been complaining about for months and see what other little jobs you can do.'

'Edith, nothing happened,' Alec pleaded.

'Aside from you making yourself look like an idiot

in your dotage? Of course nothing happened. The girl was using you.' Edith rolled her eyes at her husband's stupidity.

'All inside,' Bert commanded.

They moved inside, the crowd at the door retreating like a tide to let them through. Matron had the first-aid box ready. 'The kettle is on for warm water,' she announced.

The men were directed into seats and hot water was brought in bowls. 'I suggest you attend Dr Lytton, Nurse Ellis,' Matron instructed. 'Nurses Carter and Evans can see to the others. Oh, and I have news for you, Dr Lytton. Dr Thomas has been passed fit to resume his duties so you can return to London. You haven't exactly covered yourself in glory here.'

The doctor blushed, looking more like a naughty child than an angel sent from heaven.

'I think you're going to be happy with us now, Nurse Ellis,' Matron said.

'I think I am,' Beth agreed. She paused before adding a heartfelt, 'Thank you.'

For what? Naomi didn't know exactly what had gone on between Beth and Matron, but it wasn't hard to guess that Matron had played a part in getting the young nurse to open herself up to the friendships Churchwood had to offer. Naomi was glad of it. Beth was a lovely girl who deserved every happiness.

Alec and Jed got to their feet as soon as the nursing ministrations were over. Alec headed for the door but Jed's gaze happened to fall on Hannah, who was still cradling Rose in a corner and probably dreading being noticed by him. 'What the . . .?'

He strode forward, anger in his stance and in his fists. Oh, no.

Naomi and Bert stepped forward but Ruby got to Jed first and put a restraining hand to his chest. 'Kenny,' she called, 'I might need you here.'

Kenny came over and stood in front of Jed. 'Touch a hair on my wife-to-be's head and I'll—'

'That shouldn't be necessary,' Ruby said. 'Just stay right there, both of you.'

'Are you going to . . .?' Kenny asked.

'Yes,' Ruby told him. 'I am.'

CHAPTER SEVENTY-SEVEN

Ruby

Ruby marched up to Alice. 'May I borrow your chair?'

Alice looked bewildered but duly got up. Warning people to watch their backs, Ruby carried the chair to the centre of the room, climbed on to the seat and clapped her hands for attention. 'Quiet, please.'

Gradually, the chatter hushed until only Marjorie's voice could be heard, whining, 'As I said before, it isn't as though I'm a gossip, is it?'

'Ssh,' people scolded, nodding towards Ruby. Marjorie turned to look and finally fell quiet.

'Thanks for listening,' Ruby began. 'First, I'm going to say something you'll probably all agree with. Which is that the best thing for a child is to be born into a happy family with a mother and father who love each enough to marry and provide a stable home.'

'Quite right!' someone yelled and other voices murmured agreement.

Ruby nodded but then her mouth twisted ruefully. 'Now I'm going to say something you might *not* like. Which is this. That we don't live in a perfect world and sometimes mistakes get made. Hannah made a mistake and she's paid a heavy price for it in heartache and worry. But let's look at the other side of Hannah. I see a girl who wanted to be a teacher but had to leave school early to look after her sick mother and five brothers and sisters. Did you hear that number? Five brothers and sisters. How many of you would have coped with looking after so many at her age? Most girls like Hannah spend their time wondering if they're pretty, saving up for new dresses and hoping for partners at the next dance. Hannah looks after her family. Cooking and cleaning the house. Washing and ironing clothes. Changing nappies. Getting up in the night when the little ones cry. Getting the older ones to school. Shopping for food on a tight budget. Tending her sick mother and putting up with a brute of a father. Yes, that's you, Mr Powell. There's a whole host of things to set to Hannah's credit with just one black mark against her.'

Ruby paused, staring people in the eye with a hard challenge that made some of them squirm. 'Let's think about that black mark. It happened because Hannah fell in love and was desperately worried about her man going off to war. And what did she do when she realized she was expecting? She carried on working just as hard as ever, letting no one down. Not her mother. Not her brothers and sisters. She gave birth alone – she herself a frightened child – but managed to care for her baby by leaving her temporarily with Victoria, a woman we all know to be kind and caring. Did you catch that word I used? *Temporarily*? Hannah simply hoped for time for her man to come home and help.'

Ruby paused again then gave the sort of smile that promised her audience even more discomfort. 'Now let's take a look at *you*. How many of you can claim as many credits as Hannah? How many of you have more than one black mark against you? I haven't lived in Churchwood for long, but I know how much Kate suffered from the nasty comments and looks she received from many of you not so long ago. Instead of helping her – a young, motherless girl growing up with a miserable skinflint father who forced her to wear her brothers' old clothes – you shunned her. Then there's our children's teacher, Evelyn Gregson. Can you all say you were kind and compassionate towards her and her children when her husband deserted the army only to be killed right here in Churchwood? No, you can't. Not until Alice and her father shamed you. Even the evacuee children who live here had a tricky time at first, since some of you took against them when they needed your understanding to adjust to village ways. And what about the gossips among you?'

'She can't mean me,' Marjorie Plym said, only to be told to shush again.

'There's a lot of gossip in Churchwood and I'm sure I've come in for my share of it with my dyed hair and painted nails. Not that I'm saying you're all terrible people. You're not. You can be kind and welcoming, and you can put yourselves out to help others. What I'm saying is that you're human. You have your wonderful qualities, but you're hardly angels because you also have flaws. Black marks. How does the old saying go? People in glass houses shouldn't throw stones? Something like that. There's a saying from the Bible, too. I'm not much of a churchgoer, but maybe you could help me here, Adam.'

'The Bible has plenty to say about hypocrisy,' Adam said. 'Here's just one quotation: "Why do you look at the speck of sawdust in your brother's eye and pay no attention to the plank in your own eye?"'

'That'll do nicely,' Ruby said. 'Now, you may all be wondering why I've got a bee in my bonnet about this. It's because I don't want Hannah to feel alone in being judged by you. I want to share it with her because she isn't the only unmarried mother in the village. I'm another one. Timmy isn't my brother. He's my son, and I'm sick and tired of him having to carry the burden of secrecy around.'

A ripple of shock went around the room.

'I did wonder,' Marjorie said.

'No, you didn't,' someone told her.

'My circumstances were different,' Ruby continued. 'I wasn't in love. I was a stupid sixteen-year-old who didn't realize what her married boss had in mind when he kept her behind one evening and who didn't really know what was happening until it was too late to stop it. But I love my son, just as Hannah loves her daughter. We may have been caught out in our different ways but we're both trying to be good mothers to our beautiful, innocent children who've done nothing wrong and who deserve to live happily, free from shame.'

'You're succeeding, Ruby,' Kate shouted. 'Timmy is a credit to you.'

'I agree,' Alice called.

Beth called out, too. 'Well done for everything you've just said, Ruby. I, for one, am proud to call you my friend.'

More cries went up, 'Me too' and 'So am I' among them.

'So there it is,' Ruby concluded. 'You have two unmarried mothers in the village. Two women to turn your noses up at. If that's what you choose. I've said my piece. Now I'll leave you to think about it.'

Ruby jumped down from the chair. The applause began with Bert, his shovel-like hands making loud, hollow sounds, with others joining in enthusiastically. To Ruby's relief, she saw smiles on the faces of most people, not least May Janicki and Janet Collins.

Ruby blushed and Pearl slapped her shoulder. 'What a speech!'

Ruby doubted she'd won everyone over. That would take time and some people might always sneer, but it was clear that for the most part the village was on her side and the relief she felt was deep.

Timmy came up to her, his eyes shining. 'Does this mean I can call you Mum now?' he asked.

'It certainly does,' Ruby answered, hugging him. 'I'm *proud* of being your mum, Timmy. Proud of *you*.'

'I'm proud of you too, Mum. I like not having to pretend any more. And even if I haven't got a dad – not one that counts, anyway – I've got the best mum ever.'

'What do you mean, you haven't got a dad who counts?' Kenny demanded. 'What am I? Chopped liver?'

Timmy gaped at him. So did Ruby.

'Can I really call you Dad instead of Kenny?' Timmy asked.

'If that's what you'd like.'

Timmy nodded, gulped, and threw his arms around Kenny's waist.

Ruby smiled, before noticing that someone was standing at the open door and looking in. A stranger.

A stranger to Ruby, that was. But not, she hoped, to someone else.

CHAPTER SEVENTY-EIGHT

Hannah

Hannah's heart was beating fast. How shameful her father's behaviour had been. But how magnificent of Ruby to champion Hannah like that.

Would her speech make a difference? Perhaps to some people. But not to Aggie Hamilton. Even as Ruby had been speaking, Hannah had glanced across to Mattie's mother and seen her prissy lips purse in disgust. Still, it would be a relief to know others might have at least a polite smile for her whenever she came to Churchwood. If she came at all. She might be unable to bear it once darling Rose had gone.

Hannah had buried her face in her daughter's sweet-smelling neck as she worked through the thoughts and feelings that were racing around her head. But then instinct – or perhaps some shift in the atmosphere – nudged her into looking up again.

Her gaze reached the door and the person who was standing just inside it, an army greatcoat over his khaki uniform, a cap on his head and a kit bag over his shoulder . . .

A thrill passed through Hannah like a jolt of electricity. She swallowed hard, too overwhelmed to do anything else.

But what was *he* thinking? What was *he* feeling? Tears

pricked her eyes but the next moment he smiled at her across the room. It was a smile that warmed her like molten honey. A smile that said she could trust that he loved her still and would put things right.

He held up a finger as though indicating that he'd be with her in a moment. Then he stepped into the room and cleared his throat. 'I've just listened to a speech, and a fine speech it was. I'm glad to hear that Hannah has friends here.'

He smiled at Ruby and then at the others who called out to him, saying things like, 'We're proud to be her friend,' and, 'Yes, we are!' Victoria, Mrs Harrington, Mr Makepiece, Alice, Kate, Beth, Adam . . .

'Never mind all that.' Aggie Hamilton barged her way through the crowd and, reaching Mattie, she folded him into her arms. 'You've come home to your mother.'

'Hannah—'

'Forget Hannah Powell. That girl is . . . Well, I hate to say it, but she's—'

'Careful, Mother,' Mattie warned.

Aggie simply tutted. 'Let's not waste words on her. It's wonderful to have you home again, dearest boy. Aren't you glad to see me?'

'That's a good question. I'm not impressed by what I've seen and heard from you so far.'

Aggie was shocked into taking a small step back. 'What do you mean? Is this some sort of joking talk you've picked up in the army?'

'I'm not joking, Mother.'

'I don't understand.'

'Then let me enlighten you. Hannah Powell is the girl I love, so much so that I intend to make her my wife.'

'Mattie, you can't. *You* don't understand, either. She . . . She . . .' Aggie lowered her voice, though Hannah could still hear and so, she guessed, could everyone else. 'She has a *child*.'

'*My* child,' Mattie said. 'A baby girl called Rose.'

Aggie stared at him, wide-eyed in horror. 'That isn't possible.'

'It's more than possible. It's a fact.'

'But—'

'Hannah and Rose are my priority now, Mother. If you don't want them in your life, you won't have me in your life, either. I'm not my father, so worn down by your constant bullying that he daren't say boo to a goose. I'm my own man now and I won't let you bend me to your will. If that means walking away from you . . .'

'You can't walk away from the mother who's loved you all your life. You won't.'

'I can and I will. If that's what it takes to protect my wife and child from nastiness. The decision is yours.'

Aggie gaped at him but Mattie stepped aside and stood on the chair Ruby had vacated to address the crowd. 'I'm sorry I'm interrupting the party but I expect you've all been listening to what I've just said, so let me make my position clear to all of you.'

He paused until the room was silent and watchful.

'I love Hannah, and even though I haven't met her yet, I also love my daughter,' he said. 'I'm deeply ashamed of having left Hannah here unprotected to deal with everything that's happened over the past months, but I'm here now and I want to put things right.'

He smiled across at Hannah again and then continued. 'My mother has made her disapproval plain and I imagine there may be others among you who feel the same. Let me tell you that I'm the first man to admit that it would have been better if I'd gone about things differently. If our wedding had come before our child. If

393

we'd waited a few years, too, so the war could be behind us, I could be back here building a future, and Hannah's brothers and sisters wouldn't need her so much. But it didn't happen that way and, being two years older than Hannah, I take all the blame. So if there's anything you want to get off your chests in the way of criticism, say it to me, not her.'

He glanced at Hannah again and this time sent her a wink. 'Unfortunately, we can't rewind the clock, so even though we did things in the wrong order and at the wrong time, we can't go back and change them. We can only make the best of things as they stand now. The first thing I want to do is make Hannah my wife. Not because someone has a shotgun at my back, forcing me to do the right thing, but because I love her and can't imagine ever looking twice at any other girl. And that' – he paused for effect – 'is more than can be said of some of you men here, judging from what I witnessed when I walked up from the bus stop. Grown men, brawling in the street and making fools of themselves over a young woman who, by my reckoning, has only been using them for what she can get out of them. Grown men who should have had their minds on their families.'

His gaze lingered accusingly on Hannah's father, where it remained for a long and hostile few seconds.

Jed glowered back and bunched his hands into fists at his sides.

'Oh, I know I need your permission to marry your daughter since she isn't yet of age,' Mattie told him. 'But are you really in a position to withhold it, given your shameful behaviour with the young woman over there?' He smiled at Margueritte Moore. 'I'm sorry, miss, but I don't know your name.'

She didn't smile back. Humiliation at being exposed

as a minx had brought spots of colour to her cheeks. Hannah guessed Margueritte would leave Churchwood at the earliest opportunity and never return.

Meanwhile, Jed looked as though he wanted to explode. He settled for bitter resentment. 'I wash my hands of that girl.'

'If only that were possible, Mr Powell,' Mattie said, 'but you need Hannah more than she needs you. Hannah has me now. I'm far from being a rich man and I'm unlikely ever to be one, but I'm hard-working and there's nothing I want more than to provide for my wife and child. We're not greedy people. We'll be content with a modest lodging for Hannah and Rose while I'm away at the war, and when I return I'll do everything I can to improve our prospects.'

He glanced at her and she smiled in agreement.

'I have a few pounds put aside to make that possible,' he said, 'and I'll be making sure Hannah receives some of my service pay, too. It should be enough. But you have a sick wife and a bunch of other, younger children, Mr Powell. How will *you* cope?'

The answer was that he wouldn't cope, though he wasn't the man to admit it. 'Do as you like,' he spat, taking a step towards the door.

'Not so fast,' Mattie told him. 'If Hannah is to remain in your house, looking after *your* wife and *your* children, there are conditions.'

'It isn't for you to tell me what to do,' Jed snarled.

'Actually, I think it is. Firstly, Hannah is a package with Rose. If you want Hannah in your house, you take Rose as well. Secondly, you treat them with respect and consideration. One cruel word or one unkind act and they'll be out of there. Don't go making the mistake of thinking that I won't be able to do anything to help them once

I return to my duties. From what I heard when I first arrived, Hannah has friends now, and they'll be looking out for her.'

'I'm one of those friends,' Mr Makepiece said, crossing his arms across his middle in a way that suggested he meant business.

Others joined in and brought more tears to Hannah's eyes, this time of gratitude. Mattie looked as though he was being affected the same way because for a moment he seemed unable to speak. 'You're all . . . wonderful,' he finally said, swallowing. 'Thank you from the bottom of my heart.' He touched his chest as though to confirm the point. Then he looked back at Jed. 'Well, Mr Powell?'

'The girl is to do her duty.' He wasn't the man to admit defeat in public, even if it was staring him in the face.

'You've heard the conditions. You know what will happen if you breach them. Hannah and I will be along later to be sure you understand them, but don't let us stop *you* from leaving now. You look keen to be gone and, to be honest, your foul temper isn't contributing to the party atmosphere.'

Jed stomped out of the bookshop. And Mattie thanked the audience for listening before making his way to Hannah's side at last.

She got up and leaned into his chest as he wrapped his arms around her and Rose. He kissed the top of Hannah's head and she tilted her chin so he could kiss her lips. 'I love you,' he told her.

'I love you,' Hannah said.

'That's good to hear. Now I'd like to meet our daughter.'

'Rose,' Hannah said, passing the baby into his waiting arms. 'I hope you like the name?'

He kissed Rose's head. 'I love it. I love *her*. I'm sorry you've been through such a difficult time, darling.'

'It's been awful,' she admitted, 'but now it's all coming right.'

'You knew it would?' he asked. 'You trusted me?'

'I did, though I wobbled a little when you didn't write after I asked you to.'

'I did write. I sent an air letter card.'

'I never got it.'

'Cards are supposed to be quicker than the old regular letters, but with thousands of them being transported I suppose it isn't surprising if some get lost. Maybe it'll turn up one day.'

'It doesn't matter now you're here.'

'I can't stay for long but there must be a way to marry you quickly.' He looked around and made eye contact with Adam Potts, who came over.

'I'll be delighted to marry you by special licence,' Adam said. 'You'll need to apply for it and you'll need your father's consent, Hannah, but it can be done. Yours won't be the first marriage I've conducted thanks to a special licence. Alice Irvine's . . . Kate Kinsella's . . . You'll be in good company.'

'It'll be a simple wedding since we haven't time for anything fancy and I'd rather our money was used to help out Hannah and Rose while I'm away,' Mattie explained.

'Simple can still be beautiful. And I'm sure you'll have well-wishers.' Adam gestured over his shoulder to the people who were waiting to speak to them.

How nice they all were! But before they could step forward, Aggie Hamilton appeared at Mattie's side. 'I think there's been a misunderstanding,' she said.

'I don't think so,' Mattie challenged her. 'I've told you how things are. It's up to you to decide what you want to do about them.'

'What I mean is, perhaps I misunderstood Hannah,' Aggie said. 'You saw how her father behaved . . .'

'If this is your way of apologizing to Hannah, you're making a hash of it,' Mattie said, but Hannah read the real distress in the older woman's face and felt pity stir.

'Would you like us to put the past behind us and start again?' she asked, and Aggie gulped with relief.

'Yes, please.'

'Then why don't we begin by introducing you to your granddaughter?' Hannah took Rose back and held her out so Aggie could see her better.

'She's beautiful,' Aggie said, with a softness Hannah had never seen in her before. 'May I . . .? But no. Sorry, I can't expect . . .'

'Of course you can hold her,' Hannah said.

Aggie cradled Rose in her arms and made cooing sounds. Then she looked up at Hannah. 'I've wronged you. But we're family now. I'm on your side and little Rose's side. You'll have me to help you, going forward.'

'Thank you,' Hannah said. She touched Aggie's arm and then turned to the well-wishers Adam had mentioned. Mr Makepiece, Mrs Harrington, Victoria, Suki, Alice, Kate, Ruby, Beth . . .

Hannah introduced them to Mattie and explained how they'd helped her. 'Thanks,' Mattie said, again and again. 'Thank you, more than words can say.'

'My mum is getting married, too,' Timmy Turner announced, proudly.

Hannah smiled at him and also at Ruby. 'You deserve to be happy, Ruby. You're . . . Well, you're wonderful for standing up for me like that.'

'It needed saying,' Ruby said, and the farmer she was to marry nodded proudly.

'Ruby isn't the only one who's getting married,' the taller, clumsier land girl said. 'So am I!'

'Congratulations.'

'If you're surprised that someone like me is getting married, you're not half as surprised as me. Mind you, I won't be getting spliced if this idiot doesn't treat me well. This is Fred, by the way. He's got tin legs.'

'Fancy,' Hannah murmured.

'It means I'll only have to give him a little push if he misbehaves and over he'll go. That'll teach him a lesson.'

Hannah caught Mattie smiling at this news and smiled back before saying, 'Hopefully, that won't be necessary.'

'Hopefully not,' the land girl agreed. 'But remember, Fred, you've been warned. Now come along. I want a drink . . .'

'I must be mad, marrying her,' Fred told Hannah. 'She's horrible.'

'But you love me,' the land girl pointed out.

'More's the pity,' he said, and they went off squabbling.

Victoria and Beth stepped forward then, Victoria gesturing with her head towards the retreating Pearl and Fred. 'One of Churchwood's more colourful couples,' she said.

'Mmm,' Hannah agreed.

'I'm so glad things have worked out well for you and Mattie,' Beth said. 'And for Rose, of course. I hope you'll all be very happy together.'

'Thank you.'

'It's strange,' Beth added. 'I thought I was coming to a quiet place where nothing much happened, but Churchwood is full of interesting people. It makes me wonder what will happen next.'

'Perhaps it'll be your turn for an adventure,' Hannah said. 'Yours too, Victoria.'

Victoria smiled and her eyes sparkled as her gaze touched on the American soldier. 'I think I just might be on the way to mine, but maybe it'll be Beth's turn next.'

'Who knows?' Beth said.

'Come and dance!' someone called to Beth. It was one of the other nurses. The dark-haired one. Tables and chairs had been moved aside to create a dance floor.

'Coming, Babs!' Beth called back. She smiled at Hannah and Mattie again. 'I won't call dancing an adventure exactly, but it's a start.'

She walked off with a bounce in her step, Victoria and her American following.

'Shall we dance, too?' Mattie asked. 'It'll be our first dance ever.'

'But not the last,' Hannah said.

'The first of many,' Mattie confirmed.

Leading her on to the dance floor, he swept her into his arms.

Acknowledgements

It's a privilege to have so many people to thank for helping to bring *A Foundling at the Wartime Bookshop* into the world.

Firstly, I must thank my lovely readers. I'm so encouraged by your kind messages and reviews of the earlier books in the *Wartime Bookshop* series and my previous novels. You're wonderful.

Secondly, a big thank-you is due to the fabulous team at Transworld, not least my insightful editor, Lara Stevenson; my clear-eyed copy-editor, Eleanor Updegraff; my highly efficient production editor, Vivien Thompson, and managing editorial coordinator, Holly McElroy; and everyone involved in sales, marketing, cover design, proofreading . . .

Thirdly, huge thanks are due to my agent, Kate Nash (aka Super Agent), and all the team at the Kate Nash Literary Agency.

Finally, I must thank my family and friends, who listen to me banging on about deadlines with unfailing patience while pouring me cups of tea and glasses of wine.

Thank you, one and all!

About the Author

Lesley Eames is an author of historical sagas, her preferred writing place being the kitchen due to its proximity to the kettle. Lesley loves tea, as do many of her characters. Having previously written sagas set around the time of the First World War and into the Roaring Twenties, she has ventured into the Second World War period with *The Wartime Bookshop* series.

Originally from the northwest of England (Manchester), Lesley's home is now Hertfordshire, where *The Wartime Bookshop*'s fictional village of Churchwood is set. Along her journey as a writer, Lesley has been thrilled to have had ninety short stories published and to have enjoyed success in competitions in genres as varied as crime writing and writing for children. She is particularly honoured to have won the Festival of Romance New Talent Award, the Romantic Novelists' Association's Elizabeth Goudge Cup and to have been twice shortlisted in the UK Romantic Novel Awards (RONAs).

Learn more by visiting her website:
www.lesleyeames.com
Or follow her on Facebook:
www.facebook.com/LesleyEamesWriter

Land Girls at the Wartime Bookshop
Book 2 in *The Wartime Bookshop* series

The residents of Churchwood have never needed their bookshop, or its community, more. But when the bookshop comes under threat at the worst possible time, can Alice, Kate and Naomi pull together to keep spirits high?

Kate has always found life on Brimbles Farm difficult, but now she is struggling more than ever to find time for the things that matter to her – particularly helping to save the village bookshop and seeing handsome pilot Leo Kinsella. Can two Land Girls help? Or will they be more trouble than they're worth?

Naomi has found new friends and purpose through the bookshop and is devastated when its future is threatened. But when she begins to suspect her husband of being unfaithful, she finds her attention divided. With old insecurities rearing up, she needs to uncover the truth.

Alice has a lot on her plate. Can she fight to save the bookshop while also looking for a job and worrying about her fiancé Daniel away fighting in the war?

AVAILABLE NOW

Christmas at the Wartime Bookshop
Book 3 in *The Wartime Bookshop* series

Alice, Kate and Naomi want to keep the magic of Christmas alive in their village of Churchwood, but a thief in the area and a new family that shuns the local community are only the first of the problems they face . . .

Naomi is fighting to free herself from Alexander Harrington – the man who married her for her money then kept a secret family behind her back. But will she be able to achieve the independence she craves?

Alice's dreams came true when she married sweetheart Daniel. Now he has returned to the fighting, but Alice is delighted to discover that she's carrying his child. Will the family make it through the war unscathed?

While **Kate**'s life on Brimbles Farm has never been easy, she now has help from land girls Pearl and Ruby. But what will it mean for them all when Kate's brother returns from the war with terrible injuries? And why has pilot Leo, the man she loves, stopped writing?

As ever, the Wartime Bookshop is a source of community and comfort. But disaster is about to strike . . .

AVAILABLE NOW

Evacuees at the Wartime Bookshop
Book 4 in *The Wartime Bookshop* series

January, 1942

Victoria is on her way to Churchwood in Hertfordshire, looking for a life away from the dangers of wartime London for herself and two orphaned children. But the village residents are already dealing with their own problems . . .

Alice is working hard to get the village bookshop back up and running after the previous premises were destroyed. The new building is in urgent need of repair and a builder has been hired, but where is he and where is the money he was paid?

Kate is struggling to work out the next steps in her relationship with pilot Leo. Injured in the fighting, he has returned to convalesce with his parents, but they are rich and elegant, and Kate suspects they want their son's sweetheart to be the same – not a country bumpkin like her with barely a penny to her name.

Meanwhile, **Naomi** shows kindness to Victoria and her evacuees, but is she biting off more than she can chew, especially when she is confronted with a surprising intruder . . .

With so much trouble and uncertainty in the village, can Victoria and her little family find the safe haven they crave?

AVAILABLE NOW